IVORY NATION

A GABRIEL WOLFE THRILLER

ANDY MASLEN

TYTON PRESS

For my family.

'The things that we love tell us what we are.'
Thomas Aquinas

1

LATE SUMMER
KGALAGADI TRANSFRONTIER PARK, BOTSWANA

The elephant's butchered carcass stank. Corporal Steve 'Stevo' Wallingham fought the urge to empty his guts onto the African soil beneath his boots.

Shouldering his SA80 rifle, he approached the huge, tusk-less head. The flies swirled in a thick, angry cloud as he drew near. He looked down into the glazed-over eye, with its long, curling eyelashes. But not for long.

What screamed at him from the ravaged face was the ugly, bloody, maggot-filled crater that had until a few hours previously housed the dead animal's right tusk.

From his briefing with the head of the Botswana Defence Force's Anti-Poaching Unit, Stevo knew the poachers routinely used petrol-powered chainsaws, when they could get the fuel. If not, they'd hack away with machetes and rip-saws until the precious ivory came free. This crew had obviously had the petrol. Horrific wounds had been gouged into the flesh above, below and behind the socket.

A plaintive wail had him whirling round, grabbing for his rifle.

Behind him, Stewie and Rob were crouching, rifles at their shoulders. Moses, Eustace and Virtue were flat on their bellies, their own, more antiquated firearms – Russian-made AK-47 assault rifles – pointing into the bush.

The sound repeated, and he was surprised to see first Moses, then the other two APU men grin, then clamber to their feet. The two other Paras stayed ready on one knee, scanning the foliage just a dozen or so feet in front of them.

Crashes. A swish of leaves being pushed aside. The crackle of snapping wood, bone-dry despite the recent rain shower. Then Stevo smiled too.

A baby elephant emerged from between two acacias, whimpering breathily. Clearly the offspring of the dead bull, it eyed the humans nervously, before turning to the dead elephant. It took a few hesitant steps and bent its head to nuzzle its father's forehead. It curled its trunk around its father's and lifted the great, grey mass, before letting it flop to the ground. Again it emitted the strangely human-sounding moan, clearly a pain-filled cry of grief.

Stevo turned to Moses.

'What do we do with it? Is the mother going to come back?'

Moses shrugged his wide shoulders.

'I honestly do not know. If she is not with him now, then maybe the poachers have already killed her.'

'What about the rest of the herd?' Stewie asked.

Moses shrugged.

Rob had wandered to the edge of the brush. He came back with a long, whippy branch covered at its far end with succulent, bright-green leaves. He waved it to catch the little elephant's attention

'Hey, Dumbo! You hungry, lad? Hey? You want some scran?'

The calf turned at the sound of the Yorkshireman's crooning questions. Its gaze swivelled to the branch, but it stayed rooted to the spot. Rob got down on one knee and held out the branch.

'Come on, lad. Tha' must be feelin' peckish?'

He flicked it to make the leaves rustle. Slowly, taking tiny steps and breathing noisily, the calf approached him. The other five men remained still. With a yard to go, the calf stretched out its trunk and with the delicacy of a jeweller handling a precious gem, curled the tip around the end of the branch. Rob held firm as the calf stripped a big bunch of leaves from the thin twigs.

A crash from the edge of the clearing stopped the little beast's trunk halfway to its mouth. It turned its head at the noise, lifted its trunk and bleated out a cry. The answering roar was deafening by comparison.

Before Stevo got his rifle to his shoulder, an adult elephant, almost as big as the dead bull, burst into the clearing, trunk raised.

He had time to register the tusks, gleaming white in the noonday sun and to wonder whether this was the calf's mother. But that was all. Before his horrified gaze, the elephant barrelled into Rob, knocking him onto his back.

The scream issuing from Rob was cut off as her massive front feet smashed down onto his ribs. The awful crunch as the slender bones snapped like dry twigs was clearly audible to Stevo. Yet his finger never got beyond first pressure on the trigger. Rob was dead, foamy scarlet blood bubbling from his mouth, his upper torso mashed to pulp under the raging matriarch's feet.

The APU men had all aimed at the elephant. Moses loosed off a burst above her head. Trumpeting, she whirled around and took a couple of stiff-legged steps towards the remaining men.

Her ears were held out straight from her head and her trunk waved menacingly from side to side as if she were wielding a sabre.

'Hold your fire!' Stevo yelled.

He could feel his heart racing as he confronted the beast towering over them all. He didn't want to lose another man, but he didn't want to have to explain how his patrol had shot and killed a female elephant when their mission was to protect them.

Rob was dead. They'd mourn him properly later. But for now he wanted to extract without another casualty, human or animal.

The APU men obeyed unquestioningly, though all three kept their AKs pointed at the elephant. She was puffing out great breaths, the whites of her oddly human eyes showing as she swept her gaze along the tight row of humans.

Then her baby, who'd been cowering behind her, emitted

another of its plaintive cries and tottered over to the dead paratrooper.

Stevo watched as the little creature bent its head and stroked the dead man's cheek with the tip of its trunk. Mewling, it snuffed out a breath that flipped Rob's hair up. It walked a complete circuit of the body, trailing its trunk over an outstretched hand, the boots and finally the face again, then retreated to the shade of its mother's belly.

Hardly daring to breathe, Stevo watched as the mother bent her head and reached between her fore legs with her trunk to caress the baby's head. Then she lifted her head, glared at him, and turned away.

Releasing a pent-up breath, Stevo watched as mother and baby walked away from them, pushing out of the clearing through grass seven feet tall.

'That was close!' Stewie whispered in his strong northeast accent. 'Look at poor Rob, man. You need to call it in.'

While Stewie, Moses and Eustace covered the body and began assembling a rudimentary travois out of branches to drag it back to their Land Rover, Stevo ran a few quick calculations.

They'd covered about three miles on foot, mostly through forest. It had taken about an hour. That was when all were alive and only carrying daysacks and rifles. Now, with a thirteen-stone corpse to drag, they'd be looking at double that, at least.

Once back at their FOB, they could radio ahead to let the Anti-Poaching Unit HQ know they were down a man and would need him flying back to the UK. Then it would be the sad, silent, four-hour drive back to Gaborone.

He sighed. Poor Rob. Killed by the mother of the baby elephant he was feeding. She wasn't to know he was only trying to keep the poor little thing alive. He'd survived Afghanistan, counter-terror missions across half the world, even the regimental Christmas talent show, when he'd done a passable imitation of Elvis Presley singing 'Love Me Tender'. *You loved to sing, Rob mate.* But at least he'd met his end doing good. Not blown to shit by some medieval madman with an IED and a bloodstained copy of the Koran.

Stevie looked up.

They'd lashed two long poles together with lianas into a long, narrow V and tied shorter sticks on top of them, crosswise. Together, Eustace, Moses and Virtue lifted their fallen comrade's broken body and gently lowered it onto the travois.

Stewie looked over at him. The gaze spoke of shared missions, other bodies waiting to be CASEVACed from the battlefield, a depthless camaraderie among fighting men that would endure long after Rob's flesh had melted from his bones.

Stevie nodded back.

'Let's go,' he said. 'Stewie, you and Moses take the first half-mile, then me and Virtue'll take over.'

'What about me?' Eustace asked, pushing his camouflage cap back on his head.

'I want you to scout ahead. I don't want to meet any more elephants.'

Eustace nodded, his normally smiling mouth now set in a grim line. Holding his AK across his body, he jogged ahead and disappeared from the clearing.

Stevo turned to the others.

'Let's get him home, boys,' he said.

Machetes slashing at thick foliage, they made slow progress. Stevo checked his watch: 1415 hours and they'd barely covered the first mile.

Of Eustace, there was no sight. But he was the most experienced tracker of the three Botswanans. He'd be doing his job; reconnoitring the ground ahead and warning of potential threats.

Stevo had just lifted his side of the travois, swatting away the flies that had formed a dark, buzzing column above Rob's body, when a rifle shot rang out.

He and Virtue dropped to their knees, laying the travois flat and readying their rifles. Stewie and Moses were also crouching, rifles aimed into the enclosing brush.

'That did not sound like an AK,' Virtue said.

He was right. The report had a higher-pitched sound to it, the crack tighter somehow. They'd all heard enough gunfire, in combat or APU-versus-poacher encounters, to know the sound of one long gun from another.

Stevo ran a lightning-fast combat appreciation.

One man unaccounted for. Probably dead.

Enemy numbers unknown.

Terrain inhospitable. Visibility twenty yards max.

Our forces, four.

Split up into pairs and maintain a line.

Leave Rob. Sorry, mate.

He clicked his fingers to get the others' attention.

An index finger pointed at Stewie and Moses, then left. They nodded and crouch-walked away from him. A second signal, to his own chest then Virtue's, then right. Virtue nodded. Together they headed for a path leading away from the travois and directly opposite the route Stewie and Moses had taken.

He heard voices. They were speaking English, but in a variety of accents ranging from French-inflected East African to the unmistakable guttural sound of an Afrikaaner.

'Do we go in, boss?' one asked.

'Nah, man. Too slow. Clear them out.'

The first speaker laughed.

'Sure thing, boss. I flush them right out.'

Stevo heard a loud metallic scrape. Recognised it. A charging lever. On something big. Something heavy. Something—

The machine gunner opened fire. Stewie's head burst open like a ripe melon falling from a tree. Virtue's scream was cut off mid-stream as he was cut in half, spraying blood and tissue all over Stevo's left side.

The roar of the shooting obliterated all other sound. Stevo started firing instinctively, emptying his magazine as he swept the SA-80's barrel right to left into the brush.

Moses was firing into the trees, their broad-leaved foliage now shredded by the incoming fire to reveal a dark-skinned man standing in the back of a pickup operating a belt-fed machine gun.

Moses' face exploded outwards as a burst caught him, and his lifeless body toppled backwards, still firing the AK.

Scrabbling for a spare magazine, Stevo heard crashing. He looked up. Striding towards him was a white man in khaki shorts and a belted jacket, his eyes shadowed under a wide-brimmed hat. He held a sand-coloured assault rifle at his hip, the muzzle pointed at Stevo's chest.

'Drop it!' he shouted.

Stevo might have gone for a shot if the SA-80 was loaded, but without a mag, it was useless. He dropped it. Raised his hands in surrender.

'I'm a British paratrooper, mate,' he said, standing slowly. 'You've killed two, which is bad enough. But they'll pay a ransom for me.'

The man in khaki frowned. Stevo could see him making the calculation. Money always won with these people. It's why they did it. Selling ivory, collecting ransom cash from the British government, it was all the same to them. He'd have to endure a few days' captivity, maybe even a few weeks. Then he'd be home free and could return with more men to wipe these scum—

'Nah, man. I don't think so.'

The burst took Stevo in his mid-section. His last sight, as he folded forwards over his ruined belly, was of his guts spilling onto his boots.

Five hundred yards to the northwest, Eustace rolled onto his back. Above him, high in a sky the cobalt blue of Mama Botswana's eyes, three vultures circled. He raised a shaky hand to his right cheek. He winced as his fingertips encountered gashed skin and the mushy feeling of torn flesh and congealing blood.

The shot had clipped his cheekbone and he'd spun into the scrub, landing unconscious in a pile of elephant dung. He'd come to as the poachers, for he was sure that was who had attacked him, had driven off, laughing.

'He's dead!' a white man had shouted. 'Leave it.'

So they'd searched for his body and missed it. *Good. Thank you, Heavenly Father for saving me.*

Gingerly, he climbed to his feet, reeling as the blood temporarily left his brain. The Land Rover. He needed to reach it. He offered another prayer, this time of supplication rather than thanksgiving.

Father, help me reach the Land Rover. Let the poachers not have commandeered it or smashed the radio. Amen.

He did not bother with a prayer of intercession. He knew that the others were all dead. But if he could survive this, he could bring back help for their bodies and souls.

It was 5.45 p.m. by the time he reached the Land Rover. Not much light left. He clambered aboard and checked the radio. To his intense relief, it fired up as soon as he flicked the power switch.

Within a few seconds he was speaking to APU Control in Gaborone. With GPS coordinates relayed, and a promise of help secured, he climbed out of the cab and crawled under the chassis. Stevo had the ignition keys, so it was only good as shelter.

2

ENGLAND

In the comfortably furnished drawing room of a seventeenth-century cottage deep in the Buckinghamshire countryside, two men and two women sat watching the latest royal wedding.

Gabriel Wolfe and his girlfriend Eli Schochat occupied a well-worn buttoned leather Chesterfield sofa. On a second, their boss at The Department, Don Webster, sat beside Christine, his wife of forty-five years.

A bottle of Pol Roger sat in a battered aluminium ice bucket beaded with condensation up to the halfway mark.

Don had just refilled everyone's glasses. He pointed at the screen.

'You see that, Old Sport?' he said to Gabriel. 'Sign of the times. Whatever anyone says about this country and its institutions, it's something to be proud of.'

'Because Carty's black?'

'Exactly. Those of a Republican persuasion love to carp on that the monarchy's out of touch, unrepresentative. But what do they have to offer in its stead?'

Christine put her glass down on the coffee table.

'Don's about to deliver his "President Tammerlane" speech again.'

Don laughed.

'Absolutely not. Not after the telling off I got last time.' He turned to Eli and Gabriel for support. 'All I'm saying is, Joe Tammerlane is out of touch with the people of this country. We don't want a revolution. And do you know why?'

'Why?' Eli asked.

'Because we've already had one.'

She frowned.

'Really? When?'

'Let's say 30th January 1649. That's when Oliver Cromwell had Charles the First's head cut off,' Don said, adopting a scholarly tone Gabriel had rarely heard. 'We ended up with Cromwell as Lord Protector, which was a fancy term for a military dictator.'

Eli grinned.

'And there was I thinking you were just an old warhorse! Now I see you missed your vocation. You should have been a historian.'

'Huh. With a general election coming up, I'll probably end up having to apply for a job as a window cleaner if Tammerlane gets in.'

Christine tutted and laid an affectionate hand on Don's shoulder.

'Don't be silly, darling. Britain doesn't go in for revolutionaries, like you said. That dreadful Tammerlane's so far to the left he'll meet himself coming the other way.'

She smiled as she said this, but Gabriel noticed the way his boss's face darkened. Did the old man know more than he was letting on? The election was in two weeks and nothing was as it had been for decades.

The Labour party had self-destructed earlier in the year after the 'liberal elite' and 'blue collar' factions had engaged in civil war. And although all the political commentators were predicting a slender Conservative majority, he'd watched with interest, and no small measure of alarm, the rapid rise of Joe Tammerlane's Freedom and Fairness party.

Following the model of insurgent populist parties of both right and left persuasions across Europe, Freedom and Fairness had risen from nowhere to become the second most powerful party in the UK.

Its charismatic thirty-five-year-old leader looked like a movie star. His boyish good looks – ice-blue eyes and dark, stylishly ruffled hair – and engaging smile had netted him several million Instagram followers. His tweets were read, re-tweeted, commented on in what remained of the mainstream media and argued about in pubs and around dinner tables across the country.

That he was somewhere to the left of Karl Marx bothered nobody, so readily digestible were his promises of homes for the young and jobs for the woke, urgent action on climate change and a diversion of Government spending from armaments to the NHS.

* * *

The black-clad man at the front of the briefing room eyed each member of his squad in turn. Grim-faced, the men's cheeks blued by stubble, they stared back, caressing their weapons as if they were alive. He waited until he had their full attention.

'When you're all in position, you radio in with call sign. Tom and Kit, you're on the princess and her new husband.'

The two squad members he'd just addressed nodded.

'Rules of engagement, Skip?' another man asked.

'Simple. Anyone moving faster than a walking pace towards the happy couple, you take them out,' he said. 'Anyone inside a fifteen-metre circle acting nervously or wearing anything thicker than a sports jacket, you take them out. Anyone spotted carrying any kind of weapon, anywhere they could use it against the targets, you take them out.'

'Force level?' Kit asked.

'Lethal. Head shot if possible, otherwise centre-mass. Multiple shots authorised by Gold Commander.'

'I heard the Knights of Albion are planning a protest, Skip,' a tall, heavyset man said from the left-hand side of the group.

'MI5 are in the crowd, plus Special Branch and covert teams from the Anti-Terror Command. So long as they stick to shouting, they'll be filmed but left alone. They're keeping them well back from the route. Any more questions?'

Heads shook in synchrony.

'Good. Let's go.'

The eight men and one woman left the briefing room and headed out to the car park. Bright sunshine, unobscured by a single cloud, bounced off the white paint and blue-and-yellow chequered livery of the police vehicles. Parked in a row, three dark-blue, unmarked transit vans waited for them. Three to a van, plus their rifles. They climbed in, and three high-performance engines roared into life.

* * *

Half an hour later, all nine sharpshooters were in position, their rifles resting, variously, on the parapet of a multi-storey carpark, the training tower of a decommissioned fire station, a couple of the tallest office blocks in the town centre and a turret of Windsor castle itself.

Sarah Furey, the team's most recent, and only female, recruit, adjusted her position slightly, wedging herself more firmly into the angle between the floor and the redbrick retaining wall of the fire station training tower.

A veteran of the Iraq War, she had left the army with an honourable discharge and immediately applied to join the Metropolitan police as an authorised firearms officer or AFO. She aced the selection process, graduating top of her class and earning an approving pat on the back from the urban sniper course instructor, a former Royal Marine.

She was proud to be keeping her family's military tradition alive. Her grandfathers on both sides had served in the armed forces, as had her father and two of her three brothers. Not a day went by when she didn't mourn Robbie, the youngest, killed by an IED in Afghanistan in 2005.

A couple of the men she'd trained with had tried intimidating her, but after she'd dumped one on his arse and cold-cocked another who'd unwisely got in her face at the end of a post-course drinking session, they'd left her alone. Resentment turned to grudging respect as they saw what she was capable of.

Her tactical gear was still new-issue stiff, and she rolled her shoulders trying to ease the pressure on her left side.

'Control from Whisky Foxtrot Two-Five, in position,' she said into her cheek mic.

'Thanks, Two-Five,' came the reply, crackling in the stillness fifty metres above ground level. 'All squad members, from Control. They're leaving the church now. Radio silence apart from operational comms till they're back inside the castle.'

Sarah ran her fingers along the rifle's ergonomically designed stock. Checked her Schmidt & Bender Flashdot scope. She'd shot many different rifles in her time, including the G3K's junior siblings, the G36 and the SG 516. But the G3 was her favourite, and, she knew, that of the SAS and 14 Int in Northern Ireland. Its pedigree comforted her.

* * *

The young man with George and the Dragon tattooed onto his left arm had been a member of the Knights of Albion for three years and four months. He'd joined mainly for the fighting, stayed for the comradeship and risen through the ranks for the cause. He jabbed his finger at the TV screen, spilling his lager in the process.

'She's married a nigger!' he spat. 'Can you believe it? A fucking nigger! She's a princess for god's sake. Wasn't there one single white man on the planet she could've picked?'

Beside him, Jonathan Ballmer, the group's deputy leader, shook his head and took a sip from his own can.

'Race traitor, Marky-boy. Don't you worry, our lads will make sure the world gets our message.' He consulted his watch. 'In about two minutes thirty.'

'Excellent,' Marky-boy said, draining his lager and crushing the can between the heels of his hands. 'I can't wait.'

* * *

From his vantage point in the churchyard, James Farrow, the BBC's newly appointed royal correspondent, watched as the newly married couple emerged from the church. They smiled through a cloud of tumbling rose petals tossed skyward by enthusiastic flower girls drawn from the younger members of the royal family's growing ranks.

Princess Alexandra beamed her famously toothy grin left and right like a laser beam. Her peaches-and-cream complexion was flawless, her natural beauty heightened by the skilful application of makeup. Her blonde fringe peeped out from beneath an antique lace veil, thrown back to reveal its wearer's gleeful expression, blue eyes flashing in the sun.

Beside her, Thad Carty, the sixth richest black man in America, founder of a software firm now worth billions, beamed. His looks had been compared, favourably, to leading men in Hollywood, former presidents and Olympic athletes. His close-cropped moustache and goatee framed his widely smiling mouth.

* * *

'You OK, honey?' Carty asked his bride as they sat back against the centuries'-old leather upholstery, waiting for the coachman to settle the horses.

'Of course I am, darling. It's our wedding day.'

'Only, I saw you frowning back there.'

She shook her head.

'It's nothing.'

'Come on. Tell me. After all, I am your husband,' he said, flashing her a grin.

'That interviewer from Germany.'

'You're not still upset about that, are you?'

'No! I mean, not really. But he made it sound like I was pro-Palestinian just because I spoke at that charity event. He said I was taking a political position. And you know what Granny is like about that sort of stuff. "Leave politics to the politicians, Sasha", that's what she always says. "However much of a balls-up they make of it".'

He took her hand in his.

'Hey, come on now. You were talking about poverty. Education for those kids we met. Medical supplies. Nobody could object to that, surely?'

'The *Telegraph* did. They published an editorial, for god's sake. They said I was, and I quote, "gullible at best and misguided at worst". Told me I should stick to fashion design.' She turned and gripped his hand in hers, remembering at the last minute to keep her smile in place for the crowds and the TV cameras. 'How was I to know the charity had links to Hezbollah?'

'You weren't, baby. Nobody could have known. Let it go.'

'I can do so much more, Thad. I've got it in me!'

'I know, baby, I know. Now, let's wave to our fans. This is going to add millions to your Insta account.'

She turned away from him, smiling, waving. Then turned back again.

'That's another thing. Those awful Knights of Albion people on Twitter. You saw what they called me.'

'Hey,' he said, softly, intentionally deepening his voice. 'So, you married a black man. This is 2019. They need to get over themselves. Anyway, you've got protection, haven't you? Look around. I bet half the people in this crowd are packing heat.'

She giggled.

'Packing heat? Oh my god! Where did you learn that? The Big Boy's Book of Gangster Slang?'

3

Turning away from the scene in front of the church's magnificent front door, Farrow checked his tie knot in a handheld mirror wielded by Rosie, the new gofer, adjusted it by a fraction, and practised his smile.

'You look great, James,' she said, smiling. She was remarkably pretty. Wide-set eyes that radiated intelligence. *Like Rachel's used to.*

His producer's voice in his earpiece snapped him back to the present.

'Coming to you in five, James.'

In front of him, the camera operator signalled he was running and the sound woman nodded to him, raising the boom mike into position on outstretched arms. He listened to the studio feed. Millie Campbell, the lunchtime co-anchor, was doing her link.

'And let's go back to our royal correspondent, James Farrow. James, she looks beautiful, doesn't she?'

He switched on the smile, and looked into the camera lens.

'Millie, I think radiant is probably the most overused word to describe new brides, but in the case of Princess Alexandra, I can't think of a better one.'

* * *

Christine Webster leaned into her husband's side and sipped from her glass.

'Mmm, this really is very nice. Doesn't she look pretty, Eli?'

Gabriel watched Eli from the corner of his eye. She smiled as she answered.

'That dress. It's…'

Gabriel knew what was coming. *A meringue. No good in a fire fight. So girly*. He smiled inwardly.

'…beautiful. If she wasn't already a princess, it would make her look like one.'

OK, I did not *see that coming.*

'I agree,' Christine said. 'She's just… Oh, I know it's such a cliché, like James Farrow said, but she looks radiant, doesn't she?'

* * *

As Farrow delivered his pre-written lines, he turned from time to time to look at the bride and groom. It was true, he reflected. She *did* look happy. Twenty-three years old: the same age as his daughter had been before breast cancer drew a red line across her life, leaving twin boys motherless and her husband devastated.

The treatment that might have saved her was not available on the NHS. That's what Rachel's oncologist had told them. Austerity was still biting.

Then came the day he knew he would never forget. The short, apologetic call from the doctor.

James had rushed to the hospital straight from covering yet another royal event, raging internally at this privileged family for whom nothing would ever be 'unavailable'. He'd been stuck in traffic and arrived in time to find his son-in-law and the twins in a state of shock. The doctors had let him see his daughter's emaciated, waxen-skinned body, from which the life-force had faded and then winked out ten minutes earlier.

'James?'

He started. Millie was asking him a question. Never dry on camera. Ever. His golden rule. He smiled.

'I missed that, Millie, sorry. I was caught up in the moment.'

Her bright-as-a-button voice bubbled in his earpiece.

'I think we all are. I was asking what the crowd's reaction to the royal couple has been.'

'Well, Windsor is used to royal events, but I have to say this wedding has really brought out the best in people.'

'Even the leader of the opposition is there, isn't he? Joe Tammerlane?'

'That's right, Millie. Or supposed to be, at least. Apparently there was a train delay and, as you know, he doesn't run a car, preferring to use public transport.'

She laughed.

'Well, if this doesn't change his mind about supporting the monarchy, what will?'

Farrow laughed dutifully.

'Yes, Millie. He'd have to have a very hard heart indeed not to be moved by this magnificent spectacle.'

The screams and shouts from the crowd caught him by surprise. These weren't the usual noises of joy and welcome for newly married royal couples. Shock and anger mixed into a swelling roar.

Farrow swivelled instinctively towards the sound and quickly saw the reason for it. Two shaven-headed youths had unfurled a banner on which the words RACE TRAITOR = RACE WAR had been professionally rendered in a font that suggested dripping blood.

Four men acted as a barrier as some of the braver members of the crowd lunged towards them, intent on tearing the banner out of their hands. Farrow saw a man and a woman filming the fracas on phones. He even had time to think *very professional* before several heavily built men in jeans and bomber jackets converged on the banner-wielding group and wrestled them to the ground, still under the watchful lenses of the cameras.

. . .

Don was still extolling the virtues of the country he'd pledged his life to protect.

'The monarchy is one of the most flexible, adaptable—'

'Oh my god, look!' Christine said, sitting forward and jabbing her own finger at the screen.

Gabriel watched as the protesters with their bloody banner were briefly visible, yelling their slogans, before a group of men, clearly law enforcement, tackled them to the ground.

'Idiots!' Eli said.

'Maybe they are, dear girl,' Don said, 'but look how we treat them. They weren't allowed to get any closer or spoil the party, I'll grant you. But there are places in the world, places you and Gabriel have been to, where they'd find themselves staring down the business end of an AK-47 for pulling a stunt like that.'

She grunted, clearly unwilling to cede the point to her boss.

Furey watched the incident in front of the church through her G3K's telescopic sight. Her heart rate had settled once she realised the protesters were just intent on making a noise. They were well outside the fire zone Skip had laid down and she could already see some of Special Branch's finest pummelling the protesters into submission.

She hadn't been out of the army long, but long enough to have forgotten a lesson drummed into her. Stay situationally aware at all times. Watch for the absence of the normal or the presence of the abnormal.

The extraordinary events taking place in the crystal clarity of her scope's reticle were partly to blame. But whatever the cause, she missed the faint scrape of a boot on the concrete behind her. By the time she registered the presence of her attacker, it was too late.

His knee drove the breath from her body and the knife that swept left to right across her throat ensured she'd never replace it.

4

Together, the men dragged the cop's body to the far side of the tower. The spotter laid a black ripstop nylon groundsheet over the blood pool, then reached for his binoculars to monitor the procession.

The sniper picked up the police markswoman's G3K. He ejected the magazine and checked it, then slotted it back into the receiver with a soft click.

He rested the bipod on the parapet and began adjusting the scope. Trying to avoid thinking about his wife and children, or the woman he'd just murdered, he focused on the princess and then moved the crosshairs over to her new husband, walking slowly to the coach and waving to the crowds.

Five-fifty metres. A student's shot. Back in the day, he could have made it drunk. He could smell the spotter's aftershave. Knew he would never again be able to endure it.

The princess was first into the coach, her ivory gown arrayed around her like a bubble bath. Beside her, the *schwartze* was grinning like an idiot, waving to the crowds. *Man, you have only a few seconds left of your married life, so make the most of it.*

He breathed in and re-centred the cross-hairs on the woman's forehead. High, unlined. So clear in the precision-ground optics he could see a mole above her right eyebrow. *I'm doing this for you, Alina. I'm sorry.*

He breathed out. Squeezed his finger on the trigger, taking it to half-pressure. Three-point-seven pounds. Calibrated to his specific requirements by the armourer.

His heart beat once. He prayed for forgiveness.

It beat again. He felt the gold Star of David tremble against his chest. He tightened his finger.

Behind him, he heard the spotter's boots scrape on the concrete but ignored it, filtering out all sound.

'Put the rifle down, Dov,' the spotter said.

He released the trigger.

'What?'

Pressure from something hard on his skull, just behind his left ear, told him all he needed to know.

'OK, OK!' he said, taking both hands off the rifle.

'Now stand up.'

He turned and his eyes widened. Where he had expected to see one man, two now stood. One aimed a pistol at his chest.

'I thought you wanted me to kill her,' he said.

'Oh, I did. Tell you that, I mean. And as far as the world is concerned, you did.'

* * *

'So you're saying freedom of speech is another institution we should be proud of, boss?' Gabriel asked.

'In one. Personally, I find firebrands of any political persuasion about as welcome as a boil on the bum, as I think you know,' he said, looking meaningfully at Christine, who chuckled. 'But you take the rough with the smooth. Let them speak out. Keep them where we can see them, that's my take on it.'

Gabriel sipped his champagne. The boss was wise. Gabriel had learned more from him than any man except Zhao Xi, his mentor and surrogate father growing up in Hong Kong. He pulled Eli closer and put his arm around her shoulders. He looked sideways at her and smiled.

* * *

In the stillness between two heartbeats, when the muscle deep in his chest was momentarily still, and his body existed only as a support system for the digit curled around the short curved length of steel, he fired.

He saw her head explode in a pink spray. Nodded once. Started thinking about extraction and exfiltration.

* * *

Eli jolted upright so fast she spilled her drink.

'Oh, fuck!' she shouted.

Gabriel stared at the TV screen. The coach had stopped moving. The horses were rearing in their harnesses, forelegs flailing empty air. The soundtrack was screams, shouts and the panicky voice of the BBC's royal correspondent trying to be heard over the chaos. But it was the scene inside the carriage that held his attention.

The princess sprawled across her husband's lap. The top of her head was gone. The dress, so recently a virginal white, was now besmirched, its bodice scarlet from throat to waist. Carty was screaming for help, his face spattered with stuff that resembled pink porridge. Two men were climbing into the carriage, one already stripping off his jacket and throwing it over the mess.

Gabriel swallowed, felt his vision closing in to a black pinpoint, and the scene before faded. He was lost to a memory so painful it still caused him to wake screaming in the night, drenched in sweat and trembling so violently Eli was unable to hold him still.

The beach.

Britta.

The shot from behind them.

Her head exploding.

Toppling, falling away from him.

The second shot, ripping into his shoulder.

The screaming.

He squeezed his eyes shut, then opened them, gulped air down and drained his glass. Nobody had noticed. Everyone in the room was watching the pictures on the screen.

Gabriel looked at Don. The older man was bolt upright, staring intently at the screen, unaware that his wife was clutching his left arm. Gabriel knew what he was doing because, free now of the flashback's grip, he was doing it himself. Analysing. Looking beyond the horror, the blood, looking *into* the picture. Searching for details.

The devastation to the princess's head said large-calibre weapon. The choice of target said professional marksman. The bullet could be retrieved. It would be embedded in the coach's bodywork or the road surface. Nobody else had been shot. This was no spree killer. This was an assassination.

A hit.

* * *

Don's mobile had been ringing continuously since the moment the princess's lifeless body had slid sideways across her stricken husband's lap. As soon as one call ended, another began.

In thirty minutes he'd spoken to the heads of MI5, MI6, the Met's Counter Terrorism Command and a civil servant working within 10 Downing Street.

While they waited for him to be free to brief them, Gabriel, Eli and Christine could only do what the rest of the country was doing, and stare at the TV.

As the gut-churning few seconds were replayed from angle after angle, commentators tried to offer words of comfort. Military experts were wheeled out to make pronouncements about the likely calibre and type of weapon used by the assassin. And journalists, particularly the men, made great play of using weapons terminology with which they clearly had only passing acquaintance.

'What do you think, boss?' Gabriel asked Don, after he'd ended his latest call.

Don stroked the side of his nose, making his distinctive 'Hmm, mm-hmm' as he formulated his reply.

'We all receive a weekly briefing of the various unsavoury groups crawling around in the silt of the body politic,' he said. 'Rightists, leftists, Islamists, white supremacists, Irish republicans, anarchists. KOA pop up from time to time but they're a fringe group. About thirty members, if memory serves.'

'You saw the banner, boss,' Eli protested.

'Yes, I did. And that's all I did see. A banner. Admittedly a very professional and lurid banner,' he added. 'But a few square metres of printed vinyl do not a terror group make.'

'You going to defend their right to free speech?' Gabriel asked.

'Afraid so, Old Sport. I'm sorry, Eli, whoever put a sniper onto a tall building with a high-powered rifle, it wasn't them. I'd stake my reputation on it.'

'Well who, then?'

'That's rather the question, isn't it?'

'Anything for us?'

Don shook his head.

'Five and Six are already squabbling for jurisdiction with Counter Terrorism and Special Branch. They've convened a COBRA committee so no doubt they'll hash out a command structure. We, however, are not required.'

5

KGALAGADI TRANSFRONTIER PARK, BOTSWANA

Nick Acheson, colonel of the Parachute Regiment, and his men stood in the clearing to which Eustace, head still bandaged, had led them. As soon as he'd received the message from the Anti-Poaching Unit, Acheson had swung into action.

He'd called his oppo at the SAS in Hereford and asked for immediate assistance. Within half an hour the regiment's unmarked, matte olive-green Hercules C-130K had taken off with Acheson and sixteen SAS members on board, heading for Botswana.

There being no convenient airport nearby, the SAS men and their guest parachuted in, steering their rectangular ram-air chutes in a tight formation so they landed within a quarter mile of each other in the bush. Along with the men and their kit, the Hercules had also dropped two specially adapted Land Rovers, each mounted with a pair of ferociously effective L7A2 General Purpose Machine Guns.

Under the command of a thirty-four-year-old captain sporting a piratical red beard, the eight SAS men, together with thirty members of the Botswana Defence Force, established a perimeter around the clearing.

The Landies were circling the clearing beyond the on-foot perimeter, bearing, in addition to the gunners, a driver and two more heavily armed fighters. Any poachers coming within range could expect to be either captured or killed without mercy.

Acheson looked down at a depression in the earth, its outline demarcated by animal footprints. The earth in the centre was stained a deeper red and scraped out somewhat. Beyond it, the skin-draped skeletons of the dead elephants looked like badly erected tents.

Eustace pointed at the vaguely man-shaped space.

'I am sorry, Sir.'

Acheson shook his head.

'And you didn't find any remains at all?'

Eustace shook his head.

'No, Sir. We searched, but human remains, they are easier to carry than elephant bones,' he said, jerking a thumb over his shoulder in the direction of the skeletonised elephant carcass. 'That is why the elephant is still there. Lions, hyenas, leopards, jackals, plus all the birds of prey – they take away everything. Hyenas crack marrow bones. Strong jaws.'

A shout went up. Acheson turned towards the source. A SAS man came running with a set of identity discs.

'Sir, I found these over by the trees. Caught on a thorn bush,' he said as he handed them over.

Acheson took the proffered discs, still in the green rubber rings that prevented them from chinking together. He turned them over on his palm and learned he was holding possibly the only remaining evidence of Corporal Steven 'Stevo' Wallingham's tour of duty in Botswana. He pocketed them and snapped the press stud closed.

'Right, I want the whole area searched. We had three guys out here and there were two APU guys as well,' he said. 'If possible, I want two more ID discs for our lads and something to prove Moses and Virtue were here, too.'

The SAS man nodded and returned to his squad to brief them.

Over the next three and a half hours, the SAS and the Botswanan soldiers meticulously searched the clearing and a hundred-yard-diameter circle outside it. Sometimes they crouched to rake their fingertips through trampled undergrowth. Others stretched to pluck things free of the thorny branches of acacias. Eventually they retrieved a small trove of items that could be returned to base and matched to their deceased owners.

A battered, steel-cased Timex watch with a red, white and blue woven nylon strap; the property, according to its engraved back, of Moses Haunda.

The bullet-starred back-half of a human skull that would have to be sent to a DNA lab to establish its identity.

An elephant-hair bracelet consisting of several wiry black strands with a copper ring adjuster that Eustace recognised as belonging to Virtue.

A pitted and gouged femur, the ball-joint cracked off.

A second set of ID discs that had belonged to Private Stewart 'Stewie' Pearce-Edwards.

Several small scraps of camouflage fabric, on one of which remained the corner of a name tape bearing the letters RTER. Acheson made this deduction for himself: Private Robert Carter.

And a handful of small pieces of bone that might have been human, or animal, all of which, along with the skull and the femur, would be analysed for DNA.

Once Acheson was sure they had enough evidence to take away from the site of the massacre, he called a halt to proceedings and gathered the men around him in a wide semi-circle.

'I want to thank you for coming here and helping to retrieve the remains of your brothers in arms, and the brave Botswana Defence Force men whom they were training,' he said, looking at Eustace as he mentioned the man's slaughtered colleagues. Eustace nodded back. 'They were doing good here, combatting an illegal trade conducted by ruthless criminals. We will hold the paras' funerals in England and although I am sure you men,' he nodded at the SAS contingent, 'need to be going, I will stay for the funerals here.'

Eustace touched the colonel on the arm.

'Excuse me, Colonel. Please may I say some words?'

'Of course, please go ahead,' Acheson replied.

Eustace smiled and half-turned so he was facing the semi-circle of tired men, their faces coated in a greasy mixture of sweat and red dust.

'Moses and Virtue were my friends. We went to school together,' he began. 'Rob and Stewie and Stevo came to help us, thanks to the kindness and friendship of Colonel Acheson. They were my friends too, and friends to Botswana and our elephants. Please, I would like us to pray for them.'

In front of him, the troopers and soldiers bowed their heads and clasped their hands in varying attitudes of prayer. Acheson followed suit, listening as the Botswanan's mellifluous voice soothed his burning soul, just for a minute or two.

'Heavenly Father. Please, we beg you, shepherd into Heaven the souls of our dear friends Moses Haunda, Virtue Jonathan, Stevo Wallingham, Rob Carter and Stewie Pearce-Edwards,' he intoned. 'Let them always have clear water to drink, sweet honey and tender meat to eat, and the sun on their backs. Send them our love and our gratitude for laying down their lives. Tell them we will find their killers and avenge their deaths with great wrath. Amen.'

The chorus of amens floated upwards into the African sky. Acheson added a silent prayer of his own: 'Let me be successful in finding those bastards, Lord. Amen.'

6

LONDON

Smiling beneath the skilfully applied makeup, and sweating lightly under the TV lights, Joe Tammerlane waited to be introduced by Becca Price, *Wake Up, Britain!*'s glamorous host.

Beneath his immaculately tailored suit, he could feel his heart thrumming with anticipation. Not anxiety, instead a heightened sense of reality. He looked at her while tuning out her excitable gabble and smiling that famous smile. He could see the downy hairs on her upper lip. The weave of the multicoloured threads in her skirt. A tremulous flutter of the skin on the side of her neck where the veins ran.

He sensed his moment was approaching. The moment when everything would change. He tuned back in.

'Our next guest is a man who, until recently, was mainly of interest to the political commentators,' she was saying. 'Then, on that tragic day last week, when the nation was celebrating the latest royal wedding, he tackled the terrorist who killed poor Princess Alexandra. Ladies and gentlemen, please welcome Joe Tammerlane.'

The studio audience burst into what sounded to Tammerlane like genuinely spontaneous applause. A couple of the men whistled loudly, and he could see one older woman dabbing her eyes with a tissue.

He lowered the volume on his smile and composed his features into a suitably sober expression, part-acknowledgement of his unbidden heroism, part-sadness that he hadn't been able to act in time to save the princess.

Becca turned to him. He caught the hiss as her nylon-clad legs rubbed together.

'Joe Tammerlane. You killed the man who had just assassinated Princess Alexandra and might well have gone on to murder Thad Carty. How did you do it?'

'Can I just say, Becca, before I answer your question, that as leader of Freedom and Fairness, I want your viewers to know that I stand with them in mourning this beautiful young woman.'

Becca nodded her head, furrowing her brow.

'Of course. I think we all do.'

'I know I have been vilified by parts of the mainstream media for my views on the monarchy, but at the end of the day, what we saw was the senseless murder of a young woman on her wedding day.'

'And how *did* you stop her killer?' she prompted.

'Actually, purely by accident. I was supposed to be in the congregation as a party leader, but my train was delayed. I hoped I could reach the castle quicker by using the back roads and that's how I happened to be running past the old fire station.'

'And you saw the shooter?'

'I did. I don't know why, but I looked up as I ran past and I saw what I instantly recognised as a gun barrel sticking out of the top floor.'

'Most people would call the police. What made you decide to tackle him yourself?'

He ran a hand over his hair and shrugged.

'Honestly? I don't know. I guess sometimes you just act without weighing up the risks to your own safety. I ran for the tower and started climbing.'

'What was the scene when you reached the floor where the gunman was? We know he'd already killed a police markswoman, Sarah Furey.'

He swallowed before speaking, glancing out at the studio audience and finding the eyes of the crying woman. She nodded at him and he offered a small, sympathetic smile in return.

'I heard the shot as I was on the final flight of steps. I think I knew, deep down, who the target was. There was all that hate speech from far right terror groups. I knew it would be the princess, or her husband.'

'Was there a struggle?'

He nodded.

'He was leaning over the parapet, looking through binoculars. I honestly think he was so wrapped up in what he'd just done he didn't hear me. I saw a pistol tucked into the back of his waistband and I just grabbed it.'

'Then what happened? Is that when he hit you?'

Tammerlane fingered the wound on his cheekbone and winced. He'd asked the makeup artist to leave it visible.

'We both had our hands on the gun, and for a moment he gained the upper hand. He sort of jerked it at my face and the barrel caught me. But I managed to get it off him and somehow, instinct I guess, I pointed it at him and pulled the trigger.'

Throughout his recounting of the story, he'd paid close attention to her body language and facial expression. Behind the professional 'concerned' face he detected nothing that suggested even a shred of doubt. *Good. That's as it should be.*

'And you were arrested, is that right?'

'Not quite. I called the emergency services once I realised he was dead and the police asked me, as was their duty, to go with them to Windsor police station to be interviewed.'

'Were you offered a lawyer?'

'I was, again, as was perfectly proper for them to do. I declined.'

'Why?'

'Why?' he repeated, smiling. 'I hadn't done anything wrong. I didn't see the need. If you'll forgive me for referring to a plank of my party's policy, unlike the old fashioned socialists in Labour and their innate distrust of the state law enforcement agencies, we are totally behind them. I always say, old-school socialists are anti-police, right up to the moment their house in Islington gets burgled.'

Becca did him a favour and smiled at the joke, weak as it was.

'So what happened then?'

'Well, they asked me a lot of questions, pretty much the same questions you've been doing,' he said, flashing her the full-wattage Tammerlane grin this time and registering the widening of her pupils. 'They took my fingerprints and a DNA swab from my cheek, again, which I was happy to provide. That was it, basically.'

'Well,' she said, turning slightly so she was facing the studio audience. 'Whatever you think of his politics, I don't think there's any doubt that Joe Tammerlane deserves our nation's respect, and thanks. Joe Tammerlane, ladies and gentlemen.'

The applause this time was rapturous. Tammerlane bowed his head in acceptance and then the miracle happened: Becca stood, also applauding. Then she crouched, took his hand and dragged him to his feet so he was standing beside her.

Her eyes were sparkling with tears. In a seemingly coordinated move, the studio audience rose to its feet. He looked out at them and smiled shyly, noting that the camera operators and sound recordists were also clapping.

You're mine. You just don't know it yet.

* * *

In the days following the assassination of the princess, social media was alight with competing theories. Gabriel avoided all the platforms on principle as well as for operational reasons, but, back home in Aldeburgh he opened a laptop and loaded Twitter.

. . .

@Trexxy333

Its got 2 b the islamics, hasnt it? We shd kick them all out to those shitholes what they come from #WeepForPrincessSasha

@BrutusOfFairfield

For fucksake @Trexxy333 UR such a racist!!! Why immediately jump to that conclusion? Cd just as easily be IRA or Knights of Fucking Albion fuckwits. #WeepForPrincessSasha

@GrannyDeakins

You're wrong @BrutusOfFairfield I think @Trexxy333 is right. They want to kill us Christians. It's in their holy book. Poor Alexandra was killed for her faith. #WeepForPrincessSasha

@GreenKingJackson

@Are you always this dumb or just for special ocassions GrammyDeakins @BrutusOfFairfield @Trexxy333 ? “Poor Alexandra” was a Parasite living off working people who should kick out the “royal” family and stop idolising them. #WeepForPrincessSasha

@KOAofficial

The race traitor was put down for blood-mixing. This is the start of the race war. Whites unite for the right to fight! #WeepForPrincessSasha

Gabriel clicked on the final tweet. The profile came up on screen. Knights of Albion. Fighting to restore fairness in England for its true inheritors.

'Clever,' Gabriel said.

'Clever?' Eli repeated, coming into the kitchen and sitting beside him to read over his shoulder. 'You do see through that, right?'

'Of course I do. They're sailing close to the wind but on the right side.'

'Yeah,' she snorted. 'The far-right side.'

7

The examination room inside Westminster Public Mortuary's Iain West Forensic Suite smelled of disinfectant and the sludgy, rot-stink of death. Gathered around the green-draped figure were the forensic pathologist Dr Bill 'Mitch' Mitchell, Chief Superintendent Andrea Robinson, the Senior Investigating Officer, a photographer, three detective inspectors and a MI5 deputy commander who had introduced himself merely as 'Jim'.

'Let's begin, shall we?' Mitch said, drawing the green sheet away from the body and handing it to a mortician, who folded it into squares as if it were a freshly laundered bedsheet and laid it on a stainless-steel counter.

The detectives had, between them, worked on over two hundred murder investigations and were hardened to the sight of dead bodies. Not so the MI5 man, who rushed to a corner and vomited into a bucket, placed there especially for the purpose by the mortician.

Robinson caught the eye of her closest colleague and rolled her eyes.

'Amateur,' he mouthed back at her.

Mitch looked down at the corpse. Cause of death was obvious:

massive gunshot trauma to the forehead, though he would still investigate fully before committing himself to print.

'As you can see, ladies and gentlemen, our killer was shot through the frontal bone of the skull. The black stippling is gunshot residue, indicating a close-range shot.'

He took a slender transparent plastic wand and inserted the tip into the crater on the top part of the head.

'The head is, what? Shall we say fifty percent decerebrated?'

'Sorry, doc, what?' one of the DIs asked.

'Tammerlane blew the bloke's brains out,' a second detective said.

'Or half of them, at any rate,' Mitch said.

The mortician passed him a pair of trauma shears, which he used to cut off the man's clothing, one garment at a time. He kept up a running commentary for his digital recorder and stepped back periodically to allow the photographer to take pictures. The socks and shoes went last.

When the corpse was naked, Mitch pointed to the thin gold chain and Star of David around the throat. He then indicated the dead man's circumcised penis.

'It would appear our assassin was Jewish.'

'Princess Alexandra made that speech at the pro-Palestinian event last month, didn't she?' one of the DIs said. 'Think it's connected?'

'Let's not jump to conclusions, gentlemen,' Robinson said. 'Carry on please, Mitch.'

Mitch nodded and went back to work. After opening the thorax using the traditional Y-incision, he began removing the internal organs one by one. He handed the stomach, a soft, squashy pink bag, to the mortician, who took it to a side-bench and slit it open with a broad-bladed scalpel.

Squeezing it gently, he ejected the contents into a white plastic washing-up bowl.

'You might want to take a look, Mitch,' he said.

Mitch peered into the bowl.

'Interesting. Our man had a meal quite soon before he was killed.'

He moved the tip of a second plastic rod through the remains of the dead man's last meal. Scattered throughout the sharp-smelling liquid were small fragments of a greenish, brown, grainy substance. Deep fried, to judge from the golden brown coating on the outer edges.

He picked a piece up with a pair of plastic tweezers and brought it up to his nose. He inhaled sharply, in a short, huffing series of breaths.

'Do you know,' he said, turning to the detectives, who were wincing and wrinkling their noses, 'I believe our killer ate falafel for his last meal.'

'Can you pack up a sample please, doc?' one of the DIs said. 'We'll get Forensics on it, see if it can tell us anything.'

* * *

Back at West End Central police station, Robinson re-read the initial report on the killer, which had arrived on her desk while she'd been attending the autopsy. She shook her head. It made no sense.

He'd been carrying an Israeli ID card identifying him as Dov Lieberman. The intel team had worked fast and had come up with CCTV from Heathrow airport showing Lieberman arriving at Terminal 4 the morning of the royal wedding.

Checks with airport security had confirmed that he had arrived on an El Al flight from Tel Aviv.

With a sinking feeling in the pit of her stomach, she picked up the phone. As she waited for the MI5 man to answer, she shook her head.

'*Way* above my pay grade,' she muttered.

'Andrea, what news?' Jim said.

'The shooter arrived in the UK from Tel Aviv the morning he killed her. He is – was – an Israeli citizen. A Jew. Name, Dov Lieberman. ID number, 22-9-3-20-9-13.'

'Shit.'

'Do you want to contact MI6 or shall I do it?'

'I think it had better be you. There's always been a certain,' he paused, 'friction between our respective services.'

Robinson next dialled a number in her contacts she had only ever used once before. Her heart was thrumming in her chest. It wasn't so much she was nervous of speaking to spooks, she'd just rather have been doing something else. Like enduring a root canal. Without anaesthetic.

'Liaison.'

'This is Detective Superintendent Andrea Robinson of the Metropolitan Police. Collar number 7609.'

'Hold, please.'

She could hear a keyboard clicking. A DI put her head around the office door, mouthing 'coffee'.

'Please,' she mouthed back.

The MI6 liaison came back on the line.

'Yes, Detective Superintendent, how may I help you?'

'I'm the SIO on the princess's assassination. The shooter appears to have been an Israeli citizen. We have his ID card.'

'Name and number, please.'

'Dov Lieberman. ID number, 22-9-3-20-9-13.'

'Thank you. I'll call you back. Please do not investigate him any further until you hear from me.'

She placed her phone on her desk and ran her fingers through her hair.

The DI reappeared bearing a cup of steaming coffee.

'Thanks, Marie,' she said, and took a careful sip.

'Everything all right, guv? You look like you've seen a ghost.'

'Just been talking to a spook. That close enough?'

'About Lieberman?'

'Yup.'

'Think they'll take it off us?'

Robinson blew out her cheeks.

'I bloody well hope so.'

* * *

Her next visitor was the Met's Director of Forensics.

'Mark, what have you got for me?'

'I'm not sure, to be honest. We just got the results back on the G3. We recovered four sets of prints.'

'Go on,' she said, sitting forwards and motioning him to sit.

'Set one: Sarah Furey, the AFO. Set two: the shooter. Set three: Ty Stafford, the SCO19 armourer.'

'And set four?'

'That's the weird thing. A partial, off the underside of the telescopic sight. Not on IDENT1. I've sent it to Europol and Interpol and told them it was urgent. But what I can tell you is a fourth person handled that rifle.'

Lieberman's wasn't the only autopsy that Mitch handled in the crucial hours after the assassination. He'd also examined Sarah Furey's body. Cause of death was a massive cut into her throat by a bladed weapon. The blade, he estimated, was four to six inches long, not serrated but extremely sharp. It had severed not only her carotid arteries and jugular veins on both sides but damn-near gone through her spine as well.

8

TEN DAYS LATER

[Official BBC News transcript: 5.57 a.m.]

Dawn Bradley, Political Editor: Mr Tammerlane! Mr Tammerlane! Do you have a few minutes for the BBC?

Joe Tammerlane: Of course, Dawn. What do you want to know?

DB: The obvious question. How does it feel to have come from nowhere to the office of prime minister in three years? And with such a large majority?

JT: Well, I'd hardly call working in my father's business nowhere [laughs] but I see what you mean. The answer, Dawn, is I feel incredibly humbled that the British people have given me the chance to lead them into a bright new future.

DB: Your critics have labelled you a wolf in sheep's clothing. An ultra-left ideologue merely echoing the sentiments of the woke generation that swept you to power. How do you respond to them?

JT: I think I know who you mean. But the politicians who broke this country by clinging onto outdated notions of class war and privilege – from the right and the left – have had their chance and, quite frankly, they blew it.

I fought the election promising a revolutionary way of governing and they tried everything to smear me. They tried to paint Freedom and Fairness as some sort of Trojan horse. But I have to say to you, Dawn, and if they're watching [turns to camera and waves] – Hi, Guys! – them, too, they put their policies to the people and the people said no.

Freedom and Fairness put ours and the people said yes. Now, I'm a democrat. I believe in implementing the will of the people. I think it's clear what the people's will is.

Forgive, me but there is much work to do and I start tonight. [Checks watch and smiles] That is to say, this morning. Thank you.

DB: Thank you, Prime Minister.

9

WHITEHALL

In London, two weeks after his depressing discovery, Nick Acheson waited in an anteroom at the Ministry of Defence. He glanced up at the wall clock.

The meeting with the brand-new secretary of state had been scheduled for 10.00 a.m. It was now five past. He frowned and picked up the *Times*, which lay neatly folded on the glass-topped coffee table in front of him. He read the main headline and sighed.

PM Signals Radical Shift In Defence Priorities

The talk in the mess had been of little else since a leak from inside No. 10 had warned the chief of the defence staff about 'something big coming down the line'.

The previous morning, the prime minister had made a televised address to the nation in which he'd unveiled the first in what he called 'planks in a bridge leading to a different sort of future for this great country'.

The plank in question was ominous in its implications.

Tammerlane had announced that the impending Defence Spending Review would be postponed while, 'we explore new strategic options and opportunities for global partnerships'.

Acheson had a growing sense of unease. Discussions with colleagues in the three armed services that stretched late into the night had only served to amplify them as they compared notes, swapped theories and forecast difficult times ahead.

A young woman in a smart black suit and a severe haircut that accentuated her large dark eyes and oddly pixie-like ears crossed the sparkling granite floor to him, her heels clicking on its polished surface.

'Colonel Acheson? The secretary of state will see you now.'

Acheson got to his feet, refolding the *Times* and placing it on the tabletop, squared up to the corner and precisely five centimetres from each of the bevelled edges.

The office of the Secretary of State for Defence reeked of power and a defiant military outlook that stretched back through history to the Peninsular Wars and beyond. Dark mahogany panelling stretched from floor to ceiling, and gilt-framed oil paintings depicted the men who had fought Britain's enemies down the centuries, from Nelson and Wellington to Field Marshall Montgomery and Winston Churchill. An old fashioned globe sat in a polished brass-and-mahogany stand.

The woman sitting behind the desk looked barely older than Acheson's daughter, Sophie, who had recently graduated from Cambridge with a First in Ancient and Modern History. In an olive-green silk jacket with a Nehru collar encircling a slender neck, she might have been twenty-five, twenty-six at a pinch.

Though he didn't know her age, he knew her name. Tracy Barnett-Short. A Freedom and Fairness 'diversity champion' who had campaigned vigorously and skilfully in the election, painting the incumbent cabinet as 'over-privileged, under-qualified and unfit to lead'.

She looked up from a paper she was reading and offered the briefest of smiles. With her coffee-coloured skin, glossy dark hair swept up into a style he believed his wife would call a chignon and almond eyes, she was rather attractive he had to admit. He frowned, imagining Sophie's eye-rolling entreaty for her dad to 'stop perving over girls young enough to be your daughter'.

'Thank you for seeing me, Madam Secretary,' he said.

'Least I could do, Colonel. And let's dispense with the formalities, shall we? You call me Tracy and I'll call you Nick, how about that?'

'As you wish, M— Tracy.'

'You're here about your missing men,' she said.

'Yes. As I said in my email, we lost three paratroopers in Botswana a few weeks ago. A massacre. Poachers according to the Botswanans. I want their deaths investigated and the perpetrators brought to justice.'

She frowned.

'What did the Botswanans have to say about it?'

'They did their best but, to be frank, they're not up to it. They simply don't have the resources we do. Nor the motivation. And they were our men, not theirs.'

'The anti-poaching soldiers killed were their men, I believe,' she said, softly.

Realising he'd been caught in a trap, Acheson tried to backtrack.

'Yes, of course. But I am the colonel of the Paratroop regiment. These were my men. Brothers in arms.'

She sighed. A gesture Acheson clocked as mere theatrics.

'It seems to me that you need to check your privilege. A white man flying halfway round the world in a plane full of Special Forces soldiers dropping in unannounced to a sovereign country – a sovereign black African country – and then claiming they're not skilled or resourced enough to investigate some killings on their own doorstep. You can see how that might look, surely?'

'Minister, please—'

'Tracy.'

'Tracy,' he said, trying to keep his temper under control, 'with the greatest of respect, we can't let their murders go unpunished. Surely you can see that?'

'I'll tell you what I see.' A beat. 'Nick, I see a middle-aged white man displaying a rather unattractive, neo-colonialist attitude. Treating me, a woman of colour, like a servant, demanding action to redress his own failings as a commander.'

'No! That's completely misrepresenting what I said. The point is—'

'I'll *tell you* what the point is, Colonel,' she said, her voice as hard as a gun barrel. 'This ministry, this corrupt, imperialist, war-mongering *machine* is under scrutiny, finally, for its misdeeds. We intend to re-engineer it until it's fit for purpose. And I can tell you that military adventurism is not on our list of priorities.'

The levee broke.

'*Adventurism?* Those boys were helping the Botswanans defeat ivory poachers. Offering highly skilled, selfless and courageous assistance. They died doing their duty. It's *our* duty to find and punish their killers.'

He was leaning forward, heart bumping painfully in his chest. He knew he'd lost the battle before she spoke.

Smiling, and with no outward sign that she was doing anything more radical than ordering a cup of coffee, she said, 'As you will learn over the coming days, a great many changes are coming that will radically transform Britain's armed forces from an engine of conflict and neo-imperialism into a domestic security apparatus designed to protect the citizenry. No more *adventurism*,' she leaned heavily on the repeated word, 'no more military *assistance* to repressive regimes, and definitely no more *self-glorification* by attention-seeking commanders who should know better. Your request is denied.'

Somehow, without quite realising how, Acheson found himself outside the MOD building on Horse Guards Parade. A sudden shower had greyed the sky, and the building's sleek Portland Stone now looked dim and greasy. His heart was racing and sparks were shooting in random spirals in the periphery of his vision. Trying and failing to calm himself, he pulled out his phone and called his predecessor at the head of the Paras.

'Hello, Nick. How are you?'

'Not good, Don. Not bloody good at all. Are you in town or at Rothford?'

'Town. Been in meetings with Six at Vauxhall Cross all day. What's going on?'

'I'd rather tell you face to face.'

Acheson walked briskly to his club on Jermyn Street, swinging his tightly furled umbrella and jabbing its brass-ferruled tip at the pavement with every other step. Two green-haired climate change protestors sniggered as he passed them. He suppressed the urge to beat their heads to a pulp against the pavement.

He nodded to the doorman, outfitted in a splendid royal-blue frock coat and top hat. 'Morning, Raymond.'

'Morning, Colonel.'

Don was waiting for him in the reception area, sitting, legs crossed, in a burgundy leather armchair. He stood as soon as he spotted Acheson.

'Nick, old boy, what's up?' he said, advancing towards his younger colleague and shaking hands.

'Let's get a drink and I'll tell you.'

Five minutes later, with large gin and tonics sitting on a mahogany table between them, Acheson took a pull on his drink. He looked around. The room hadn't changed, he imagined, for several hundred years. A new coat of buttercup-yellow paint on the walls every now and then, he supposed, and new upholstery and curtains.

But the wood panelling, much like that enclosing the new secretary of state for defence in her fiefdom, the heavy, old fashioned armchairs, the glass-panelled book-cases with their collections of leather-bound military histories, journals and classics, and the equally venerable gentlemen sitting alone, in pairs or quartets, chatting in low murmurs: these, he felt, represented the DNA of the place.

Beyond these four walls, though, change was happening. Oh, yes. It was definitely bloody happening.

Not entirely trusting himself to speak without his voice cracking or trembling, he began.

'The lunatics have taken over the asylum, Don,' he said.

Don raised an eyebrow.

'Our new government, you mean?'

'In the person of Tracy Barnett-Short.'

The older man nodded and took a slow sip of his drink, regarding Acheson over the rim.

'This about your boys in Botswana?'

'Yes it bloody is!' Acheson said, unable to control the volume of his voice and earning a handful of disapproving stares from beneath bushy white eyebrows, or over the lowered pages of the *Times* or the *Daily Telegraph*. 'I've just come from the MOD. Asked her to look into the massacre and the bloody…' he paused to sigh out a breath, 'woman basically accused me of incompetence. Sent me packing like a naughty schoolboy. Jesus, Don, I wanted to kill her, I was so angry.'

Don nodded, then wrinkled his nose.

'Not sure offing the big boss would exactly smooth your path to the general staff, Nick, if I may say so.'

Acheson burst out laughing. He glared back at the retired army officers staring at him.

'No,' he said, when he'd recovered himself, 'you're probably right. But, Don, what the hell is going on?'

Don shrugged his shoulders. To Acheson, he looked old. His hair was all grey now, and receding at the temples.

'I think,' he said finally, 'people like us may be heading for a period of retrenchment. Our new political masters seem bent on creating a People's Republic of New Britain. They'll want an army, those kinds of people always do. But I dare say their focus will be on suppression of dissent at home, or support for their left-wing friends abroad, rather than anything more, what shall we call it, glorious.'

'How are things with your outfit?' Acheson asked.

'Not good, if I'm honest. We're governed by the Privy Council, as you know, so there are friendly opposition voices in the discussions, but the new PM and his cronies are intent on, what did he say to me? "Root and branch reforms of the security apparatus".'

'So you're still active?'

'Very much so. Took out an Islamist terror cell last month, as a matter of fact. Very satisfactory outcome.'

'Don,' Acheson said, leaning forward and dropping his voice, 'can you help me?'

Don smiled, leaning in towards Acheson.

'I thought you'd never ask,' he murmured. 'Want me to put a team together?'

'You can do that? Without alerting the PM or his bloody attack-dog at Defence?'

Don nodded.

'You know everyone thinks The Department is the ultimate in off-books wetwork outfits?'

'Yes.'

'It isn't.'

'No?'

'No. When I took over from Harry Macintosh I foresaw a time when the pols might decide we need our wings clipping, so I set up an arms-length outfit.'

Acheson grinned and felt relief flooding his system.

'You've got a Plan B, haven't you?'

Don returned the grin.

'Always.'

'Care to share?'

'Remember when I was CO of The Regiment?'

'Yes.'

'I created a cadre of lads who had, what shall we call it, something extra? Called them the Black Dogs. Gave 'em a little black diamond arm patch. They all loved it.'

'You replicated that at The Department?'

'Hmm mm-hmm, yes I did. Even got one of the original lads working for me. Chap called Wolfe.'

10

BIRMINGHAM, ENGLAND

The mourners at Stevo's funeral divided neatly into two distinctive camps. Family, dressed for the most part in black, and comrades and friends from the Paras. Like them, Gabriel wore his khaki No. 2 Service Dress uniform. The maroon lanyards and cap badge placement over the left eye indicated they were members of 1 Para, known informally as 'Fitness 1' for their role supporting the SAS in the Special Forces Support Group.

The sky, which for so many months had abandoned every other colour but blue, had turned the ashy grey of woodfire embers. A chill in the air had noses running and eyes watering, disguising the tears that flowed copiously as the vicar delivered the graveside prayers.

As his final 'amen' was repeated by the mourners, four paratroopers took hold of the ropes beneath the flag-draped coffin and lowered Stevo to his final resting place in the soil of the country he had loved so much.

At the edge of the crowd, Gabriel and Eli stood in a tight group with Don, Colonel Acheson and a man the latter had introduced simply as John. In his sixties, thick silver hair parted on the right, he had the upright bearing of a former soldier, although, Gabriel reflected, it could just as easily be the result of yoga or simply good genes.

Acheson, Don and Gabriel all wore medals on their chests. John did not, which, given his age, also moved Gabriel to conjecture that if he *had* served his country, it was in the security or intelligence services.

Gabriel turned and smiled at Eli. For a woman who always tended to wear bright colours when not in camo, she looked severe in her funeral outfit of a knee-length dress, black tights and heels. But black suited her.

As the other mourners drifted away from the graveside, Acheson turned to Don.

'Do you mind if we speak out here?'

'Not at all. Best privacy in the world.'

'I've known John since schooldays,' Acheson said, looking at his friend who stayed silent, letting Acheson explain his presence. 'We were at Manchester Grammar School together. I went into the army, John business. We always joke that I got the glory, John the money.'

Along with Eli and Don, Gabriel smiled dutifully, though the joke was barely worth it.

'Nick's right,' John said in a deep voice in which the flattened Mancunian vowels were clear. 'Mineral mining may not be as glamorous as what he does, but it pays well. Now I want to help him out by donating some of it. All I need to know, Colonel Webster—'

'Don, please.'

'Don, is how much and in what form. I can do bank transfers, cash or bloody big bars of gold. Just let me know how much, when and where you want it and it's yours.'

Now Gabriel understood. They were meeting the mission's banker.

'That's very kind of you, John,' Don said.

'Kind?' John repeated, his silver eyebrows jumping upwards. 'Listen, I'm something of an old fashioned bloke, if you take my meaning. A monarchist. A free marketeer. A patriot. And bloody proud of all three. This crew of communists who've lied their way into power will be gone in a few years. In the meantime, I'll not stand idly by while they refuse to avenge British lads killed helping the Africans better themselves.'

'Has Colonel Acheson talked to you about the sums we might need?' Gabriel asked.

'No. And it doesn't matter. You want a private jet? Helicopters? Guns? Vehicles? Give me your shopping list and I'll give you a trolley dash round whatever supermarket you chaps,' he interrupted himself as he turned to Eli, 'and ladies use when you're getting tooled up, or whatever you call it.'

'It could run into seven figures,' Gabriel said, not wanting to find himself and Eli stranded thousands of miles from home with a backer who suddenly choked off the money supply.

John smiled, putting deep crinkles around his icy-blue eyes.

'Shall I tell you the fookin' great thing about being a billionaire, lad?'

'Go on, then.'

'Me fortune's growing faster than I can spend it! You want a million quid? It's yours. Ten million! Why not?'

Then he burst out laughing, the sound made physical in a rising swirl of condensing breath in the chill air.

The meeting broke up at that point, with Don promising to liaise with Acheson and John over their 'trolley dash'.

* * *

Driving back to Aldeburgh in the big black Camaro Gabriel had inherited from a dead friend, Eli asked the question Gabriel had been worrying at like a ragged fingernail.

'How do you feel about operating outside the law?'

He frowned.

'Honestly? I'm not sure. We've always had the explicit backing of the Government and therefore the implicit backing of the Crown.'

'Whereas now we're operating as Don's private army.'

'Exactly. No cover from the MOD. No backup from the security services. No Get-Out-Of-Jail-Free card.'

'Do you believe in the operation?' Eli asked.

'Of course!'

'So do I. If those boys were IDF, Israel would have people on the ground in Botswana within days tracking their murderers.'

'So would we if Mr Tammerlane hadn't just taken up residence in Downing Street.'

'I don't trust him. You heard what he said on TV the other day about Israel.'

Gabriel nodded. They'd been holed up in their hotel room watching a Sunday morning interview with the new prime minister. Tammerlane had insisted that, while he would do everything in his power to prevent any form of racism getting a hold in Britain, people had to recognise that the state of Israel was nothing short of an apartheid state and had to be treated as such by the international community.

Eli had sworn at the screen and descended into a black mood it had taken most of the day and a very good dinner to lift.

'He has a majority, but we still have Parliament,' Gabriel said now. 'They'll temper his worst excesses.'

'I hope you're right,' she said. 'Uri called me yesterday while you were talking to Acheson and the other Paras at the wake.'

Gabriel's pulse jumped up. Uri Ziff was Eli's old boss at the Mossad and had made no secret of his desire to hire her away from Don.

'What did he want?' he asked, keeping his voice level.

'What do you think? "Eliya, things don't look so good in England. Come back. Your country needs people of your calibre. Now more than ever",' Eli said in a rough approximation of Uri's fruity baritone.

'What did you say?'

'I said, I'm living with the man I love. And he loves England. So here we stay.'

Gabriel stretched out his right hand and laid it on her thigh.

'I love you, too, El, but…'

'But what?'

'I don't know. I don't think Tammerlane's England is my England. If he starts stirring up hatred for Israel, well, you know where that could end. I won't put you through that.'

'You think we should have suitcases by the front door?'

'No. The house in Hong Kong has everything we need.'

'Ah. That other bastion of democracy.'

'You're right. Maybe I should sell it. Buy somewhere new.'

'But it was Zhao Xi's house.'

'Exactly. His *house*. Master Zhao lives in here,' he said, thumping his chest. 'The place in Hong Kong is just a building.'

'Take me there.'

'What?'

'Take me there! I want to see it. I want to meet Mei.'

She was referring to Gabriel's sister, long believed dead after a botched triad kidnapping in the eighties. Gabriel had only recently found out she was living on the island and working as a bodyguard for the boss of the White Koi triad, now deceased.

He nodded.

'Let's get the job in Botswana out of the way, then we'll go.'

* * *

Gabriel parked the big black muscle car on the gravel beside his simple, brick-built house on the Suffolk coast. The small garden was enough for a couple of steamer chairs where he and Eli could enjoy a glass of wine together, and that suited him fine.

With the V8 ticking as it cooled, he retrieved their bags from the boot and set them down. He inhaled and let the smells of salt and ozone flood his lungs.

He turned and looked towards the sea and its grey-green waters, topped with white horses. As he had known she would, Britta stood there amidst the cobbles, her fire-red hair loose and whipping around her head in the offshore wind. She lifted her right hand and waved. He lifted his hand out from his body to reciprocate, realised Eli was standing beside him, and let it drop.

'You all right?' she asked, interlacing his fingers with hers.

'I was thinking about Britta. She was on the beach.'

'Just now?'

'Yes.'

'Is your PTSD back?'

'I don't know. Delayed reaction?'

'Can you find time to see Fariyah?'

He shrugged.

'Would it help?'

'It did before.'

He sighed.

'OK. I'll try. It depends on Don, though. How fast he gets everything together for the mission.'

Eli bent and picked up one of the bags.

'Come on. Let's go in and have a brew.'

He shook his head.

'I have a better idea.'

Upstairs, Gabriel closed the bedroom door and turned to face Eli. He held his arms wide and, smiling a little, she stepped inside his embrace. He buried his nose in her long auburn hair and breathed in her scent that he had come to know so well: lemon and sandalwood.

Reaching up to the nape of her neck, he found the tag of the long brass zip closing her dress and dragged it, inch by inch, down along her spine. When he reached the swell of her bottom he dropped the tab and hooked his fingers around the soft black fabric on each side and drew them apart.

Eli shrugged once and the dress fell from her shoulders. She shimmied to the left and right causing the dress to slide over her legs and puddle at her feet. She took a step back and put her hands on her hips, then executed a slow turn until she was facing him again.

Holding Gabriel's eyes in hers, she unfastened her bra and

dropped it to one side. He allowed himself the luxury of taking in every curve, the swell of her breasts and the hardening brown nipples.

Without breaking eye contact, she stooped just enough to ease her knickers down over her thighs, her knees, and her calves until she could kick them free with an expert flick that sent them sailing across the bedroom and into the lidless laundry basket.

Gabriel grinned. It was a trick he didn't think he'd ever tire of.

'Now then, Mr Wolfe,' she said. 'Are you going to watch a poor Israeli girl get goosebumps standing here for your pleasure, or are you going to get undressed too?'

Gabriel shucked off his suit jacket, hooking it over the bedpost. The tie followed, after a few twirls and a wink that set Eli's giggles off.

One by one he undid the buttons on his white shirt before sliding his trousers and underpants off together.

'Come here,' he said, when he was naked.

Eli closed the gap between them and put her hands on his shoulders. Gabriel held her around the waist, braced his knees and lifted as she jumped up.

She reached down with one hand and found him, guided him into her, gasping as she leaned out from him, and arching her neck to expose her throat.

Slowly they began to move together, she raising herself up and then letting herself push down onto him, he moving her hips rhythmically in his grip, easing himself into her tempo.

As she approached her climax he leaned forwards and lowered her onto the bed, driving himself deep into her as she came before his own climax erupted, causing him to cry out.

'Oh, Eli! I love you!'

Afterwards, they lay entwined for an hour, watching the light fade outside and listening to the gulls keening and the halyards clinking against the masts of the boats in the next door boatyard. It was to be a long time before they would experience such peace and contentment again.

11

PADDINGTON GREEN

Amid the muted conversations and hum of centrifuges in the lab at Paddington Green Police Station, lead forensic scientist Lucian Young adjusted the focus of his microscope.

The picture sharpened. He looked at the array of particles one of the CSIs had lifted from the concrete platform at the top of the fire station training tower. At x10 magnification, they resembled boulders, crusted and rugged, varying in size but all tinged in various shades of rust-red and speckled with silvery flecks like diamonds.

Soil. He'd already analysed dust and grit from the same location. The samples were completely different, both in morphology and colour. The concrete samples were sharper, with larger plate-like areas of reflective mica. And they were grey and yellow.

He increased the magnification to x100 and moved the slide around beneath the lens. Different boulders swam into focus, though all displayed identical characteristics. Then he saw something that piqued his curiosity.

'Hello,' he said. 'What are you?'

The object capturing his attention was black, curved, shiny and ended in a needle-point. The blunt end was ragged. Had it been broken off? He pressed a button on the side of the microscope and took a high-resolution digital photograph.

After printing out a large-format copy, he took the sample over to a bank of high-tech equipment tended by a young woman in a white coat. Her blonde hair tied up in high mini-bunches gave her the appearance of a science club schoolgirl.

'Jess, can you run this soil sample through the gas chromatograph and mass-spectrometer for me, please?' he said.

She nodded wordlessly, accepted the slide and placed it reverently on her desk.

Lucian returned to his own desk and made a call. The ringing was cut short before the first digital purr ended.

'Magda Szabo.'

'How's my favourite forensic entomologist doing?' Lucian asked with a smile.

'Lucian?'

'One and the same. I've got a toughie for you.'

'Ooh! Sounds interesting. From a body?'

'For once, no. We're working on Operation Birch. I've got a soil sample from the sniper nest and—'

'Soil? I'm insects.'

'…and I've found something that looks like a stinger. It's no more than a tenth of a millimetre long.'

'And you were wondering if I could identify it for you.'

'If you had time.'

'You have picture, yes?'

'You want me to email it to you?'

'I'll have answer for you as soon as I can. I'll do it straight away. There are various databases I can consult.'

* * *

Two hours later, Lucian's mobile rang. He glanced at the screen and smiled.

'That was quick, Magda,' he said.

'It's Operation Birch. I would be sitting on my hands for this?'

'Of course not. So. What can you tell me?'

'It's very strange.'

'Come on, Magda, don't keep me in suspense. What is it? A spider fang? A wasp sting?'

'Neither. It is mandible. Right mandible, to be precise. From termite.'

He could hear the triumph in her voice. And understood why.

'A termite? You're sure?'

'What? You doubt your, what did you call me, "favourite forensic entomologist"?'

'Sorry, no. Of course not. What kind, could you tell?'

'Absolutely! It is soldier of species *Macrotermes michaelseni*.'

'Habitat?'

'Very interesting, given you found it in Windsor.'

She paused.

'Please, Magda!'

'Sub-Saharan Africa. You know those big mounds?'

'Yes.'

'He is one of those. Long way from home, yes?'

Lucian nodded as he thanked her and ended the call.

A bloody long way from home.

He stared at the picture he'd printed out. At this magnification, the jaw looked like a particularly vicious knife blade, albeit one snapped off the hilt.

'What's that?' Jess asked, as she arrived by his shoulder.

'That,' he said, 'is the right mandible of a soldier termite. Exclusively found in Sub-Saharan Africa.'

'That's interesting,' she said.

'I know.'

'No, I mean it's interesting because I've been working on the soil sample you gave me.'

'Go on,' he said, feeling that a second revelation was only seconds away.

'I compared the mass-spec and gas-chroma results to the UN's

Harmonized World Soil Database. There's a ninety-two percent probability it comes from the Okavango Delta in Botswana.'

'You're joking!'

She grinned.

'Actually, yes, I am. It matches the soil in the flowerbeds in Hyde Park.'

'Shit! I thought we were onto something.'

She burst out laughing.

'Sorry, boss, but you're so easy to fool. No, it really is from Botswana. There's a spike in the copper content that's so distinctive it's like a fingerprint.'

Lucian's fingers flew over his keyboard as he tapped in a search query: Okavango Delta termite.

The very first search result Google returned was 'Master Builders of the Okavango'. It led to an article about mound-building termites.

He turned and thanked Jess, then picked up his phone.

'Stella?'

'Hi, Lucian, what's up?'

'Someone in that sniper nest had recently been in Botswana.'

'What?'

'I've got two data points that confirm the presence of soil from Botswana on the top floor of the training tower. A termite mandible and the soil sample we found it in.'

'Bloody hell!'

'I knew you'd be pleased.'

'You're a genius, Luce. I'm taking this to Callie.'

12

Tammerlane looked up from his papers. He smiled broadly and rounded his desk to shake hands with his visitor.

'Anthony! Please, take a seat.'

As commissioner of the Metropolitan Police, Anthony Redding was the public face of the investigation, known as Operation Birch, into the assassination of Princess Alexandra.

'Thank you, Prime Minister.'

'Call me Joe, please,' Tammerlane said with a smile.

'We have some rather disturbing intelligence. About the killer's identity.'

'Go on,' Tammerlane, said, cupping his chin in his hand.

'It appears that he was an Israeli. Name of Dov Lieberman,' Redding said, his hooded eyes maintaining contact with the PM's.

'Mossad?'

'No, Sir. He was a schoolteacher. Physics, apparently.'

'A physics teacher?' Tammerlane repeated, arranging his features into an expression of disbelief. 'What, you're telling me assassinating British princesses was a *hobby*?'

'No, Sir. He was a marksman in the IDF. They all do national service in—'

'Yes, yes, I know. Bloody warmongers.'

'Well, that's how he came to be such a good shot.'

'You haven't told me why, Anthony.'

'Why, Sir?'

'Yes! Why did he do it?'

'I'm afraid we don't know. We've asked the Israelis for his home computer, any laptops, devices at his home, but we're still waiting.'

'Yes, and I'm sure you'll be waiting a lot longer. Thank you, Anthony, for coming today. Leave this with me. I think we need to rattle the can a little.'

* * *

The Downing Street press officer approached the microphone and waited for silence. The breeze flapped at a page of A4 in her hand but, otherwise, everything about her was poised, immobile, immaculate, from her tied-back blonde hair to the pencil skirt of her black suit.

'Ladies and gentlemen, the prime minister.'

Tammerlane smiled at the assembled journalists. Then he frowned and gripped the lectern. He waited for the harsh whine of the cameras' digital shutters to quieten before he spoke.

'I have just come from a meeting with the commissioner of the Metropolitan Police Service. He brought me the most disturbing intelligence imaginable. Princess Alexandra was assassinated…' He paused and shook his head, frowning deeper. 'No, let's be blunt here, *murdered,* by an agent of the apartheid state of Israel. A former military sniper acting covertly in the guise of a teacher.'

He waited for the brief susurrus of journalistic whispers to die down before resuming.

'Britain is a sovereign nation. Whatever your views of the monarchy, and mine are no secret, it is an act of state-sponsored terrorism to deploy an assassin on foreign soil and murder one of its citizens.'

He found a TV camera and stared directly into its lens, pointing a finger as he spoke.

'As of now, Britain is breaking off diplomatic ties with the terrorist state of Israel. We are expelling diplomats and closing its embassy. All Israeli citizens are given notice: you have one month to leave this island.

My home secretary and her colleagues at Defence, International Trade and Overseas Development will be announcing further measures later. Thank you. That is all.'

* * *

'What the fuck just happened?' Eli said to Gabriel as she stabbed the remote's off button.

'He's mad.'

'That's me done. You know that, right?'

'I know. I can't think.'

'Well I can! I'm going upstairs to pack. This country just put out a Jews Out! sign and I for one am not going to wait around until they start knocking on doors at three in the fucking morning!'

'Eli, wait!'

She whirled round.

'No! *You* wait. I'm leaving.'

'He's posturing. There'll be legal challenges. It's unenforceable. Parliament will never allow it.'

Breathing heavily, chest heaving, Eli took her foot off the first step. She came and stood right in front of Gabriel.

'He's the prime minister. With a huge majority. He's also a hard-left dictator-in-waiting with a hard-on for Israel.'

'What about the mission?'

'I'll do that. It's in Africa anyway, so I assume Tammerlane's tentacles don't stretch that far. But that's it.' A tear crept down her cheek. 'Gabriel, you know what's coming, right?'

Unwilling to believe it, yet unable to process the press conference and deal with the grief of the woman he loved at the same time, Gabriel defaulted to operational mode.

'Let's both pack. We'll head down to Rothford and stay there till we deploy. If it makes you feel any better, while Tammerlane's in charge I have no desire to sit around and watch him dismantle everything I love about this country.'

'You mean it?'

'Yes, I mean it.' He held her upper arms and looked deep into those grey-green eyes. '*You* are what matters to me. If it's all going to get shitty here then we decamp somewhere until it's over. People like Tammerlane don't last for ever.'

'No. But they last long enough.'

* * *

Gabriel cut the Camaro's engine at the gate to MOD Rothford, the army base in the Essex countryside that housed, alongside its official residents, the small team that comprised the leadership and support staff for The Department.

'Morning, Sir. Mr Wolfe, isn't it?'

'That's right, Corporal. Andy, isn't it?'

'Yes, Sir. Miss Schochat with you?' the uniformed soldier asked, bending to peer in through the open window. 'Morning, miss.'

'Morning, Corporal,' she said, flashing him a grin that Gabriel had rarely seen since Tammerlane had swept into power. 'How are you?'

'Very good, miss, thank you.'

'We're here to see Colonel Webster,' Gabriel said.

'He's expecting you, Sir. Said you'd find him on the range.'

'The range?'

'Yes, Sir. Said it was about time the old warhorse got his eye in again.'

Occupying a tree-screened acre or so on the north-eastern edge of the base, the rifle range was usually the preserve of uniformed recruits or squads undergoing specialist weapons training. Today, alongside the men and women in their twenties, in combat gear, Don Webster stood in a bay, an instructor by his side.

The air reeked of the sharp tang of burnt propellant and hot brass. Ejected cartridge cases flew in all directions, their spinning sides flashing in the smoke-filtered sun.

Two dozen or so SA 80 assault rifles being fired on full auto made talking at conversational volume impossible.

'Don knows something,' Eli shouted to Gabriel as they walked up to the rear of the line of shooters.

They stood a few yards behind Don. Unlike the regular soldiers along the line, Don was firing single shots. Gabriel looked down the range. His boss was shooting at a target at the five-hundred-yard mark. A female silhouette.

After squeezing off a shot, Don turned, smiled and handed the SA 80 to the instructor.

'Morning, boss,' Gabriel yelled, when they were within two feet of each other.

'Morning, Old Sport, Eli. Let's go to my office,' he added, pointing at the administration block for good measure.

Inside and with mugs of freshly brewed coffee and a plate of biscuits sitting in front of them, Gabriel waited for his boss to speak. Eli beat him to it.

'Did you get bored of paperwork, boss?'

Don grinned.

'To tell you the truth, I did. Have been, in fact, since I took up the job. Needs must, eh?'

'That the only reason you were brushing up your marksmanship?'

Don steepled his fingers under his nose.

'Hmm. Mm-hmm. A teacher makes a five-hundred-and-fifty-yard head-shot through a ten-mile-an-hour crosswind over hot urban streets. Smelled fishy to me, so I checked with Six. Lieberman left the army in 2012 and I got to wondering how feasible it would be for someone that rusty to make that kind of shot.'

'And?'

'Well, *I* couldn't. And I went through a hundred rounds trying.

Paul Brooke is the best firearms instructor on base, and even with him spotting for me I couldn't shoot for shit.'

Gabriel frowned, processing the information.

'What are you saying?'

'Not exactly sure, Old Sport. But I've put in a call to the Met. Asked if we could take a look at their analysis of the rifle.'

He pushed a thin brown cardboard folder across the desk. Gabriel read the top sheet and the fingerprint analyst's clipped sentences. He passed it to Eli, who scanned the notes then closed the file.

'The fourth print. You think there was a second shooter?'

'I don't know,' Don said. 'But at worst we know that there was someone else involved. I checked with the Met. The rules on handling firearms are strict. Only the armourer and the AFO to whom the weapon is assigned handle it.'

'Tammerlane?' Gabriel asked.

'His prints weren't on it. The Met asked him to provide a set for elimination purposes.'

'Lieberman was a fall guy,' Eli said.

Gabriel could hear the hope in her voice. That, even now, there was a chance normality could be restored. His heart was a weight in his chest. Because he didn't see it.

'I've passed on my concerns to the Met, along with a few carefully chosen thoughts on the marksmanship issue,' Don said. 'They told me they'd bear it in mind, but you know what the cops are like. At the moment it's an open and shut case. Ballistics match the round to the G3K. They have a dead man with his prints on the murder weapon. And a witness in the person of our own, dear prime minister.'

'But surely they can see it doesn't make sense!' Eli said, raising her voice. 'Israel's a *friend* of Britain. Why would the Mossad assassinate a princess?'

Sensing Eli's mounting impatience, Gabriel changed the subject.

'What about the mission? Are we good to go?'

'There, we *do* have clarity,' Don said. 'I've booked you on a Virgin flight for tomorrow evening. Leaves at five past eight. You transfer in Johannesburg then on to Gaborone. You arrive 10.35 a.m. the following morning.'

'Kit?' Eli said.

'Waiting for you in Gaborone. Our friend John has a contact in the region,' Don said. 'Chap runs a private security firm called Kagiso Group. Our intel team have checked them out. They look after Western interests in the region. Pipelines, factories, mines, that sort of thing. He's sending a driver for you.'

'What about a cover story?' Gabriel asked.

'The old standby: freelance journalists. We've prepared IDs for both of you. Poaching's a big issue so it makes sense you'd be out there researching for a story.'

Eli shifted in her chair. Gabriel caught the movement out of the corner of his eye and turned. Her brow was furrowed and there was a tightness around her eyes.

'Boss,' she said, 'there's something I need to tell you.'

Don smiled at her.

'What's that?'

'Uri Ziff asked me to go back to Israel. To rejoin the Mossad. I'm...' She paused and reached out with her left hand to find Gabriel's. She gave his hand a hard squeeze. 'I'm seriously considering it.'

'Because of this business of Tammerlane's?'

'I work for you, but my passport's Israeli. I only have a month to...' she swallowed, '...get out.'

Don nodded. He opened his desk drawer.

'Do you *like* working for me?'

Her eyes flashed.

'Of course I do! You know that. I already turned him down once.'

'I do know. But has anything changed? Apart,' he added quickly, 'from Tammerlane.'

'No.'

'Here,' Don said, sliding a brown envelope across the desk.

'What is it?'

'Open it and find out.'

Gabriel watched Eli reach for the envelope and slide her thumbnail, her bitten thumbnail he noticed, under the flap.

She tipped up the envelope and out slid a brand-new British passport.

She looked at Gabriel, then at Don.

'You said my citizenship was a grey area for now,' she said with a grin.

'From grey to blue,' Don said, with a smile. 'I pulled a few strings at the Home Office. Couple of people there owe me favours.'

She opened it and flicked to the photo page. Held it out for Gabriel to inspect.

'It's definitely you,' he said, earning a punch to the arm.

Then the frown returned.

'Legally, I can stay. But what if this is only the start, boss?' she asked. 'What if it's Israelis today, Zionists tomorrow and Jews the day after that?'

'I honestly don't think it will come to that, Eli,' he said. 'But I understand your anxiety. We look after our own here. If you ever decide you need to leave,' he glanced at Gabriel, who nodded to the unspoken question, 'along with Gabriel, I will personally arrange a flight anywhere you need to go. With an armed escort from our friends in Hereford, if necessary.'

Eli flicked her index finger at the corner of her right eye.

'Thanks, boss.' She sniffed. 'I mean it. And I *will* let you know. I promise.'

Gabriel looked at her and took her other hand in his. He knew, in that moment, that he would leave everything behind to be with her.

Don smiled.

'That's settled then.'

13

BOTSWANA

On the last leg of their journey to Botswana, they'd overflown thousands of square miles of scrub, savannah and forest. Nothing but green and reddish-brown from one end of an in-flight movie to the other. So to emerge from the jetway into the air conditioned splendour of the arrivals hall at Gaborone's Sir Seretse Khama International Airport came as a shock to Gabriel.

He turned to Eli.

'Why do I feel we've just landed in Geneva?' he asked.

She grinned.

'I know. Look at all that marble. We could be anywhere in the world.'

All around them, people were talking loudly into phones, chattering excitedly, or wandering through the glittering space deep in conversation. Business types, mothers in flamboyant traditional aprons, skirts and tops dragging children by the hand, students in colourful western-style outfits. The whole place was a hive of activity.

Gabriel nodded, looking around for someone holding a welcome card with their cover names written on it.

He found what, or more precisely who, he was looking for. A young black man in a shimmering light-grey suit and narrow black tie standing beside a life-size sculpture of an elephant set amid rocks and grass at the centre of an intricate maze-pattern of black and silver granite floor tiles. He was holding up an iPad displaying their cover names.

JENSEN/CAMARO

Eli nudged Gabriel. They wheeled their cases over to the young man. As soon as he spotted them making their way towards him, his mouth widened into a broad grin, revealing flashing white teeth among which a gold canine twinkled.

'You are my customers?' he asked, still smiling and holding out his hand.

They shook. Gabriel rested his wheeled case and patted his chest.

'I'm Jensen.'

'And I'm Camaro,' Eli said.

'Very pleased to make your acquaintance. Welcome to G-City. Phefo Sibanda at your service,' he said. 'My name means "windy", on account of my mama gave birth to me in a storm. She say the damn thing nearly blew me out of her belly!'

Smiling, Eli pointed at the sculpture.

'Are those real tusks?'

Phefo nodded vigorously.

'You better believe it, my lady.'

They examined the sculpture from all angles, and Gabriel noticed the empty black tubes in the tusks where nerves had once run. He read from a plaque mounted near the elephant's head.

'It says these were all found on elephants that had died of natural causes.'

'Must be worth a fair bit,' Eli answered.

'Three hundred and thirty million pula, my lady,' Phefo said. 'That's about thirty million dollars.'

'Wow! Has anyone ever tried to steal it?'

'No. Too many police. But maybe you see why poaching is such a problem in Bots?'

Phefo led them proudly to a white Mercedes E-Class saloon parked under the shade of a tree in the airport's open-air carpark. On the drive into the centre of Gaborone, which Phefo had taught them to call G-city, Gabs or Mageba, Gabriel's phone lit up with a text.

Welcome to Bots! Phefo will pick you up at 9.00 a.m. tomorrow and bring you out to our compound. George Taylor.

'Is George Taylor your boss?' Gabriel asked Phefo.

'He's everybody's boss. The *big* boss!' he answered, with a laugh.

After ten more minutes' driving Phefo made a right turn off Julius Nyerere Drive onto Chuma Drive, a wide dual-carriageway lined on one side with trees and the other by a low, white concrete wall. Low-growing shrubs dotted a scruffy pink gravel median strip.

The white wall on the left was replaced with a neatly trimmed hedge. Phefo hit the brakes to make a left turn beneath a squat pink concrete gateway that reminded Gabriel of Stonehenge: two slope-shouldered uprights supporting a wide, flat rectangular capstone, all cast with geometric designs.

'Here we are, Sir, my lady,' Phefo said. 'Welcome to Avani Gaborone Resort and Casino.'

Their luggage retrieved from the boot and a discreet twenty-dollar tip passed from Gabriel's palm to Phefo's, they made their way inside. A tall, broad-shouldered porter marched over, picked up their cases as if they were filled with feathers, and deposited them on a gold luggage trolley.

While they waited to check in, Gabriel nodded at the trolley.

'D'you remember when we used one of those to carry our rifles into that hotel in Kazakhstan?' he asked Eli.

She grinned back at him.

'What was our cover that time?'

'Intelligence analysts.'

Her eyes widened.

'That's right! We were Mr and Mrs,' she paused, 'Edmonds, was it?'

'Esmond.'

'Yeah. Mr and Mrs Esmond.'

Gabriel felt a rush of emotion surge through him, out of nowhere, like a summer storm.

'You know, Eli…' he began.

'What?'

'Yes, Sir, Madam? Checking in?' a young female voice asked from the desk.

They broke eye contact and turned towards the receptionist.

Passports photocopied, room keys assigned and all the usual rigmarole dealt with, they found themselves in a cabin looking out onto a swimming pool fringed with palm trees.

Eli flopped back onto the huge bed, arms spread wide.

'Well, this could be worse,' she said.

Gabriel lay beside her, head propped up on one elbow.

'Not bad for a couple of contract killers, is it?'

She frowned.

'Is that what you think we are?'

'Why, don't you?'

'No!'

'What, then?'

'I don't know. Agents, I suppose. Or operatives, if you prefer.'

'But when push comes to shove, we're the ones pulling the trigger or slipping the knife in, aren't we?'

'Yes. But the people we're up against aren't innocent victims. They're enemies of the state. That's what The Department does.'

He leaned over and kissed her softly.

'I totted up the number of people I've killed in the last two months. How many, do you think?'

'Gabe, don't do this, please,' she said.

'Go on,' he said, persistent now. 'How many?'

She huffed out a breath.

'I don't know. Six?'

'Thirteen.'

'Unlucky for some.'

'And how many do you think were enemies of the British state?'

Eli clamped her lips together.

'Fine,' he said. 'I'll tell you. None. Not one. Everyone I killed in Russia was for personal reasons. Everyone in China because I owed a triad boss a favour.'

Now Eli did speak.

She hoisted herself up into a sitting position and cradled his face between her palms.

'Gabriel Wolfe! Stop beating yourself up over this. The Russians killed Britta. They were trying to kill you, in case you'd forgotten. As for the Chinese, I don't know what to say. Maybe it wasn't your finest moment, but you said Fang Jian kidnapped your sister all those years ago. And as for the Communists, fuck them!'

He sighed.

'OK. You're right. Sorry.'

'What were you going to ask me when we were checking in?'

'What?'

'In the queue. You started to ask me something, then the receptionist called us.'

He shook his head.

'Can't remember. Hey, let's go for a swim. That pool looks inviting.'

Eli frowned.

'Hmm. Fine. Last one in's a rotten egg!'

Stripping his shirt off, Gabriel laughed.

'Very good! Have you been mugging up on British slang?'

'A girl's got to do something while her man's gallivanting around the world fighting the bad guys!'

She unclipped her bra and stepped out of her knickers, caught Gabriel staring frankly at her and executed a neat pirouette, hands out from her sides.

'Like what you see?' she asked, winking at him.

'The swim can wait,' he growled at her.

'Oh, no, mister!' she said, evading him as he made a grab for her waist. 'I need to cool off. And so do you!'

She unzipped her suitcase and fished out a coral-pink bikini. Moments later, she was swinging the sliding door across and running for the water.

Much later, sated by food, wine and sex, and with Eli sleeping beside him, Gabriel stared up at the ceiling. A cobalt-blue gecko skittered across its textured surface before freezing into immobility.

He remembered Eli's words earlier. *Perhaps you're right, El. China wasn't my finest moment but I put an end to Colonel Na's reign of terror. And as for Fang and Liu, they were crooks, both of them. Liu was corrupt, too. They conspired to kill me after I'd done their dirty work.*

He noticed the gecko wore sergeant's stripes on its front legs. And then he heard a voice he hadn't heard for a long time.

She's got a point, boss. Can't just sit there while the bad guys try to fuck you over, can you?

He turned his head and there, in the dark corner of the room, over by the wardrobe, sat a handsome black man in the motley camo and olive-green webbing of a SAS trooper.

Hello, Smudge. Didn't we say goodbye in Camberwell New Cemetery?

Can't keep a good man down, boss, Smudge, or the hallucination, replied with a broad grin.

Does this mean my PTSD is back?

Nah, boss. Not unless I am. And I'm dead and buried, aren't I?

So I'm dreaming?

Not for me to say. Though I reckon your shrink might have something to say about it. What's her name, Fariyah?

Yeah. I haven't been to see her for a while.

You should. Do you good. Here, he said, nodding in Eli's direction. *She's all right, isn't she?*

Gabriel glanced over at Eli.

She's fantastic, Smudge. I mean, she's brave, she's smart, she's sexy…

Well then…

What?

When are you going to make an honest woman of her?

I nearly asked her earlier.

What stopped you?

The receptionist.

Smudge grinned. Gabriel was relieved to see that his lower jaw, shot off by a militiaman's Kalashnikov round, stayed in place.

Come on, boss. You know that ain't why. What's the problem? You love her, don't you?

Of course! You know I do.

Right. And she loves you.

It's not that simple, mate.

Nothing's simpler. You just go down on one knee, look up into those beautiful eyes of hers and say, Eli Schochat, will you marry me?

Look what happened to Britta.

What, you think you cursed her by proposing? Boss, I don't want to be crude here, but she dumped you! When Kristersson killed her she was engaged to Jarryd, not you.

Is true, a gravelly male voice with a Russian accent interrupted. *Plus, Britta was never target. We wanted you dead, not her.*

Hello, Max, Gabriel said.

Max Novgorodsky, a Russian gangster Gabriel had shot in revenge for killing Britta, lolled in an armchair, his head replaced by that of his pet wolf, Pyotr.

Max got to his feet, baring yellow fangs that dripped with saliva. He approached the bed. Gabriel's heart rate spiked as that hideous mouth widened still further.

The wolf-man flung out its right arm. Long, ragged claws raked across Smudge's face and neck, slicing deep into arteries and releasing a flood of scarlet that sprayed into the air.

I'm coming for you, Gabe, Max said. 'Gabe! Gabe! GABE!'

Gabriel screamed.

'Gabe, Gabe!' Eli was saying, over and over again. She was shaking him and staring into his eyes. For a second her mouth was the wolf's mouth, unnaturally wide and lined with sharp-pointed teeth.

Gabriel twisted away from her, straining to get free of her grasp.

Then her features resolved into that familiar face he'd grown to know so well, and to love.

'Oh, God, El, I had a nightmare.'

'No shit! Look at you, you're drenched,' she said. 'Come on, let's get you a towel and then we'll change the sheets.'

***

Gabriel opened his eyes. He checked the time: 7.00 a.m. The memory of the nightmare was clear in his mind. He could still hear Smudge, still see the monstrous apparition that had been Max/Pyotr.

Eli was already up, and showering. Gabriel climbed out of bed and looked at himself in the full-length mirror screwed to the wall. He took a deep breath, forced a smile onto his face, and walked into the bathroom.

'Morning,' he said, cheerily.

'Morning. How are you feeling?'

'I'm fine. I'm sorry if I scared you last night.'

'Huh. It'll take more than that to scare me. But I am worried about you. Is everything OK?'

'Yeah, it's fine. *I'm* fine.'

'Really. You're not just saying that?'

'Truly. It's all good.'

'Right. In that case, why don't you get in here and soap my back for me, then we'll go and get a proper breakfast. We've got poachers to catch.'

14

Gabriel and Eli stood outside the hotel's main building at 8.55 a.m., waiting for Phefo.

They'd opted for a universal casual look that journalists, NGO staff and the smarter sort of adventurous tourist sported, from Bolivia to Bangalore: khakis, polo shirts and well-worn hiking boots. Each had a daysack, though these contained nothing more dangerous than a camera, notebook and bottles of water. All the 'interesting' kit, they'd be picking up later in the morning.

Around them, tourists, businessmen and a few businesswomen chatted loudly, slapping each other on the back or exchanging business cards.

Nobody gave them a second glance. Why should they? All around them louder, more colourfully dressed and clearly wealthier individuals gave off brasher social signals that drew the eye and faded anyone less gaudy into the background.

A cheerful double-toot made them turn round. Phefo's sleek white Merc purred to a halt at the kerb. He was out of the car and round to hold the door open for Eli before she could reach for the handle.

'There you go, my lady,' he said with one of his trademark, gold-flecked grins.

She winked at Gabriel as she got in. To Gabriel, the meaning was clear: *as with gate guards at MOD Rothford, so with drivers in G-City!* Gabriel followed her into the car's chilly interior.

'Strapped in, Sir, my lady?'

'We're good,' Gabriel said, nodding to Phefo in the rear-view mirror.

'Where's the Kagiso Group compound?' Eli asked as Phefo powered away from the hotel gateway, accelerating steadily down Chuma Drive, another tree-lined boulevard.

'About twenty-three kilometres. We own the land to the northwest of Mokolondi Nature Reserve,' he said. 'There's heavy traffic on Willie Seboni, so I'll take you the direct route, on the A1. Normally it's way slower but, man, the jam's a G-City special. That's what we call them, you know?'

As they left the downtown area, the flashy modern buildings and gaily painted villas in peach, lemon-yellow and sky-blue, gave way to a few straggling kilometres of corrugated-iron shacks and food stands, and then nothing but Botswana's beautiful countryside. On both sides of the road unbroken prairie-like flatland was punctuated by stands of broad-leafed trees and thorny scrub. Distant blue-tinged mountains promised cooler, higher ground.

For the next twenty-five minutes, Phefo acted as combination tour guide and acclimatisation specialist. Finishing a story about where to get the best barbecue chicken in G-City, he turned onto a red clay back road. Even with the Merc's superior suspension, the ruts and potholes made their presence felt.

After a couple of juddering miles, he rolled to a stop in front of a pair of tall steel gates, topped with razor wire. More wire stretched left and right, before disappearing into the trees. A sheet metal sign bolted to the bars read:

KAGISO GROUP
PRIVATE PROPERTY

NO ADMITTANCE WITHOUT
ID OR AUTHORISATION

Another read:

!WARNING!
!LIVE FIRING EXERCISES AT ALL TIMES!
!DANGER OF DEATH!

Phefo punched a code into a stainless-steel box mounted on a post to the right of the gates. With a clank from their well-greased hinges, the gates slid open on runners set flush with the red earth.

Gabriel rolled his window down. Hot air gusted into the car's cool interior. He listened carefully and, yes, there it was. The distant but unmistakeable sound of small arms fire. His heart thrilled to it and his right index finger twitched involuntarily.

Ever since leaving the SAS, he'd had occasional invitations to join outfits like Kagiso Group. Either directly from their owners, always ex-military men, or indirectly, from former comrades or ex-soldiers tapping into veterans' networks.

He'd always said no. Partly because his job for The Department kept him occupied. Partly because some of the private security firms weren't too choosy about their clients.

Brutal dictator putting down an uprising with government troops and mercenaries? Of course, Sir! Yours for a cool couple of million. Unscrupulous energy firm suppressing local protests at chemical spills? We have the men, the muscle and the motivation. Sign here.

But here he was, about to accept logistical support from one of those self-same operations. *Yes. To find the killers of a bunch of Paras. My conscience is clear. On this one, at least.*

The car pulled up in the centre of a tramped-flat red earth

square. A white-painted single-storey building occupied the whole of one side. Its double glass doors and etched Kagiso Group logo – an eagle clutching a rifle in its talons – suggested this was the HQ. On the adjacent sides, more white buildings, some with windows, some blank-walled: stores or training rooms, Gabriel guessed.

The fourth side was empty. The red track they'd arrived on stretched away through the bush.

Gabriel and Eli climbed out of the car and accepted their daysacks from Phefo, who'd gone straight to the boot. They both stuck bush hats on and donned sunglasses.

'Greetings!' a male voice shouted. 'Welcome to Mokolondi.'

Gabriel and Eli turned. A tall, thickset white man was striding towards them, hand outstretched. No hat, just a sun-browned scalp bisected by a jagged silver scar from crown to forehead. Deep fissures in his cheeks and radiating from the outer corners of his eyes gave his complexion the look of a dried-out river-bed. He wore camouflage fatigues and sand-coloured combat boots, laced to mid-calf.

'George Taylor, at your service,' he boomed as he arrived, and grasped first Gabriel's hand then Eli's. 'Late of Hammersmith, London, and the Royal Regiment of Fusiliers. Now a proud resident of Mageba and CEO of Kagiso Group. Means "peace" in Tsetswana, by the way.'

Gabriel and Eli each shook his hand and introduced themselves.

'Do you live out here?' Eli asked.

'Part of the time, dear lady, yes,' Taylor said. 'Home's a delightful little villa on Nelson Mandela Drive. Come on, you must be thirsty after the drive.'

He led them over to the building bearing the Kagiso Group logo. As Gabriel had guessed, it was the HQ, complete with receptionists, a waiting area, an IT suite, and a variety of conference rooms.

'Impressive,' he said, as Taylor showed them each function housed within the building, from telecoms and briefing rooms to lecture hall and guest rooms.

'Thanks. We like to think so. We get heads of state, generals,

CEOs of Fortune 500 companies coming through here. It projects an air of competence. Reassures them their dollars are going to be well spent.'

'How many men do you have under your command?' Eli asked.

'In total, nine hundred. We have deployments that could call for anywhere from a team of four to a couple of hundred. Right now, we've got three hundred and seventy-five on call. The rest are in the field.'

'All based in Botswana?' Gabriel asked.

'No. We have twenty here right now. The rest are based at other locations. But this is our African operational base. As I'm sure you can imagine, most of our work is somewhere on this wonderful continent.'

He took them out to the back of the building. A sweeping deck looked out across the countryside. Wicker chairs and a glass-topped table sat beneath a huge triangular canvas sail strung on galvanised steel poles.

They sat, and a minute or two later, a woman appeared, dressed in a traditional black-and-white maid's uniform, complete with frilled apron and cap. She set down a tray of frosted mugs of beer.

Taylor beamed up at her.

'Thanks, Mary. Can you tell chef we'll have lunch at one, please?'

'Yes, Mr Taylor,' she said with a smile, before leaving them to enjoy the cold beer and unbroken view of trees and scrub that stretched to the horizon.

'Cheers!' Taylor said loudly before downing half of his beer.

'Cheers!' Gabriel and Eli said in unison.

'How did you meet John?' Taylor asked.

'Didn't he tell you?' Gabriel replied.

'Why don't *you* tell me?'

Gabriel frowned. 'We met at the funeral of one of the lads who were massacred. Guy called Steve Wallingham.'

Taylor smiled, seemingly satisfied.

'Sorry. Just doing my due diligence. I like to know who I'm dealing with. And you're ex-regiment, is that right?'

'Eight years. I was badged in in 2005 and I left in 2012.'

'How about before that?'

'Paras.'

'Ever see action in Africa?'

Gabriel nodded.

'I was part of Operation Barras. September 2000 in Sierra Leone. We supported the SAS against the West Side Boys. You ever hear of them?'

'Nasty bunch,' Taylor grunted, taking another pull on his beer.

'They'd taken British hostages,' Gabriel said. 'We recovered the hostages and some British army trucks and blew the West Side Boys' heavy weapons to shit.'

Taylor turned to Eli.

'How about you, Eli? You must have something special about you if you ended up out here,' he said, sweeping his free arm in a wide semi-circle.

'IDF then the Mossad. Now I work with Gabriel in a government role.'

Taylor gave a low, appreciative whistle.

'Mossad, eh? Kidon?'

He was referring to the secretive unit within the Mossad responsible for targeted assassinations of Israel's enemies. Those recruited to join the "tip of the spear" were drawn exclusively from Israeli Special Forces.

Eli smiled.

'If I told you that, I'd have to kill you.'

Taylor stared at her for a couple of seconds, then laughed loudly, startling a pair of grey-and-turquoise parrots that had perched on the edge of the sail canopy.

'I believe you would, too,' he said, finally, wiping his eyes with a spotless white handkerchief. 'Although whether you'd get out of Bots in one piece is another matter.'

She inclined her head.

'I think I'd manage.'

After a little more banter, Taylor straightened in his chair and slapped his hands down on his knees.

'You didn't come all this way just to swap war stories,' he said. 'Do you want to follow me? We'll go and meet Frank.'

'Frank?' Eli asked.

'Onagweyo. Our quartermaster.'

They walked together along a track for a hundred yards until they reached a white-painted blockhouse, roughly sixty yards to a side. Recent rains had splashed red mud up against the first foot of the walls, giving them the look of bloodstained plaster.

Inch-thick steels bars striped the windows, which were backed with a reflective film, preventing anyone from seeing in. A steel plate reinforced the door and the lock looked serious enough to withstand anything less powerful than a thermic lance.

Taylor smiled.

'Welcome to Toyland,' he said, as he entered a code into the stainless-steel box mounted on the wall.

15

Once inside, Gabriel and Eli nodded with the respect of professional soldiers. Beyond a plain grey steel front desk, they could see sturdy drilled-metal racks of equipment. Uniforms, Bergens, boots, canteens, zipped battlefield first aid kits, olive-green steel boxes, fat, camouflaged sausages that looked like tents – all the enterprising paramilitary team would need to do anything from protecting a goldmine to staging a small military coup.

Taylor called out.

'Frank?'

A tall, solidly-built black man in sand-coloured fatigues rounded a corner and smiled when he saw them. He came hurrying over and shook hands with Eli and Gabriel.

'Frank, I want you to meet Gabriel and Eli. They've come over from England to investigate those murders over in Kgalagadi,' Taylor said.

'Bad business,' Frank said, shaking his bald head. 'You going to find the bastards who did it?'

'We hope so,' Gabriel said. 'That accent. Are you from South London?'

Frank's eyes widened.

'I am, as it happens. Brockley. Don't normally get officer-class types with that sort of ear for accents, 'specially ones from my neck of the woods.'

Gabriel smiled.

'I had a friend who came from Peckham.'

Frank nodded, as if that were all the explanation he needed or wanted. He half-turned and extended an arm.

'Welcome to my little empire,' he said. 'Want the tour?'

'Yes, please,' Eli said.

'I'll leave you in Frank's capable hands,' Taylor said. 'Come and find me once you've finished up here.'

Frank led them down the central aisle, pointing out different items like a proud department store manager aiming to impress important customers.

Gabriel inhaled and smiled as his brain processed the universal aroma of military kit: grease, gun oil, cold steel and brass and musty canvas.

'Nice, isn't it?' Frank said, catching sight of Gabriel's half-closed eyes.

'Wonderful. Did you serve with George then?'

'Ten years. Best bloody battlefield commander I ever saw. Never asked us to do anything he wouldn't do himself.'

'The mark of a good leader,' Eli said.

Frank nodded.

'One time, just outside Kandahar? We're closing in on a Taliban machine gun nest. They'd had us pinned down for six hours, so Major Taylor says, "Right, lads, I've had enough of this. We're going to wait till nightfall, then go up there and annihilate the fuckers."

'We waited till it got dark, then we made our move. It was all going to plan, then they hit us with a searchlight. They lit us up and only me and Major Taylor survived. Our machine gunner, Dicky Salmon, got his head shot off. Major Taylor grabbed his GPMG, and him and me ran on.

'I chucked a grenade towards their position and Major Taylor, he got the GPMG on his hip and opened up. I arrived a few seconds after him and started feeding the belt to stop it jamming, you know?

'We killed them all. Four with the GPMG, then when we ran through the first belt, him and me, Major Taylor I mean, we went for it. The major, he used to go into battle with this tomahawk. He won it in a bet with a US Marine Corps gunnery sergeant. He did two of them with it. Split their heads open like fucking melons. Then we—'

Frank stopped mid-sentence. He frowned, and scratched his bald dome. Gabriel saw his Adam's apple bob up and down in his throat, picked up on the increased muscle tone in his facial muscles, caught the minute flicker of his eyes.

'You OK, Frank?' Gabriel asked.

'Yeah. Yeah. I'm fine. Sorry, you shouldn't get me started on old war stories.' He inhaled. 'Right. What say we go and look at the *real* toys?'

He led them to a section of the building protected by a further set of locked steel-reinforced doors. Beyond lay the heart of the armoury: the firearms.

Racks of assault rifles: a United Nations of models. Russian AK-47s with their antiquated wooden stocks and fore-ends, and more modern guns, from American M4s to British SA80s and German G3Ks.

Beyond the assault rifles, submachine guns and compact carbines more suited to firing from within vehicles or in confined combat situations.

Finally Frank pointed to rows of pistols and knives.

'Take your pick,' he said, simply.

For Gabriel, the rifle was a simple decision. If he'd had backup from a battalion armourer, or a supply line, the SA80 would be his choice any day of the week, in any situation. But he didn't know how long he and Eli would be in the bush, alone, with only their personal weapons and limited ability to clear jams.

'I'll take an AK with a folding stock,' he said.

'Good choice,' Frank said, lifting down one of the gleaming

rifles, fitted with a telescopic sight. 'Old as the hills and just as reliable. Drive a tank over one of these and you'd still be able to shoot it.'

'No IWI ACEs?' Eli asked.

Gabriel smiled. Eli was loyal as always, to products of Israel Weapon Industries.

'Sorry, no. It was based on the AK originally, you know that?'

'Yeah, but I'm an IWI fangirl. OK, I guess I'll have an AK too.'

'Smart. You can share magazines that way. We use mags from the AK-103.'

'What's the ammunition load?'

'You get three hundred and ninety rounds in thirteen mags. The most you can get with a twenty-two-pound carry weight.'

'We'll have more in the truck, yes?'

Frank nodded. Then ducked under the racking and came out with two leather scabbards. He drew the blade from one, a fifteen-inch, spear-pointed bayonet with a blood-channel grooved along each side.

'For when the rounds run out,' he said.

Gabriel and Eli nodded silently. They'd both been in contacts that outlasted the ammunition. Then, fire fights turned into knife fights, fist fights or whatever-you-can-lay-your-hands-on fights.

They spent another ten minutes selecting pistols – a SIG Sauer P226 for Gabriel and a Glock 17 for Eli – plus rucksacks, a tent and sundry survival equipment, and they were done.

As they were leaving, Gabriel drew Frank to one side. He called out to Eli, 'Go ahead and find Taylor. I won't be long.'

Once the door had closed on silent hinges behind Eli, Gabriel turned to Frank.

'Earlier, when you were telling us about you and Major Taylor taking out the machine gun nest, you stopped.'

Frank ran a hand over his shining scalp.

'Yeah, I was running off at the mouth with me old war stories. I mean, we've all got 'em, right?'

'We do. Look, please don't take this the wrong way, but are you OK?'

Frank's brow crinkled.

'What do you mean?'

Was he about to step into a minefield and risk upsetting the armourer? Gabriel ploughed on.

'I mean, in your head. Listen,' he continued, holding up a hand as Frank's mouth opened, 'I left the army after my last mission went badly wrong. That guy I mentioned, the one with the same accent as you? He was killed. We had to leave him behind. I struggled with PTSD for years afterwards. I'm still not out of the tunnel. I'm just saying, if you needed someone to talk to…'

He left the words hanging in the air between them like gun smoke drifting across a battlefield.

'You got all that from me tailing off mid-story?' Frank asked after a long pause.

Gabriel shrugged.

'You get to recognise the signs.'

'PTSD,' Frank said.

'Yes. I still see a shrink from time to time. I do yoga, all kinds of weird shit to keep myself sane.'

Frank's shoulders, which Gabriel had watched creep towards his ears as they were talking, suddenly dropped. He sighed out a breath and ran a hand over his skull again.

'Lot of my mates are suffering. You know, back home. Couple topped themselves. Divorced. Drinking problems, nightmares, anger issues, all of it.'

'Are you? Suffering, I mean?'

Frank blew out a whistling breath through narrowed lips. He shook his head.

'I was. Drink, mainly. But other stuff. Then I hit my wife, didn't I? Broke her jaw. She asked for a divorce. I didn't stand in her way. How could I? I might have killed her in my sleep.'

'Kids?'

'Two. Scott and Zara.'

Frank reached into an inside pocket and took out a worn, brown leather credit card wallet. Extracted two photos. A girl and a boy, both smiling from beneath comically oversized Santa hats. Behind them a Christmas tree was swathed in decorations. Tinsel and fairy lights spread protective branches over mounds of brightly wrapped presents.

Gabriel took the photos and studied the children's faces. So happy. So untroubled. The girl had a gap where an incisor had yet to come through. He handed them back.

'Nice-looking kids.'

'Yeah. They're older than that, now.'

'Do you see them much?'

Frank shook his head.

'I came out here to try and save myself. I had to get away. I love them so much but I was worried I might hurt them, too. Sometimes it gets too much. Then I just grab a Jeep and go off into the bush with a rifle and a box of ammo and shoot until I'm calm again.'

Gabriel pulled out his wallet and took out a card, which he handed to Frank.

'That's my personal number,' he said. 'If you ever need to talk.'

Frank nodded and sniffed, once.

'Thanks. You'd better get going,' he said. 'The major'll be wondering what I've done with you.

Gabriel found Taylor with Eli on the outskirts of the compound. Eli was firing single shots at metal targets mounted on the bone-white branches of a lightning-struck tree some sixty yards distant. The steel circles plinked and spun as she hit them steadily, working left to right.

She turned as Gabriel walked up, and grinned.

'A beautiful girl shooting an automatic weapon,' Taylor said. 'If there's a better sight in the world, I've yet to see it.'

'How's it feel?' Gabriel asked Eli.

'Sweet. Like one of our old Galils. Want to try it?'

Gabriel took the AK from her. The wooden pistol grip was warm from her hand. He tucked it against his shoulder and sighted on one of the targets, crystal-clear in the scope's reticle. A warm, sweet-smelling breeze was blowing left to right and he made a best-guess adjustment to compensate.

He fired. Missed. Swore.

Behind him, he heard Taylor whisper to Eli, 'Looks like your friend hasn't been keeping up his range practice!'

Gritting his teeth and refocusing on the target, he took better care this time. He emptied his head of everything but for the tiny black circle mounted beneath the splintered branch tip. He squeezed the trigger to first pressure.

Something moved on the branch above the target. He moved the crosshairs up a little. Shuddered.

16

LONDON

Detective Superintendent Calpurnia 'Callie' McDonald looked up from the report she was reading. Seeing who was standing in the doorway, she grinned, her red-lipsticked mouth widening.

'Well now, if it isn't my most dedicated detective chief inspector,' she said, her Edinburgh accent as clear now as it was the first day she moved south from Lothian and Borders Police. 'Please tell me you have something I can take to the commissioner? I swear to you, Stel, the bloody woman's going to be the death of me!'

Stella closed the door behind her and sat in the chair facing Callie. The two women had a long and complicated history stretching back to the time Stella had virtually single-handedly rolled up a conspiracy stretching to the top of the British legal system.

Callie had protected Stella when all looked lost and then promoted her to head the Special Investigations Unit inside the Met.

'The shooter was in Africa. Recently,' Stella said.

Callie's eyebrows shot up.

'Really? Because what I'm hearing is that he was an Israeli.'

Stella shrugged, then handed over the single sheet of paper Lucian had given her.

'The one doesn't preclude the other,' she said. 'He might have trained there. It's Botswana, by the way.'

'You can be that specific?'

'A soil sample and the jaw of a termite confirm it, apparently. I want to go out there, boss.'

Callie placed the paper on her desk.

'Why?'

'It's a lead, isn't it? If the shooter was out there, someone might know him, or know something about him.'

'What, you think they all just hang around together, sharing a bottle of wine in the International Assassins' Club?' Callie said in a sarcastic tone of voice. Then she coloured. 'Oh god, Stel, I'm sorry. That was uncalled for. I'm just under the cosh, ye know? Everybody up to and including the prime minister is looking for answers and everyone on Birch is running on caffeine and adrenaline.'

Stella smiled. Walked over to a filing cabinet. Extracted a bottle of Glenlivet single malt and a couple of cut-glass tumblers. She poured a finger into each glass and handed one to Callie.

'It's fine,' she said, taking a sip of the whisky.

'Really?'

'Really. Anyway, I've got a plan that doesn't involve palling around with the barman at the Assassins' Club.'

Callie rolled her eyes.

'A plan. Am I going to like it?'

'You might,' Stella said, regarding her boss over the rim of her glass.

Callie sighed.

'Go on, then.'

'Remember Don Webster?'

'Oh, Mr Leave-it-to-the-big-boys, you mean? How could I forget?'

Their paths had crossed before and Don had managed to put

Callie's nose out of joint before retreating with a suitable apology and asking for her help.

'He's kept in touch ever since that business with the Russians,' Stella said. 'In fact, he's offered me a job on a couple of occasions.'

Callie's eyebrows arched even higher.

'Has he now? Why, the bloody nerve of the man! I told him no poaching the first time I met him. I hope you said no.'

Stella grinned.

'I did. But I'm thinking he could help us out for a change. You know, get me into Botswana and provide some intelligence backup. I get the sense they work from a different rulebook to ours.'

'Backup? Hmm,' Callie said. 'And you'd turn him down if he tried poaching you again?'

'As long as you keep giving me interesting jobs, boss,' Stella said with a wink.

'Och, you cheeky wee thing!'

* * *

Don was driving home in his Jensen Interceptor when his phone rang. He'd had one of the guys in the motor pool retrofit a hands-free kit, hiding the modern controls on the dash.

'Don Webster,' he said.

'Don, it's Stella Cole.'

'DCI Cole! How nice to hear from you. How's life in the Met?'

'At the moment, hectic. The small matter of Operation Birch. And please call me Stella.'

'I saw your guv'nor on the news last night. The hyenas were out for blood.'

'Which, and forgive the lack of small talk, is why I'm calling you.'

'Fire away, Stella.'

'Our forensics team just identified the source of a speck of soil found in the sniper nest. It came from Botswana.'

'Hmm. Unusual place for an Israeli physics teacher to be travelling. Could it have come from the PM, do you suppose?'

'We asked his office for a list of his official engagements in the week leading up to the assassination.'

'And?'

'Radio silence. I checked his Twitter feed. No holiday snaps from Botswana, either. I'm wondering whether Lieberman was a teacher at all. What if the prime minister is right and he was a Mossad agent all along?'

'I have to say, from what I know of the workings of organisations like the Mossad, that seems unlikely. Anyway, what can I do to help?'

'I want to go to Botswana. If the shooter was there in the days before the killing, someone might have seen him. I mean, how many Israeli physics teachers can there be in Botswana?'

Don smiled. Were the stars aligning to help him out?

'Do you remember my chap, Gabriel Wolfe?'

'The moody one with the scar?'

'That's him.'

'Yes. I like him.'

'He's over there at the moment, along with another of my operatives, Eli Schochat. They're on an unrelated mission, but still…' Don said, suddenly wondering just how unrelated they really were. 'She's Israeli herself, so you two might put your heads together about the Mossad connection.'

'Can you hook me up with them?'

'Leave it with me. Get yourself over there; you'll fly into Gaborone and I'll have them pick you up at the airport.'

'Great, thank you. I'll sort out a hotel and let you know where I'll be staying.'

'No. Don't do that. I have a better idea. We're currently benefiting from the largesse of a wealthy friend of The Parachute Regiment. I'll book you a room where Gabriel and Eli are staying. Save the Met a few quid.'

'Thanks again. I can feel my Favours-Owed-to-Don-Webster file bulging at the seams.'

'Not at all.' He paused, just for a second. 'Stella, there is one thing you could do for me. Not really a quid pro quo, but just, hmm-mm-hmm, as a friend.'

'What? Anything.'

'Keep this to yourself, would you? My little band of jolly cut-throats aren't precisely operating within our remit at the moment.'

He heard Stella laugh.

'Don't tell me the off-books brigade have gone off their own books?'

Don smiled.

'Something like that.'

'My lips are sealed. My own career hasn't always been a tribute to protocol.'

'So I gather. Come and see me when this trip of yours is over.'

'I promised my boss I wouldn't let you lure me away from her, Don. Plus there's a queue,' she said.

He could hear the good humour in her voice. Smiled to himself.

'Who said anything about luring? I was thinking we could have a spot of lunch and I could debrief you. Just to satisfy my own curiosity.'

'And no hiring-talk.'

'No hiring-talk. I promise,' he agreed. *Not unless the timing seems right.*

'One more thing, Don.'

'Fire away.'

'I was thinking of adopting cover as a BBC journalist while I was out there,' Stella said. 'Not officially, just if I need to go poking around. Do you think that would work in Botswana? I'm guessing you have more experience in these things than me.'

'Normally it would be my go-to legend. Dear old Auntie Beeb is still a globally respected institution, even if her standing at home gets the old dent kicked into it from time to time.'

'But?'

'But I happen to know they only maintain a bureau in Johannesburg these days, so you'd be a bit off the beaten track. Fewer problems as a freelancer. It's what my two are using.'

* * *

Tammerlane sipped his whisky. The clock in his private office chimed three times. Through the window he watched thin blades of cloud slice across the full moon.

Ensconced in a sagging leather sofa on the other side of a walnut coffee table sat his right-hand woman, Ruth Evans. The new chancellor of the exchequer raised her chin. It was a gesture he'd seen her use a thousand times in the House of Commons.

'What is it, Ruth?'

'When are you going to talk to the king?'

'When the moment is right. The old boy needs to know the jig's up first. That way, when we introduce the Great Republic Act, he'll go quietly.'

'You should talk to him now, Joe. Before he can mobilise support. Alexandra's death won't serve as cover for ever, you know.'

'Yes, Ruth, I do know, thank you,' he snapped. 'This is going to play out exactly as we planned.' He began counting off points on his fingers. 'The royal family's under threat from external forces. For their own safety, we're reconstituting the UK as a people's republic. They get to live out their lives away from the glare of publicity and ongoing terrorist threats. We quieten the great unwashed with welfare handouts, free tuition fees, and whatever else you can bribe them with in your budget.'

'Yeah, well there's a problem with that.'

'Problem?'

'There's no money.'

'What do you mean, "no money"?'

'I mean we have what we need to keep the lights on, but since we came to power, foreign investors have been pulling out of government bonds, the pound has lost a third of its value and, well, to cut a long story short, we're running out of cash.'

'Borrow it.'

'The IMF would cripple our plans, Joe. They're a capitalist cabal. They'd—'

'I'm not talking about the IMF.'

'Then who?'

'The Chinese. They own half of London already. Talk to them.'

He watched her as the idea percolated through her brain. Working out the angles, figuring out how to sell the idea to the Great British Public. He smiled, and waited.

Finally, her eyes lit up.

'I'll call Beijing in the morning.'

He smiled lazily and finished his whisky.

'It's 11.a.m. there, Ruth. Why don't you call them now?'

Once he was alone, Tammerlane picked up his phone and called up a speed-dial number. The face beside it, filling the little circle, was tanned beneath a hat, the brim folded up on one side. Blue eyes stared out challengingly. Lush vegetation beneath a startling cobalt sky in the background suggested somewhere hot.

The name beneath the image said Julius.

17

BOTSWANA

With infinite care, a large hairy-bodied spider was stalking a scarlet songbird. The spider placed one leg at a time on the smooth, barkless wood. Gabriel estimated its span at seven inches: a monster.

Seemingly oblivious to its imminent demise, the bright-plumaged bird carried on chirruping, its sharp-pointed beak scissoring open and shut.

Gabriel hated spiders. He always had. Nothing freaked him out more than having to allow one of the creatures to crawl along an arm or over his face while on a lurk.

I'll show you.

Centring the crosshairs on the mottled grey thorax, he squeezed off a shot.

Wood chips flew out from the branch. The bird took flight, emitting high-pitched cries.

Eli and Taylor laughed out loud.

'That was worse than the first shot!' Eli said. 'I think George is right. You need to get in some serious practice.'

Gabriel turned to them, handing her the AK. He smiled.

'Not at all. I hit the target dead-centre. Come and see.'

They followed him down the improvised range until they reached the tree. Up close, Gabriel could see it was obviously a favourite for marksmanship practice. Its trunk and branches were scarred with hundreds of pockmarks.

The spinning metal targets were equally well used. Their rotating plates were dented and scored with silver lines.

'So? Where'd your shot go?' Eli demanded.

Gabriel wasn't looking at the branch. He was scouring the ground around the tree. Finally he saw what he was looking for and toed it into plain view from its resting place in the dust.

'There!' he said triumphantly.

Four legs lay in the dirt, attached to a fragment of hairy exoskeleton. Some way away he saw two more legs, separated this time from the spider's body.

Taylor bent and picked up one of the three-inch-long legs. He waggled it at Eli.

'Huntsman,' he said. 'One of the little buggers bit my chef only last month. Poor bloke was in the sick bay for the rest of the day. Thought he was having a heart attack.'

Eli nodded, pursing her lips.

'Not bad shooting. Shame you had to kill a poor little spider just to show off, though.'

'Poor—?' Gabriel repeated. 'It was about to attack a defenceless little bird. Anyway, you heard what George said. They're monsters.'

'Speaking of monsters,' Taylor said, 'what do you think about the new prime minister back home?'

'I don't know how he pulled it off. First winning the election and then this amazing stroke of luck that he just happened to be running down the street at the exact moment the shooter took out the princess. The more I think about it, the more fishy it gets.'

Taylor laughed humourlessly.

'Like a bucket of herrings left in the sun for a week. You buy the Israeli angle?'

'On the face of it, you have to. I mean, he was up there. His prints were all over the rifle.'

Gabriel hesitated.

'But?' Taylor prompted.

'But, why? That's what Eli and I can't see.'

'Exactly,' Eli said. 'There's no earthly reason why Israel would want to assassinate a princess. That "pro-Palestinian" bullshit is just the media cooking up conspiracy theories. Oh, and by the way?' she said, spreading her hands wide. 'If they did, do you *really* think they'd do it that way? I mean, come on! This is the Mossad we're talking about. They'd do it so it looked like a heart attack, or an accident. They wouldn't send a sniper.'

'I agree,' Taylor said, simply. 'I think Tammerlane's a very dangerous man. Mark my words, his next move will be to sideline the monarchy and call a referendum on going for a republic. At best,' he added, frowning. 'It's one of the reasons I'm planning to relocate the business out of the UK.'

Still discussing UK politics, Taylor led them away from the shooting range to a hangar-like building.

'Motor pool,' he said, sliding a full-height wooden door to one side on greased rollers.

Gabriel nodded his appreciation. Beside him, Eli whistled. Inside the dimly lit space they could see twenty or so military spec vehicles from Jeeps and Land Rovers to armoured Bradley Fighting Vehicles.

'You're journalists, right?' Taylor asked.

'That's the legend,' Gabriel answered.

'In that case, I think these babies might be a little too, what shall we say, OTT? You could just about explain the weapons away, but not one of these. Come with me.'

He strode between a couple of Land Rovers wearing green-and-brown camouflage.

The trio emerged in front of a handful of white-painted Toyotas. A couple of Hilux pickups on extra-large tyres and jacked-up suspension, and three Land Cruisers, the pickups' bigger, bolder SUV cousins.

'The poachers mostly use these, plus just about every militia and terrorist group from Boko Haram to the Lord's Resistance Army,'

Taylor said. 'Toyotas are the Kalashnikovs of the automotive world. Bullet-proof engines, pretty much literally. Fixable with whatever you've got to hand. Take one of the Hiluxes. I'll have one of my boys load it up with spare gas, water, the usual.'

Two hours later, Gabriel was piloting the pickup through the Gaborone traffic, thankful for the visibility from the high-up driving position. He turned to Eli.

'Now all we need is a guide to the kill site.'

'We should head over to the Anti-Poaching Unit.'

'Now?'

'Why not?'

'You think the kit's safe in the back?'

Eli pursed her lips.

'Hotel first, then we'll call them and make an appointment.'

Gabriel nodded.

'Better.'

Taylor had packed their materiel in nondescript black nylon holdalls. They hefted the heavy bags onto their shoulders and entered the blessedly cool reception area, making their way to the stairs without attracting so much as a glance from the other guests thronging the marble-floored space.

Sitting in an armchair in their room, Gabriel launched a browser on his laptop and Googled 'Botswana Defence Force'. He called the main switchboard number.

'BDF. How may I direct your call today?'

'Hi. Can you put me through to the Anti-Poaching Unit, please.'

'Hold the line, please.'

Gabriel smiled at Eli, who was field-stripping her AK-47. The phone clicked.

'This is Major Edward Modimo. To whom am I speaking?'

Gabriel gave his prepared lines.

'Major Modimo, my name is Alec Jensen. I'm a freelance journalist. I'm travelling with a colleague in Botswana. We're researching a piece on the illicit ivory trade. We'd like to interview you about the BDF's anti-poaching efforts.'

Gabriel heard the major sigh. He held his own breath.

'A journalist? For which media outlet? The *Times* of London? The BBC? Buzzfeed?' he added, with barely concealed contempt.

'As I said, I'm freelance, but yes, the piece is for the *Times*. An in-depth report.'

'Your colleague. He is a photographer?'

Sensing a way in, Gabriel improvised.

'Yes, absolutely. Although he is actually a she. We'd obviously want some good photos of you and your men.'

'Do I need to visit my barber?'

Gabriel hesitated.

'I'm sure, Major, your appearance will be—'

The major laughed.

'I am joking, Mr Jensen. Yes, come and see me. In three days' time, if you will. Wednesday. Be here at ten hundred hours. Goodbye.'

Gabriel put the phone down.

'That was easy,' he said. 'We need to buy a camera.'

Eli slotted the bolt home in the rifle and laid it on the bed beside her.

'Come on then, "Alec",' she said, getting to her feet. 'Bags I drive this time.'

The manager of Hi-Tek Electronics began apologising as soon as Gabriel and Eli entered her shop. A slender lady in her late forties, with a sharp gaze behind lemon-yellow glasses, she was immaculately dressed in a pale-grey skirt and white blouse, a string of scarlet beads at her throat.

'Welcome, Sir, Madam. The air conditioning just broke down. Sorry for the heat.'

'It's fine, really,' Eli said with a smile.

'How can I help you today?'

They emerged thirty minutes later with a brand-new Canon digital SLR in a white carrier bag emblazoned with the shop's logo.

Eli laughed.

'I thought she was never going to let us go!'

'She was just proud of her shop,' Gabriel said.

'I must have looked at ten cameras.'

'You have to admit, she was a good saleswoman.'

'Good? She was brilliant. I hope our benefactor doesn't blink when he sees the receipt.'

'From what I saw of him, he'd probably find the money down the back of his sofa.'

18

Waiting for the Met Police detective, Gabriel and Eli stood side by side next to the ivory elephant. The arrivals hall vibrated to the mingled sounds of joyous family reunions, excitable children and executives competing with each other to dominate their conversations.

'There she is,' Eli said, pointing to a lone white woman dragging a wheeled suitcase across the polished granite floor. 'Stella!'

Stella turned towards the sound and grinned when she saw Eli, who was striding through the crowds to meet her. Gabriel followed in her wake, eyes flicking left and right, alert to threats.

The two women shook hands, then Eli enveloped Stella in a hug. Stella turned to Gabriel.

'What's it to be, a hug or a handshake?'

Gabriel opted for a hug, marvelling, not for the first time at how many badass women he'd met in his life.

We need to get together, Sis. Soon.

'You're going to love the hotel,' Eli said, as she led the trio to the carpark and the Mercedes they'd rented that morning. 'Fantastic pool, excellent restaurant. And a couple of really cute staff members.'

'Hey!' Gabriel said, eyes wide in mock-outrage.

'Almost as cute as Gabe,' Eli added, winking at Stella.

'I can't wait,' Stella said, grinning at Eli.

Once they arrived at the hotel, they agreed to let Stella check in and get herself unpacked, then meet at the pool bar for a beer at midday.

Under a rush-roofed cabana, Gabriel, Eli and Stella sipped from bottles of ice-cold St Louis Export lager, the pride of Gaborone's Kgalagadi Breweries.

Stella frowned, and swiped a hand across her face.

'Are you all right?' Eli asked.

'Just a little jet-lagged. So,' she said brightly, 'what's the plan?'

'What's *your* plan?' Gabriel asked. 'Don told us you were out here following up a lead on Princess Alexandra's killer.'

'We found a soil trace and an insect mouthpart in the sniper nest. Believe it or not, our forensics guys narrowed it down to here. I'm thinking an Israeli physics teacher would have stood out as much in Gaborone as we do. Somebody might have seen him meeting someone, because one thing I can tell you, he wasn't acting alone. Someone paid him to do it.'

'Or forced him,' Eli said.

'Or forced him,' Stella agreed.

'I just can't see it,' Eli said. She spread her hands wide. 'I mean, even if he *was* a Mossad agent, why? I mean, what *possible* reason could the Mossad have for assassinating a member of the British royal family? It doesn't make any sense.'

'She'd recently given a speech at an event backed by Hezbollah,' Stella said. 'The Palace put out a press statement saying she hadn't been aware of the connection and was speaking on humanitarian issues, but it was widely reported as a pro-Palestinian speech.'

Eli snorted.

'Listen, Stella, if the Mossad went around killing every prominent Brit who spoke out in favour of the Palestinians, there'd be piles of corpses in the House of Commons, the media and half the bloody academic world from London to Edinburgh.'

'Eli's got a point, Stella,' Gabriel said. 'The Mossad go for hard targets. Like we do. Terrorists, gun runners, people financing terror, organisational leadership.'

'Then give me a motive. Why did Dov Lieberman travel from Israel to London, via Botswana, in order to assassinate a princess?'

'I don't know. But I'm going to find out. I know some people who'll be more than willing to help.'

'Thanks,' Stella said. 'I was hoping you'd say something like that.'

'You can help us out in return,' Gabriel said.

'Sure. How?'

'We're going out to the place where the Paras were murdered tomorrow morning. Having a detective along would be really useful.'

They met again in the hotel reception at 7.00 p.m. Beyond the glass doors the hotel's lights shone out into the darkness, illuminating a few acacias on the far side of the road.

'Where shall we go to eat?' Gabriel asked.

'I'd really like to go somewhere the locals go,' Stella said. 'I hate the stuff these hotels serve up. Chicken Kiev, burgers, Caesar salad. You could be anywhere in the world.'

Eli smiled at Stella.

'I agree. Let's go and find that barbecue place Phefo mentioned. What was it called?'

'Koko Loko,' Gabriel said.

'How far is it?'

Gabriel checked the distance on his phone.

'Mile and a half.'

'Walk or drive?'

'Let's walk,' Stella said. 'I love getting a feel of a place.'

. . .

Koko Loko occupied a corner site in a busy part of town. The restaurant's fascia blazed across the street, a backlit riot of orange, green and yellow plastic lettering.

From as far as fifty metres away, Gabriel could smell the smoky, spicy aroma of grilling chicken wafting from its wide-open front door. The sound of laughter and good-natured shouting between tables drifted over, along with the cooking smells.

A sound system set up outside behind the rickety aluminium tables blasted out an infectious, melodic music: guitars, offbeat drumming and a high-pitched man's voice singing in Tsetswana.

Eli pointed up at the sign.

'Cute.'

'Koko means chicken in Tsetswana,' Gabriel said.

Eli rolled her eyes. She turned to Stella.

'Gabe speaks a million languages.'

They laughed and Gabriel felt lifted by the good-natured mood.

'Nyet ya ne! Bù, wǒ bù zhīdào! Nee, ek doen nie!'

Stella's eyes popped wide open.

'What?' she exclaimed.

'I just said "No I don't". In Russian, Cantonese and Afrikaans.'

Eli snorted.

'Typical of you to research the local lingo.'

'Which has got us out of at least one scrape since we've been together.'

Their banter was interrupted by a smiling man in a flower-print shirt and an apron tied round his waist.

'Ladies, gentleman, welcome to Koko Loko. I am Jimmy, the boss around here. Table for three, yes?'

Seated outside at a table Jimmy brought out from the interior, Gabriel, Eli and Stella ordered a St Louis each. Jimmy was adamant they should let him choose for them.

'You won't be disappointed,' he said with a grin.

Ten minutes later a waitress, long braids wound up into a glossy coil on the top of her head, brought their food. She wove through the other diners with a huge oval tray balanced expertly on one upturned palm.

'We have mixed barbecue,' she said, placing a vast platter of perfectly charred cuts of chicken, pork and lamb in the centre of the table. She pointed at a stainless steel-dish of a fluffy white substance halfway between rice and mashed potato. 'This is phutu pap. It's ground maize. Plus Jimmy's special sauce.' Next she indicated a brimming jug that released a rich smell of tomatoes and garlic. 'This is morogo. Some folk call it African spinach. It's cowpea leaves. Very tasty. Lots of protein,' she added, winking at Gabriel. 'Build up your muscles.'

Left to their food, Stella glanced at Eli, then turned to Gabriel.

'I think the waitress likes you, Gabriel. All that bit about protein.'

'Yeah,' Eli added, stripping the flesh from a chicken wing. 'I'd better keep an eye on you.'

Gabriel pretended to think about what she'd said, staring upwards and stroking his chin.

'You may have a point, Stella,' he said. 'She was very pretty.'

Eli's eyes popped wide.

'Bastard!' she said, punching him on the arm, none too kindly.

'Hey! You started it.'

'Yes, but I was joking.'

'So was I!'

'What have you been up to since we last spoke?' Stella asked Gabriel. 'Tell me about your sister.'

Gabriel finished a mouthful of chicken and took a swig of his beer. He scragged his fingertips over his scalp.

'Good question. Leaving aside all the boring operational stuff, the main event was that I discovered I had a sister,' he said. 'A triad kidnapped her when she was a baby and trained her up to be a bodyguard for the big boss. We were reunited in his office.'

Where she ran him through with a Samurai sword before he could kill me.

Stella raised her bottle to him and clinked the neck of his.

'Wow! Congratulations! That's amazing. And, somehow, a very "you" kind of story.'

'Thanks. I think.'

'What's she like? It must have been quite an experience if you'd never really got to know each other.'

He hesitated. Yes, what *was* Mei like? Stella's second question was even better than her first.

'She's tough, a really good fighter. Smart. Fearless. But—'

'But what?' Stella asked, glancing at Eli, who was frowning as she concentrated on Gabriel's words.

'I don't know. In fact, that's just it! I *don't* know. Not really. We spent some time together at my place and started to tell each other our stories, but then I had to get back to the UK.'

'Did you feel a connection?'

Gabriel nodded.

'Yes. Absolutely. In fact, there was one point in her boss's office where I think we were communicating without words.'

'Well, that's good, isn't it? That means there's something deeper there.'

'I guess so. And she reminds me of my mum. She has the same eyes.' He took a pull on his beer. 'How about you? What's been keeping you occupied?'

Stella laughed, causing a few nearby customers to turn round in their chairs, smiling good-naturedly.

'I don't know if you see much news, but you must have heard about the serial killer in London last year. The media called her "Saint Death" because she was doing her victims in like they were Christian martyrs.'

Gabriel nodded.

'She was crazy, right?' he asked.

Stella shrugged.

'Not for me to say.'

'Didn't I read you killed her in self-defence?' Eli asked.

'Yup. She never made it as far as a courtroom, though I'm pretty sure we'd have got a conviction.'

'What did you use?' Eli asked.

'A spiked metal fence post.'

Eli pursed her lips and nodded in appreciation.

'Good riddance to bad rubbish, yes?'

Stella frowned. She swigged some beer.

'I'm a cop, so I shouldn't say this. But, yes. Basically. Mim Robey was a psychopath. She killed or helped her brother kill a dozen innocent people.'

While the two women discussed the rights and wrongs of killing psychopaths, Gabriel looked around the restaurant.

For all we know, the people we're looking for are right here, sucking chop bones.

He ran through what little he knew about the targets.

They're involved in the illegal ivory trade.

They're at the sharp end – literally – shooting and butchering elephants right here in Botswana.

They must have a supply route to get the ivory out of Botswana.

They're making sufficient returns to justify the risks.

They have enough men, weapons and discipline to get the better of a troop of Paras supporting APU guys.

Surely they must have known that hitting the Paras would bring a shit-ton of trouble down on their heads? Did they care? Are the stakes so high they're willing to go all-out?

The obvious answer to the riddle was that this was organised crime. International organised crime. And where one illegal commodity was involved, he was pretty sure they'd find other flows of 'trade', from arms and drugs to people trafficking.

That made him think of some of the unsavoury characters he'd met in the previous few years, from Russian gangsters and triad bosses to corrupt politicians and tycoons with a morality-bypass.

None of it made him comfortable. But of one thing he was sure. Of all the categories of villain Don had sent him up against, or he'd ventured into battle against on his own account, *he* was enjoying barbecue chicken in a lively G-City chicken joint. And *they* were all dead.

19

The following morning, Eli knocked on Stella's door. Stella came to open it, phone clamped between cheek and shoulder. She smiled at Eli and pointed to an armchair.

Eli listened to one side of the conversation.

—

'Yes, boss.'

—

'Nothing we couldn't handle.'

—

'It doesn't mean anything. Just a figure of speech.'

—

'I'm making a start first thing tomorrow.'

—

'I'll try the big hotels first. Chat up the bar staff.'

—

'OK, I promise.'

—

Stella ended the call.

'Hey, Eli,' she said. 'That was my guv'nor, back in London. She just wanted a progress report. I had something I wanted to ask you.'

'Go ahead. This whole trip's about mutual assistance,' Eli said with a smile.

'Is there any way you can tap your old contacts in the Israeli intelligence community to find out more about Dov Lieberman? He's the one concrete lead I have.'

Eli answered immediately

'Of course! I'll call Uri Ziff. He's *my* old guv'nor,' she said, uttering the last sentence with a dreadful Cockney accent that made Stella laugh.

'Thanks? Coffee?'

Eli nodded, already calling Ziff's number.

'Eliyah! How's my favourite expat? When can I tell our human resources people to find you a flat in Tel Aviv?'

Eli laughed.

'You never give up, do you? The answer to your first question is, fine. I'm in Africa, with Gabriel. The answer to the second is, not yet.'

'No? OK then. So why the call? Not that I'm not happy to hear your voice,' he added. 'It's about the assassination.'

Eli had no need to ask which one. Only one recent killing had gone viral so fast it had travelled round the globe before the sound of the gunshot had died away.

'He's insane, you know that?' Uri asked.

'Tammerlane?'

'Yes, Tammerlane!' Uri paused. 'I'm sorry, Eliyah. It's been a trying few days, as you can probably imagine.'

'It's fine. I get it. But he's not mad. Just very, very dangerous.'

'Yes! For Jews! He's begun kicking us out. First Israeli citizens, but then, who knows?'

'And I'm ready to go, Uri, believe me. I'm not going back to the UK. Not while he's in power.'

Uri huffed out an irritable sound.

'You'll have a long wait, then.'

'So be it. But that wasn't why I called. Not precisely. There's something fishy about the whole business.'

'You think?'

The exasperation in Uri's voice was tangible.

'You've been looking at Lieberman.'

A statement, not a question. Eli knew what her old employer would be doing, regardless of any investigations conducted by the police or Shin Bet, the internal security service.

'Of course. It's early days, but we think we're onto something.'

'What?'

'Oh, Eliyah! If only you worked for me, I could share all our intelligence with you in a morning briefing. But you work for the Brits now, don't you? This is sensitive stuff.'

'Uri Ziff!' she said with mock outrage. 'How could you play that card with me? Especially when I am in Africa helping a Metropolitan Police detective chief inspector work the case.'

Uri sighed.

'Strictly confidential, yes? I'm treating you as an employee on temporary sabbatical in the UK, yes?'

'Thanks, Uri. I won't let you down.'

'You'd better not! So, here's what we know. Lieberman is – was – a physics teacher at David Ben Gurion High School in Haifa. After completing his military service in the IDF, where he gained a qualification as a designated marksman, he returned to civilian life and did a teaching degree at Tel Aviv University.'

'Which is all great background, but—'

'Don't be so impatient! It was always your one weakness,' Uri said. 'Ten days ago, his wife and children went missing. He kept it quiet but we talked to her employer and the children's school. No sign of them ever since. No CCTV, no airline tickets bought with her credit card, no passport scans at any border crossing or port or airports, nothing.'

Eli connected the dots at lightning speed.

'He was being coerced. They kidnapped his family, threatened to kill them unless he did the hit.'

'Impatient, yes, but also a quick study. That's our working assumption, too.'

'Do you buy the idea of Tammerlane just happening by at the right time to kill him?'

Uri sighed. Eli caught the familiar scratch of his big hand scrubbing at his stubbly jaw.

'It's a possibility. Our analysts are divided. Personally, I think it stinks.'

'Me too. Here's something in return. My contact here told us the British cops found some soil specks in the sniper nest.'

'And they're African.'

'Ha! I'm not the only quick study. Yes, they're from Botswana.'

'What was Lieberman doing in Botswana?'

'That's what our friend from the Met,' Eli smiled at Stella, 'wants to find out.'

The call with Uri finished, Eli invited Stella to join her and Gabriel in their room to discuss an idea for the next day's activities.

20

The following morning, Stella pulled up at the tree-shaded front gate of the Sir Seretse Khama Barracks on Monganaokodu Road. She killed the Toyota's engine as the soldier on the gate strolled over from his post, AK-47 held nonchalantly at his hip.

'Yes, madam,' he said. No smile. The suspicious look of military base gate guards the world over.

'Carl Jensen and Rachel Camaro to see Major Modimo,' she said, jerking her thumb over her shoulder, where Gabriel and Eli sat in the centre row of seats.

'Who are you?' he asked her.

'Security.'

He glanced at the bulge on her right hip beneath her untucked shirt. She'd strapped a zipped nylon pouch onto her belt earlier and the effect was convincing.

'They have an appointment?' he asked, apparently satisfied by her one-word answer.

'At ten.'

'Wait here,' he said. 'Please,' he added, as if he realised he'd forgotten his manners.

Stella watched him enter a tiny brick kiosk and pick up a phone. He emerged a couple of minutes later.

'Park over there,' he instructed her, gesturing with the muzzle of his AK towards a red-earth square fronting an office building. 'Major Modimo's office is inside.'

He walked back to the barrier and pushed on the steel counterweight, swinging the red-and-white striped pole up to admit them.

'Thanks,' Stella said through the open window as she inched the Land Cruiser over the threshold. She followed a track edged with white-painted rocks to the rudimentary carpark.

She parked, and all three clambered out of the Land Cruiser's air conditioned interior into the already searing heat of a Gaborone morning. A stork strutting across the compound, its rosy beak as long as a combat knife, eyed them warily before taking wing and flapping noisily up to perch on a rooftop.

They entered the whitewashed office block. A young female soldier in beige dress uniform, her braided hair tied in tight at the nape of her neck, looked up from a folder and smiled.

'You are here to see Major Modimo?' she asked.

'Yes,' Gabriel said. 'I'm Alec Jensen.'

'And I'm Rachel Camaro,' Eli said.

They both held their press passes out for inspection, but the young woman waved them away with another smile. She ignored Stella. The gate guard must have filled her in on 'the security'.

'Wait here, please,' the soldier said, before picking up her desk phone, a heavy-looking unit in a shade of institutional green Stella remembered from her parents' first house.

'Major Modimo. Your guests are here. Yes, Sir.'

She replaced the handset in the cradle and smiled up at them.

'Major Modimo is coming to collect you personally,' she said, in a tone of voice that suggested this was very far from an everyday occurrence.

The tread of boots on polished tiles sounded loudly from a corridor behind the reception area. Gabriel straightened. Beside him Eli did the same, and he noticed approvingly the way Stella took a couple of steps back to stand behind and to his left.

The man who rounded the corner and approached the small group forced Gabriel to hurriedly reset his expectations. He realised he'd been expecting a carbon-copy of another African officer who'd extracted him and Britta from a firefight in north-western Mozambique a few years earlier. Major Anthony Chilundika had been tall, solidly built, heavily moustachioed and possessed of a jovial booming voice: a Sandhurst-trained combat commander with the manners and appearance to match.

Major Modimo presented an altogether different model of army officer. No more than five feet seven and ten stone, he nevertheless looked good in his immaculately tailored camouflage fatigues. His steel-rimmed glasses and neatly trimmed goatee gave him the cerebral look Gabriel associated with intelligence and strategy types.

They shook hands and, after the introductions were out of the way, the major ushered them along a narrow corridor to his office.

Sparsely furnished, with a desk and three mismatched chairs, the room was clearly a purely practical space. Gabriel saw none of the trappings of success so many people at the top of hierarchies – military or civilian – collected. No gold pen and pencil sets. No extravagant artworks or ceramics. No expensive leather-upholstered sofas or glass-topped coffee tables.

He did, however, register a framed photograph of the major smiling and shaking hands with a man Gabriel recognised from the briefing notes Don had supplied: Jerome Tsebogo, Botswana's current president. Beside it, another photo of the major, an AK-47 on his hip, standing with three soldiers behind the corpse of a black man, sprawled on the ground beside a tusk as long as he was.

The major spoke, jerking Gabriel's attention back to the present.

'You are in Botswana writing an article for the *Times* of London about the illicit trade in ivory, yes?'

'That's right, Major,' Gabriel said. 'As you know, the people of Britain are very concerned that these magnificent animals should be protected. It's a very topical story.'

'It is also a very complicated story, did you know that?'

'I'm not sure I know what you mean.'

'The farmers up north are not so happy about Botswana's healthy elephant population. A single bull can destroy an entire year's crop in one night. They come into villages and smash the place up. They kill people, too.'

'We'd want to present all sides of the story, obviously.'

'Yes, and I'm sure your readers will love to hear *that*,' Modimo said with unmistakable sarcasm. 'Poor blacks killing beautiful elephants *just*,' he made air quotes, 'to protect their livelihoods.'

This conversation wasn't going at all the way Gabriel had envisioned.

'We heard about the murders of your men by poachers. And the three British paratroopers. We thought we could start there. If you could arrange for us to visit the site of the killings.'

'I have already detailed a squad of my best men for protection. I will accompany you,' Modimo said.

He turned to Stella.

'You are security?'

'Yes, Major.'

'You have a weapon?'

She smiled.

'Civilians are prohibited from owning handguns in Botswana, Major. As you know.'

Gabriel could see the major trying, and failing, to suppress a smile.

'Of course, my dear lady. And your employers, which one, I wonder? Techpoint? Logistics International? Kagiso Group? They will not, how shall I put this delicately, have reached an accommodation with my colleagues at police headquarters?'

Stella lowered her eyes and returned his smile. Said nothing.

Modimo laughed.

'Well, no matter. For the purposes of this little,' he paused, 'adventure, I will furnish you with a firearm. I assume, even though you aren't carrying, you know how to shoot?'

'I do.'

'Excellent. Let us proceed, then. My men are on standby and eager to get into the field.'

Outside, seven soldiers were standing in the shade of a tree. A couple were smoking. They were laughing and bantering. As soon as the major arrived, the cigarettes were hastily stamped out, the laughter ceased, and all seven snapped to attention.

'At ease, men,' the major said. 'These are our visitors from England. Mr Jensen, Miss Camaro and,' he turned to Stella, 'my apologies. I didn't ask your name.'

'O'Meara.'

He turned to face his squad again.

'And Miss O'Meara. Corporal Kobisa, find Miss O'Meara a rifle.'

'Yes, Sir.'

The man sprinted off and returned shortly afterwards bearing a wooden-stocked AK-47. He skidded to a halt in front of Stella, who thanked him and shouldered the rifle.

Modimo pointed to the Land Cruiser.

'I should take your car if I were you. More comfortable than anything the BDF can provide.'

He laughed.

'Would you like to travel with us, Major?' Gabriel asked. 'We could use the time to learn more from you about ivory poaching.'

The major smiled.

'Elegantly put, my friend. Saving my poor rear end from a fifty-mile ride on military suspension, eh? Yes, why not. Thank you.'

The major turned to his men, issued a few orders in Tsetswana and then, as the soldiers climbed into the truck, returned to Gabriel's side.

'Follow that truck!' he said, laughing again.

Gabriel took the wheel and Modimo sat beside him. Eli and Stella climbed into the Land Cruiser's spacious rear compartment.

'There,' Major Modimo said, pointing to a spot about five hundred yards to their left.

Ahead of them, the truck was already turning, leaving the track and bumbling across the rough, rock-strewn ground, avoiding acacias and tall, brick-red termite mounds. Gabriel followed its tyre-tracks, looking past it to the place Modimo had indicated.

At a distance, the object might have been a bonfire waiting to be ignited. A pile of whitish sticks arranged in a rough pyramid. As they neared their destination, the object resolved into the skeleton of an adult elephant. Behind a low-growing thorn bush, Gabriel spotted a second skeleton and then, hidden by that, a third, much smaller than the other two.

He brought the Land Cruiser to a stop behind the truck and climbed out.

Major Modimo issued his orders. Even without Tsetswana, Gabriel could translate it. It's what he would have said.

Establish a perimeter. Anyone appears, give them a warning. If they don't stop, shoot. Once in the air. Then to kill.

They walked over to the largest skeleton. Not a scrap of flesh remained, just bleached bones shrouded in a thick, desiccated hide. The front of the skull had been sawn clean off. The spongy interior was revealed across a dead-flat plane of bone, its edges scored by a chainsaw's teeth.

All around the carcass, the ground had been gouged out in scrapes and scoops. They reminded Gabriel of the gouges in his lawn back in Salisbury when his old greyhound Seamus would dig up the grass for chafer bug larvae.

'What are they?' he asked.

'When the meat is gone, and beetles have consumed every last morsel of edible material that remains, vultures eat the blood-soaked earth. Mother Nature is very efficient out here, Mr Jensen. How does the line go in the film? The circle of life?'

Gabriel nodded, reflecting that, for these poor beasts, the circle had been accelerated unjustly by men's insatiable greed for money, not a predator's natural appetite for food.

Behind them, Eli was using the Canon. Photographing the skeletons but also the ground, documenting the entire site in a series of identically framed pictures they could upload to a laptop and study for clues back at the hotel.

'If you don't mind, I will wait in the Land Cruiser,' the major said. 'I have been here more times than I care to remember. Take your time. We will return to the barracks when you are ready.'

Five minutes later, Stella called over.

'Alec, Rachel! Over here!'

They hurried over.

Stella was crouching between two widely spaced acacias. She pointed at a series of zig-zag tread marks in a smooth area of dried mud.

'Must have rained a little before they drove out here. I can take a cast of that.'

She headed over to the Land Cruiser and returned with a black nylon holdall in one hand and a plastic container of water in the other. She set the water down and unzipped the holdall. From its crowded depths she brought out a plastic bag of white powder, a large plastic measuring jug and a block of grey modelling clay, all purchased the day before in Gaborone.

Gabriel watched as she began pulling lumps of modelling clay off the main block and rolling out fat sausages. These she flattened into inch-high strips. She erected low walls around a foot-long section of the tyre-track and squeezed and smoothed the joins with her thumbs. She mixed up the Plaster of Paris in the jug until it reached a gloopy consistency that reminded him of melted ice cream. Pronouncing herself satisfied, she slid a pair of purple nitrile gloves on and poured the thick white liquid into the enclosure and eased it to the edges with her thumb.

She looked up at Gabriel and Eli.

'In this heat it won't take more than thirty minutes to dry,' she said. 'I'll photograph it and send the pics back to London. My forensics guy might be able to get us a make and model.'

'Let's keep searching while it dries, then,' Eli said. 'No offence to Major Modimo or the Botswana Police Force or your former colleagues, Gabe, but they could have missed something. And Stella's a professional.'

They spread out, each taking a 120-degree slice of a circle. On hands and knees, they began a fingertip search of the ground. They were looking for something, anything, that might provide a lead to the identity of the poachers.

Gabriel could feel the heat burning into him. They'd brought plenty of water, and drunk their fill before starting work, but, even so, he could feel his tongue sticking to the inside of his mouth.

A flicker of scarlet caught his eye: a small bird, identical to the one he'd saved from the spider. He followed its flight as it flitted from bush to acacia and back again. Finding a perch to its liking, it began stroking its beak from side to side on the branch, as if sharpening a knife on a whetstone. Something else caught Gabriel's eye. A smooth, curved, bone-white surface.

21

He got to his feet and walked over to the thorn bush, causing the bird to depart, peeping with what he imagined was annoyance.

Rolling his shirt sleeve down and donning a leather glove, he snaked his hand into the depths of the thorn bush, wincing at the sharp pain as an inch-long dagger impaled his forearm. He managed to extract the thorn using his other hand and continued pushing his right arm deeper into the bush.

Finally the bone was within reach. He placed his fingers around it and pulled steadily. The high, whispery squeals as he dragged it past thorns set his teeth on edge. As it came free, he realised it wasn't a skull at all.

He was looking at a complex curved piece of plastic. No more than three millimetres thick, it was white on the convex side and a dull black on the concave. One edge was smooth and clearly shaped by machine, but on one side, the plastic had been fractured or torn away somehow.

'What are you?' he murmured, holding it in the sunlight and turning it this way and that.

He rubbed it on his shirt to remove the thin scrim of red dust. Now he saw it. The paint wasn't plain. It was pearlescent. As he tilted it, a second colour, a pale mint-green, glistened through the white.

The insight popped into his head unbidden. A flashbulb going off.

'Auto trim,' he said triumphantly. He turned and called over to Eli, who was on her hands and knees about thirty metres away.

'El—' he stopped before he uttered the second, betraying, syllable. *Shit, stay focused, Wolfe!* 'Rachel, I found something.'

Eli got to her feet and ran over.

'What *is* that?' she asked.

He gave it to her.

'I think it's a bit of vehicle trim.'

Her eyes narrowed as she scrutinised the fragment of plastic.

'You think it's from the poachers' vehicle?'

'Who else would it be?'

She nodded, pulling on her earlobe and turned the plastic over.

'There's mud in it,' she said. She turned away from Gabriel. 'Hey, O'Meara, get over here!'

Stella trotted over. She swiped a hand across her forehead.

'What is it?'

'Alec here found this,' she said, passing the plastic to Stella. 'Look at that.'

She pointed to the crust of red mud lodged in one of the intricate little mouldings on the black side.

'You said you tracked Lieberman to Botswana because of a soil sample,' Gabriel said. 'Do you think you could repeat the trick to track the poachers?'

'I suppose we might be able to. But in all probability, it'll be local and won't tell us anything beyond what we already know.'

She produced a clear plastic bag from her pocket, dropped the trim into it and sealed it.

They spent another hour at the site, but turned up no further physical evidence.

'We should get back,' Gabriel said. 'There's nothing else here for us.'

'Wait!' Eli said.

'What?'

'Aren't you forgetting something?'

Gabriel shrugged. 'Not following you.'

'The pictures! Major Modimo's got a thing for them, or didn't you notice in his office?'

She strode off to the Land Cruiser and pulled open the passenger door. Gabriel and Stella watched as she spoke briefly to the major, who then emerged from the cab, smiling at Eli and gesturing towards his men.

As they rejoined Gabriel and Stella, Eli said, 'The major thinks a photo of him and his men standing guard while we examine the skeleton would be a good start.'

Gabriel grinned. He and Eli knelt by the crudely disfigured skull while the soldiers struck a variety of martial poses, grim-faced, rifles pointed out at imaginary enemies. Hands on hips, the major faced Stella, who wielded the Canon, shooting dozens of pictures, so that the camera's electronic shutter buzzed as loudly as the insects that swarmed around them.

'Now, how about one of me with the ladies,' the major said.

He stood between Eli and Stella, encircling their waists with his arms and grinning as Gabriel fired off a few more shots. He saw Eli wince. *Why?*

'And one of us shaking hands, Mr Jensen,' the major said.

One of the soldiers asked shyly if *he* could pose with Eli, and before long each man was requesting a photo with Eli, Stella, Gabriel or all three. Finally, after agreeing she would upload all the shots to the major's PC at the barracks, they finished up and prepared to leave.

The last job onsite was for Stella to lift the plaster cast of the tyre track, bag it and lay it gently on the Land Cruiser's rear row of seats.

They were back at the barracks two hours later.

After retrieving the camera's SD card from the slot on the major's surprisingly up-to-date computer, Stella turned to go. The major was looking oddly at Gabriel. She couldn't read his expression.

'I am a great reader, Mr Jensen,' he was saying. 'Charles Dickens is one of my favourite authors. The great Chinua Achebe. Many American writers, too. Ernest Hemingway. Alex Hayley. Stephen King. But not just fiction. I like to keep abreast of current affairs, too. As well as the *Botswana Guardian*, I read the *International Herald Tribune*. And the *Times* of London.' A beat. 'For whom you are writing your story. Remind me of the editor's name again.'

'Raymond Shaw,' Gabriel answered smoothly. Basic background for a legend. Get your colleagues' names straight.

'Ah, yes. Mr Raymond Shaw. I called the *Times* while you were conducting your search.'

Stella's gaze flicked from Modimo to Gabriel, to Eli, and back again. It was like watching a poker game between three very experienced players. Nobody displayed a tell. The major continued.

'Here's the funny thing. I mentioned I was hosting two journalists writing a piece for the *Times*. I asked to speak to one of the commissioning editors.' He paused. 'Guess what?'

'What?' Gabriel said, smiling.

'Nobody in that department had any knowledge of this piece you claim to be writing. I gave them your name and that of your colleague, here,' he said, nodding at Eli. 'They had never heard of you. I explained I had seen your National Union of Journalists cards so they ran your names through their database. The oddest thing. You aren't in it.' He leaned forwards. 'Tell me. Whoever you are. Did you think we were just a bunch of simple African soldiers, ready to swallow whatever—'

'Major—' Gabriel began, but Stella cut him off.

'Major Modimo, we owe you an apology. And an explanation. Can we sit?'

The major sat behind his desk and motioned for the others to take a seat each.

'I'm waiting,' he said, 'with bated breath.'

'I'm sorry we had to mislead you. My colleagues aren't journalists, as you correctly deduced. And I don't work for a private security firm, though Kagiso Group has provided us with some logistical support. May I?' she said, gesturing to a patch pocket on her trousers.

'Please,' he replied, inclining his head.

She pulled out a black leather ID folder and opened it. She passed it across the desk to him.

His eyes widened as he looked at it, before handing it back.

'Detective Chief Inspector Stella Cole. Of the Metropolitan Police. This is genuine?'

'It is. You can call my office if you like.'

'No need. Somehow I believe you. Why are you in Botswana, Miss Cole? And who are these people?' he added, pointing at Gabriel and Stella.

'I am part of Operation Birch. It's the investigation of the murder of Princess Alexandra. No doubt you read of it. Perhaps in the *Times*?'

He nodded, allowing her mild flattery.

'Go on.'

'A lead brought me to Botswana. My colleagues are investigating the murders of the British soldiers here. But not as journalists. They are part of the British security apparatus. I regret I cannot tell you more than that and, once again, forgive me, us, for the subterfuge.'

Gabriel held his breath. Unlike previous encounters in similar situations, there was no question of fighting their way out. Major Modimo might have them arrested, but that would be a relatively simple matter to iron out. No, this was about not destroying a fledgling relationship that could be mutually beneficial.

Modimo drew in a breath.

'We lost two good men out there,' he said. He eyed Gabriel, Eli and Stella in turn. 'Married men. With children. The British Paras lost their lives and I am truly sorry. They were doing good out here. But Moses and Virtue, they were *my* boys.' He thumped his chest. 'So do what you have to do. I will not stand in your way, although I cannot be seen to be helping you in an official capacity any longer. Find the people who committed this heinous massacre. Find them and deal with them.'

His meaning was clear. Gabriel nodded.

'We will, Major. That's a promise.'

'Then go. And God be with you.'

'That was a smart call,' Eli said to Stella as Gabriel drove away from the barracks.

'Thanks. He's a smart guy. If we'd tried to lie or bluff our way out of it he'd have stuck the cuffs on us. I'm here on official business, but Don told me you two aren't. Seemed like the best idea to keep things sweet with the major.'

'Did he pinch your bum when we were having our picture taken?'

Stella snorted.

'Oh my god, he did! You too?'

'Right on the softest part. Cheeky bugger!'

Gabriel drove on, shaking his head

22

Stella placed the hardened lump of Plaster of Paris on the desk in her room. Using a complimentary toothbrush from the bathroom, she flicked away the particles of soil and grass that had stuck to the plaster. The treads were deep and sharp-edged. *New tyres*. It was a wide track, too, suggesting a 4x4.

Using the Canon, she took a series of shots of the tread marks from directly above and at a couple of different angles, laying a hotel ballpoint alongside the marks for scale.

She emailed the shots to Lucian back in Paddington Green with a short message.

Hey Luce,

Greetings from Botswana!

I took this cast in the national park. Any chance you could identify the tyre brand and/or vehicle?

I'm couriering you a paint sample, too. Hopefully the two will tie together.

Take care and say hi to Gareth for me.

Stel x

Using the tip of the craft knife she'd bought as part of her improvised forensics kit, she sliced away an inch-square piece of painted plastic from the trim piece Gabriel had found. She wrapped it in the shower cap provided by the hotel management then wound it round with a dozen sheets of toilet paper before sticking the whole thing in an envelope.

The hotel's business centre turned out to have everything the would-be forensic analyst would need, including padded envelopes and an efficient young man called John, who promised Stella he'd have the packet FedExed to London that same afternoon.

She called Callie.

'What's up, wee girl?' her boss answered, her crisp Edinburgh accent a sudden shock after all the African voices Stella had been listening to recently.

'I've sent a paint sample to Lucian. It could be connected to the case. Can you make sure nobody bullies him into giving their work higher priority?'

'Don't you worry. I've got half the bloody top brass breathing down my neck back here, Stel.' She paused. 'And the other half are calling for my head.'

Stella felt a pang of guilt for misleading her boss. *But the paint could be related to Operation Birch. Stranger things have happened.*

'I'm going out tonight, shake the tree a little. See if anything falls out. Judging by what I've seen so far, an Israeli physics teacher would stick out here like a vegan in a police canteen.'

'Aye, well, get what you can and get back here, Stel. I'm not paying for ye to go on bloody safari!'

With Callie updated, that just left the soil sample. And Stella had an idea. She Googled 'geology Botswana university'.

The very first hit returned the exact same search term, attached to the Geology department of Botswana University in Gaborone. She checked the address on her phone. 4775 Notwane Road was a five-minute drive or a thirty-minute walk. Stella ran to keep fit, and to keep her head straight. She'd once walked six hundred miles through America's northern states in three months. She decided to walk.

First she needed to make a call.

Wearing a pressed white shirt over pale-grey chinos and trainers, she arrived at the Geology department feeling warm but not unpleasantly so. The breeze blowing east to west through the city kept her cool and the lack of traffic and openness of the landscape meant it was more of a pleasant summer stroll than a route march.

Trees grew everywhere, and every twenty yards or so a huge flowering shrub threatened to overspill its garden and push the unwilling pedestrian into the traffic. Fallen Bougainvillea blossoms like papery pink lanterns littered the pavement. She stopped to smell the white feathery flowers on a drooping-branched tree and smiled as an intense orange hit wove its way into her nostrils.

Opposite the blue-and-green sign for the university, a group of local women had set up stalls selling cold drinks, beers, sandwiches and fruit. She made a mental note to buy something on the way back to the hotel.

Having explained on the phone who she was and what she was trying to achieve, the head of the Geology department had proved not just willing but eager to help her.

After introducing herself to the receptionist, Stella went to wait by a display of brochures advertising the various courses available to students.

A few minutes passed, then a female voice made her turn round.

The woman crossing the polished floor towards her was in her late twenties, her hair straightened and cut short. She was smiling, her wide-set eyes magnified by heavy-framed glasses.

'DCI Cole?'

Stella smiled.

'Yes. Dr Montho?'

They shook hands.

'Please call me Lydia.'

'Stella.'

'Good. Formalities out of the way, come to my office. I can introduce you to one of my most promising students.'

Waiting for them in Lydia's office, a neat, professional space filled with green plants and rock samples, was a tall young woman, her braided hair piled on top of her head and secured with a lilac headscarf. She stood as they entered.

'Stella, I'd like you to meet Zela Chilume, one of my most able researchers.'

Stella shook hands with the statuesque student.

Lydia ushered them to comfortable armchairs.

'You said on the phone you needed help with a soil sample.'

'Yes.'

Stella retrieved the evidence bag from her pocket. She laid it on the low coffee table between them.

'I found that inside a piece of vehicle trim in the national park. I'd love to know if it's local or not.'

Zela leaned forwards. She looked up at Stella.

'May I open it?'

'Be my guest. It's why I'm here.'

Zela slid a thumbnail into the Ziploc fastening and held the open bag to her nose, sniffing at the contents. Then, in a move that surprised Stella, she moistened the tip of her index finger with her tongue and dipped it delicately into the powdery red earth. She brought it to her mouth and once more extended her tongue, like a cat tasting something suspicious.

Lydia smiled at Stella.

'You are pulling a face, Stella!'

'Can you really identify the location of a soil sample that way?' Stella asked.

'Not precisely, no. That would be ridiculous. But the local earth is high in iron. It has a distinctive taste, a little like blood, you know? When you suck a cut.'

Stella did know, having inadvertently tasted more blood than she would ever care to admit. She limited herself to a nod.

'I think it is local,' Zela said. 'I can taste the iron. But we need to do a full analysis to be sure.'

'We have a gas chromatograph and a mass spectrometer,' Lydia said proudly. 'Thanks to a wealthy donor who studied here and went on to make a fortune in mining.'

'How long do you need?' Stella asked.

'I can start right away,' Zela said. 'We have comparison charts for all local soil types and for those of our neighbours.'

'Neighbours?'

'Namibia, Zambia, Zimbabwe and South Africa. Lydia compiled the database for her PhD. It is known throughout Africa for its detail and comprehensiveness,' she said, grinning at her mentor.

'Give us twenty-four hours,' Lydia said, smiling.

Stella's mind fizzed at an incoming idea.

'Lydia, could you introduce me to someone in the Physics department?'

'Of course,' she said, with a smile. 'Come on, it's just a five-minute walk across campus.'

They strolled across a Tarmac quadrangle between still and brick buildings. Groups of students chattered, laughed, listened to music through shared headphones or read books beneath shade trees.

At the department of Physics, after a short tour and directions from a couple of earnest male students in lab coats, Lydia introduced Stella to a short, round-faced man.

'This is Dr Ralph Nkosi. Ralph, this is Detective Chief Inspector Stella Cole. She's from the Metropolitan Police, in London.'

He shook Stella's hand.

'What brings you to my department, Detective Chief Inspector Cole?' he said in a deep voice in which Stella detected the rasp of a tobacco habit.

'Just a single question, really. Have you entertained any visitors to your department from Israel, recently? Specifically a high school physics teacher named Dov Lieberman?'

He frowned and shook his head.

'I'm afraid not. I wish it were otherwise, but our last international visitor was in 2015. A Swedish researcher. But Israel? No. I am sorry.'

Stella shook her head.

'Don't be. It was just a wild guess.'

Stella found Gabriel and Eli by the pool when she got back. They'd grouped three loungers in the shade of a rush-topped beach umbrella in a quiet corner of the pool area.

The temperature had increased during her meeting at the Geology department and she was sweating, despite having bought a can of orange drink and a pot of fragrant, cubed fresh mango to consume on the journey back.

Eli smiled up at her from her lounger. Stella had time to admire the younger woman's body, honed, she imagined from years of combat and intensive militant training.

'You should get your cossie on,' Eli said, then paused, brow furrowed. 'That's what you call them, isn't it? Swimming costumes, I mean?'

'Well, yes. But strange though this might seem, I didn't pack one.'

'They sell them in the resort shop. Come on,' she said, getting to her feet and wrapping a diaphanous blue sarong round her chest. 'I'll help you pick one out.'

* * *

Gabriel opened his eyes. Eli and Stella were approaching from the direction of his and Eli's room. Stella wore a high-cut orange one-piece swimsuit. He took in the flat belly, toned legs and arms. Though older than Eli by around ten years, she looked more than capable of taking care of herself. He felt confident the three of them would be more than a match for a bunch of poachers, however they encountered them.

'Well?' Eli said, when she and Stella arrived. 'What do you think? She looks great, doesn't she?'

'You do,' Gabriel said. He pointed to her left arm. 'Nice scar. War wound?'

Stella grimaced.

'You could say that. Mim Robey gave it to me.'

Gabriel peered at the puckered ribbon of skin.

'Looks like something a golok would do.'

'A what?'

'It's what we called a machete in the SAS.'

Stella nodded.

'Yes. That.'

They spent a few minutes checking out the knife, machete and bullet wounds on each other's skin, before Gabriel, laughing, changed the subject.

'Now that we've established we've all been in the wars,' he said, 'Stella, what did you get from the boffins at the university?'

'They'll have a report for me on the soil sample by tomorrow. I've couriered a paint sample to Lucian, too. He's the top forensic scientist at Paddington Green. No idea how long that'll take, but the lad in the business centre said the courier service to the UK is "One hundred per cent efficient" – his words – so we'll just have to hope and pray. You?'

'Eli and I reckon the best next step, for both our investigations, is to hit the bars. Not the swanky tourist ones—'

'The dives where the pond life hang out,' Stella finished for him.

'Sorry,' Gabriel said. 'Forgot you're a cop for a minute.'

'Must be my cossie,' Stella said, winking at Eli, who grinned back.

'Tonight?'

Stella nodded.

'I was on the phone to my boss earlier. She seems to think she's paying for me to be out here photographing wildlife. I need to find out what I can and get back to London.'

'I suspect that where we're going, you'll see plenty of wildlife,' Gabriel said. 'Scavengers…'

'Predators,' Eli added, joining in.

'And lots of creepy crawlies,' Stella finished. 'Eight? Nine?'

'Nine,' Gabriel said.

23

At 9.15 p.m., Gabriel parked outside one of the downtown hotels. He retrieved a briefcase from the boot then whistled to a couple of skinny kids in Adidas T-shirts, shiny football shorts and sandals and held out two five-dollar bills.

'Watch the car for us, boys,' he said. 'If it's unmarked when we get back there's another five each for you, OK?'

'OK, Mister,' the taller of the two said. 'No problem!'

'Good. Now, another question. Where do the gangsters hang out in G-City?'

'Gangsters?'

'Yeah, you know, the bad guys.'

The shorter of the two boys shrugged.

'What are you talking about? No gangsters here, man.'

'Come on,' Gabriel said with a smile. 'Don't tell me a streetwise dude like you doesn't know where the action is?'

The boy grinned and held out his palm.

'Questions, free. Answers, five dollar.'

Smiling, Gabriel proffered the extra note.

'Spill.'

The boy slipped the note into his pocket.

'Oasis Lounge. Very shiny. On Gandukuni Street.'

Gabriel patted his informant on the shoulder and rejoined Eli and Stella.

'No need for a bar crawl,' he said. 'Our friend back there told me the place we need to hit.'

With the car as secure as they could make it, the trio set off towards Old Naledi, the centre of what the guidebook described as Gaborone's version of Boston's Combat Zone.

Gabriel and Eli wore the universal outfit of hired muscle the world over – jeans, boots, black tees and lightweight black jackets. Stella walked between them, head held high, sharply dressed in a dark-grey silk jacket and matching trousers, plus four-inch heels that brought her up to Gabriel's height. She swung a black briefcase from her right hand.

Stella stumbled on an uneven patch of pavement.

'These bloody heels!'

'You're the big boss,' Eli said. 'We can't have you in combat boots, now can we?'

'Cheeky mare! Just make sure any trouble gets out of our way fast, cause there's no way I can fight in these.'

'Oh, I don't know. You could always take them off and stab the fuckers.'

Gabriel had trodden many such streets in his career, some as a soldier, others as a department agent. Reckoning that two former Special Forces soldiers and a clearly badass Met Police detective would be more than a match for any low-level gangbangers, he walked on, confident they'd find what they were looking for without incident.

The fact that he and Eli were carrying George Taylor's pistols tucked into their waistbands was also a comfort.

As they walked, the three Brits shared stories, bantered and commented on the sights and sounds of this part of Africa, new to all of them. Insects competed with frogs to make the loudest racket, their overlapping squeaks, buzzes, rasps and chirrups a continuous high-pitched drone.

. . .

In Gabriel's experience, inner-city drinking establishments that didn't bother with bouncers sent out plenty of other signals to potential troublemakers. He remembered a sawdust-floored Republican bar in the Falls Road in Belfast. Posing as a Russian arms dealer, he'd had to fight to control a fluttering heartbeat as all around him the 'men of violence' drank Guinness, ate Tayto-brand crisps and planned attacks on their Protestant neighbours, the British Army or the RUC. McGinty's front door had been unguarded.

Oasis Lounge fell squarely into the same category as McGinty's. Outside, young black men leaned against shiny BMWs and Mercedes with oversized chrome wheels and blacked-out windows. The cars' stereos were turned up loud, pumping the fast, bass-heavy jazz the locals called Afropop into the warm evening air. Girls in vest-tops, micro-miniskirts and heels far higher than Stella's stood in groups of three or four, laughing and smoking and swigging beer from long-necked bottles.

From inside, yet more music set the air vibrating: harmonising guitars over a lively dance beat and a high-pitched male voice singing in Tsetswana. Above the double doors, neon palm trees flicked from side to side, flanking the name of the bar, which was picked out in orange and lime green. 'Oasis' flashed in random patterns designed to give anyone looking for too long a migraine.

'Confidence,' Gabriel muttered, just loud enough for Eli and Stella to hear, as they approached the group of men bantering under the sole streetlight.

He noted approvingly the way Stella strode one pace ahead of him and Eli, head held high.

'This bar's not for tourists,' one of the young guys said, pushing himself off the bonnet of his Beemer. 'Plenty of upscale joints in Extension Ten.'

Stella whipped her head round and glared at him, closing the distance between them to less than a foot for good measure.

'Good. Because I'm not a tourist. Now get out of my fucking way.'

Gabriel closed in to Stella's left side, as Eli mirrored the move on the right.

The young man hesitated, then kissed his teeth with a raised chin and sidled back to his friends.

Ignoring the threatening murmurs, Gabriel followed Stella inside. The place smelled of expensive perfume, aftershave and tobacco smoke. Subtle lighting created an intimate atmosphere, enhanced by circular leather-benched booths around the walls.

A band occupied a corner of the bar, painted black to demarcate the performance space and framed by two pole-mounted PA speakers. Two guitarists, a bass player, drummer and singer were playing a lilting mid-tempo number. The singer nodded at Gabriel as he caught her eye.

They attracted a fair number of curious and even hostile gazes from the all-black clientele, but that was to be expected. Clearly this was the right place. Tailored suits and expensive-looking designer gear were much in evidence. Lots of gold, plenty of ice sparkling at women's necks, wrists and earlobes, chunky watches on display beneath pulled-back shirt cuffs. Tall glasses of champagne, ice buckets, cigars.

'Follow my lead,' Stella said.

Stella marched up to the bar as if she owned the place. She raised an index finger and crooked it when the barman turned her way. Gabriel and Eli turned outwards and surveyed the room.

Stella was gratified to see that most of the starers turned back to their own conversations, drinks or card games.

'Yes, madam, what can I get you?' the barman asked her.

'Champagne. A bottle. And two glasses.'

He raised his finely arched eyebrows.

'Two? Not three? Is one of your,' a pause, 'friends not drinking?'

'Neither of them is. And they're not my friends. They're my employees.'

'Then—'

She leant over the bar and dropped her voice.

'One for me and one for the guy I need to talk to about ivory.'

He stood a little straighter.

'I don't know what you mean, Madam. I'm sorry. Let me get you the champagne.'

He arrived back in front of her a few minutes later with a bottle of Moët in a sweating ice bucket and two flutes on a tray.

'That will be one hundred dollars US, please, Madam,' he said with a small smile.

Stella turned to her left and spoke to Gabriel.

'Case.'

He nodded, maintaining the unsmiling expression beloved of personal protection officers all over the world. The case made a satisfyingly loud thump as he plonked it down on the wooden bar top.

Stella popped the catches and lifted the lid, making sure the barman got an eyeful of the neatly arranged, blue-banded stacks of fifty-dollar bills. She slid two from beneath one of the paper ribbons and handed them over. As he extended long, delicate fingers to take them, she slid a third note into the breast pocket of his white jacket.

'Thank you,' she said, closing the lid. 'Send him over to my table, would you? I have a business proposition for him.'

The barman's gaze flicked over her left shoulder before he regained eye contact with her. He thanked her for the tip and turned away to serve another customer. She waited at the bar while Gabriel and Eli found an empty booth then beckoned her over.

Stella opened the champagne and filled the two flutes to within half an inch of their rims, before scrunching the bottle back into the ice.

'You think he bought the act?' Eli asked.

'Yep. Whoever he is, our man's in the room. Or someone who can take us to him is. Just wait.'

She took a sip of the champagne. Remembered a bottle she'd shared outside a bar in Taormina on her honeymoon. The man with whom she'd shared it was dead now. So was their daughter. But that was in the past. She slammed the heavy door in her mind that protected her from her memories.

They didn't have to wait long.

24

Bald pate shining in the gleam of the recessed lighting, the man on his way to their table slipped his six-foot-plus, heavily-muscled body between the tables with a dancer's grace.

When he reached the table, he smiled and bowed. Gabriel caught a glint of gold on his left wrist beneath the French cuff fastened with a polished knob of white.

'Good evening,' he said to Stella, ignoring Gabriel and Eli. 'I am Peter Mafombe.' He spread his hands wide. 'This is my place. May I join you?'

Stella held out a hand, palm upwards.

'Be my guest, Mr Mafombe.'

He pulled out a seat on the open side of the booth and leaned across the table. He steepled his fingers beneath his chin.

'I am afraid you are labouring under a misapprehension, Miss…?'

'Call me Joyce.'

He smiled again.

'Joyce. There is no ivory trade in Botswana. It is banned under CITES. That's the—'

'Convention on Trade in Endangered Species, yes, I know.'

Gabriel had one eye on Mafombe, and one ear on his conversation with Stella. The other two organs he employed to survey the rest of the bar. Eli would be doing the same.

He saw fewer pretty young women in revealing outfits. And more muscular men standing in small groups, glancing in his direction.

The double doors, which had been flung wide when they entered, were now closed. The band was still playing, but the musicians were exchanging worried glances.

Gabriel's pulse ticked up a notch. He let his right hand, currently lying on the tabletop, slide off the polished wood and rest on his lap. Just below his waistband.

'Then, forgive me,' Mafombe said, 'but why do you come to my bar asking about ivory?'

'Because blood diamonds are too hot these days and I need a new asset class to invest in.'

'Blood diamonds? I have not heard of them. Are they some kind of ruby?'

'Right!' Stella said, getting to her feet. 'I've had enough of this. We're leaving.'

Gabriel and Eli stood in a fast, coordinated movement that had Mafombe rearing back in his chair. Behind the bar owner, the men Gabriel had been observing straightened their postures. He saw hands edging towards pockets, or the backs of waistbands. Prepared himself.

Mafombe stood too, turning to pat the air at the men readying themselves for something more kinetic than playing cards and chatting up women. They stood down.

Mafombe turned back to Stella, all smiles. He stroked a palm across his skull. Pointed at the second flute.

'May I?'

'Did the barman tell you who it's for?'

'He did.'

Stella shrugged as she sat back down.

'Then you know the answer,' she said.

Gabriel glared at a couple of the young men still arrowing

hostile glances in their direction, then lowered himself into the leather banquette's embrace once more.

'I will take *half* a glass,' Mafombe said, finally, lifting the champagne to his lips.

Gabriel watched the man's Adam's apple hop as he swallowed. Visualised the blood vessels pulsing beneath the skin.

Mafombe placed the glass on the table with a click.

'Blood diamonds, eh?' he asked, placing his fingertips on the base of the flute and circling them to swirl the remaining champagne. 'Where did you used to get them?'

'Sierra Leone. The DRC. Ivory Coast. Wherever the sellers weren't too greedy.'

She sipped her own champagne and sat back with a smile, a high-roller in the murky world of illegal commodities. Gabriel mentally revised his opinion of her – upwards – once again.

'But no longer,' Mafombe said.

'Like I said. Too hot right now.'

'And ivory isn't?'

Stella smiled.

'Let's just say it's time my organisation diversified its investment portfolio. Now, can you take me to the man whose champagne you're drinking or not?'

Mafombe checked his watch; a Rolex, Gabriel now saw.

'Why don't you sit back and enjoy the show? I have to make some calls. In an hour we can go, yes?'

Stella inclined her head.

'One more thing, Mr Mafombe.'

'Please, call me Peter.'

'Peter, I'd like you to have a word with your friends over there,' she said, jerking her chin over his shoulder. 'Tell them to back off. Otherwise I fear for their safety. My colleagues here are well-armed and well-trained. You can guess where.'

Gabriel fixed Mafombe with a dead-eyed stare. The guy was probably making an educated guess. South Africa. Wrong. Russia. Wrong. America. Wrong. Israel. Right. Belgium. Wrong. The UK.

Right. People like 'Joyce' didn't wander into places like the Oasis Lounge without some extremely effective protection.

As he got to his feet, Mafombe smiled down at Gabriel, acknowledging his presence for the first time. He looked at Eli, then back at Stella.

'Enjoy the music, Joyce. I'll send over some beers for your,' a beat, 'colleagues.'

Gabriel watched as he threaded his way through the crowd, pausing here and there to whisper into cocked ears. Stances softened. Stares drifted away. Laughter replaced silence. The bar exhaled a sigh of relief.

'Ever do any amateur dramatics? Because that was a bravura performance,' Gabriel said to Stella once they were alone again.

She grinned.

'I played Tinker Bell in a school production of *Peter Pan* once,' she said.

'Is Captain Hook going to come through?'

'I think so. The barman will have told him how much cash I brought in here. Money talks with guys like that. He'll want a cut of whatever deal goes down.'

Peter Mafombe was as good as his word. He slid into the booth next to Eli exactly sixty minutes after their first encounter. He spoke across her to Stella.

'You are in luck, Joyce. *My* colleague wants to meet you.'

She inclined her head.

'Good. When and where?'

He waggled his head from side to side.

'Not so fast, Joyce. There is an arrangement fee.'

'A what?'

'He is not a man to be hurried. And he wants to be sure you are serious. Twenty thousand US. The meeting will be next week some time. I will tell you when and where once he has the payment.'

Stella stared at him. Gabriel registered the relaxed pose and muscle tone. How was she doing it? Deep in enemy territory and she looked like she was having a drink in her local.

'Five thousand,' she said.

'Fifteen is the lowest he can accept. He told me so himself.'

'Seven and a half.'

'You expect me to take such a piss-poor offer to my colleague? He is the big man hereabouts in ivory. Thirteen.'

'Nine.'

Gabriel could see where the haggling would end up. He assumed Mafombe could, too.

'Eleven.'

Gabriel heard the hint of a question mark. Fatal.

Stella shook her head.

'Nine,' she repeated, more firmly this time.

'– and seven fifty?'

'– and a half.'

She reached for her glass and drained it. Then turned to Gabriel, moved closer and whispered into his ear.

'Lovely weather we're having for the time of year.'

He nodded, allowing a smile to steal across his face. He glanced round Stella at Mafombe, then placed his lips close to her ear.

'I hope we get the chance to see some wildlife while we're out here.'

Mafombe's eyes flicked between the two of them. He checked his watch, then started twisting the cufflink on his left wrist. Finally he sighed.

'You drive a hard bargain, Joyce. Nine and a half. I take it to my colleague, then I call you with details of the meet.'

Stella nodded at Eli, who lifted the briefcase onto the table and popped the catches with a double snap. Stella raised the lid, shielding the contents from prying eyes elsewhere in the bar.

She lifted out a handful of bundles and passed them to Mafombe. He ran a long-nailed thumb across the edge of one of the stacks of bills, smiled and nodded, then stuffed them into his inside pockets.

'Wait!' she said sharply.

She pulled a ballpoint pen from the inside of her jacket and grasped his hand. She turned it over and wrote a number on his palm.

'Call me with the details.'

He stood, then bent down towards Stella.

'You are not afraid I will simply take your money, and to hell with the meeting, Joyce?'

She smiled up at him, a forgiving expression such as a patient school teacher might bestow on a slow but harmless student.

'You are going to call me with the details by midnight tomorrow,' she said quietly, maintaining the smile. 'Fail, and we'll come back here with a couple of RPGs and blow you, your customers, your house band and the Oasis Lounge into tiny, little,' a brief pause, 'fucking pieces.'

Mafombe patted his breast pocket, over the money. Nodded once, then turned on his heel and worked his way back through the crowd.

Gabriel waited until Mafombe had disappeared.

'We should go. Now. You beat him down on the arrangement fee, but my guess is, a man like that isn't used to having his pride kicked so hard. There'll be trouble unless we're quick.'

'I agree,' Eli said. 'Let's go. Nice and easy, but nice and fast, too.'

Gabriel and Eli formed a wedge and pushed their way gently but firmly through the drinkers and the dancers until they reached the doors and stepped out into the warm night air.

25

'Stay alert,' Gabriel said, as they began walking away from the Oasis Lounge, down the street and back towards the spot where they'd left the car.

After five minutes, when they hadn't seen anyone, Gabriel permitted himself to relax a little. The absence of streetlights meant visibility was poor, but the moon was bright, giving them enough light to see.

'How far to the hotel?' Stella asked.

'Half a mile? A bit less?' Eli said. 'Those kids better have done a good job of watching it.'

'No reason why they shouldn't, is there? It's a pretty standard way of earning a little pocket money. Plus Gabriel asked them,' Stella replied. 'Even in London, there are places where the local villains-in-waiting do it. There's a code of honour.'

'It's a mini-protection racket.'

'Exactly! "Bad area, this, Miss",' Stella said, roughening and lightening her voice into a Cockney squawk. '"You pay us some cash and we'll stop your nice shiny motor getting its paintwork keyed or your rims nicked".'

'They'd actually steal your wheels?' Eli asked with a grin.

'When I'd just qualified as a DC, one of the lads left his patrol car parked in a very dodgy estate in East London while he went to attend a domestic. He came back and the local pond life had stolen the rear wheels. Put the poor sod's Mondeo up on bricks!'

'Aren't they locked on, though?' Eli persisted, laughing now.

'Of course! But these little gangs, they build up a set of locking wheel nuts for all the popular makes.'

Gabriel laughed, too, though his eyes were still roving the street ahead, watching for side roads, darker patches of shade, anywhere potential trouble could be lurking.

He inhaled deeply as they passed a creeper that enveloped a single-storey whitewashed house. A wrought-iron ornamental lamppost lit the scene with pale-yellow light.

The overwhelming smell of oranges and honey swirled up into his brain and made him smile. Yellow trumpets with maroon centres hung from pale stems and he watched as a fat-bodied moth resembling a hummingbird hovered just beneath one, poking its rapier-like proboscis deep into the centre of the flower.

'Smell that,' he said.

The two women craned their necks upwards and sniffed at the exotic blossoms.

'Wow!' Eli said. 'It reminds me of a flower that grows in Israel. I don't know its scientific name, but in Hebrew, we call it Lotus Sweetjuice.'

Stella took another sniff. She nodded.

'I know what you mean. I think it's a—'

A deep male voice interrupted.

'What is this? Two beautiful ladies out for a stroll, is it?'

Gabriel cursed himself for not being more alert. *Should have heard him coming up on us.* From the corner of his eye he registered Eli and Stella adopting non-threatening postures. Non-threatening, but with their weight balanced between their feet. Hands loose by their sides.

Five men faced them, in a loose group. Their dress suggested some sort of gang affiliation. Baggy black basketball vests, each bearing the number 9 crowned with a Nike swoosh. Spotted bandannas tied around their foreheads. Suspicious bulges at the waist beneath the vests. All wore squishy-soled running shoes. Gabriel couldn't remember if he'd seen the men in the Oasis Lounge.

The man at the centre of the group grinned. Taller than Gabriel by a head, impressively muscled arms folded across his chest, he jerked his chin at the flowering plant.

'Who is he?' the man asked Eli, pointing at Gabriel. 'Your hairdresser?'

The other four men chuckled. Unable to keep still, they shifted from foot to foot, stroking their close-cropped heads and exchanging sidelong glances.

Was it worth reasoning with them? Gabriel dismissed it as a waste of effort. He knew what they could see. Three dumb Western tourists who should have known better than to walk G-City's streets after dark. Probably loaded with dollars, fancy watches, iPhones, credit cards, the works.

'If you think you're going to mug us, you're going to come off worst.' He pointed to Stella. 'Metropolitan Police.' To Eli. 'Mossad.' Finally, he jabbed a thumb into his own chest. 'British Army.'

The gang leader followed Gabriel's pointing finger on its three-stop trip round the incomers' forces. Then he threw his head back and guffawed.

'Man, you tell a funny story. I give you that,' he said. 'Now, hand over all your shit and we'll let you go back to smelling the sweet flowers of Botswana.' He looked at Stella's briefcase. 'You a sales lady? Got some nice aftershave in there? Face cream for my girlfriend?'

Another chorus of cackles from his subordinates.

Eli took a sharp step forward, causing the closest of the five men to take a step back. She smiled.

'What are you carrying under the vests, boys?'

With a grin, the leader lifted the hem of his garment. Gabriel saw a gun butt. From the look of it, a small-calibre revolver. The others revealed knife hilts protruding from their waistbands. No match for the Glock or the SIG, but he really didn't want to start a firefight that would lead to the muggers' deaths.

'That enough for you, my lady?' the leader asked, resting his right hand on the gun butt and grabbing his crotch with his other hand. 'I've got something much bigger down there. Maybe I show you what it can do to a little girl like you.'

'Very impressive. Shame such a big man as you feels the need to carry a gun just to rob three tourists. Especially when two of them are women. What's the matter, you worried we'll kick your arses?'

His eyes widened. Then he threw back his head and laughed for the third time.

Which was a mistake.

The sound died in his throat, as Eli's blade-like right hand chopped across his larynx. She stepped in close and jerked her knee up hard into his groin, dropping him to the ground. Two punches to his left temple and he was out cold.

Gabriel and Stella moved in together as if they'd been fighting side by side for years. Clearly the heels weren't an impediment.

He felled one man with a kick to the knee that sheared the tendons and ligaments with a loud crack.

Stella head-butted a second, stunning him so that he fell backwards, hingeing at his ankles. A third man punched Stella in the face, but his aim was off and the blow barely grazed her cheek. Gabriel was dodging knife thrusts from his man, waiting for the chance to inflict a deadly blow of his own.

'That's enough!' Eli shouted, bringing the remaining fighters, Gabriel and Stella included, to a stop.

She pointed the little revolver into the face of the only gang member still standing. The terrified would-be mugger's hands shot skywards.

'Don't kill me!' he stammered.

'I'm not going to,' Eli said. 'Unless you try anything. In which case I'll shove this little popgun up your arse and pull the trigger. Now, on your belly.'

He pressed his palms together at his sternum.

'Please. I am begging you.'

'Now!' she shouted.

He dropped to the ground, hands clasped above his head.

Eli whipped a bundle of cable ties from her trouser pocket. In a series of economical moves, she linked his right wrist to that of his nearest neighbour, then repeated the process until all five men were daisy-chained together around the ornamental lamp post.

She flicked out the chamber and emptied the six rounds into the palm of her hand. The now-useless revolver she dropped into the centre of the group. She collected their knives and dropped them into a plastic dumpster nearby.

Then, as calmly as if the whole episode had never happened, she pulled out her phone.

'Hello? Yes, police? Come to the junction of Old Lobatse Road and Samora Machel Drive. You'll find five gangbangers handcuffed round a lamp post. They have an illegal firearm.'

Despite the obvious string of questions chirping from the phone's tinny speaker, she ended the call.

'Let's go,' Eli said.

Ten minutes later, they regained the safety of the well-lit streets of the commercial district and the Avani. The Mercedes was exactly where they had left it. Gabriel glanced at the wheels; all on the Tarmac, not a brick in sight.

Reaching the car, he whistled, loudly. A 'Hey! We're back!' signal to the protectioneers.

He needn't have bothered. The two boys were already crossing the street to meet them, hips rolling, hands thrust deep into their shorts pockets.

'Everything cool?' he asked the taller boy.

'Chilled, man. Icy,' the kid said, affecting a half-decent American accent.

He held his hand out.

Gabriel pulled two ten-dollar bills from his wallet and slapped them down into the budding entrepreneur's palm.

'Good job. Thanks.'

'You betcha!' he said, pointing a finger at Gabriel then clicking his tongue as he dropped his upraised thumb. 'Gotta blow, Joe.'

'Gotta scram, Sam,' his partner piped up.

Shaking his head, Gabriel blipped the fob to unlock the car. He, Eli and Stella climbed inside.

As he pulled away, he heard Stella sigh from the back seat.

'Well that was intense.'

* * *

The next morning, Gabriel answered a knock on the door to find Stella standing there with a triumphant smile on her face.

He beckoned her in and closed the door. Eli emerged from the bathroom.

'Hey, what's up?'

'Guess who just called "Joyce"?'

'Mafombe came through?'

'He did. Friday. Back at the Oasis. Four in the afternoon.'

Eli smiled.

'Good. We can get a couple of steps closer to the killers.'

'On which subject, now we've got a lead on the poachers, can you guys help me work on finding whether Lieberman ever came through here?'

'Of course,' Gabriel said. 'I don't know why, but I get the weirdest feeling it's no coincidence we're all out here together. What are the odds, after all?'

Stella shrugged.

'He didn't visit the university. That was just a wild guess.'

'I've had a look up as we've been walking around. No CCTV apart from outside some of the big hotels,' Gabriel said.

'I know. Not quite the surveillance society we've got back home.'

'Could you try calling Uri again?' Gabriel asked Eli.

26

TEL AVIV

The three men and two women clustered around the desktop PC had over two hundred years' service between them defending Israel against its enemies.

Uri Ziff stared at the screen. To his left he could hear the breathing of his immediate superior, Director Avigael Peretz, as she scrutinised the action unfolding in slow motion. To his right, Saul Ben Zacchai, the prime minister, remained silent, though his pungent aftershave gave plenty of signals he was in the room.

'Back it up again, please,' Uri asked the young intelligence analyst operating the controls for the CCTV playback.

The keyboard clicked, the mouse whispered across the mat and the footage restarted.

Two men, clad in baseball caps and dark clothes came into shot as they walked along the narrow balcony that led to the front door of Flat 27, 19 Yahalal Street. They kept their faces turned away from the camera mounted on the underside of the next floor up. Both were slim, both tall, both walked with the weight-balanced gait of professional men of action.

They stopped outside Lieberman's home. The broader of the two stretched out a finger and rang the doorbell. A few moments passed, then the door opened, framing Sarah Lieberman. She brushed a stray strand of hair behind her ear, smiling and nodding as the man who had rung the bell spoke.

Then her expression changed. Her forehead crumpled and her mouth turned down. Eyes wide, she began gesticulating at the men, her mouth working. She nodded in response to another question and stood aside to let the men in. The door closed.

Unbidden by his superior, the analyst fast-forwarded the images for approximately five minutes then slowed the playback once more.

The front door opened and Sarah Lieberman emerged, holding her three-year-old son, Shmuel, by the hand. Her face was a mask of panic, eyes tight, mouth a stiff line. The boy was crying. The two visitors came next, one holding a baby wrapped in a white blanket in his arms.

The group turned left and hurried along the balcony before disappearing from the camera's view.

The analyst clicked a couple of keys and a new rectangular playback window opened on the screen. It showed a white SUV with blacked-out windows driving away from a parking spot outside the Liebermans' apartment block, heading west towards the coast.

The analyst stopped the film and turned to look at Uri over his shoulder.

'We picked up the SUV sporadically after that. Last contact on 91, heading towards Damascus.'

Uri patted the young man on the shoulder.

'Thanks, Yacob. Good work.'

The senior officers and the prime minister retired to a glass-walled conference room.

'What happened, Uri?' Saul asked.

'I think it's fairly obvious. Two Syrian agents tricked Sarah Lieberman into coming with them by posing as security agency employees. Us or Shin Bet. Spun her some story about Dov being in trouble. "No time to explain, you're in mortal danger. Come with us."'

'And this happened when, exactly?' Saul asked.

'Three weeks ago.'

'So, two before the princess was shot.'

'Yes.'

'Did Lieberman report that his family were missing?'

'No. We checked with the school. He turned up for work every day just like normal. The headteacher said he even ran the after-school Physics club on the Wednesday afternoons. She said he looked a bit off-colour, but he told her he had a cold.'

'You think the Syrians blackmailed Dov into committing the assassination?'

'I do. We have him leaving Israel on an El Al flight for London the day before the hit.'

'Avigael, do you believe that bullshit Tammerlane put out about just happening to be passing by and seeing the shooter's rifle barrel?'

She put her fingertips to her pursed lips.

'You know the training, Saul. "There's no such thing as coincidence. If something smells fishy, start looking for fish",' she said.

'Then what? Tammerlane was involved in a plot to murder a member of the British royal family? Why?'

'You saw the news! It was a pretext to break off diplomatic relations with us. He's expelled our citizens. He's a lifelong enemy of Israel!'

Saul patted the air.

'Calm down, Avi, I get it.'

'Plus, I heard a whisper from our friends in London that Tammerlane's making noises about a referendum on the existence of the monarchy.'

Saul smiled.

'It's fine. That's my view as well. I just wanted to hear it from your lips.'

'Fine. So hear this, too. After Dov took the shot, Tammerlane killed him. Otherwise he could have spoken out.'

'Would he, though?' Uri asked. 'Even if the Syrians gave him back his family, they could have threatened to kill them at any time if Dov opened his mouth. He was a teacher, remember. He had no training for this sort of thing.'

'It made Tammerlane look like a hero,' Saul said, emphasising the final word. 'He won the election with a landslide after that. One of the most royalist countries on Earth elected a republican. *I* should have his luck. Sorry,' he added, as his two most senior foreign intelligence officers looked at him wide-eyed.

'The wife and kids are dead, too,' Uri said.

Saul and Avigael nodded. No loose ends. The training.

Uri's phone vibrated in his pocket. He pulled it out and glanced at the screen.

'Can I take this? It could be important.'

Saul nodded. Uri accepted the call.

'Eliyah. I'm with the prime minister and Director Peretz. What is it?'

'I'm in Botswana with Gabriel Wolfe and a Metropolitan Police detective chief inspector. She's investigating the assassination.'

Uri felt his pulse accelerate.

'Go on.'

'They found dirt in the sniper nest. It came from Botswana. She's trying to find out whether Lieberman was here in the days before the killing. Have you guys found anything that could be helpful?'

Uri heard the distinctive click of a puzzle piece slotting home.

'As a matter of fact, Eliyah, we have. No way was Dov Lieberman in Botswana. Or anywhere else outside Israel for that matter.'

'You're sure? Sorry, Uri,' she said, immediately. 'But, you're confident? There's no way he could have got away for even a couple of days?'

'It's fine, and yes, I am one hundred per cent confident. Dov Lieberman was never in Botswana.'

He looked back at Saul and Avigael who were both regarding

him with raised eyebrows. He gave them a thumbs-up as he ended the call.

'Well?' Saul asked.

'Lieberman wasn't the shooter,' Uri said with a broad smile.

'How do you know?'

'The British police found soil in the sniper nest. From Botswana.'

'Tammerlane?'

'No. As far as we can tell, he was in the UK the whole time.'

'Then, the soil—'

'Must have come from a third person. *They* took the shot then disappeared, killing Lieberman to leave a false trail.'

'Could have been a spotter,' Saul said.

'For a professional, that was a short-range shot. No need for a spotter. Anyway, these guys work alone, as you know. Ours do.' He huffed out a breath before continuing. 'Saul, I say this with the greatest respect to you, as a friend and the prime minister: think about it logically. Did we order this hit? No! Was Dov Lieberman, high school physics teacher and family man, a professional hitman? No! Did he have any personal reason, any reason in the world, to fly to England and murder a princess? No! Plus, we saw his family being kidnapped! I am telling you, he was set up. A patsy.'

Saul was nodding with each emphatic point Uri made.

'This is excellent news, Uri,' he said. 'We can work with this. We need to get our diplomats onto the radio, the TV, whatever. This blows Tammerlane's narrative into pieces.'

'Yes, it does. But if it wasn't Lieberman, then who was it, Saul?' Uri asked. 'Who killed Princess Alexandra?'

Saul turned to Avigael.

'I want all efforts directed to finding the real shooter. All resources we can spare. And all we cannot.'

* * *

Eli pocketed her phone. Turned to Stella and Gabriel. She tried but failed to prevent the smile cracking her cheeks.

'What did Uri tell you?' Stella asked.

After Eli had filled them in on the details of the call with Uri, Gabriel scratched his head.

'Are you going back to the UK then?' he asked Stella.

She frowned.

'Lieberman didn't come here. But the real shooter did,' she said. 'And I have my meeting with Mafombe's contact. I'm going to stay on for a few days, see if I can find out anything. Mafombe can help there as well. He seems to know everybody who's somebody in G-City.'

'You don't think that would be pushing it?' Eli asked.

'I think it absolutely *would* be pushing it. That's kind of my job,' she added with a smile.

27

That night, after Gabriel and she had made love, Eli rolled onto her side and propped her head on her right palm. Gabriel looked up at her and twirled a lock of her auburn hair around his finger. Her eyes were shining in the moonlight flooding their room through the open curtains.

'What?' he said.

'Do you think he'll rescind the order about Israelis having to leave the UK?'

'I don't know. I hope so. I guess Stella will speak to her boss, then the Met will release the information and that'll take the focus away from Israel. You're all right though, now. Don got you a British passport.'

'It's not about that, though, is it, Gabe? Even if I, personally, can come and go as I please, it's what lies behind it that worries me.'

Gabriel didn't answer straight away. He ran through a couple of scenarios in his head first.

'He might. With evidence pointing away from Lieberman, the police will be looking for a new suspect. Unless Tammerlane says it was him who was in Botswana, which would be odd, then he has to concede he got it wrong.'

Gabriel hesitated.

'But?' Eli asked, brows knitted.

'But he's not a normal politician. We know he's anti-Israel. Has been since he was a student. I can't see him giving it up so easily.'

'What can he say? The forensic guy said that soil came from right here.'

'He could say anything. The sample was cross-contaminated. It was left by someone else way before the hit. The analysis was flawed. It was planted by the Mossad. Anything.'

Eli pouted.

'Great. Thanks for the encouragement.'

He drew her down and into an embrace. He spoke against the top of her head, releasing thoughts that had been circling in his brain like vultures over a dead elephant.

'It's going to be fine. Unlike Tammerlane, you and I have actually met Saul Ben Zacchai. No way would he have sanctioned the hit. Or Uri or Avigael either. It's a false flag operation.'

'Organised by who then? Tammerlane?'

'He's done pretty well out of it, wouldn't you say?'

'You're serious, aren't you?'

Gabriel stroked her hair, feeling her heart beating against his own chest.

'Terrified by the kidnappers into compliance, Lieberman arrives in London. He makes his way to Windsor.' Gabriel paused, rearranging the pieces on the deadly board game he was playing in his mind.

'He climbs the tower, overpowers and kills the police markswoman, and sets up his sniper nest. A second man climbs to the top of the tower, kills Lieberman and takes the shot himself. Tammerlane arrives and the shooter leaves. The police arrive to discover Tammerlane covered in a dead sniper's blood. Open and shut case.'

'Hang on,' Eli said sleepily. 'How did the cop die?'

'The markswoman?'

'Yeah.'

'I don't know.'

'Probably wasn't a shot. That would have alerted people. Probably someone would've called 999.'

'A knife then. Or he used his bare hands.'

'We need to ask Stella in the morning.'

Gabriel came out of the shower, rubbing furiously at his hair. Ensconced in an oversized armchair, Eli was flicking through the pages of an African fashion magazine. He caught a glimpse of beautiful black models clad in leather trousers and traditional printed fabric tops.

'Ready for breakfast?' Eli asked him, looking up.

'I was up early. Already had mine.'

She frowned.

'I didn't hear you get up.'

He came to her and kissed her, then wrapped his arms around her waist.

'That's because I am a trained master of *Yinshen fangshi*,' he whispered. 'I could cut your throat from ear to ear in the night and you wouldn't know until it was too late.'

She grinned and reached down between his legs. He winced as she took hold of his balls in her cupped hand.

'Oh yeah? Don't you think being manually castrated might make that a little difficult?'

She increased the pressure.

'Fine, fine! Let me go.'

'Let me go…' Eli drew out the final word and lifted her chin in an unspoken question.

'Please!'

'Please, Eli Schochat, Queen of My Heart and Supreme Fighting Machine.'

Squeeze.

'Yes, that, OK! Let me go.'

Squeeze.

'Say it.'

'Let me go please, Eli Schochat, Queen of My Heart and Supreme Fighting Machine.'

Laughing, Eli released him. He massaged the afflicted area.

'We need to talk to Stella,' she said. 'About the dead markswoman.'

'You go,' he said. 'There's something I want to do.'

'What?'

'Call Mei.'

'Will she be up? What time is it in Hong Kong?'

'It's midday there. She'll have been up for hours. My sister's an early riser, despite her job.'

'What, you mean running a triad?'

'She doesn't run a triad.'

'Er, hello? She took over the White Koi after she killed Fang Jian.'

'She's turning it into a legitimate business.'

'And how's that working out for her?'

'That's what I want to find out.'

Eli left after calling Stella and arranging to meet at the poolside breakfast terrace. With the room to himself, Gabriel called Mei. He listened to the clicks and hisses on the line as satellites, fibre optic cables and copper wires routed the call from G-City to Hong Kong. The ringing tone sounded like a cat's purr in his ear. He imagined his sister sitting at a wide desk at the Golden Dragon casino, a laptop open in front of her. The white leather 'Lotus Blossom' uniform she'd worn while protecting Fang Jian exchanged for a simple business suit.

Through the window, he watched Eli crossing the grass from the row of chalets to the breakfast bar. Stella was already sitting at a table, reading a newspaper. She stood as Eli arrived. The women embraced, then sat and picked up menus. They looked over in his direction. Stella waved. He raised his left hand in acknowledgment.

He smiled, even though he knew they'd not be able to see his expression. And then he realised something that he found shocking. Pleasing, but shocking. *I'm happy. Goddamn it, I'm actually happy.*

His country was in the grip of a hard-left government led by someone who Gabriel trusted less with every passing second. His girlfriend was on the cusp of leaving England for Israel. The organisation that had given him a renewed sense of purpose was under threat from Tammerlane's zealots. And yet…

And yet, I'm looking out at the woman I love talking to someone I think of as a friend. I'm waiting for my sister to pick up. My sister!

'Gabriel?'

Mei's voice startled him. Regaining his composure, he switched to Cantonese.

'Hi, Mei, yes. It's me. How are you? How are things with the WK?'

'I'm good. Work is hard, but I'm getting somewhere. Lots of hurdles to jump. Especially with the police. How are you, Big Bro?'

'I was just thinking. I'm good. I'm happy.'

He heard the smile in her voice.

'That's good! Really good. Where are you?'

'Botswana. Ivory poachers murdered some Paras— British soldiers. And some local soldiers, too. Eli and I are tracking them down.'

'Ha! I wouldn't want to be in their shoes. Did you…' Her voice burbled for a second, then came back sharp and clear as if she were sitting by the pool with Eli and Stella. '…ivory?'

'Sorry, Mei, you faded out there. It's an ivory poaching gang we're chasing, yes.'

'China is the world's biggest market for ivory, did you know that?'

'I do now.'

'You should come out. I can introduce you to some people. They're further down the supply chain from the poachers. They might give you some clues to follow.'

Gabriel hardly needed to think. Grinning, he shot back his answer.

'I will. That's a great idea. I'll call you when I arrive.'

. . .

He went outside to join Eli and Stella. Each woman had an empty plate in front of her. He spied fragments of herb and a couple of tiny chunks of fried onion.

'That looks nice,' he said. 'What did you have?'

'Omelettes,' Stella said. She turned in her chair. 'You see that woman there?'

Gabriel looked over to where a short, plump woman with braids piled on top of her head was working several pans at a series of portable gas burners.

'Yes.'

'Get her to make you one. They're amazing.'

Feeling hungry after all, Gabriel made the short journey to the omelette chef and asked for peppers and chicken.

'Coming right up!' she said with a brilliant smile as she began cracking eggs into a bowl.

'The forensic evidence on Lieberman looks really shaky,' Eli said as Gabriel sat back down.

'Shaky, how?'

'Tell him, Stella.'

Stella took a swig of coffee.

'The police markswoman had her throat cut.' Stella paused. 'Her name was Sarah Furey, by the way. The pathologist said it was a very sharp knife. Some sort of hunting model, or a combat knife. You know, the kind the gangbangers use.'

'Did they find the knife on Lieberman?'

Stella nodded.

'They did, but in the light of what we've found out here, we may have a problem. His fingerprints were all over it, but they were plastic prints. You know what that means?'

Gabriel shook his head.

'You've got three basic types of prints. Latents are where the print is made in the skin oils from the perpetrator's finger pads. You reveal them with dust or magnetic powders, or by fuming with superglue. Patents are where someone's got their fingers covered in a medium like ink or paint or blood and when they touch something they leave a visible print. Plastics are where they touch something that takes an impression, like wet paint or fresh window putty.'

'And Lieberman's prints were made in the blood, is that what you're saying?'

'Yes.'

'So he touched it *after* it was used to cut her throat.'

'That's what it looks like.'

'Wait a minute. That blows a mile-wide hole in the police theory that he was the shooter. Someone else must have murdered her.'

Stella shook her head.

'It's not that simple. Lieberman's prints were all over the rifle. The SIO, which isn't me, by the way, is saying Lieberman must have got blood between his hand and the hilt when he was murdering Sarah.'

'What about burnt propellant on his hands?' Gabriel asked.

'There was some gunshot residue, yes.'

'Which could have been transferred from the real shooter to Lieberman,' Eli said.

'It's possible,' Stella conceded.

'I've got some news,' Gabriel said, breaking off to thank the waitress who brought his omelette over.

'On the case?' Eli asked.

'Mm hmm,' he said, biting into the fluffy, spicy creation he realised was the best omelette he'd ever tasted. 'Mei said she knows people in the ivory trade. Apparently China's where it all goes, or most of it. I'm going out there. See if I can get a lead on the poachers from that end of the chain.'

Eli frowned. 'What about the meeting? We're Stella's,' she glanced at Stella, 'I mean *Joyce's* bodyguards.'

'I'll be back by then. This is literally a flying visit,' he said. 'It's a fifteen-hour flight from G-City to Hong Kong via Johannesburg. I can be there and back in three days. Four at the outside. And I really want to see Mei.'

'I'm sure you do,' Stella said. 'You should go. Eli and I can do some digging. I want to know who runs the various rackets in G-

City. And whether our mystery shooter really did stop here for a while and scuff his boots in the soil. We'll keep ourselves busy and then we'll go in mob-handed and find the bad guys.'

Stella frowned.

'What is it?' Gabriel said.

'There something we haven't talked about.'

'What's that?'

'What happens when you find the people who killed the Paras?' she asked.

Gabriel looked into her eyes. Searching for a glimmer of complicity in those blue-green irises. 'Interesting. You're not assuming we'll be arresting them.'

'You don't have the legal power.'

Gabriel paused before answering. 'We'll bring them to justice.'

Stella nodded. The glimmer brightened, just for a moment. 'That sounds about right.'

'How about if, I mean when, you find the second shooter?' Gabriel asked her.

'Much the same,' she said airily. 'Have him arrested, extradite him back to the UK, have him charged, sent for trial and, hopefully, a long prison sentence. Just like you're going to do with your guys.'

There! Was that the ghost of a wink?

Eli drove Gabriel to the airport. They stood, entwined, beside the ivory elephant. She kissed him, hard, on the lips.

'I'm going to miss you.'

'Me, too. Miss you, I mean. Stay safe.'

She nodded.

'Get going or you'll miss your flight.'

After a second, lingering kiss, Gabriel headed towards check-in and a reserved first-class seat on a Cathay Pacific flight to Hong Kong. First stop, Jo'burg.

28

GABORONE

The Syrian assassin watched his vibrating phone creep towards the edge of the table. The glass top amplified its buzz to that of an enraged insect. Just as its centre of gravity approached the chipped edge, he picked it up between long, manicured fingers.

He glanced at the Caller ID, saw a codename he'd assigned his client, and felt his jaw muscles tighten. Rule One: you don't call me after a job is completed.

'What is it?' he said.

'I need to know you're clear.'

'Clear?'

'Yes, clear. You know, out of the UK.'

'You think I hang around? Do the tourist thing? Visit Buckingham Palace? Take selfies?'

'No, of course not! Sorry. Where are you?'

'That, my friend, is no concern of yours.'

'But you're safe, yes?'

'Neither is that.'

'Please, work with me on this.'

'Look, my friend. You paid for my services. I delivered. I tell you what. You're curious. So am I. Answer me one question and I'll answer yours.'

'OK, fine. Yes.'

'Why no middleman?'

'What?'

'People like you, normally they use go-betweens. Deniable, you see? But you, you come direct. I want to know why.'

A pause. Long enough for the Syrian to look up and signal the hovering waiter for another mint tea.

'Deniable, yes. But also leaky. In this game, the only way to ensure total secrecy is to do it yourself. Happy?'

'Yes. I am in Gaborone.'

'That's Botswana.'

'Yes, I know.'

'Why are you there?'

'Like I said, my friend, that's not your concern.'

'That's where you're wrong. The police here are investigating the shooting and there's no way I can intervene. Not overtly. They found a link to Bots. You need to go. Find another bolthole.'

'Bolthole? You think I'm hiding?'

'Isn't that what you people do? Lie low for a bit.'

The Syrian bit back an urge to hang up.

'I can't speak for anyone except myself. But I am not *lying low*, as you put it.'

'What, then?'

The Syrian sighed. He supposed it wouldn't do any harm to let 'Leon' in on his plans.

'A detective is here. From London. She is asking questions. The wrong questions. I am here to ensure she does not leave with answers.'

'You're going to—'

'Never mind what I'm going to do!' the Syrian snapped. 'Do not call this number again.'

He looked up, rolled his eyes as the waiter, an elderly man with tightly curled silver hair, placed the glass of tea on the table and picked up the empty.

'My ex,' he said. 'Some people don't know when it's time to let go.'

The waiter smiled. A man-to-man, 'I hear you, Brother' kind of smile.

29

HONG KONG, GABRIEL'S HOUSE

Gabriel raised his glass to Mei. She tipped the rim of hers until they clicked together.

'Cheers!' he said.

'Cheers, Big Bro.'

He took a sip of the champagne. Off-dry, stewed apple, hazelnuts. Delicious.

'Are you ever going to stop calling me Big Bro?'

She grinned.

'How does BB sound to you?'

'It sounds great. BB King's one of my favourite guitarists, so I'll take that.'

He set his glass on the table. The moss was spongy beneath his bare feet and he enjoyed the sensation as he curled his toes down into the soft mat. Away in the distance, pale-blue mountains floated in the mist, their bases obscured by white cloud.

The air on the hill smelled fragrant – perfumed creeping flowers, pine, and top notes of seawater from the harbour below.

'I hope we can spend some time together,' Mei said.

'Me, too. Apart from business.'

'Yeah. Because there's something I want you to do for me.'

'Anything.'

'Will you take me to see Michael's grave?'

'You haven't been yet?'

She shook her head.

'I didn't want to go alone. I want you there with me.'

'We can go now, if you want?'

Mei looked up. The whites of her large eyes were as clear as porcelain. She returned her gaze to her 'big bro'.

'Yes, please.'

Gabriel led Mei along a wide gravelled path that led away from the cemetery's car park. They passed the office building and chapel, with its non-denominational stained-glass window in blue, green and gold glass. Above their heads, clouds had clumped into gloomy, rounded masses, their greenish-grey undersides pregnant with threat.

Ahead, the gravestones stood in serried ranks, the grass between them mown down to a half-inch of startling green. Here and there, mourners stood or knelt by the graves of their loved ones, singly or in pairs. Gabriel turned his head towards a keening sound.

A young woman, no more than thirty, stood on her own by a small white headstone topped with a carved angel. A net veil obscured her face; in his mind's eye he saw red-rimmed eyes, tears on her cheeks, bitten lips. She clutched a white handkerchief in black-gloved hands.

Your husband? Please, God, not your child.

She turned suddenly and he caught a flash of her eyes behind the veil as she stared straight at him. He looked away and walked on, relieved when Mei threaded her left arm through his right.

He steered Mei around a tall laurel bush, clipped into a perfect cone, and nodded the way ahead.

'He's just down here, on the right.'

Reaching Michael's grave, Gabriel stepped off the path, releasing Mei's arm, and stood, head bowed.

The grass here was cut just as neatly as elsewhere in the vast, stone-filled field. Gabriel looked at the grass under his feet. It was pale, the vibrant green changed to a dull grey. Who turned the colour down? He shook his head. The vibrancy returned.

A few dried-out sprigs of pink magnolia sat in a glass vase before the gravestone. He read again the sparse, gold-filled phrases carved into the small slab of polished black granite.

Michael Francis Wolfe.
Nineteen eighty-five to nineteen ninety.
Beloved son and brother.
Taken from us too soon.

'Master Zhao used to bring those,' he said, pointing at the flowers. 'They're the last bunch he brought here. I'm never going to move them.'

'Do you remember him?' Mei asked. 'Michael.'

'Now I do. It took a while. For years I believed I was an only child. I told you before, right?'

'Some, yes. I don't remember all of it. What was he like?'

Gabriel closed his eyes, inhaled and exhaled in a soft sigh. He felt neither pain nor grief. Something had broken inside of him during the two weeks when he'd retreated from reality in the aftermath of Michael's death. But he missed him. Missed the *idea* of him.

'He was funny. Mischievous. A proper little brother. Always getting into trouble. His school uniform always looked like he'd been in a scrap. He used to love playing rugby. That's how he died. He went in after a ball I kicked into the harbour. He drowned.'

'You're OK talking about it now?'

Mei phrased it as a statement, not a question.

'Yes. For so long, I thought it was my fault. It was mixed up in my head with stuff that happened just before I left the army. Then Kenneth Lao told me the truth.'

'Mum?'

'Yes. Mum. She was drunk when she should have been watching us. It wasn't her fault. Not really. She went to pieces after Fang kidnapped you.'

Mei nodded. She stepped forward and placed a hand on the gravestone's curved top. She knelt, placed her lips against the stone and closed her eyes. Gabriel watched as she communed with the soul of their dead brother. After a minute, she straightened in a single, flowing movement and rejoined Gabriel.

She took his arm again.

'I want to see their graves, too, BB.'

'Mum and Dad's? They're in England.'

'I know. I want to see them.'

'I'll take you as soon as this operation is over.'

'Pinky promise?' she said, holding out her right little finger.

Amused at his sister's childlike gesture, Gabriel nevertheless hooked her finger with his and squeezed.

Back in the car, Gabriel started the engine, then turned to face Mei.

'What about the people you said you could introduce me to?'

'I'll make some calls. Things are changing in my world. Now I'm taking WK in a different direction, I can talk to some of Fang's old rivals. They want what we have so they're keen to do deals. All kinds.'

'I need to be back in Botswana by Friday.'

'It's Monday today. You'll have plenty of time. Anyway, if you're a couple of days late, Eli can cope, can't she? After all, isn't your girlfriend a, what did you call her, "a real badass"?'

Gabriel smiled because Mei had slipped into American-accented English to utter this last, pungent phrase.

'Let's make sure she doesn't need to be this time.'

. . .

Back once more in the bar of the Golden Dragon, Gabriel felt an entirely justifiable sense of *déjà vu*. Only this time, the boss wasn't a gangster plotting his murder with a corrupt Chinese Communist Party high-up. It was his little sister.

The barman recognised Gabriel and came over with a smile. He held a sweating martini glass by the stem and placed it in front of Gabriel on one of the casino's trademark gold cocktail napkins with a black-scalloped edge.

'Tanqueray Number Ten, not too dry, three olives,' he said.

'Thanks, Tony.' Gabriel sipped the ice-cold drink and smiled. 'Perfect.'

Gabriel picked up the glass and threaded his way through the crowd of well-dressed gamblers to the door leading to the private offices.

Mei had redecorated Fang's office. Gone was the heavy Chinese rug with its deep- plum-red stain where its owner had bled to death. Gone was the gold-painted antique furniture. Gone were the gold dragon lamps, each snarling reptile clamping a light-globe in its slavering jaws.

In their place, polished wooden floorboards, a white carpet, modern steel-and-glass desk, blond wood filing cabinets and a half-dozen contemporary light fittings that Mei told him she'd commissioned from a rising glass artist on the mainland.

She came round from behind the desk and hugged him. In her working dress of tailored western-style suit and heels, she could have passed for a business executive rather than a triad boss. But then, as she'd explained, that was the plan.

'The Mafia did it. People go legit all the time,' she'd said to him on his previous visit.

'Your guest not here yet?' Gabriel asked, taking a seat.

'He'll be here shortly. He just texted me. Stuck in traffic.'

Gabriel had to smile. Even top-level gangsters weren't immune from Hong Kong's notorious jams.

Five minutes later, the office door swung inwards to reveal the Golden Dragon's security manager. He extended his free arm and in walked a very short, very thin man who, Gabriel judged, had to be in his eighties.

Mei rounded the desk for a second time and crossed the expanse of white carpet. She bowed and extended her right hand, which the old man took, executing his own, smaller bow.

'Mister Cho, I'd like you to meet my brother, Gabriel,' she said, leading the old man over to Gabriel, who had stood in anticipation. He bowed as the man closed the four-foot gap between them.

'Mr Cho runs the Four-Point Star triad,' Mei said over the old man's shoulder.

Cho barely came up to Gabriel's shoulder. He raised his chin and scrutinised Gabriel's face, his deep-brown eyes moving restlessly over each feature.

'Your sister is a tigress. Very powerful lady now,' he said in English. 'You are lucky. I do not come to meet any *gweilo*.'

The slang term for a westerner could have been an insult, but Gabriel dipped his head a second time, acknowledging his outsider status.

'I am pleased to meet you, Sir,' he said in Cantonese. 'Thank you for agreeing to see me.'

They sat. Mei produced drinks.

'You are interested in ivory?' Cho asked.

'In the people who poach it. Who kill for it.'

Gabriel sketched in the details of the operation to capture the poachers. When he'd finished, Cho stroked his chin with a liver-spotted hand.

'The Four-Point Star controls the ivory trade into China. Also Singapore, Thailand and Japan. But we are just importers here. We also own a factory in the United Arab Emirates. They process the raw material, which comes in from Africa via a market in Vientiane. You know it?'

'Laos, yes,' Gabriel said.

Cho nodded, agitating the wispy white hairs above his ears.

'Globalisation,' he said, smiling to reveal crooked brown teeth. 'Not just good for car makers and drug companies, eh?'

'Can you permit me to visit your factory in the UAE?'

Cho glanced at Mei. Gabriel saw his pale eyebrows lift fractionally. I can trust your brother? they said.

'Gabriel is discreet,' she said. 'I give you my word he will breathe nothing of what he sees. Also, I will be in your debt. You know my plans for the WK. Maybe we can find a way to divest some of our holdings to your control.'

'Mister Cho,' Gabriel said. 'What my sister says about my discretion is true. Other people may wish to pursue your operations. I only wish to avenge my fallen brothers. You knew my mentor, perhaps. Zhao Xi?'

Cho nodded.

'Everyone in Hong Kong knew Xi. He was a fine man.'

Gabriel placed his right palm over his heart.

'I swear on his memory, and that of all my ancestors, that I will say nothing of what I see.'

Cho interlaced his fingers in his lap. He straightened his back.

'The manager is a man named Yusuf. I will email him to tell him you are coming. I accept your promises and your oath. But I will also send you with one of my men. It will remove the need for,' he unlaced his fingers and waggled his hand in a seesaw motion, 'additional security measures. You are happy with this?'

'I am. And thank you.'

Gabriel took the window seat on the Cathay Pacific flight to Dubai. He yawned: his body clock was still set to Gaborone time. The presence of a thickset Four-Point Star minder to his right, reeking of garlic, did nothing to prevent his falling into a deep sleep as the Airbus A330-300 left the tarmac, climbed and banked into a crystalline-blue sky.

Nine hours later, a stewardess leaned across the burly minder and touched Gabriel lightly on the shoulder to wake him before landing.

30

GABORONE

Mid-morning, and Eli and Stella were sitting at a roadside fruit stand just a few yards down Chuma Drive from the resort. In front of them, on a table constructed from upturned wooden crates sat two big bowls of fruit salad: mangosteen, melon and a soft-fleshed, aromatic fruit the female vendor had called 'Mama's Kiss'.

Apart from the occasional truck loaded with timber or battered blue oil drums, the road was quiet at this time of the morning.

A young boy, eight or nine, strolled past on the far side of the asphalt. In front of him, a fat-bellied goat ambled along, kept moving by the boy's insistent application of a stick to its hindquarters. The boy waved to them as he passed.

'Good morning!' he called out in English, beaming them a thousand-watt smile. 'How are you?'

'Fine!' Eli called back. 'How are you?'

He stopped, and his grin widened.

'I am fine! How are you?'

Eli smiled.

'I am fine! How are you?'

'I am fine! How are you?'

Feeling the game could continue indefinitely, she changed tack.

'My name's Eli. What's yours?' she called out.

'I am Abednigo Tsonga. I will be best football player in all Africa!'

'Good luck!"

He smiled once more, switched the goat across its backside, and waved over his shoulder as he walked away.

'Nice to be so untroubled,' Stella said. 'He's got his goat, his dream. Lives in this beautiful country.'

'You sound envious.'

Stella shrugged.

'He looked happy. I wouldn't mind that sort of simplicity in my life.'

'You'd be bored inside a week.'

Stella wrinkled her nose.

'I think you're right. I just wish you weren't.'

'Life can't be too bad, can it? Hey! I just realised. All I know about you is the work stuff. You're this kind of super-cop who punched a serial killer's ticket. What about who you are as a woman?'

Stella smiled and scooped another spoonful of Mama's Kiss into her mouth. A squirt of juice escaped her lips and she rolled her eyes as she wiped it from her chin.

'What do you want to know?'

'I don't know. Your story. What made you who you are today?'

Eli saw a cloud flit across Stella's face. *Damn! Have I just trodden on something fragile?*

'Until a few years ago, I would have said my story was pretty conventional,' Stella said. 'School, university, teaching, then I joined the police. Fast track to detective inspector. Great things expected of me.'

'Something happened, didn't it?'

'You could say that.'

Eli reached over and placed her hand over that of the woman she realised she wanted as a friend.

'Stella, if you don't want to talk about this, it's fine. I just go charging in where angels fear to tread. Always have.'

Stella shook her head and smiled at Eli.

'No, it's fine. And call me Stel. My other friends do.'

Eli smiled, feeling a flush of pleasure. Here was someone she could relate to, the first woman in England with whom she'd made that connection.

'Stel it is, then.'

Stella inhaled sharply. Looked up and down the road even though they were alone, apart from the fruit stand lady, who was snoozing under a wide pink, yellow and green beach umbrella.

'I guess with what you and Gabriel do for a living I'm safe saying this, but I've killed more people than Mim Robey. A lot more. Sometimes I get the heebie-jeebies when I think about it.'

'Not innocent people, though, surely?' Eli said.

Stella shook her head.

'No. Not really. Some were murderers. Others were accessories. A few were trying to kill me.'

'There you are, then,' Eli said. 'You shouldn't worry.'

'As simple as that?'

'Why not? Listen, Stel, you said your story was conventional. Mine's a little less conventional. After school I went into the IDF to do my national service. I really enjoyed it. The camaraderie, the training, all of it. But also the action. I was good at it and they recruited me into Special Forces. From there, I went into the Mossad. The real sharp end. Literally. In fact, the Hebrew name for my old outfit means tip of the spear.'

'Have you killed many people?' Stella asked.

Eli ate a spoonful of mango.

'Mm-hmm,' she mumbled, then swallowed. 'Lots. It goes with the territory. But they were all enemies. Either mine or my country's, although it always came down to the same thing in the end. Now I'm with Gabe in The Department, and you know how *that* works.'

'But I'm a police officer. We're supposed to uphold the law, not take it into our own hands.'

'Who were these people you killed?' Eli asked.

'This is off the record?'

Eli grinned. 'Given what I've just told you, I'd say you can trust me to keep my mouth shut.'

Stella sighed out a breath.

'It all started when my husband and baby daughter were killed by a hit and run driver.'

Over the next fifteen minutes, Eli listened, rapt, as Stella shared her story. Of madness. Of a burning desire for revenge. Of a discovery that shook her faith in the legal system. Of a series of actions that gradually restored it.

'…and now, although I'm still a successful senior detective, there are people higher up the food chain who'd like to see me gone.'

'But why?' Eli said. 'If you're so good at what you do.'

Stella smiled but Eli didn't see much happiness in it.

'Because I'm a permanent reminder of an episode they'd rather forget.'

'Ever thought of leaving?'

Stella nodded.

'Often. Your boss has more or less offered me a job on at least two occasions.'

'But you're still at the Met.'

'Yep. It's something I said to a friend of mine when she interviewed me on the radio. Deep down, I'm still just a girl in blue.'

'Then focus on the job at hand,' Eli said. 'From the sound of it, the people you killed more than deserved it and justice wouldn't have been done if you'd gone through official channels. They'd have got away with it. You did the right thing.'

Eli watched a sly smile steal across Stella's face.

'What?' she asked. *Because that looks like the genuine article.*

'That's what Jamie says.'

'And who is Jamie?' Eli asked, cupping her chin in her hand and rolling her eyes. 'A *work* colleague?'

Stella's grin widened.

'He's my…boyfriend. God, that makes me sound like a twenty-year-old!'

'No it doesn't! Gabe's *my* boyfriend.'

'Yeah, and how old are you? Twenty-five? Twenty-six?'

'Twenty-nine, actually.'

'Well, I'm forty-one.'

'Call him your partner, then.'

Stella shuddered.

'Ugh! I hate that word.' She put on a ridiculously over-the-top posh voice. 'Yah, like, Jamie's my partner, actually?' *Jamah's ma partnah, arch'lah.* 'We, like, met on a yoga retreat in Madagascar?' *Yogah rahtraht in Mahdagahskah.*

Eli snorted with laughter, sending a morsel of soft pink fruit flying towards Stella face. Stella squawked a 'Hey!' and ducked, but the episode sent both women into a fit of giggling that woke up the sleeping fruit vendor. She smiled indulgently in their direction then settled her straw hat over her eyes again and reclined against the back of her blue plastic lawn chair.

Stella's burner phone rang, shattering the calm in the wake of the outbreak of laughter. She looked down, then up at Eli. Only one person had the number.

Eli stretched out her hand.

'Let me answer it.'

She cleared her throat, stood up and shook her head, before lifting her chin and answering the insistently ringing phone.

'Yes?'

'Joyce?'

'Joyce is on another call. Who is this?'

'Peter Mafombe. Who are you?'

'The help. What do you want?'

'My contact changed his mind. He wants to meet Joyce tonight.'

'No good. We agreed Friday.'

'He's gonna be up country, Friday. Business.'

'This *is* business.'

'Look, lady, if your mistress wants to meet Mr Ivory, tell her to be at the Oasis Lounge tonight at seven or forget it. This is not a negotiation. Clear?'

Eli counted to three.

'Clear.'

She punched the end call button.

'Shit!'

'What is it?'

Eli sat back down.

'The creatively named "Mr Ivory" just brought the meeting forward.'

'To when?'

'Tonight. Seven.'

'So we do it ourselves. Three would have been preferable but it's like we were saying, we're neither of us shrinking violets, are we?'

'No. But I'd prefer the odds stacked just a little bit more in our favour.'

'You've got your Glock, plus that pea shooter you took off that mugger. We'll just style it out.'

Eli barked out a short laugh.

'Fine! But I tell you, Stel. If anybody makes a move, I'll style his fucking eye out.'

* * *

Back at the hotel, Stella's force-issued phone delivered two pieces of intelligence. Dr Montho called from the university to confirm the soil from the inside of the vehicle trim was definitely local. And Lucian sent her a text.

Trim is Range Rover.

On their second trip to the Oasis, Eli and Stella drove all the way. Figuring it might be a good idea to have their wheels close at hand, Eli parked the Toyota right outside the club. They'd discussed whether the Merc would make a better statement but, in the end, the Toyota's rugged practicality and lack of brand kudos would make it a safer bet.

She blipped the throttle a couple of times, raising the revs to a deafening roar before killing the engine. Through the windscreen she watched the assorted lowlifes, swagger-merchants, wannabe gangsters and gangsters' molls for a few seconds.

A couple of the boys moved closer, hands grabbing crotches, trousers at half mast like teenagers all over the world. They made complicated gang signs with knitted fingers and waved through the dusty glass.

In a coordinated move they'd practised back at the resort, Eli and Stella swung the doors wide and jumped out before slamming them again with a stuttered double-bang.

They'd paid just as much attention to their outfits as to the choreography. 'Joyce' was in her business suit, but this time with low-heeled boots beneath the trousers. She'd tucked the little revolver into the back of her waistband.

'The help' wore black jeans tucked into black combat boots and a black, sleeveless vest beneath a black silk bomber jacket. In a holster on her waist the Glock sat, stripped, cleaned and oiled, with a full magazine and topped off with one in the chamber.

Each woman also had a slender-bladed knife tucked into her right boot.

Eli singled out the biggest lad in the group of drinkers by the front door. She pointed at him.

'You!' she shouted.

He placed a palm flat on his chest and raised his eyebrows. Me?

'Come here.'

The tone of authority was unmistakable to everyone gathered around the two women. Eli was used to giving orders and watched with satisfaction as his feet began to carry him towards her before he'd had a chance to think it through. *Still got it, El!*

Recovering some of his poise he sauntered over, taking his time, winking left and right at his friends. He stopped in front of her, hands loose by his side. Looked her up and down. Kissed his teeth.

Then he smiled, a slow, lazy grin that stretched his lips wide, revealing perfect teeth, even and straight.

'You, ah, want something, darling?'

'How much do you make in a week?' Eli snapped out the question.

'None of your damn business.' It came out *nun ya dam bidness.*

She stretched out a fist towards him making him jerk back. Rolled it over and opened her finger to reveal a rolled $50 note.

'Watch the truck and you get another when we come out.'

He stared at her for two or three seconds, popped an unlit match into his mouth and gripped it between his teeth. A cheap gangster move from an old forties Jimmy Cagney flick, but somehow he made it work.

He took the note and pocketed it. Nodded briefly.

Eli took a gentle but firm hold of the front of his shirt and drew him closer. Up close she smelled clean male sweat and a tang of tobacco.

'It would be in your interests to be here when we come out,' she murmured into his left ear.

Having done what she could to arrange security for the truck, Eli led Stella past the newly respectful crowd and into the Oasis Lounge. The band from before were playing and the singer nodded to Eli as she made eye contact.

Before they reached the bar, Peter Mafombe materialised at Stella's side, dressed in a shimmering shot-silk suit that changed from powder blue to maroon as the folds and creases caught the bar lights.

'Joyce!' he said, beaming. He extended his right hand and shook Stella's vigorously. He turned to Eli. 'And the help.' He bowed a little from the waist.

Stella turned left and right then looked back at Mafombe.

'Where is he?'

'In the back. Come with me, please.' He looked over at the barman, whose eyes were locked onto his. 'Bring some beers,' he shouted. The barman nodded and turned to the low-level row of fridges behind the bar.

Eli hung back, allowing Stella to precede her through the door at the back of the room. She pressed her forearm against the gun beneath her jacket, feeling its reassuring bulk against her ribs. Nobody was looking at them. Nobody shot them death stares, despite their being the only two white people in the bar. Or, she suspected, the entire neighbourhood.

Beyond the door, a dark, narrow corridor stretched for twenty yards. Stickers – for bands, nightclubs, car accessories and political parties – spattered the wall at shoulder-height all the way down. A fire door closed off the end, secured with a dull-steel push-bar and a green-and-white emergency exit sign.

'Down here, please,' Mafombe said over his shoulder, indicating a door to his right. A skirted stick figure had been chalked onto the matt-black paintwork. Beneath it, the word '*Basadi*'. Eli didn't need Gabriel's linguistic skills to translate it. 'Women.'

Mafombe stood aside and pushed the door open.

Eli's heart rate had jumped significantly as soon as they'd left the relative safety of a crowded bar. Now it ticked up still further. The ladies' toilets? What was this? She pushed the side of her jacket behind the Glock's butt and rested her hand on it.

Stella was playing her part to the hilt. Somewhere the woman had deep reserves of *chutzpah*, because she strode across the threshold as if she owned the Oasis Lounge instead of Mafombe.

Eli followed her in and stopped dead.

31

To the right of a row of three cubicles a tall man leaned against the single sink. He smiled at her. His beige silk suit, rust-and-cream-checked waistcoat, open-necked gold shirt, tan-and-white wingtips and gold-topped cane gave him the appearance of a 1920s New Orleans jazzman.

Flanking him were two beautiful black women with the lean, muscular look of Olympic athletes built for strength as well as speed. Heptathletes. Or javelin throwers. Each wore a bored expression: lazy eyelids coloured white and peacock blue, weighed down by exaggerated false eyelashes.

Mafombe left, letting the door bang closed behind him. Eli suppressed the urge to look behind her.

'Good evening,' the man said in a mellow baritone voice that could have secured him a gig in Sun City any night of the week. 'My name is Joshua. You must be Joyce,' he said to Stella before taking her hand and bringing her knuckles gently to his lips.

She inclined her head.

'A pleasure to meet you, Joshua. Is this your usual place of business?' she drawled, encompassing the toilet cubicles, sink and battered metal tampon dispenser with a sweep of her left hand.

He laughed, a deep, indulgent sound. Beside him, the two black panthers, as Eli had mentally named them, allowed themselves the briefest of smiles.

'Ha! Very good, Joyce. My usual place of business,' he repeated, chuckling. 'No.' His smile vanished.

He took a sudden, quick pace towards Stella. Eli willed her to stand her ground and couldn't stop a frown from crossing her face as Stella leaned back, then righted herself with a half-step.

'My, my,' the man calling himself Joshua said. 'Not nervous, are we? The bigshot white lady with the briefcase full of cash and the diesel-dyke bodyguard?'

He jerked his chin contemptuously in Eli's direction as he spat out the insult.

She stared at him, her mouth a grim line, clenching her teeth to make her jaw muscles bulge. But her pulse was racing.

Stella's next move surprised Eli. And clearly the man in the beige suit.

She stuck a pointed finger hard against his sternum, just in the V of his waistcoat's neckline. His eyes widened and, to each side, the athletes tensed.

'Keep your language civil, Joshua.' She pushed hard with her finger. 'Or I'll have to teach you some manners. I came here to do business with Mr Ivory,' Stella made air quotes, 'not to have my staff insulted. So why don't you tell me what the fuck is going on so we can sit down and talk about making money together?'

Genius move, Stel! Eli said mentally. *Either we're in, or we're dead.* She prepared herself for a fight. The women facing her wore tight jeans and tighter vests. She saw no evidence of any weapons. In a way, this worried her more.

Joshua had clamped his lips. His jaw was working. Eli looked at the cane. He was squeezing the gold knob – a lion's head – so hard his knuckles were poking up through his skin. She experienced a surge of adrenaline. *It's a sword stick!* She altered her stance, moving her right foot behind her left a little to shift her weight. She'd aimed for a casual move but realised she hadn't carried it off.

The Olympians were glaring at her. And Eli realised they'd

walked straight into a trap. *You don't* need *weapons! We're in here. God knows who's waiting on the other side of the door. You know we could never fight our way out. Shit! The Toyota's probably having new plates screwed to it in some backstreet bodyshop right now.*

Joshua broke the silence.

'Take your clothes off. Both of you.'

'I beg your pardon?' Stella said, her hand sliding around her right thigh and towards the small of her back.

'Move that slender arm one more centimetre and Galele here will snap it in two,' he said.

The nearer of the two women took a step closer to Stella.

'Joshua,' Stella said, placating now. 'I came here to talk business. Not to star in some cheap voyeur fantasy. Either we're going to do business or we're leaving.'

He held his hand up to silence her.

'And we *will* talk business,' he said. 'But I am a cautious man. You don't survive long in G-City if you're not. Galele and Naomi will search you. I will leave. Any weapons you are carrying will be returned to you when our meeting is concluded.'

Without waiting for an answer, he squeezed between Stella and the sink, shot Eli a look of the purest malice and left.

Stella, maintaining her role as boss, looked at Eli.

'Let's get it over with,' she said.

Standing naked, side by side, the two women watched as Galele and Naomi rifled through the pile of clothes on the floor. Galele placed the Glock, revolver and the two knives to one side. She stood and kicked the clothes towards Stella.

'Get dressed.'

* * *

Eli felt more naked without her weapons than she had done without her clothes. She'd spent part of her childhood on a kibbutz where attitudes to nudity and sex were refreshingly frank and unconcerned. God gave us these bodies, and there's nothing to be ashamed of, being the general drift.

With Galele and Naomi behind them, she and Stella walked along the corridor before stopping at the fire door. A door to the left seemed the obvious move.

'In there, yes,' Naomi said.

Eli pushed through the door. What she saw on the far side jacked her adrenaline levels into the stratosphere.

32

Through a sweet-smelling fug of marijuana smoke, Eli saw a couple of bare-chested guys sitting, legs spread wide, on a saggy old sofa. Off to one side, two more, wearing replica Manchester United football shirts over narrow chests. Sitting at a round table, Joshua looked up at Eli. No smile this time.

It wasn't the men themselves that had elevated her fight-or-flight response.

The responsible parties were the AK-47s each carried or had resting beside his right arm.

The men on the sofa grinned lazily up at her and Stella. One had teeth missing at the sides of his mouth, giving him the comical look of a cartoon rabbit. The other had gleaming gold where his canines should be.

Afrobeat pounded from a boombox placed on the windowsill, its scratched silver paint and oversized speaker grilles placing it dead-centre in the eighties. Eli shook her head. It was a miracle of Japanese electronics the damn thing was working at all.

The room was lit with candles, whose untrimmed wicks led to wildly flickering flames. Shadows danced across *Playboy* centrefolds tacked to the walls.

As well as the cigar-sized reefers the men were smoking, they were taking pulls from long-necked bottles of beer. One belched grandly, an arm swept wide as the guttural sound emerged from between grinning lips.

Joshua rose from the table. He strolled over to Stella, hand extended. He shook her hand, then Eli's. She registered the position of each of the four guards in her peripheral vision while smiling at 'Mr Ivory'.

'I hope Galele and Naomi treated you respectfully,' he said to Stella.

'They were perfect ladies. I hope I can rely on you to be the perfect gentleman,' she said.

He gestured to the table, where two extra seats had been drawn up.

'Sit. Beer?'

'No thank you.'

He shrugged and slid into his own chair, signalling one of his men to bring him another bottle.

'Fine by me if you don't want to drink my beer,' he said, before picking up the bottle sitting by his elbow and draining it.

He smacked it down on the table with a sharp rap. Eli was pleased to see that Stella didn't even blink. Rejecting the proffered chair, she took up a position with her back to the wall where she could keep all four guards in view.

'Right,' Stella said. 'We waited for a convenient time. We came to this shithole of a bar for the second time. And we submitted to a strip-search. Let's talk ivory, shall we, or were you planning on jerking my chain a second time?'

If her bolshie speech upset the spiffily dressed Botswana, he didn't show it. He just grinned again.

'Brave words for a woman who just gave up her gun and is sitting in *my* boardroom. With my board of directors watching,' he said. 'What do you think, Edward?' he called out over Stella's right shoulder. 'Has this nice white lady got bigger balls than you?'

The man he'd addressed got up from the sofa, grabbed his AK

and sauntered over to the table. He stopped just inches from Stella, so his groin was at the level of her face.

'She just pussy like they all, boss,' he said. 'She give you disrespect,' – *dizrispec* – 'I teach her some manners.' He grabbed his crotch for good measure and grinned at the other three men.

His friends cackled with laughter. Eli reckoned the dope had more to do with it than the witticism. She scowled at him, counting the many ways she knew to relieve a man of his genitals.

Without turning her head by a fraction, Stella jabbed her right elbow out hard and fast, straight into the place Eli had been mentally attacking. Eli smirked as the man, so cocksure just a few seconds earlier, doubled over, both hands cupping his insulted scrotum. She shot a warning look at the second sofa-dweller, whose hand was straying towards his AK.

'Don't!' she barked.

His hand stopped in mid-air, but his eyes stayed focused on Joshua. The question was clear to all who could see him. *Do I kill them, boss?*

Stella was still on the offensive. She leaned across the table and pointed a red fingernail at Joshua's face.

'Tell your man to get the fuck out of my face. If he tries anything like that again he'll be singing soprano in the church choir.'

Joshua raised his eyebrows. He leaned over the side of the table.

'Edward. Go and sit down. I'll speak to you later.' He straightened. 'My apologies, Joyce. I was only joking with what I said earlier.'

'Yeah? I'd buy a new joke book, if I were you. Now, for the last time. What can you tell me about ivory?'

'Well, now. I can tell you a lot of things. I can tell you I have a stockpile worth ten million dollars. I can tell you I am connected to some very rich Chinese gentlemen who love ivory more than gold. I can tell you that I have thirty-seven men under my command who are completely and utterly ruthless. When your resume has "child soldier" on it, you are not scared of a few poorly paid government troops.'

'Ten million, eh? So you can cut me in on the action, can't you? For a suitable level of investment.'

He spread his hands.

'Ah, Joyce. If only it was that simple.'

'What's making it complicated? You're a businessman, aren't you? I'm a businesswoman. I've got cash, you've got ivory. What's the problem?'

'The problem is my business partners. You think this is like the Wild West out here in deepest, darkest Africa? No law, no honour, just winner takes all and the Devil take the hindmost?' He shook his head. 'No. It's not like that at all. I have contracts. Supply. Wholesaling. Processing. Distribution. Security. Sales and marketing. Exclusive deals.'

'So you're running a proper little company. Good for you. I can take two million dollars' worth right now. I've got cash at my hotel or I can even wire it to you.'

'Do you know what my partners would do to me if I went outside our exclusive agreement, Joyce?'

'Would they sue you for breach of contract?'

'Very funny.' He called out once more. 'Joyce thinks my partners would take me to court if I double-crossed them, boys.'

The men laughed. A nasty sound. While she'd been watching Stella, the standing pair had picked up their rifles. The men on the sofa, Edward still clutching his balls with one hand, held machetes. Both were glaring at Eli. She mentally named them First and Second Machete.

They'd all stubbed out their joints. And though their eyes were still pink from the effects of the drug, she detected a fixity of purpose in their gaze.

Her pulse sped up. She calculated distances, angles. Lines of fire. In a small room like this, opening up with automatic weapons would be suicidal. The machetes, though. Those could be wielded to devastating effect without risking wounding or killing their own side.

She pushed off from the wall, balancing her weight equally on the balls of her feet. Getting ready to move.

Joshua was speaking again.

'No. No courtroom. No lawyers. No judge. They would take me out into the bush, far from G-City. They would use knives on me. Like the ones my boys here have. Not kill me. Just cut my hamstrings, my Achilles tendons. Remove my hands. Then they would sit in their Hiluxes and wait. You know what for?'

'An ambulance?'

Eli mentally applauded Stella's bored response. It was worth a Best Actress Oscar.

'Jackals. Hyenas. Lions. Vultures. They'd watch them tear me to pieces and film it on their phones. Then they put it on YouTube. A warning, you know? I have one I downloaded last year.' He pulled his phone out of an inside pocket. 'You want to see it? The screaming is very loud when a hyena cracks his skull open.'

'I'm good. So tell me, Joshua. If you're not going to deal, why are we here?'

'To give you some advice and to suggest a different kind of partnership.'

A machete blade clanked hollowly against the wooden arm of the sofa.

Eli was already moving slowly but purposefully towards the four guards. 'The advice is, go to the market. Down the supply chain. Vientiane. Laos. That's where you can pick it up wholesale and still make some profit.'

'Thanks,' Stella said, getting to her feet. 'We'll try that.'

'Wait!' Joshua said, raising his voice. 'You haven't heard my proposal yet.'

Eli could see two machetes glinting in the light from the guttering candles and two AKs held level across their owners' flat stomachs. Shit! Hadn't Stella worked it out? They were in trouble. *Big* trouble.

'No need,' Stella said, backing up. 'Ivory's the only proposal I'm interested in, and you can't deliver that.'

Joshua shook his head. The smile had gone, replaced with a predatory expression. A narrow-eyed stare that said, 'I'm coming for you'.

'I think, seeing as I have been so generous with my market intelligence, you two ladies should show your gratitude. I was thinking you could entertain me and my boys here for an hour or two.'

'Get fucked,' Stella said, turning and heading for the door.

'I intend to,' he said, the wolfish leer widening. 'What do you say, boys? Shall we teach these little white pussies how G-City boys make love?'

'Come on, Eli, we're leaving,' Stella said in a low, tight voice as stoned leers turned into looks of animal lust.

'No. You are not,' Joshua said, holding up a finger.

One of the guards with an AK slid round the periphery of the room and barred Eli and Stella's route to the door.

Everything happened fast.

33

Eli backed up towards the guard at the door.

Without turning her head she bent, twisted, then reared up at him and straight-armed him under the point of his chin. A classic Krav Maga move. People never expect to be hit by someone facing away.

As he went down, she chopped him hard across the side of the neck, crushing the nerves running beside the thick ropy blood vessels and paralysing him. She pulled her right foot back and kicked him so hard in the side of the head that she felt the jolt as an electric current running from her foot to her hip.

Stella had leaped into the centre of the room, then taken one of the machete guys before he'd had a chance to lever his lanky frame out of the sofa.

Her booted right foot lashed out and hit him in the face, snapping his nose with a sound like bubble wrap. Beside him, Second Machete was swinging his foot-long blade at Stella's leg.

Which was no longer there.

Instead, his vicious blow embedded six inches of the blade's edge into his friend's thigh, severing half a dozen blood vessels which spouted blood up to the ceiling.

Over the screams of pain, Stella jumped up onto the sofa and with a yell of pure warrior spirit stamped down on Second Machete's groin.

Joshua was out of his seat and reaching into his waistband.

If he'd been dealing with an ivory smuggler and her hired help, he might have got the chance to put a round or two into one of them.

So it was his poor fortune to be facing Eli Schochat and Stella Cole.

His gun arm came up, fingers wrapped round the grip of an ageing Browning Hi-Power. Aiming for the back of Stella's head.

'Stel, down!' Eli screamed.

She kicked Joshua's wrist so that the shot spanged off a ceiling light. Ricocheting, the bullet smashed the window and passed, harmlessly, into the night.

Also unfortunately for Joshua, Eli was now the proud owner of the door-guy's AK-47.

She struck him across the forehead with the muzzle, tearing a huge flap of skin free that flopped down like a veil, blinding him. She cut off his scream with a monstrous blow to the stomach with the rifle butt, dropping him in a crumpled heap of bloody white silk.

A burst of automatic gunfire deafened her. She spun round. The last remaining guard had jumped onto the sofa and sprayed a three-second burst at Stella. She'd rolled for cover behind Joshua's desk, and although the rounds smashed into the heavy wooden top, none penetrated.

Eli grabbed a fallen machete and flung it at his head.

The blade whickered through the air and hit his left temple, slicing off his ear and a sizeable portion of his scalp. It clattered onto the desktop and skidded off the far side.

With a howl, he whipped round, blood spraying outwards in a spiral. He jammed his finger down on the AK's trigger. The magazine was empty in seconds.

Several rounds found the two men on the sofa. Second Machete lost half his face in an explosion of pink mist. First machete took one in the throat and one in the chest. He died drowning in his own blood, which frothed from his grimacing mouth.

Then the shooter's eyes rolled up in their sockets.

He toppled sideways, head lolling from a gaping wound as Stella smashed a machete into the side of his neck. The blade jammed between two cervical vertebrae. She stood back as he fell, taking the blade with him.

The gun smoke had thickened the atmosphere to a thick blue fog. Eli's ears were ringing as she turned a full circle, AK cocked and ready at her hip. Her nose was prickling and itching at the sharp smell of burnt propellant and hot brass, and the coppery tang of blood.

Out of the five men who'd been preparing to gang-rape them, three were dead, one was out cold and one, their leader, was slumped against a chair, cradling his face with both palms and struggling to replace his floppy brow in its rightful place beneath his hairline.

His suit jacket was scarlet from lapels to waist. The front of his trousers looked as though he were auditioning for a punk band, streaks and spatters of red forming criss-crossing streaks across the shimmering white fabric.

Eli strode over to him and lifted his chin with the AK's muzzle. His eyes were wide, and although he held onto his forehead with one hand, he raised the other in supplication.

'Please. Don't kill me. There's money over there, in the safe. Take it. I can give you the combination. It's—'

'Shut up! We don't want your money.'

Outside the door she could hear people shouting. Someone was hammering to be let in. Eli turned, flicked the fire selector switch to single shot and fired once into the very top of the door.

The hammering stopped.

She returned her gaze to Joshua.

'Three questions. Three answers. Tell the truth, you live. Lie, you die.'

'Sure, sure,' he said, in a panicky voice.

'The market in Vientiane. Address?'

'It's an old Catholic church on Tad Thong Road. By…' he gasped, 'by the river.'

'Good. When is it held?'

'First Monday of every month.'

Eli paused for a moment. *That gives us a week.*

'What's the security?'

'I do not know what you mean. What security?'

'Oh dear. And we were doing so well.' Eli took a half-step closer. She pointed the AK at his stomach. 'Goodbye, Joshua.'

'No! Wait! The market boss is called John-Antoine Vong. You need a password. It's…' He hesitated. 'Mekong.'

Eli stood.

'There,' she said. 'That wasn't so hard, was it?'

She stamped down hard on his right instep. He screamed and clutched his foot. She crouched in front of him.

'Mekong? Really? Every fucking tourist in the place would be saying it.' She got right in his face, so close she could smell his fear-sweat and the blood that was slowly congealing on his cheeks. 'Last chance, Joshua. Password.'

'I am looking for the Pompidou Centre,' he grunted.

'What?'

He repeated himself. 'That's what you say. Then the door guy, he says, "You're a long way from Paris". And then you say, "But Vientiane is cheaper." Then you're in.'

Eli stood. Satisfied. It was too random for him to have made it up.

'Stel, you ready?' she asked.

Stella was hunched over one of the dead guards.

'Hold on,' she said, then she stood up and turned to Eli.

Eli winced. Had Stella just taken a trophy? But there was no ear or nose clasped between her fingers. Just a couple of flick-knives and a small chrome revolver.

She held them out to Eli.

'Leave the Kalashnikovs, but take these.'

Eli nodded. She collected the AKs and dropped out the magazines. These she stuffed into her bag.

'Ready?' she asked.

'The window, I think,' Stella said.

Eli nodded. *Smart.* She rammed one of the unbroken chairs under the door knob then bent and, with a grunt, lifted the unconscious door guy onto its well-worn seat.

She cleared the sharp glass teeth from the window sill with one of the AKs then dropped it inside as she scooched herself up and over and into the street. Stella followed, handing Eli one of the knives.

'Let me have the gun,' Eli said, holding out her hand.

'Fuck off! It's an Airweight. A Model .38? Believe me, I know how to use one of these.'

Eli grinned as some of the adrenaline began to leave her system.

'OK, "Joyce", but let's be quick.'

Stella reached the front of the Oasis Lounge. So automatic gunfire clearly didn't put off the usual crowd. The young man they'd paid to look after the Hilux was still there, with his friends, a bottle of beer in his right hand, his left resting on the hip of a girl in a white string vest over a fluorescent-orange bra.

'Lively tonight, yes, Missus?' he said, to caws of laughter from the crowd.

'I wouldn't know.'

'That's Old Naledi for you,' he said with a grin. 'Best neighbourhood in G-City.' He turned and pointed at the Hilux. 'There's your wheels. Just like you left 'em.'

'And here's your money. Just like I promised. You want to earn a little extra?'

'Sure. What you want me to do?'

Eli pulled another fifty from her pocket. She held it up where he could see it.

'If the cops arrive, tell them four white guys arrived in a white Range Rover and shot the place up. They took off that way.'

Eli pointed in the opposite direction to her route back to the hotel.

He winked. Plucked the note from her fingers and stuck it into the waistband of his Calvin Klein boxers, of which a good three inches showed above his belted jeans.

'They were big guys, officer,' he said. He held his hand flat about a foot over Eli's head. 'Up to here. Built like tanks. South Africans.'

She smiled.

'Attaboy!'

As they regained the relative safety of G-City's commercial district, a police car shot past them in the opposite direction, lights flashing, siren wailing. Eli turned to Stella.

'Trouble in Old Naledi.'

'I heard some South Africans have been running riot.'

Eli grinned. Stella grinned back. Eli swerved to avoid a pothole deep enough to drop a body into.

'Shit!'

Half a block behind them, the Syrian watched their tail-lights weave for a second. His own lights were dark.

34

He estimated he had killed about eighty people. Of those, he had assassinated precisely fifty-eight. The approximation came from his exploits in uniform where his prowess with a heavy machine-gun had led to a large but unspecified number of deaths.

As he observed the two British women in the Hilux, tracking east along Kudumatse Road, he mentally revised his commercial total to sixty. Unprofessional, he knew, to count his chickens before they died in a welter of blood and tissue, but really. Two women, British women at that! Well, it was hardly a rough day at the office, now was it?

For this particular piece of wetwork, he'd selected a pistol. The scratched and dented but perfectly serviceable Colt 1911 was nothing fancy. No Picatinny rail housing a light or reflex sight. No suppressor or muzzle brake. No adjustable backstrap. No under-barrel laser. Just a couple of pounds of black steel housing seven .45 ACP hollow-point rounds in the magazine.

But they'd been made in their millions and found their way into the hands of criminals as well as soldiers and law enforcement professionals from Argentina to Zimbabwe.

In other words, the perfect disposable weapon that would point a million fingers, none of them at him. He'd bought it a week earlier from a dealer in Block 8, a sketchy Gaborone neighbourhood that made Old Naledi look like Manhattan's Upper East Side.

He stretched out a hand and patted the venerable semi-automatic, where it lay beside him on the Corolla's dirty grey velour passenger seat.

The hotel lay a couple of miles to the north. The women would have to pass through Bontleng Extension, a four-square-mile neighbourhood where the Africans had run out of money, energy or both to install and power streetlights.

He planned to make the hit roughly in the centre.

After the truck shimmied around a pothole big enough to dump a body into, it resumed a steady path and speed – thirty miles per hour – towards Avani resort. They crossed Old Lobatse Road and entered the kill zone.

The Syrian nodded with satisfaction. Like most of his peers, he was a meticulous planner. How else to command the high fees that kept him in mistresses, sports cars and fine wines? He watched the pinkish-red tail-lights make a right and followed the women into a narrow street lined with cinderblock houses roofed with rushes or corrugated iron.

A dog darted out from an alley, barking at his front wheels. He had time to swerve but held his line, nodding with satisfaction at the dull thump from the rear tyres. He watched the cur limping away in the rear-view mirror. The dog was lucky. *They* wouldn't be. They had five minutes to live.

He accelerated to forty-five, then braked suddenly, shot down a side street and floored the throttle, driving along an unnamed, dirt-surfaced street running parallel to the road the women had chosen. At the far end, he cornered hard again, took another right then jammed on the brakes and slewed the car to a halt. He yanked the bonnet release catch, stuck the Colt in the back of his waistband under his jacket, ran round to the front of the car and raised the bonnet.

With his head stuck into the engine bay, which smelled of hot oil, he could look sideways under the bonnet and watch the Hilux approach on the other side of the road.

Seventy yards to go. Sixty. Fifty.

He straightened, looked round as if in surprise and waved his hands in the air from side to side. The universal 'I need help!' gesture of broken-down motorists.

For good measure, he pasted an embarrassed yet hopeful expression onto his face. He'd practised in the bathroom mirror back at his hotel until he had it just right. Eyebrows drawn together. Eyes widened. Half-assed smile.

Forty. Thirty. They slowed. *Good. Come to me.*

Twenty. He heard the Hilux's brakes bite onto the pads.

They stopped.

Of course they stopped! *I'm not white, like you, but I'm sure as hell not black like these Africans.*

He turned the volume up on the helpless yet harmless expression until his cheeks quivered with the effort.

Through the windscreen he could see the women conferring. He was no lip reader but it wasn't hard to decode the conversation.

We should help him.

What if he's dangerous?

He doesn't look dangerous. Besides, there are two of us.

I don't like it.

Come on, the poor guy's broken down in the shittiest neighbourhood in this shithole country.

The woman with the lighter complexion, the detective, settled the matter. She opened her door and climbed out. Stayed behind the comforting slab of steel, though. OK, so she wasn't completely innocent in the ways of the world.

'What happened?' she called out.

'My car. It broke down,' he answered, using his BBC World Service accent. Arab desk, obviously. 'I'm terribly sorry, but you wouldn't be able to run me back to my hotel, would you?'

He stayed where he was. No threat. Not yet. The Colt felt good, pushing against his lumbar spine. Comforting. He put his hands behind him and rested them on the front wing. *Look*, they said. *Even less of a threat.*

'What's wrong with it?' she asked. Staying behind the door.

The other woman, the one with the darker complexion, stayed in the cab, staring at him through the windscreen. Arab, like him? Israeli? It didn't matter. She was dead.

'I'm not one hundred per cent sure, to be honest. I'm a journalist, not a mechanic. I think it might be something electrical.'

He inched his right hand behind him until he could brush the back of it against the Colt's grip.

'A journalist? Who for?'

'What?' He could feel his smile slipping. Jacked it back into place. She was ten yards away. Not the easiest of shots, especially as he'd have to hit her through the window glass. But not impossible. Not for him.

'Who do you work for? The BBC?'

'Yes. I've got my ID here. Hold on a second.'

He reached behind him, still smiling, and curled his fingers round the Colt's chequered grip.

The cop turned to the woman in the cab. She said something. The other woman nodded. The cop started to climb back into the Hilux.

He brought the Colt round in a tight under-arm swing so that the barrel brushed his right thigh on the way up. More economical than a roundhouse move.

The driver was gunning the engine. He had split seconds before the cop slammed her door and they took off.

His first shot shattered the windscreen. *Fuck!* The round passed harmlessly between their heads, blowing a hole in the rear glass before disappearing into the trees.

He fired again, a double tap. The truck was moving. No time to think. She was bearing down on him. He jumped to one side, firing again. Four more hollow-points slammed into the truck.

He meant to dodge the onrushing vehicle and give chase in the Corolla. But something grabbed the sleeve of his jacket. He whirled round to see the cuff buttons caught in the angle between the front wing and the bonnet prop.

The Hilux's rowdy engine note boomed in his ears. He wrenched at his jacket and the sleeve tore. Scrambling to find safety, he tried to climb onto the roof.

The slabby front end of the pickup caught his left leg, mashing it against the Corolla's door. The driver hauled the wheel right, rolling him all the way along the car's grimy body, crushing him between a combined three and a half tons of Japanese steel.

He screamed as his right shoulder dislocated, then again as the ligaments in his right knee parted in a series of pops he felt rather than heard.

The Hilux screeched its way past the Corolla's rear bumper, dragging it off its mounts. He fell to the road, clothes ripped from his body. Something hurt deep inside his abdomen and the right half of his field of vision had disappeared.

They'd stopped again. And he knew why.

He had a spare magazine in the front pocket of his trousers. They hung from his belt in shreds, but the lining was intact and he could feel the hard rectangle of metal jammed against the top of his thigh.

He tried to straighten enough to insert two fingers into the pocket and retrieve the magazine. A dark, bad feeling uncoiled like a snake from the region of his kidneys. He gasped with the pain.

Time slowed down. His ears were ringing.

The magazine came free. Somehow he'd maintained his hold on the Colt, even as the bitch driving the Hilux had crushed him half to death. His hand was trembling so violently it took him three tries to drop out the empty magazine.

With shaking fingers, he upended the pistol and tried to feed the magazine into the grip.

It was hard with only half his sight. His hand kept disappearing into the vanished sector. Finally it slid home. He pushed it hard to seat it, ignoring the snake and its needle-pointed fangs that dug into his side.

He raised the Colt in the direction of the Hilux.

Then it flew from his grasp. He couldn't understand how. When the driver's second kick landed, he realised.

She loomed over him, a half-woman, wearing a half-expression of fury. In her half-hand, a half-revolver. A tiny thing. Chromed. Little more than a toy.

She squatted in front of him.

'You're bleeding badly and it looks like you've got an internal haemorrhage as well,' she said. 'You're going to die unless we take you to a hospital. Who are you? Where are you from?'

He'd spent his adulthood taking the lives of others. Now death had come calling, he realised he wanted to save his own.

'My name is Nazir Aboud al-Javari. I am Syrian.'

'You're not a journalist, are you?'

He shook his head and the world lurched. He swallowed against his rising gorge.

'I am an assassin,' he whispered. 'I need a hospital. Take me and I will pay you whatever you ask.'

The other woman, the cop, got to her knees in front of him. Half a face looked at him. The visible eye was narrowed with concern. She was holding something up to his face. Something black. Shiny. A bright white light dazzled him. He squinted into the light.

'You…illed…rincess…dn't you?' she asked.

Her voice warbled, dropping out like a bad short-wave radio connection. He nodded, then retched as the snake surged halfway up his throat.

'Who hired you?' she shouted. 'Who? The Israelis?'

He shook his head. 'No. Not…them.'

He turned to one side and vomited blood onto the road. When he looked back at her, the visible half of her face began to shrink, a receding pale oval. And he was a boy again, at the National Museum of Damascus on Shukri al-Quwatli Street with his father. In the little auditorium, they sat with half a dozen other people watching a speeded-up film of the phases of the moon. The dark half grew larger and the shining silver oval shrank, first to an ellipse, then a crescent, then a sliver like a curved knife blade and then, finally, like an eye closing, it winked out. All dark now.

His father spoke in the blackness of the auditorium, fragrant with cigarette smoke.

'Come, Nazir. Time to go home.'

'I want to watch again, Father. From the beginning.'

His father held him gently by the elbow.

'No. Your mother is waiting, she —'

* * *

Stella stuck two fingers under the man's jaw, probing for the artery, then held them there while she searched for a pulse. She closed her eyes. Nothing.

She retrieved the Colt and stuck it in her waistband. She stood up.

'Dead?' Eli asked.

'Dead.'

'Shit!'

Stella shrugged.

'It's actually not so bad. I recorded his confession.'

'Will that be enough?'

'Should be. Deathbed confessions are pretty solid in terms of the law of testimony. No further reason to lie.'

'How did you know he wasn't a journalist?'

Stella shrugged.

'Partly, he just didn't look right to me. There was something off about his body language. His accent was all wrong, too. BBC journalists haven't spoken like that for decades.' She paused, winked. 'Plus, Don told me the BBC's only African bureau is in Johannesburg.'

Eli's eyes widened.

'You really had me going there! I thought you'd been taking tips from Gabe and all his Oriental mind-control shit.'

Stella grinned.

'Me? Nope. Just a hardworking copper who knows how to ask the right questions. Now, shall we stay here with another dead body, or get going?'

Eli looked around. Despite the racket they'd created, the street was still dark. Nobody had come out from one of the shacks to see what was going on. In an area like this, residents would know better than to investigate the sound of gunfire or automotive accidents in the middle of the night.

She nodded.

'Come on.'

Together they ran back to the Hilux. The assassin they left for whoever reached him first, the cops, or the hyenas.

Back at the resort, Eli texted Gabriel a short summary of the day's events.

* * *

The following morning she drove the Hilux out to the Kagosi Group compound and returned the materiel to Taylor, plus one Smith & Wesson Airweight Model .38. One of his men drove her back to the resort, dropping her off at reception with a smile and a wave as he floored the throttle to swerve the pickup round in a tight, rubber-burning circle on the tarmac.

She and Stella checked out, drove the rental Merc to the airport and, after a little research on the part of the sales clerk, bought two one-way tickets to Vientiane. They paid for access to one of the lounges and kept their heads down inside its cocooned, sound-deadening confines, drinking gin and tonics and eating salty plantain chips until their flight was called.

A TV was playing a rolling 24-hour news channel in the corner. The crawl caught Eli's eye. She rose from the leather armchair and wandered closer to read the yellow-on-red text.

Murder and mayhem in Old Naredi… Local businessman and four

other men brutally attacked at Oasis Lounge, three slain…police searching for four Afrikaaners…

She nodded. *Good boy, you earned your extra fifty.*

35

DUBAI

With the rental Jeep Wrangler's air con blowing icy air into the cabin, Gabriel pulled out from the Hertz parking lane at Dubai airport. His taciturn companion grunted out directions at each intersection.

In total, Gabriel reckoned the man, who hadn't given his name, had spoken no more than twenty words. Even when they'd stopped at a roadside grill to get breakfast, he'd merely pointed to a sandwich and drink and handed over his money to the cook in silence.

Gabriel named him *Jiàntán* – 'chatty'.

The drive took an hour and five minutes, including ten for the breakfast stop. The E88's tarmac was glassy-smooth, and Gabriel relaxed, steering with a single finger resting lightly on the bottom of the wheel.

To each side, the flat, sandy landscape extended to the horizon, punctuated here and there by scrubby bushes low to the ground and the sun-bleached skeletons of long-felled trees. Gigantic red wooden spools lay in groups every five miles or so. What were they?

Electrical? Left over from when the highway was cabled for streetlight?

Jiàntán jerked a stubby forefinger at the windscreen.

'Left.'

Gabriel nodded and turned off the highway onto a dirt road that curved lazily eastwards. He smiled to himself. *Twenty-one.*

Even off-road, the Jeep's suspension and four-wheel drive had little work to do. After half a mile, the track began breaking up, before disappearing altogether. Now the stocky 4x4 could dig in and prove its worth. Gabriel let the wheels slide over the sand, enjoying the sensation of the four-wheel drive system finding-losing-finding grip and powering ahead all the while, its turbodiesel engine making light work of the terrain.

A snaking line on the horizon resolved into a ridge of rock and sand. Beyond its crumbling edge, Gabriel saw a dried-out riverbed – a *wadi* – as he crossed a short stretch of metalled roadway that spanned it. He glanced left and followed the ancient watercourse until it disappeared beyond a distant dune.

The sandy track replaced the Tarmac and he searched the way ahead for a building or some other sign they might be nearing the factory.

The track split in a soft, curving Y and Jiàntán indicated the right-hand fork. After five hundred yards he pointed to the right. A long, low concrete building, painted the same colour as the greyish sand it stood amidst, squatted behind a row of low-growing trees.

'That's it?' Gabriel asked.

Jiàntán nodded and unclipped his seatbelt. Within seconds a warning chime bonged inside the cabin. Gabriel ignored it and swung into an access road leading from the track to the factory's front gate.

No guard came out to question them. Gabriel saw no dogs prowling on the other side of the chain-link fence, then mentally slapped his forehead. *Idiot! It's fifty Celsius out there. A dog would fry from the inside out.*

A metal squawk box mounted on a wooden post seemed the likeliest method of gaining admittance.

Gabriel turned in his seat.

'Shall I go?'

Jiàntán grunted. Stayed put. Gabriel climbed out, grinning, and flinched as the wall of bone-dry heat smacked him in the face.

Feeling runnels of sweat dripping from his armpits and the space between his shoulder blades, he thumbed the button beneath the speaker grille.

He looked round while he waited for someone to answer. Even through his sunglasses the sun was blinding, bouncing off the sand, the white-painted building beyond the wire, the Jeep's white paintwork.

'*Tahduth.*' Speak.

'*Aismi hu Gabriel Wolfe. Yusuf yatawaqaeni.*' My name is Gabriel Wolfe. Yusuf is expecting me.

He heard a harsh buzz from the speaker, then the latch to his right clunked. Sand must have entered the hinge mechanism: the gates screeched as they juddered apart.

Gabriel climbed back into the Jeep's chilly interior, pushed the gear sector into drive and eased between the gates and on towards the white-painted, windowless building housing the Four-Point Star's ivory-processing operation.

The front of the building was as bland as the side of a refrigerator – an unbroken expanse of white-rendered concrete that stretched for a hundred yards end to end. A single door interrupted its minimalist surface. Gabriel parked the Jeep in front of it. To each side, white cars and 4x4s were lined up in a straggling row. No need for accurate parking when there was this much space to play with.

If Gabriel had been expecting a reception area, he was soon set straight. The whole of the inside of the building was an open rectangle of floor space. It had been crudely subdivided into workstations comprising cheap-looking desks, swivel chairs from some bargain-basement office supplier and rudimentary, belt-driven drills. Power came via overhead cables slung from the suspended ceiling.

At each of the workstations, of which there must have been fifty, a masked operator sat, head bent to the task of transforming elephant tusks into purchasable objects.

A couple of the blue-masked workers glanced up as he and Jiàntán entered the factory, but they soon returned to their work. From his right, Gabriel heard footsteps above the multiplied thrum of the drills.

He turned to meet their host.

The man bustling towards him was in his late fifties and wearing traditional Arab dress. His belly interrupted the smooth fall of his white robe. *Thawb*, Gabriel translated mentally. Beneath the hem, his feet were shod in brown leather open-toed sandals. His red-and-white checked headscarf – *ghutrah* – was held in place with a black rope – *agal*.

Behind gold-rimmed square glasses, Yusuf's brown eyes gleamed and he was smiling broadly. He held out his right hand and took Gabriel's.

'*As-salaam 'alaykum, Gabriel*,' he said, pumping Gabriel's hand vigorously.

'*Wa alaykum salaam, Yusuf*.'

The handshaking went on, as was traditional.

'You speak excellent Arabic,' Yusuf said, in English.

'And you speak excellent English.'

Finally, Yusuf relinquished his grip on Gabriel's hand. He looked over his shoulder and nodded perfunctorily at Jiàntán.

'Let us keep to English, Gabriel. It is the international language of business, is it not?'

Gabriel nodded.

'It is, but I am happy to speak in Arabic if that would be easier for you, Yusuf.'

Yusuf's eyes widened.

'No! Not at all. I speak English with my clients in Hong Kong. It is good to practise, yes?'

Gabriel smiled.

'Agreed. Mr Cho sends his regards.'

'Please return mine to him when you next see him. He is well?'

'Yes, as far as I could see, he enjoys good health.'

'That is good, that is good,' Yusuf said. 'Come, you must be thirsty. I have prepared refreshments in my office.'

He reached down and took Gabriel's hand in his and led him, companionably, along one side of the factory, to a partitioned-off corner.

'Wait outside,' Yusuf barked at Jiàntán.

The office was blissfully cool after the unpleasant warmth of the main processing area. A low mosaic-topped coffee table occupied most of one side. Its multi-coloured tiled surface was covered with small silver and brass dishes. Each contained a different sweetmeat.

Gabriel saw deep-fried falafel the size of golf balls, filo pastry tubes from which fragrant lamb and mint poked out at either end. Olives, black and green, and swimming in a reddish oil. Flatbreads, their upper surfaces pocked with black bubbles from the oven. Dishes of baba ganoush and hummus, the smells of charred aubergine and garlicky chickpeas rising from the little bowls and making Gabriel's mouth water.

A silver pot steamed on a second table and, beside it, glass cups in silver cages stood ready, laden with fresh mint leaves.

Yusuf swept a hand wide over the table.

'Eat! Eat! Whatever you like. Mint tea?'

'Yes please. That would be lovely,' Gabriel said. The roadside sandwich he'd eaten earlier felt like an age ago.

Yusuf beamed, took one of the low armchairs and watched intently as Gabriel scooped up some hummus on a triangle of flatbread.

'It is acceptable?' he asked, his forehead creasing. 'We get it from a restaurant up the road. They are not the best, but they are the nearest.'

'It's wonderful,' Gabriel said, and he meant it. The dip was creamy and spiked not just with garlic but a pinch of chilli.

Yusuf poured boiling water into two glasses, pushed one towards Gabriel and took one for himself.

The smell of fresh mint coiled its way into Gabriel's nostrils and from there to his brain, stimulating memories of his parents' herb garden at the trade mission house in Hong Kong.

'Mr Cho said only that I should make you welcome, Gabriel,' Yusuf said, waiting until Gabriel had taken a sip of the mint tea and set his glass down. 'Nothing more. How may I be of service to you?'

'First of all, I would like to give you this,' Gabriel said, retrieving a small wrapped parcel from his jacket pocket.

He handed it to Yusuf, who took it reverentially in both hands. He looked up at Gabriel and smiled.

'It is rare to find someone who takes so much time and trouble to observe the correct behaviour, Gabriel,' he said. 'Most are all about this,' he added, rubbing the pads of thumb and forefinger together.

Gabriel inclined his head.

'I am a guest in your country, and your factory. Please, open it.'

With delicate movements that belied his stubby fingers, Yusuf unwrapped the gold tissue paper. As he spread the corners of the sheets open on his palm he inhaled softly.

He plucked out a small jade carving of a salmon leaping. Gabriel had bought it in Hong Kong's jade market the day he left for Dubai.

'I hope you like it,' Gabriel said. 'As you run an ivory-carving workshop I thought you might appreciate the artistry.'

Yusuf looked up. His eyes were glistening behind his glasses.

'This is beautiful. Thank you. You are a collector of netsuke yourself?'

'I was left a small collection, but I haven't added to it.'

Yusuf stood and placed the little green salmon on a shelf beside an intricately worked carving of an elephant inside whose latticed sides a baby elephant stood.

He returned to his chair.

'Tell me, Gabriel, what brought you to my humble factory?'

'Some poachers in Africa murdered a group of British and Botswanan soldiers. Ivory poachers. I have been charged with bringing them to justice. I need to find out who was responsible for the massacre.'

Yusuf's face, so full of pleasure only moments earlier, clouded over.

'Ah, Gabriel, I wish I could help you. And, believe me, I am sorry for the loss of your comrades' lives. But I do not know any poachers. All our ivory comes in by way of Vientiane.'

Gabriel frowned.

'So, nobody up the supply chain ever comes here? You don't deal directly?'

Yusuf shook his head, making his red-and-white *ghutrah* sway against his round cheeks.

'I am sorry, my friend.'

Gabriel tried not to let his disappointment – or his suspicion – show. He wanted to push as hard as he could. Surely a factory manager would know who was supplying his raw materials, Laotian market or not?

'And you've never heard whispers about the ultimate supplier for your ivory?'

Only now did a flicker of irritation disrupt Yusuf's previous genial expression.

'It is like I said, Gabriel. No. I order tusks from my contact in Vientiane. He arranges to buy it and ships it here.'

Gabriel finished his mint tea and placed the glass down on a few clear square inches of mosaic with a hard little clink.

'Three British soldiers were murdered, Yusuf. The people I work for will not stop until their deaths have been avenged. Not just the killers but anyone who helped them. Do not put yourself in harm's way to protect these men.'

Yusuf spread his hands wide.

'Gabriel, even if I *did* know these poachers, why would I tell you their names? You will kill them and cut off my supply. I am a businessman. I need to protect my livelihood. I have a family to provide for. A wife, children.'

It was a mistake. Gabriel knew it. And he could see that Yusuf knew it, too. Gabriel said nothing. Sometimes it was the most effective way of getting people to talk. Some people just couldn't bear the pressure.

'Look,' Yusuf said, finally. 'I am not saying that I *do* know these people.' He cleared his throat and took a sip from his glass of tea. 'But just suppose I did, I would be taking a huge risk giving them up to you. A huge business risk. I would lose a great deal of money.'

Gabriel stared at Yusuf. Watched the way his eyes, glistening with tears at his gift a few minutes earlier, now had a greedy glint. Yusuf was just like those others. The ones for whom it all came down to *this*. He mentally rubbed the pads of his thumb and forefinger together.

'I can pay you for information,' Gabriel said. 'If you have any.'

Yusuf shook his head.

'You misunderstand me, Gabriel. Money can always be replaced, yes? But favours are a currency beyond value. I tell you a name and you owe me a favour. A man as well connected as you will know many powerful people.'

Gabriel didn't even have to think.

'No favours. Sorry.' *The last one I repaid nearly got me killed and a village full of Chinese peasants massacred.*

Yusuf pooched his lips out in a moue of disappointment.

'That is a shame. But, as I said, I was only speaking, what is that English word, hypo…?'

'…thetically.'

'Exactly! Hypothetically.'

Gabriel returned the smile. Time for one more roll of the dice.

'I'm sorry, Yusuf. That was rude of me to push when you had already answered my question. Look, at least I can cross this place off my list. Thank you for your time. I don't suppose, while I'm here, you would show me around? I am fascinated by the whole process.'

Yusuf smiled again, his moment of irritation forgotten.

'Of course! It would be an honour. Come! Come!'

After the quiet of Yusuf's office, the hum and rattle of fifty electric motors, boring, burring, cutting and polishing ivory was deafening.

He looked at the bent heads with the blue paper masks over their noses and mouths. *How do they take it without going deaf?*

He followed Yusuf as he pointed out particularly intricate or large pieces of ivory. Unprocessed tusks were stacked on wooden pallets against one wall. Gabriel saw dark rust-red stains on the roots and pictured the mangled and mutilated heads of these great beasts. He felt a sudden surge of anger and reproached himself for sucking up to Yusuf. *Needs must.*

A cry of pain made him look up.

36

A woman working on an entire tusk, three feet from root to tip, had reared back in her chair. Her face above the mask was pale. She was clutching her left hand. Blood seeped from between her fingers.

'Stupid woman!' Yusuf yelled in Arabic as he rushed over. 'Don't get blood inside the tusk, it'll never come out.'

The woman was rocking back and forward in her chair and Gabriel saw blood streaming now, from between her fingers and onto the concrete floor. Yusuf was shouting for a first aid kit and in the woman's corner of the factory, work stopped while her co-workers crowded round to comfort her, or just to watch.

Gabriel looked back at the door to Yusuf's office. It was standing open. Of Jiàntán there was no sign. He must have gone off to get something to eat or drink.

While Yusuf knelt at the woman's side trying to get her to release her bleeding hand, Gabriel turned and strode back the way they'd come. He glanced over his shoulder then slipped inside the office.

A grey steel filing cabinet occupied one corner. He tried the top drawer. It didn't yield. *Shit*! The desk held an ageing PC, black and dust-covered. Gabriel jiggled the mouse to wake it up. His reward, a dialogue box asking for his password.

He pulled open the drawer beneath the desktop. A few pencils, a calculator. Some rubber bands. A packet of breath mints.

He caught movement in the corner of his eye. A pennant, six inches by eight, fluttered in the cool breeze from the air conditioning unit. He hadn't seen it earlier because the bookcase to its right had blocked his view.

Glancing over his shoulder, he crossed the office to get a better look.

At first he took it to be a sports trophy of some kind, the type of gift opposing team captains exchange on a football pitch. Shield-shaped, with a white fringe running along the sloping lower edges, it depicted a white sun flaming over a green hill. A quartered ground of turquoise and orange completed the design. But it was the wording running along the top that interested Gabriel. He peered at it.

Boerevryheid an Regte

He recognised the language: Afrikaans. The first part of the first word was easy enough to decipher. *Boer*: the descendants of German, Dutch or Huguenot settlers in the Transvaal and Orange Free State.

The rest he was less sure of, although *Regte* looked a lot like the German word for 'right': *recht*. He heard hurrying footsteps behind him. Yusuf's voice, calling his name. He pulled out his phone and took a couple of pictures, willing his fingers to stay still as he focused on a close-up.

He stuffed his phone back in his pocket and moved his gaze to the ivory elephant carving beside which Yusuf had placed the jade salmon.

'Gabriel! I thought I'd lost you.'

Gabriel turned, smiling.

'I was in the way over there,' he said, jerking his chin towards the door. 'Is the lady going to be OK?'

'She is fine. A little cut, nothing more. I tell them to be careful but they don't listen.'

Gabriel looked over Yusuf's shoulder, where the factory workers had all returned to their tasks. How much was he paying them? Was he paying them at all? Were they trafficked? He realised he had no time to worry about the fate of the ivory-carvers. Yusuf was eyeing him as a hawk might eye a mouse.

'Yusuf, I want to thank you. For making time to hear my request, even if you were unable to help,' Gabriel said in Arabic.

Yusuf bowed slightly.

'You came on the highest recommendation. I will tell Mr Cho of your trip the next time I see him.'

Gabriel returned the bow, eager to leave and have someone back at The Department check out the pennant. Yusuf escorted him as far as the front door and shook hands once more, releasing Gabriel's hand after only fifteen seconds.

Gabriel found Jiàntán outside, leaning against the side of the Jeep and smoking. Apparently impervious to the heat, he pushed himself upright, took a final drag on the cigarette then dropped it and ground it out under his toe.

'You drive for a change,' Gabriel said in Cantonese.

With Jiàntán behind the wheel, Gabriel scrutinised the image on his phone screen. A white sun. A green hill. Turquoise and orange quadrants. Ideas were shimmering in his mind but refusing to coalesce into something he could get hold of.

He returned to the slogan or motto. *Boerevryheid an Regte*. He tapped the browser icon, then swore as he realised he had no signal. Then he smiled. He didn't need it. He was a damn linguist after all. OK, so Boer he knew. The Boer people. Afrikaaners. Regte meant right. Or rights, plural, maybe. Boer rights.

Boer rights. A protest movement of some kind? A pressure group. The Zimbabweans under Mugabe had expropriated white-owned farms and handed them to the president's cronies. Maybe

South Africa's ANC-led government was trying the same thing. Or planning it.

How about the iconography? A white sun. Well, that wasn't too hard to decode. Suns set, but they rise, too. And this one was high in the sky and shining down on the land. A white sun might mean white dominance. No, wait. He had it. A green hill lit by a white sun. It was a homeland. A white homeland. No, not a white homeland. A whites-*only* homeland.

Boerevryheid an Regte was a white separatist movement. And their pennant was hanging in the office of a man running an ivory-carving factory about halfway down the supply chain for poached ivory. Equidistant between the killing grounds of sub-Saharan Africa and eager customers for finished goods in China and the Far East. He realised with a twinge of guilt that Master Zhao had a small sub-collection of yellowed ivory figurines on a shelf in his house on the hill.

The sun – the real sun – was high in the sky. Not white, but blazing yellow, searing the ground and everything foolish enough to slither, crawl, walk or drive across it. He checked his watch. The rose-gold Bremont he'd bought to replace his beloved Breitling told him it was a few minutes before 11.30 a.m.

Back at the airport, after they'd returned the Jeep to the mildly puzzled-looking clerk at the Hertz office, Gabriel turned to Jiàntán.

'I'm not flying back to Hong Kong. Have a good flight.'

Jiàntán shrugged and grunted. His meaning was clear. *Whatever. You're not my responsibility anymore.* The big man turned on his heel and ambled off towards one of the many bars.

Gabriel sighed out a breath. He found a quiet spot and chose a seat facing the runway where he couldn't be overlooked or overheard. He checked his phone. The signal was strong. The screen lit up with an incoming text. He smiled. It was from Eli.

Contacted by Syrian contract killer. Confessed to the hit on video.

Now dead. Also, got lead on poachers. Vientiane. Meet us there ASAP. El x

He took a few moments to digest her six terse sentences. Imagined Eli and Stella taking on and killing a contract killer in some Gaborone backstreet. *All roads lead to Laos.*

He tapped out a reply.

Good work. You or S hurt? I have lead too. See u in V. G x

Next, he called Don.

'What's up, Old Sport?'

'It's kind of two steps forward one back, but I have got a potential lead to the poachers.'

'Go on.'

'I'm in Dubai. I just visited an ivory-carving factory out in the desert. The manager was reluctant to talk about his suppliers, but I think he meets them, at least occasionally,' Gabriel said, as he watched a Boeing 777 taxiing in front of the expanse of plate glass. 'He had a pennant in his office. From South Africa. If I send you a picture, can you have someone take a look? I need intel on the source. I think it's something to do with a Boer separatist movement.'

'Send it over,' Don said. 'And don't be too hard on yourself, either. This is excellent work. I'll let Nick Acheson know. He'll be delighted.'

'Thanks, boss.'

'Where are you headed now?'

'Vientiane. There's a market there. My guess is some kind of wholesaling operation.'

'Eli emailed me. That's where she and Stella are headed.'

'I know. I just got a text. They found the princess's killer.'

'So I gather. I've watched his dying declaration. It's convincing.

Our friends in the security services plus the Met are assessing it as we speak. At least Lieberman's off the hook, poor fellow.'

'I haven't had a chance to see much news, boss. What's happening?'

He heard Don's breath whistling in and out through his nose.

'Things could be better. They could be worse, too, of course. Don't know if you heard, but Tammerlane went to Buckingham Palace for urgent talks about the royal family's security. The official line is he's worried for the king's safety. He's *asked*,' heavy emphasis, 'him to cancel all public engagements until further notice.'

'Has he gone along with it?'

'Apparently. And now Tammerlane's started summoning the chiefs of staff to Number Ten individually. Seems he has some sort of strategic realignment in mind.'

'What kind of strategic realignment?'

'The kind where Britain's independent nuclear deterrent gets mothballed. The kind where our armed forces are scaled back and refocused on domestic security. The kind,' Don's voice sounded heavier somehow, 'where certain of my former colleagues are meeting in St James's clubs to discuss their options.'

Even though the line was secure and double-encrypted, Gabriel knew Don wouldn't go any further in explaining what he meant. He didn't really need to.

Unlike in places like Cuba, Venezuela, or the multiplicity of African states that had fallen for Marxism in a big way, Britain's armed forces would never fall into line behind an extreme left government, still less a prime minister looking for ways to defang them.

But still, Tammerlane's confining the king to quarters troubled him. The phrase 'house arrest' came to mind. He didn't like the image it suggested.

37

LONDON

The press secretary stepped forward and addressed the gathered journalists through the floor mic.

'Ladies and gentlemen, the prime minister.'

Tammerlane smiled at the young party official and took up position at the mic. He waited for the whirring and clicking of electronic shutters to cease before speaking.

'Thank you. As you know, this great country of ours has suffered one terrible shock already this year. And you only have to look at social media to see that the threats our citizenry face daily are swelling like a tsunami gathering force in the deep ocean. I speak not only of escalating terror threats, especially from right-wing extremists, but subversion from foreign actors.

'In the light of these threats, and my declared aim of keeping the people who granted me the privilege of leading this country into a bright new era of fairness and equality, I am today announcing the formation of a brand-new government department.

'As from today, the Home Office, a relic of post-colonial thinking, is no more. In its place rises a bright citadel, where the rights of the people are put before imperial ambition and warmongering. Ladies and gentlemen, as the leader of Freedom and Fairness, and your prime minister, I am proud to announce the formation of the Department of Domestic Security.'

The room was utterly silent for two seconds, then a barrage of questions erupted.

Tammerlane patted the air for silence.

'Please!' he barked, a harder edge to his voice than the gathered journalists had heard before. 'Let me introduce you to the new Secretary of State for Domestic Security, Joni Last.'

He turned to his left and beckoned a young woman to join him before the media. She strode out from the wings, dark eyes flashing, her black hair cut so short her scalp was visible in the harsh lighting for the TV cameras.

'Thank you, Prime Minister,' she said. 'My first act as the Secretary of State at DDS is to announce a temporary suspension of the normal communications channels between the media and government ministers. We are concerned that foreign state actors have infiltrated sections of the media and while we investigate there can be no unfettered access to policymakers. However,' she said, raising her voice above the growing chorus of complaints, 'I am also creating a centralised Government Media Office through which all requests for information can be placed for evaluation and response.'

'This is outrageous!' a male journalist bellowed above the din. 'You're creating a police state.'

She smiled at him as Tammerlane left the stage.

'Not at all, Philip. Although I am glad you brought up the subject of law enforcement. It has come to our notice that the current policing protocols are not fit for purpose. Yes, for everyday crimes against the person and property, there is a role for traditional policing.' She paused. 'But as Joe has said, we live in an era of unprecedented threats to the state. Therefore, and also effective immediately, I am announcing the creation of a new force: The Internal Security Directorate. Its operatives will report to me, and through me to the prime minister. Their remit is to police matters of state security within the boundaries of the rep—' She stopped, glanced at Tammerlane. He shook his head, a minute gesture.

'Within our borders,' she continued. 'That means counter-terrorism, which is now removed from both the Met and MI5, intelligence gathering on subversives, and agents of destabilisation. They will have additional powers of detention and investigation beyond those of the police, but—'

'You can't be serious,' another journalist, a woman, called out. 'You're talking about secret police! Parliament will never permit it!'

'Parliament doesn't need to *permit* it, Jacqui. It's happened. The senior management team is in place, and we have already recruited a cadre of operational officers and staff to begin work immediately.

'Look, I know some of you, especially from the right-wing press will be eager to paint this as some sort of internal coup, but nothing could be further from the truth. As Joe has said all along, our goal is to create and maintain a stable, secure and fair state in which the people's will is respected, and the people themselves are protected. I can't for the life of me see what's wrong with wanting to protect the people, can you?'

* * *

Fifty-three miles northeast of the press conference, Don turned off the TV in his MOD Rothford office. Beside him, Nick Acheson blew out his cheeks.

'Did we just see what I think we saw?'

Don steepled his fingers under his nose, breathing heavily.

'I believe we did. He's really going to do it.'

'But we can't let him, Don! I mean, this is a coup. Pure and simple.'

Don's answer was forestalled by the phone on his desk, which had started ringing. Staring at Acheson, he lifted the receiver.

'Yes, Molly.'

The woman on the other end, his secretary of a year and a half, sounded nervous.

'Colonel, it's, well, it's the prime minister.'

Heart thumping, Don straightened in his chair, shooting Acheson a look and mouthing, 'Tammerlane'.

As Acheson's eyes widened, Don cleared his throat.

'Prime Minister.'

'Why so formal, Don? Call me Joe. And there's no need to be nervous.'

Cursing himself for not clearing his throat before answering, Don tried again.

'I think I'll stick with Prime Minister. Old habits and all that.'

'Fair enough, Colonel. Though it's an honorific, isn't it? I mean, you're not serving anymore, are you?'

Bastard! Such a simple question, but booby-trapped just as surely as an IED beneath a dead body. But Don Webster, late of the SAS and the Parachute Regiment before that, hadn't survived thirty years in uniform by rolling over corpses and taking a face full of shrapnel.

'What can I do for you, Prime Minister?'

'Surely you can guess?'

'Not sure I can, actually.'

'Very well. I'll spell it out for you.' A beat. 'Dobbin.'

As his nickname left Tammerlane's lips, Don knew the jig was up. Tammerlane had been digging. Deep. And someone had spilled their guts.

'All ears,' he managed.

'This little outfit of yours. What was it called? Ah, yes. The Department. Such an innocuous-sounding moniker,' he said, his voice dripping with sarcasm. 'Makes one think of IT. Or HR. Anyway, you're cancelled.'

'What?' Don said.

He'd known what was coming. Nevertheless, hearing it brought him to a peak of anger he hadn't felt for a long time.

'You heard, Webster. I'm shutting you and your evil little death squad down.'

'You can't. We report—'

'To the Privy Council. Yes, I know. Hey! I have an idea. Why don't you call your handler there and ask her what's going on.

Then call me back. Your secretary, Molly, was it? She has my number.'

The line went dead.

Don had to squeeze his eyes shut to dispel the mounting sense of unreality that had built during the short conversation with Tammerlane.

'What is it?' Acheson asked, sitting forward in his chair, his forehead creased with concern.

'Bloody hell, Nick. He's shut me down. Hold on, I need to make a call.'

He pulled out his own phone and swiped through the contacts until he reached the woman he wanted. She answered before he'd even heard the first ring in his ear.

'You heard, then?' was all she said.

'Hattie, tell me you have some sway in this. The Privy Council—'

'Is no more. He disbanded us, Don.' Her voice caught, and for the first time since Joseph 'Call me Joe' Tammerlane had swept to power, Don felt something he hadn't felt for a very long time. Fear.

Don gripped the phone tighter.

'What?'

'There *is* no Privy Council. It's been advising the monarch since the thirteenth century and Tammerlane drew a red line through it like an unnecessary item in the budget.'

As she explained Tammerlane's brutal action, Don listened with half an ear. But his mind was on other matters. The assassination. The BBC interview just after his election victory. The press conferences. The fawning newspaper headlines. The postponement of the Defence Spending Review. The interviews on breakfast TV. Nick's mauling at the hands of Tracy Barnett-Short.

Britain was sleepwalking straight into a coup, just as Acheson had said. And unlike the ill-fated attempt some years earlier by the blonde billionaire, Sir Toby Maitland, this had been achieved with the ballot, not the bullet.

'Hattie, I have to go. I'm so sorry. I'll be in touch.'

He called the number Tammerlane had given him.

The reply spoke volumes. Calm. Confident. And with an amused undertone. Like a cruel child caught out pulling the wings off flies and not caring.

'This is Joe.'

'What have you done, Tammerlane?'

'I see respect has left the building. No "Prime Minister" this time, Don? So much for old habits.'

'We'll stop you. You won't get away with this.'

Even as he said it, Don realised how much his threat rang hollow.

'Won't get away with this?' Tammerlane echoed, clearly amused. 'Don, this isn't *Scooby-Doo*. I'm re-fashioning this country to be fit for the people. And, purely out of interest, who is this "we" you're talking about?'

'The heads of the armed forces. The intelligence community. The people who are true patriots, loyal to the Crown and to this country.'

With a heavy feeling in his gut, Don realised that he already knew the essence of what Tammerlane would say next.

'You're an old soldier, Don. And I respect you for that. But I cut my teeth in business. And the one thing I learned was that the man who holds the purse strings has all the power. In this case, that would be me,' he said. 'How long do you think those people you speak of will stay loyal once their wages stop arriving in their bank accounts, hmm? Because the chancellor of the Exchequer has just made one or two adjustments to the Government payroll. I think you'll find you and your cronies in your gentlemen's clubs may have the fire in your belly, but those you control…well, let's just say I can hear them asking which way to the nearest Job Centre.'

Tammerlane's mocking tone was replaced by the steady hum of a dead line.

Don looked straight at Acheson.

'It's over. He's won.'

38

VIENTIANE, LAOS

Gabriel stepped out of the air conditioned arrivals lounge ready for, but still knocked back by, Vientiane's soupy air. The airport information board had declared that the outside temperature was 32 Celsius. The humidity, approaching one hundred per cent, made it feel hotter still. Each breath was like drowning on dry land, so thick and wet was the atmosphere outside.

Palm trees grew in a long avenue leading away from the terminal. Everywhere, lush green plants competed with each other, and their human neighbours, to take up as much space as possible. The sounds of the city assailed Gabriel's ears just as the heat had attacked his skin. Mopeds buzzed, high-mileage diesel engines clattered, dogs barked and pavement hawkers yelled.

He walked towards the end of the queue for taxis, unfastening another button on his shirt. Before he'd righted his suitcase, a uniformed attendant in a hi-vis vest and peaked cap rushed over.

'Sir! Sir!' he called from two paces out. 'You need taxi? You are American?'

'English. But yes, I do need a taxi. Is this the right queue?'

The attendant nodded, but then scowled at the fat woman in front of Gabriel who was regarding them both with barely concealed interest.

'These are peasants here from the country. You do not queue with them, Sir. Here.' He grabbed the handle of Gabriel's suitcase. 'I take this for you. Follow me, Sir, follow me.'

With head held high and shoulders back, the attendant swept imperiously past the queue, ignoring the shouts and what Gabriel imagined must be fairly salty Laotian curses.

Feeling a mixture of guilt and relief, Gabriel followed him, shooting the odd apologetic glance and shrugging his shoulders. *What can I do? He took my bag!*

At the head of the queue, the attendant blew ferociously on a silver whistle. The next cab trundled alongside him. The attendant turned to Gabriel.

'Where are you staying, Sir? Crowne Plaza? Hilton? InterContinental?'

'Beau Rivage.'

The attendant beamed.

'Ah, Beau Rivage. Beautiful hotel. Very good choice.'

He turned to the driver who was waiting with his window rolled down, a hand holding a cigarette dangling out.

'Beau Rivage. *Il est Anglais. Conduit prudemment!*'

Gabriel smiled to himself. Whether the attendant told all the cabbies to drive carefully, or just those carrying '*les Anglais*', he didn't know. But he was grateful, just the same.

With his suitcase loaded into the boot, and a five-dollar bill passed discreetly to the parking attendant, he slid into the car's stuffy interior. In the absence of working air con, the driver had opted for an incense burner on the dashboard, which emitted the fragrant smell of frangipani into the cabin.

Gabriel paid the driver, retrieved his suitcase and stood on the pavement as it roared away into the traffic, horn honking, all thoughts of '*conduit prudemment*' clearly forgotten.

Behind him, the Mekong stretched away in a graceful curve. A few fishing boats and pleasure craft plied the wide brown waterway. On the far bank, the Thai bank he reminded himself, nothing but jungle, stretching down to the water's edges as far as the eye could see.

Before him, the hotel entrance, a pagoda made of thick bamboo logs painted a deep blush pink. A matching sign proclaimed Hotel Beau Rivage Mekong in purple type on a paler-pink background.

Gabriel passed beneath humming power lines that dangled dangerously close to the ground. His scalp prickled and he caught the after-lightning smell of ozone.

He checked in and made his way to the room Eli had booked for them. Standing outside, he felt a delicious squirm of excitement in the pit of his stomach. *Jesus! Haven't felt like this since going on teenage dates.* He raised his right hand and knocked with his knuckle.

He heard footsteps, then the door opened inwards and there was Eli, grinning from ear to ear. She'd put her hair up, a style she knew he loved. And she was wearing makeup: sooty kohl around those grey-green eyes, and mascara to emphasise them still further.

'Hello, beautiful,' he said.

'Hello, handsome.'

She threw her arms around him and squeezed him so tightly he felt the breath leave his body.

'Whoa! Let me go, I can't breathe.'

He managed to struggle inside and closed the door behind him with his heel.

Eli kissed him, hard on the mouth, then again, more softly. She smelled of sandalwood and lemon. Gabriel closed his eyes and let himself be lost in the moment, savouring the taste of her, the feel of her body pressed flat against his. Felt the stirrings of an erection. She pressed against him harder and brought his ear close to her lips.

'I want you. Right now.'

Afterwards, Eli propped herself up on one elbow. Her up-do had turned into a half-up-half-down-do, auburn spirals sticking to her neck. Her eyes were shining.

'You OK?' Gabriel asked.

'Yes. Actually, no. I'm not OK. OK is for ordinary people. I'm…' She looked up at the slowly revolving ceiling fan, '…*nifla*!'

'*Nifla*? That's Hebrew, right?'

'Duh! It means awesome. That's how you make me feel, Gabe.' She leaned down and kissed him. Not with the fierce passion of their lovemaking. This was soft, her lips yielding to his.

'*Ani ohev otakh*,' she said. 'I love you.'

'*Ani ohev otakh*,' he repeated with a smile.

How was it possible to live this life and still find time to fall in love again? He asked himself the question, then dismissed it. It just was. Eli just…was. It worked, and that was what mattered.

'What time is it?' she asked.

'Midday. Where's Stella?'

'She went into town. I said we'd meet her in the bar later. She's going to text me when she gets back. Let's save mission talk till we're together. It'll save doing it all twice.'

'Agreed. Now, Miss Eli Schochat, I don't know about you, but I'm feeling so *nifla* I think I'd like to go again.'

Eli's eyes popped wide. She grinned.

'Why, Mr Wolfe, what a big…' she reached beneath the covers and squeezed him, '… you have.'

'All the better to ravish you with,' he growled.

Later, while Eli slept beside him, Gabriel checked his emails. Just one, from Don.

Subject line: Pennant

Hello Old Sport,

Interesting little souvenir your man Yusuf had in his factory. It's from the Boer Freedom and Rights Party. That's what the Afrikaans means.

The BVR is a white separatist movement based in the Northern Cape. Small, but vicious. They've been implicated in the murder of several black politicians and at least two journalists.

The leader's a charming young fellow. Goes by the name of Julius Witaarde. Surname means 'White Earth' if you can believe it. Sounds like a *nom de guerre* to me.

Believe or not, we don't have anything else on them. Not really our sphere of interest, you might say. Six wasn't much help either. The BVR is, and I quote, 'SLAFA': 'small, local and far away'.

Follow it up.

Yours, aye,

Don

* * *

Guests at Beau Rivage could always opt to dine in the city, but not many bothered. The Spirit House restaurant offered some of the best cooking in Vientiane and the best view. Traffic in diners came the other way.

Tables on a terrace across the road from the hotel looked out over the vast Mekong as it flowed towards its delta in Vietnam, eight hundred miles to the south.

One of those tables, separated from its neighbours by ten feet, thanks to a US-currency-smoothed intervention with the restaurant manager, was currently occupied by Gabriel, Eli and Stella.

Beneath a wide parasol, citronella candles did a reasonable job of keeping the mosquitos at bay, assisted by liberal applications of weapons-grade insect repellent. To the west, a sunset of orange, pink, purple and green had drawn dozens of tourists to take photos. Charcoal-grey clouds speared horizontally across the sky.

A bottle of Chassagne-Montrachet sat in an aluminium ice bucket, its sides beaded with condensation. Gabriel had selected it, white burgundy being his favourite wine. Its creamy toast-and-butter and apricots' flavour reminded him of long evenings sitting in the garden in Aldeburgh with Eli.

'Cheers, ladies!' he said, raising his glass. They clinked rims and drank. 'So, now we're all here, do you want to tell me about G-City?'

Stella and Eli took turns describing their final, fateful meeting in the Oasis Lounge. When Eli reached the part where the Syrian contract killer had tried to set them up, Gabriel sat forward.

'Syrian?'

'That's what he said. We think he was telling the truth, don't we, Stel?'

Stella nodded.

'He was close to death and he knew it.'

'Did he say who hired him to kill the princess?'

'No,' Eli said. 'He died right after we asked him.'

'He denied it was the Israelis and we got the whole confession on film,' Stella added. 'It's back in England being processed by our forensics people.'

'What about you, Gabe?' Eli asked. 'What did you turn up in Dubai?'

'Not a lot, to be honest. The guy running the processing factory hinted he might know people, but I think he was bluffing, trying to get something for nothing. But, I did take this.'

He pulled out his phone and showed them the picture of the pennant.

'What does that say?' Stella asked, executing a deft reverse-pinch on the screen to enlarge the image. 'Boer what?'

'*Boerevryheid an Regte.* It means Boer Freedom and Rights. They're a white separatist movement in South Africa.'

'You think they were involved somehow?'

'They're doing business with the boss of an ivory-carving factory. That means they're involved in the illegal trade. South Africa is Botswana's southern neighbour, so there's a good chance their involvement is at the sharp end. Or, as my new friend Yusuf would probably call it, the top of the supply chain.'

'They're poaching,' Stella said. 'Makes sense. Movements need money. Ivory's incredibly valuable.'

'And they'd have guns, too, Hunting rifles, shotguns, whatever,' Eli added, sitting forward.

'I'll tell you what else is interesting,' Stella said. 'It's been on my mind since the other night.' She sipped her wine. 'That is, actually, the nicest bottle of wine I have ever tasted.'

'Come on,' Eli said, 'don't keep us in suspense.'

'Sorry. Why was the Syrian guy in Botswana? Bit of a coincidence, don't you think?'

Eli opened her mouth, then closed it again. She frowned and put a finger to the top of her nose.

Gabriel leaned closer and dropped his voice, even though the nearest person was several yards distant.

'Let's work it backwards. He kills the princess in Windsor. We think he meets and kills Lieberman there, too. He left soil from Botswana in the sniper nest.'

'So he'd come from there. We know Lieberman didn't,' Eli said.

'But why? Why was he in Bots in the first place?'

'Another hit?' Stella asked.

'I don't see it, do you? Those guys are expensive hires. Crime in Bots seemed to be mostly low-level thuggery.'

'Apart from the ivory poaching,' Stella said. Then her eyes lit up. 'That's it! What if al-Javari was involved, too?'

'In the poaching?' Gabriel asked.

'Yes!'

'How?'

'I don't know. Was he protection?'

'Wait,' Eli said in an urgent whisper. 'Don't forget the BVR angle. You've got South African white separatists and a Syrian contract killer active in Botswana at the same time. He killed Princess Alexandra. It looks at least possible that they were involved in killing the Paras and the Botswana guys. Two sets of foreign killers in one place. They're linked. They must be.'

Stella closed the distance between her and Eli still further, shuffling her chair closer.

'Slow down, Eli. I agree it looks suspicious. But we have no evidence linking him to them. It's all circumstantial.'

Eli sat back and folded her arms across her chest.

'They are. I'm telling you. I can feel it,' she hissed. 'I know about contract killers and I know how the need for a homeland drives people on, sometimes beyond where they should go.'

Gabriel finished his glass and signalled to the waiter for another bottle.

'Aren't we forgetting something?' he asked.

'What?' Eli said.

'The client for the shooting,' he said. 'Who paid al-Javari?'

'That,' Stella said with finality, 'is the sixty-four thousand dollar question.' She leaned forwards. 'There's something I wanted to tell you. I heard from my boss, Callie, earlier. She wants me back in London. Now we know it was al-Javari, there's nothing more for me to do out here. I need to be back there, where our resources are.'

Gabriel saw Eli's face fall as Stella delivered the news. He realised how close the two women had become over the previous couple of weeks. He liked Stella, too, but Eli and she had formed a close bond. Strengthened, no doubt, by fighting their way out of the Oasis Lounge and then offing a Syrian contract killer.

'Can we meet up in London?' Eli asked.

'Sure!' Stella said with a smile. 'It would be a great idea for you to talk to Callie. Give her your take on events.'

'I meant,' Eli hesitated, 'socially.'

'I'd love that,' Stella said, smiling. 'When you're back, call me. We'll go out for a few wines.'

Eli nodded, then went to Stella and hugged her. As he watched the two women embrace, Gabriel felt some of the tension that had knotted up his guts leave him. He inhaled deeply and sighed it out. He was thinking about the soil. Three men and one woman had been on that training tower. What were they missing?

39

Three days later, Gabriel was returning from the Avis office on Rue Setthathirath behind the leather steering wheel of a long, low Mercedes CLS in a dazzling white paint job. He'd cruised back, enjoying the admiring stares of little boys, who grinned and waved as he purred past them. He smiled and waved back, trying out his Laotian through the open window.

'Suh-bye-dee!' Hello!

'Sa bai di bo?' How are you?

The boys would grin even wider, revealing dazzling teeth and clap their palms together at their sternum in a respectful *nop*, shouting back the greeting, sometimes in French, others English.

'Hello! How are you?'

'Bonjour! Ça va?'

Only closing the window when the heat became oppressive, he took a right on Quai Fa Ngum towards the Beau Rivage. The street in front was thronging with tuk-tuks, mopeds, ox carts and taxis, all fighting for a few square metres of roadway. He was forced to slow the big coupe to a crawl amidst the chaos.

White-feathered chickens clucked from the confines of a blue plastic crate lashed to the seat of a Honda 50. On another, a woman with a baby strapped to her front clamped a bulging string basket of melons between her knees as a toddler standing up on the seat behind her dug its pudgy fingers into her shoulders. Yellow dogs with grey muzzles darted in and out of the traffic, occasionally snapping at the bare calves of moped riders and earning angry kicks for their troubles.

A sharp rap on the glass by his left ear jerked him to full alertness. He turned his head to see a round brown face surmounted by a beige and green peaked cap looking in at him through the darkened window. He thumbed the switch.

The traffic cop's face wasn't just the beautiful shade of caramel all Laotians bore; it was overlaid with a reddish tinge, and sheened with sweat. *Poor bugger. I'd be hot, too, if they made me wear that get-up.* Over the cop's shirt, beneath which a white tee-shirt was visible, he wore a zipped-up pocketed vest and a hi-vis TRAFFIC POLICE tabard. White nylon gloves, tight at the wrist, completed the uniform.

Gabriel smiled up at the sweaty cop.

'*Suh-bye-dee.*'

'*Americaine*?' the cop asked.

'*Non, monsieur. Anglais.*'

The cop nodded, beaming.

'Princess Diana. Very pretty lady.'

It was hard to disagree. Did the cop know Diana was dead? That her distant relative by marriage was, also? He decided not to find out.

'Is there a problem, officer?' he asked.

'Today market day. Traffic very, very bad.'

'Yes. I can see.'

The cop favoured Gabriel with a long look, directing his gaze in the direction of his inside jacket pocket.

'You want go faster?'

He leaned his right arm on the Merc's windowsill so that his hand, fingers opening like a flower, draped inside.

Gabriel nodded. From his wallet he fished out a five-dollar bill. It vanished inside the curling petals. Smiling, the cop withdrew his arm then turned and marched into the centre of the knot of stationary mopeds, carts and tuk-tuks in front of the car.

He reached down to his hip. For one horrific moment, Gabriel imagined he was about to pull the black pistol from its polished leather holster and start shooting.

Instead, it came up gripping a silver whistle. Several long, shrill blasts followed. All eyes were on the cop. In a voice loud enough to wake the dead, he began bellowing, first in Laotian, then French, ordering the assorted road users to clear the way.

Little by little, and with much good-natured jostling and bantering, they parted before the Merc's predatory grille like the Red Sea before Moses.

Waving his thanks, and praying fervently they didn't take him for what he so obviously was, an arrogant, rich Western tourist, Gabriel eased the car onwards until he escaped the jam and found the relative freedom of an uncongested part of the road.

* * *

Before leaving for the ivory market, Gabriel and Eli changed into the outfits they'd bought especially for the trip. They'd decided to make an impression rather than going for anything subtle. In Gabriel's case, a pinstriped suit, canary-yellow tie and matching pocket square and polished black Oxfords.

'Well?' he said. 'What do you think?'

She pursed her lips.

'Merchant banker.'

'OK, then, let's see how you interpreted the brief,' he said.

Eli disappeared into the bathroom. Ten minutes later, as he was checking his watch for the third time, the door opened and she emerged.

Gabriel's eyes widened, involuntarily.

'Wow!' was all he could manage.

Eli stood before him, one hip cocked like a fashion model. She wore a black silk flying suit, zipped up the front and fastened at the neck with press-studs. On her feet, calf-length black leather biker boots with stainless-steel toecaps. She'd pulled her abundant hair back into a bun fastened high on the back of her head. Heavy black eye makeup and red lipstick added to the combination of sexiness and menace.

But it was the item dangling from her leather belt that captured Gabriel's attention.

40

An eighteen-inch black polished baton lay along her right thigh. From its tip protruded two stubby metal contacts.

'Is that what it appears to be?' he asked.

'Amazing what you can find if you know how to ask nicely,' Eli said. 'Four thousand volts. From a very nice man called Monsieur Nam. Apparently his main customers are in farming. I got this, too,' she said, reaching behind her back and pulling out a short folding knife with a thin blade the shape of a claw.

'Karambit. Very nice. I don't suppose you got anything for me?'

Eli pouted.

'Aww, did Gabwiel think I'd forgotten his pwesents?'

She disappeared into the bathroom and emerged clutching a black plastic carrier bag.

Gabriel accepted it and emptied the contents out onto the bed. A second karambit, a blued-steel knuckle duster and two small canisters about the length of his palm.

He pointed at the canisters.

'Mace?'

'PAVA. According to the manager of Vientiane Police Supply Store, the cops here have to buy their own PPE, sorry, personal protection equipment. It's a very concentrated pepper spray. Incapacitation guaranteed if you can hit them in the eyes, severe restriction of action if you get them in the nose or mouth. One each.'

Feeling much more comfortable knowing that between them they had enough hardware to be deadly in any close quarter encounter, yet hoping they wouldn't need it, Gabriel led the way to the car.

He took a seat in the back, while Eli sat behind the wheel. She twisted around in her seat.

'Let's go over it one last time.'

'I'm the buyer,' Gabriel said. 'Representing Russian interests in England. You're my driver-slash-bodyguard.'

They'd argued it back and forth over the preceding couple of days, but Gabriel had swung it by reminding her of Fang Jian's Lotus Blossoms. There was something about female bodyguards that threw off male adversaries.

'We make a sample purchase today, say we're going to present it to our big client in London and, if he likes it, come back for a bulk shipment,' Eli said.

'And while we're there, we make discreet enquiries about the BVR. Say we're interested in investing upstream, too,' Gabriel finished. 'You think it'll work?'

'It'll have to. This is our last remaining lead.'

The big Mercedes was silent inside, apart from the faint whisper from the air conditioning. Eli drove west along an unnamed road that tracked the Mekong's Laotian bank. Very occasionally, they'd see a fishing boat. The thin brown-skinned man holding the tiller or casting nets would pause in his labours, shade his eyes then hold up a long, lean arm in greeting.

On the Thai side of the river, palms, huge, fat-trunked ferns and other unnameable trees blocked out any view inland. Gabriel had trained for jungle warfare in Brunei. They'd spent days, then weeks living in one hundred percent humidity, either alone or in a small patrol.

The days were spent fighting through foliage laced with saw-toothed edges, four-inch-long thorns, or leaking poisonous sap that raised blisters the size of poker chips on any exposed skin. He'd become accustomed to, though not happy about, sleeping in dry clothes then waking, packing them into a waterproof bag and squelching his way into the previous day's wet outfit.

He'd been prepared for it. And it was only training, after all. As the jungle across the water rolled past, he imagined himself a farm-boy from somewhere like Kansas, drafted into the hell that was Vietnam.

One day you were driving a John Deere across a wheat field that stretched to the horizon, yellow-gold below and a dazzling blue above. The next, up to your waist in stinking swamp water, slapping away mosquitos the size of sparrows, your horizon truncated to two feet in front of your nose. Slashing at the grabbing, coiling, entangling vegetation while all the time fearing the bullet, grenade or shit-tipped punji stick that would end your life before it had properly begun.

How would they have coped? He feared he knew the answer. Not just from watching documentaries and reading military histories, but from talking to vets of that conflict during trips to the USA. Alcohol. Marijuana. Heroin. Suicide.

'We're here,' Eli said from far away, breaking the spell and jerking Gabriel back to the present. 'Tad Thong Road.'

He looked forward. She rolled imperceptibly to a stop in a clearing before an ornate stone-built church, its squat square tower surmounted by a cross whose horizontal member had slipped out of true and now hung at twenty degrees off true. A rose window above the gothic doorway depicted the crucifixion in stained glass. Here and there, irregular black stars interrupted the scene of Christ's passion on Calvary.

Theirs was by no means the only vehicle in the improvised car park. It might have been an advert for a high-end rental outfit, or a millionaires' car show. He saw a couple more Mercs, also a Bentley Continental in glittering metallic kingfisher blue, a brace of Lamborghini Urus SUVs, one black, one gun-metal, and a midnight-blue Range Rover, emblem of understated but still magnificent success from the shooting parties of Scotland to Rodeo Drive in Beverly Hills.

Eli climbed out of the front seat then came round to hold the door open for Gabriel. Two guards flanked the church doors, AK-47s slung over their impressive shoulders. They wore the regulation stony gaze of their breed. Plus in the left-hand man's case, a broken nose, and in his companion's a jagged scar bisecting his right eyebrow and continuing down across his eye socket to his cheek.

Broken Nose held up his right hand, palm outwards. He stepped forward, unslinging his AK as he came towards them. Behind him, Jagged Scar did the same, yanking the charging lever back for added drama.

Eli stood to one side.

'I am looking for the Pompidou Centre,' Gabriel said, in English.

'You're a long way from Paris,' Broken Nose said.

'But Vientiane is cheaper.'

Broken Nose grunted.

'No firearms.'

Gabriel held his suit jacket wide then lifted the back and executed a full circle. Eli turned slowly on the spot. Though his eyes lingered on the baton, Broken Nose waved them in with a grunt.

Inside, it was apparent the congregation had already gathered. Sitting in groups in the pews or standing in huddles were gathered an array of men and the odd woman who fitted Gabriel's mental category, 'foe'.

He saw portly men in the Arab combo of *thawb* and *ghutra*, looking for all the world like oil sheikhs, which, he supposed they might well be. Other Arabs dressed in conservative, western-cut business suits. Black guys wore beige and mustard suits, sporting plenty of bling at neck and wrist.

All eyes were on Gabriel and Eli as they entered the formerly sacred space. The gazes were at the least curious, if not hostile. But they had been allowed in, so they had sufficient credentials to buy. Conversations started up again, and Gabriel picked out a swirl of languages and accents, including in one corner a Belfast accent thick enough to need subtitles.

Gabriel and Eli sat at a pew right at the back of the church. Above them, a sad-eyed Madonna looked down on them, as if reproaching them for being part of such a gathering.

Gabriel jerked his chin up at the blue-robed statue.

'If her son were here, he'd have a fine time kicking over the tables, don't you think?'

She moved towards him.

'If he did, I hope he'd bring some muscle. This lot would crucify him for sure, if he tried it.'

A loud clapping from the front of the church silenced the chatter.

A tall Laotian appeared at the lectern. He was bald and the dome of his skull gleamed in the light entering through the stained glass windows.

'Gentlemen,' he intoned, 'and, ladies, welcome. My name is John-Antoine Vong. We are ready for you now. If you would like to make your way to the vestry, the vendors are ready for you.'

The buyers not already standing got to their feet and everyone headed for a narrow doorway in the gloom at the far end of the church. Gabriel and Eli hung back, then followed the last of the main crowd.

Once inside the vestry, Eli gasped.

The room, forty feet by sixty, was racked out to beyond head-height with industrial steel shelving. Every ten feet or so, the shelving broke with a gap. In the centre of each section stood a man armed with a clipboard, pen, and walkie-talkie.

But it was the objects piled, stacked and layered on the shelves that had drawn the air from Eli's lungs.

Gabriel tried to take it all in, without looking surprised. Five-foot tusks carved to represent a procession of animals entering Noah's Ark. Buddhist temples of such intricate tracery it was impossible to imagine the filigree had been achieved by human hand. Intricate geometric ornaments on which octagons tessellated with squares, hexagons interlocked and double helixes like DNA strands curled around each other in a seemingly endless spiral.

Buyers and sellers were clearly used to the process and the noise level rose as orders were placed, pages on clipboards were flipped over, commands were issued into walkie-talkies and haggling broke out.

'I'm going to have a look around,' Eli said.

The owner of the Belfast accent spoke from close beside Gabriel's left side.

'First time, eh?'

Gabriel turned to see a man a few inches shorter than himself looking up at him. Sandy hair cut short and parted on the right, pale-blue eyes, a couple of days' beard growth tinting his red cheeks grey.

'Yeah. Not yours, then?'

'Me? No, pal. Been coming here for a few years. Best source of untraceable cash on the planet just now. Take a shitload of this gear and, two months later, you can turn it into Semtex, AKs, whatever you might need for your own personal struggle, know what I mean? So, what's yours?'

Belfast winked. Gabriel favoured him with a grim smile in return.

'What's my what?'

'Struggle.'

'No struggle. I'm buying for clients.'

'Clients, eh? Chinese?'

'Russians.'

'Plenty of money, those oligarchs.'

'Enough to keep me in business. Listen, my name's—'

'Let me stop you right there,' Belfast said, holding up a hand. 'No names, no pack drill, know what I'm saying?'

Gabriel shrugged.

'Fair enough. I have another line of business. Can we talk somewhere a little quieter?'

Belfast's pale eyes flicked left and right, then settled back on Gabriel.

'How about where we came in? Place is quiet now.'

Gabriel followed him back into the main part of the church, not before catching Eli's eye and signalling for her to follow them.

Belfast wandered all the way out of the church into the car park.

'What is it you wanted to talk about?'

'I heard there's a certain South African political outfit involved upstream in the trade,' he began. 'I have some very powerful contacts who want to meet their leader.'

'Sorry, mate, no idea what you're talking about. Cigarette?' he said, holding out a pack of Marlboro.

Gabriel shook his head.

'They'll kill you.'

Belfast laughed, a high-pitched chuckle.

'Aye, well something sure as hell will.'

He lit up, inhaled deeply, then blew it out skywards with a satisfied sigh.

Gabriel had done this dance before. He knew the steps.

'These contacts of mine are wealthy as well. They would be prepared to compensate anyone who could help with an introduction. But,' he hesitated, 'if you're not the right person, forgive me. I'll go and talk to one of the others back there.'

'You think I can be bought, is that it?'

'I didn't say that. I can see you're engaged in a political project of your own. One involving,' he paused briefly, as if searching for a delicate way of phrasing it, 'non-conventional means of reaching your goals. Well, so are my contacts. They believe they could learn from the South Africans.'

He watched Belfast running the mental numbers. Calculating odds. Assessing risk and reward. Gabriel was pretty sure he knew which way the dice would land. They were miles from anywhere in a backwoods deconsecrated Catholic church on the Thai-Laotian border. He looked across the water. Anyone without the right password would end up floating downstream with a couple of ounces of lead in their body. Which meant Gabriel was clean. It was a no-brainer.

'And when you say "a certain South African political outfit"...' Belfast said.

'BVR. That's the—'

'*Boerevryheid an Regte.* Yes, I know. In my line of work, it pays to know who else is engaged in a struggle, even if they are a bunch of racists.'

'You don't approve, then?' Gabriel asked, marvelling that Belfast could afford scruples, given his 'line of work'.

'*We* are fighting to right a historic wrong imposed on Ireland by Oliver-fucking-Cromwell and enforced by the British Crown ever since. *They* are—'

'Fighting for a homeland where they can live according to their customs without interference by an over-mighty, corrupt majority-governed state they don't recognise.'

Anger flashed across Belfast's face, then it was gone. Gabriel felt sick to his stomach. Why was he having to stand here discussing politics with someone he was sure would think nothing of shooting dead his former comrades-in-arms? Not to mention blowing up women and children with car bombs, nail bombs or whatever else he could fashion from his ivory-into-Semtex supply chain.

Belfast took another deep drag on his cigarette.

'Aye, well, maybe we should leave politics to the politicians, eh? I'm just a lowly foot soldier. Suppose I *could* point you at the right person. What sort of compensation are we talking about?'

There it was again. The little green light of greed winking at Gabriel, this time from the depths of Belfast's eyes.

'I am authorised to offer ten thousand dollars.' Gabriel patted the inside pocket of his suit jacket. 'Cash. Here and now. If,' he paused, 'the information is solid. Anything less than diamond-hard would lead to some very,' another pause, 'unfortunate consequences.'

Belfast glared at him. His colour disappeared, leaving his cheeks pale behind the stubble.

'Are you *threatening* me?' he said in an incredulous tone of voice.

Gabriel smiled down at him.

'Do I need to threaten you?'

Belfast's stare intensified and Gabriel had time to observe a squiggled blue-green vein pulsing beneath the translucent skin at his right temple. His lips tightened to a mean line.

Gabriel counted in his head.

One…two…three…

He visualised drawing the karambit and laying Belfast's face open.

41

Belfast laughed.

'Fuck you, you English cunt!' he said, smiling now. 'You've got a pair of brass balls on you, I'll give you that.'

'So you *can* help.'

'Show me the money.'

Gabriel reached into his suit pocket, let his knuckles glide over the karambit's knurled grip and withdrew the bundle of hundred-dollar notes. No thicker than a deck of cards, it wouldn't look very impressive unless the viewer could see the 100s printed in the corners of the topmost note.

Gabriel made sure Belfast got a good long look before replacing it in his pocket.

'So?' Gabriel said.

'Let me make a call.'

Gabriel watched as Belfast wandered away to the edge of the clearing before pulling out a phone. The man's head nodded, shook, bobbed again. His free hand described random movements in the air, chopping down, holding up the index finger, patting an imaginary animal. Finally, he nodded emphatically, before ending the call and walking back to Gabriel.

'It's on. My BVR contact says he'll send one of his guys to meet you.'

'Here?'

'No. Jo'burg. Be there day after tomorrow. A bar called the Blue Springbok on Smit Street. Seven in the evening.' He held up his phone and took Gabriel's picture, then tapped the screen a few times. 'There! Just sent him your mugshot. Now he knows what you look like.'

It was a good idea, a little bit of tradecraft, but it came over like a threat. Gabriel Wolfe didn't like being threatened. In that moment he made a decision.

'Thanks. I suppose you want your money.'

Belfast grinned. The little green light came back on.

'That would be nice, yes.'

Gabriel made a show of looking around. He stared at the guards on the door, who were eyeing them with bored expressions.

'Not here. Let's go over there, behind the church. Out of sight of Tweedledum and Tweedledee over there. Wouldn't want them getting any ideas.'

Belfast looked over Gabriel's shoulders.

'Aye, maybe not. I saw them take a guy's hand off at the wrist a couple of months back for trying to cheat one of the vendors.'

Gabriel nodded his head towards a stand of palms choked with low-growing ferns and creepers to the left of the church. The two men walked side by side until the vegetation thickened and pressed against the ancient stone walls of the church. He stood back and let Belfast precede him.

Belfast pushed his way between two palms and kicked his way through the undergrowth until he emerged into a small space no more than six feet square. It smelled strongly of urine and Gabriel realised they'd stumbled into what passed for an outside toilet.

The little man turned, hand out.

Gabriel placed the bundle of notes in his palm.

'You don't mind if I count it,' Belfast said. A statement, not a question.

'Not at all. Tell me, you said you're a foot soldier. You chalk up many kills?'

Belfast grinned, though he didn't lift his gaze from the notes rustling between his thumbs.

'One or two, you know? Squaddies, mainly. Couple of RUC. Eejits wouldn't know one end of a—'

The rest of the sentence was lost in a gargling wheeze.

Blood sprayed out in a translucent fan from the rent in Belfast's throat, spattering against the glossy leaves of a fern with a sound like rain. He turned, eyes wide, clutching his throat, searching Gabriel's face for an explanation.

Gabriel held up the karambit, whose blade was smeared red.

'Fuck you, and fuck your project,' he hissed, before kicking Belfast in the chest and sending him toppling backwards into the soft embrace of the lush green undergrowth.

Gabriel pulled a couple of the larger leaves over the body, then reached in and took Belfast's phone. He stepped back. He couldn't do much about the blood spatter, but of Belfast himself, there was no sight. He cleaned the blade on the ground, then folded it and replaced it in his pocket.

He found Eli near the doorway, deep in conversation with a dark-skinned woman dressed in a chocolate-brown trouser suit, her thick black hair tied back in a ponytail.

'Time to go,' Gabriel said.

Eli nodded.

'A pleasure to meet you, Maria,' she said.

The two women shook hands and then Gabriel and Eli were walking smartly back to the Merc.

'Everything OK?' Eli asked.

'Yes. But we shouldn't hang around. I just killed a guy.'

'What? Where?'

'Back there. He set up a meet with a BVR contact in Johannesburg. Two days' time.'

They reached the car. Eli climbed behind the wheel and Gabriel sat beside her. As she swung the car around in a circle, past the

Bentley's imposing front grille, a couple of white men emerged from the church, their heads turning from side to side.

'Drive,' Gabriel said. 'Nice and easy.'

Back on the riverbank road, Eli glanced up at the rear-view mirror.

'Nobody behind us. You think they were looking for him?'

'I don't know. But I don't want to find out. Give this beast some juice and let's check out. We need to get out of Vientiane.'

42

JOHANNESBURG

'What time is it?' Gabriel asked.

He was sitting on the bed towelling his hair. They'd checked in an hour earlier and he realised he had no sense of time or date beyond what his watch or phone told him. The perils for criss-crossing so many time zones in such a short space of time.

'Six-thirty,' Eli replied. 'It's a ten-minute taxi ride, I checked.'

She was sitting in an armchair, feet tucked beneath her, reading a book.

Gabriel dressed in pale chinos, a white shirt and a navy linen jacket. He slipped his bare feet into tobacco-brown boat shoes.

'How do I look?'

'I like that better than the suit. Too formal. That's much more you.'

Gabriel nodded. He patted his pockets reflexively. They'd left their newly acquired hardware behind in Vientiane.

Catching the movement, Eli grinned.

'You'll be fine. After what you got up to at the church, not being armed is probably better all round.'

'He deserved it.'

'I know. But you need to get to the BVR. Killing people won't help.'

Gabriel crossed the room, planted a kiss on her lips and drew back.

'I'll see you later.'

'Take care.'

'I will.'

* * *

The taxi driver knew the Blue Springbok and dropped Gabriel outside at 6.50 p.m. Gabriel entered the bar, passing beneath an electric-blue neon outline of South Africa's own antelope. Inside the place was busy, but not noisy, the early evening crowd consisting largely of office workers, to judge by the clothes. He made his way to the bar and ordered a glass of chenin blanc.

He found a corner table where he could observe the rest of the bar. With his back protected by two walls, he felt about as relaxed as was possible. Low-level jazz, something with sax and piano, was issuing from ceiling-mounted speakers. He looked up: one was suspended directly overhead. *Good, a little extra cover for our conversation.*

He sipped the chilled wine. It was delicious. He caught a brief sensation of eating pear drops before he tasted pineapple and peach.

A young woman in a white jacket and enormous gold hoop earrings came towards the table. She was smiling.

'Excuse me, is anyone using this chair?' she asked, laying a hand on the back of one of the two others at the table.

Gabriel smiled back.

'Not that one, but leave me the other.'

'Sure,' she said, 'thanks.'

She dragged the chair over to another table. As she moved out of his eye line he saw a new patron enter the bar and felt the familiar twinge in his gut. Showtime.

The man stood six foot six minimum. Broad shoulders and a

narrow waist said 'bodybuilder'. His blonde hair was cut short in a military buzzcut and his lowering brow gave him a simian appearance. A white shirt clung to his massive pectoral muscles, its rolled-up sleeves revealing thick forearms fuzzed with reddish-blonde hair.

Gabriel watched him scanning the bar. Prepared himself for the conversation that would take him closer to whoever had murdered the Paras.

A scream to his right jerked his head round. The woman who'd asked to take the chair had jumped to her feet and was running across the bar towards the gorilla. His face lit up with a dazzling smile and as she arrived he held his arms wide. She leaped at him and he caught her, lifting her up so that she could wrap her legs round him.

They kissed energetically, then he set her down and she led him, beaming, to the group of people at her table,

'Guys, this is Marco,' she said, to smiles from her friends. 'The man I'm going to marry.'

Handshakes, fist-bumps, kisses on cheeks, then the group settled down. Gabriel shook his head, smiling to himself and took another sip of his wine while tuning out their excitable conversation.

'Do you think she'll wear ivory on her big day?' a quiet voice enquired.

Gabriel turned round.

A man stood beside him, about half the size of the bridegroom-to-be, an open expression on his tanned face.

Gabriel cursed inwardly for allowing himself to be blindsided so easily. Without a pre-arranged password or code phrase he'd have to rely on subtler means of establishing the bona fides of his contact.

'I suppose she might. Though white's more traditional.'

Non-committal. No offer to drag up a seat, which would be odd if the stranger was only passing the time of day.

'Passing through?' the man said, his dark eyes focusing on Gabriel as a bird might observe an insect.

'Yes. I was in Laos a couple of days ago.'

'Lovely country.'

'Very.'

The stranger gestured at the remaining spare chair.

'May I?'

'Gabriel nodded.

'Please.'

The stranger signalled a passing waitress. She arrived seconds later.

'A glass of wine please. What is that?' he asked Gabriel.

'Chenin blanc. The Stellenrust 2015.'

'Excellent choice. I'll have the same.'

Once the waitress had departed, the stranger held out a hand.

'Oscar Coetzee.'

'Alec Jensen.'

They shook. The little man's grip was stronger than his size suggested.

Coetzee pulled out a phone, swiped the screen then held it out, the screen towards Gabriel.

'The light was different in Vientiane to here. Greener. It makes you look a little, forgive me, sickly,' he said.

Gabriel nodded.

'Stinking country was full of gooks anyway. I was glad to get away,' he said, as if uttering racist sentiments in public was commonplace in the rainbow nation. The waitress returned with a glass of wine

Coetzee held it aloft.

'*Gesondheid*!' It came out *Guh-sont-hate*.

'Cheers!'

They clinked rims. Coetzee took a mouthful of the wine and swirled it round his mouth before swallowing.

'Man, that's good. But there are better South Africa wines, you know.'

'I'm sure there are. Do you have connections in the winemaking business?'

'We make it where I come from. The Northern Cape. No reds, though.' He paused. 'Only whites.'

'That's good,' Gabriel said. 'I prefer whites.'

'Tell me, Alec, what brings you to South Africa?'

'Tourism. I've heard it's a great country.'

Coetzee nodded.

'Used to be much better. Until *they* took over and fucked it up,' he added in a quieter voice.

'Agreed. Listen,' Gabriel wiped a slick of sweat from his top lip, 'I have some associates back in England who share your views on that particular subject. They want to extend a hand of friendship. To you and,' he paused, then dropped his own voice, 'the BVR.'

Coetzee frowned.

'Sorry, the who?'

'Oh, right, I get it,' Gabriel said, dropping his right eyelid in the most fractional of winks. He leaned right across the table so he was nose-to-nose with Coetzee. 'Never mind. As I said, my associates and I want to show solidarity with our white brothers and sisters. It's part of a global movement we're spearheading. I'm sure you can imagine its core beliefs.'

Coetzee smiled politely as if he'd been confronted with someone speaking a foreign language. But Gabriel could see it for what it was. A blind, in case anyone who shouldn't be was listening in. Smart, he had to admit.

'I'm afraid I don't know what you're talking about, Alec. But as I said, you clearly know your wines. Why don't you come up North and I'll give you a tour around our winery? I think you'll be impressed.'

Gabriel smiled.

'I would like that very much. Very much indeed. When?'

'How about the day after tomorrow?'

'Works for me.'

'Where are you staying? I'll come and pick you up.'

'The Marriott on De Korte Street.'

'Shall we say 8.00 a.m.?'

'Perfect. Just one thing. I'm travelling with a companion. Protection, you might call it. My job is purely administrative, you see, and she, well, she is more experienced in the,' he rubbed his chin, 'more *dramatic* aspects of my work.'

Coetzee shook his head.

'Sorry. No friends, no companions, no bodyguards. You alone or forget it.'

Gabriel pretended to hesitate. Inwardly he was glad Eli was off the table. He knew it was wrong, some kind of long-dormant chivalry, but all of a sudden he didn't want to put her in further danger.

He nodded after what he judged was a suitable interval.

'Fine. No companion.'

Gabriel found Eli in the hotel bar. She'd put on a simple white cotton dress that showed off her olive skin, tanned now to a soft honey colour. And she'd put her hair up, revealing turquoise earrings that matched a string of beads round her throat. As he walked in, Gabriel noticed that several of the men present, and a couple of the women, were casting glances in her direction. He smiled. *She's mine, though.*

She kissed him.

'How did it go?'

'Like a charm. We made a date for the day after tomorrow. He's taking me up country. Presumably to vet me and see whether my "associates" and I will be of use to the cause.'

She smiled.

'Great! So when do we set off?'

'It's not "we". It's me. I said I was travelling with protection but he said it was an invitation for one.'

Eli shook her head.

'That's a really bad idea, Gabe. You don't know what you're walking into. Listen,' she said, raising her voice, so that a few of the nearer patrons turned their heads. 'Listen,' she repeated, quieter, 'these people, they're dangerous. What if they suspect you're a journalist or a government spy? They'll torture you or kill you. It's what I'd do.'

He moved closer to her, breathing in her perfume.

'One, yes I do know what I'm walking into. What I've walked

into a hundred times before. And I've always walked out again. Two, I know they're dangerous. That's why we're here. But I'm dangerous, too. And three, they may well be suspicious. I'd be worried if they weren't. But I don't think they'll go for the nuclear option. Not if I show them a gesture of goodwill first.'

'What do you mean?'

'I'm going to talk to Don. Have John wire me some money. I'll take it with me as a love gift. We know they need cash. It'll work, El, believe me.'

Eli's lips parted. He waited for her to object. But she said nothing. Just leaned forward and kissed him.

'Do what you have to do then come back to me. That's an order.'

After a late dinner, Gabriel and Eli sat outside under a full moon, sipping brandies. He looked up at the stars, billions of pinpricks in a black velvet blanket. Were *their* stars meant to align? Did Eli see things the same way he did? What if she decided to leave the UK anyway, despite the new British passport? Would he follow her?

He wanted to say yes, wanted to be so sure he would leave behind the country he loved. The job, too. Though he was sure he could find a role in Israel that would give him the same kind of satisfaction as working for The Department.

And yet.

Would it be that easy? Eli felt she wanted to return home. But England was *his* home. He wanted to stay, he realised. Stay and fight. Tammerlane couldn't last for ever, could he? He'd fuck it up like extremists always did, and then the voters would kick him out in four years' time.

He had a flash of insight. A nightmarish vision. Tammerlane suspending political 'business as usual' in the light of some new threat. Declaring a state of emergency. Instituting 'special measures'. Government spokesmen reassuring querulous journalists that normal service would be resumed as soon as was practicable, all the while removing obstacles to their boss remaining in power.

Was that possible? Really? In the UK? It had happened in Africa, hadn't it? More than once. Strongmen elected by an enthusiastic populace who then found they enjoyed holding the reins of power so much they felt it was only right they should tighten their grip.

'Penny for them.'

'Huh?'

He turned. Eli was looking at him with a half-smile.

'Where did you go? I asked you the same question three times. You just zoned out.'

Gabriel sighed.

'I was thinking about home.'

'Aldeburgh, you mean?'

He shook his head.

'Britain. Tammerlane worries me.'

'Worries? Is that all. Because he scares the shit out of me.'

'What were you asking?'

'I think I should get back. If you're making the trip to see the BVR leadership alone, there's nothing for me to do here. I can't just sit around sunbathing. I'll see what Don has for me.'

Gabriel nodded, and finished his brandy.

'Probably best. You can always fly back.'

She tipped the snifter to her lips and drained the last few drops. She stood and took his hand.

'In that case, I need you upstairs, right now.'

43

Two days later

With Eli gone, Gabriel found he was better able to concentrate. His first stop the following day had been a luggage store, where he bought a cheap aluminium-look attaché case. An hour later, he emerged from the Western Union office on Hanover Street swinging the now-heavier case by his left thigh.

He wasn't bothered about his lack of hardware. As a self-declared 'admin' type, it would be out of character to carry anything more dangerous than a pocket calculator. His hands and feet were deadly enough until he could get his hands on something with an edge, a point or a trigger.

But he did want different clothes. A trip to a sporting goods outlet furnished him with a couple of pairs of khaki cargo pants, soft cotton shirts and a tough but lightweight jacket. A thirty-litre daypack, a water bottle, a first aid kit, a wide-brimmed bush hat and a pair of leather hiking boots rounded off the deal, delighting the salesgirl in the store who smiled broadly as she rang his items up on the till.

'Going camping?' she asked.

Gabriel nodded. 'Hunting trip.'

'Great! Hope you do OK.'

Gabriel smiled.

'Oh, I'm sure I will.'

Now he was waiting in the Marriott's reception, reclining in an armchair and waiting for Coetzee. Between his feet sat the daysack, stuffed with a spare outfit and some extra underwear and socks. The attaché case sat on his knees. He'd arranged to collect the rest of his luggage from the hotel on his return to Johannesburg.

He checked his watch: 7.55 a.m. The lobby was full of people, but then he saw Coetzee, sliding between knots of executives, tourists and hotel staff.

He smiled and held out his hand. Placing the attaché case beside him, Gabriel stood and they shook.

'Ready to go, Alec?' Coetzee asked.

'Absolutely.'

Coetzee gestured at the case.

'What's in there?'

'Paperwork.'

Coetzee snorted and rolled his eyes.

'What are you, man, a bloody secretary?' He laughed loudly. 'Come on. It's a fair drive out to the airstrip.'

Gabriel followed Coetzee out of the lobby. A white Range Rover was parked with its back end hard up against a flowering shrub, the purple blossoms it had shorn from the branches lying in a carpet around its base. Gabriel looked at the passenger-side front wing. It looked pristine. Not a dent or a scratch. He made a show of getting muddled about which side was the driver's, then, as he rounded the front of the SUV, fumbled his daysack and dropped it by the front tyre.

As he bent to retrieve it, he looked closer at the trim protecting the corner of the wing. Also undented. But whereas the other trim piece was dusty, this one was gleaming. He could even see a strap of pale-blue protective film adhering to one of the edges. *New, then. That's interesting.*

He grabbed the daypack and straightened and made a 'silly me' gesture to Coetzee, rolling his eyes and holding his free hand to his temple like a pistol.

'We drive on the left here, man. Just like the *old country*,' Coetzee said in a mocking tone.

44

Gabriel stowed his bags on the back seat then climbed in. He inhaled the smell of about three cows' worth of soft leather, overlaid by the pungent stink of tobacco.

Coetzee climbed in and immediately shook a cigarette out from a packet. He lit up and sucked hard, then offered the pack to Gabriel as he released the lungful of smoke with a sigh.

Gabriel shook his head.

'No thanks.'

'No? Fair enough. Can't get enough of them, myself,' Coetzee said, as he selected drive and nosed out onto the access road leading to the street.

A black couple stepped off the kerb in front of him, wheeling their luggage to a waiting taxi.

'Get out of the way, you fucking kaffirs!' he said. Then he turned to Gabriel. 'That's one thing you won't have to worry about where we're going.'

Gabriel smiled. 'Good.' Steeled himself. 'Fucking blacks. Think they own the place.'

'Yah, well they practically do,' Coetzee said, turning right and then pushing the Range Rover hard through the traffic. 'It won't be long before they're stealing white-owned farms, just like Mugabe did in Zim. And that's not a prediction, my friend. That's just a statement of fact.'

Fighting down the urge to break the man's nose with his elbow, and nausea at the language he was being forced to use, Gabriel managed to keep up his side of the race-baiting conversation as Coetzee drove northwest out of Johannesburg.

As the smart suburban streets gave way to longer and longer stretches of unpopulated countryside, Gabriel found himself relaxing. To their right a mountain clad in thick vegetation loomed over the otherwise flat landscape, which continued, uninterrupted, for hundreds of miles.

Tall pencil-shaped cypresses dotted the landscape, which, with its mix of grassland and wooded areas might just as easily have been England. England blown up to a thousand times its usual size, but still. Driving on the left reinforced the impression, which was only broken when he saw a woman with a basket balanced on her head walking by the side of the road.

Coetzee swerved over the white line towards her. Gabriel hissed out a breath and he saw her face contort with fear as Coetzee shot past her at sixty.

'Ha! Gave her a nice little shock, didn't I?' Coetzee crowed as he regained the left-hand carriageway.

After another hour, Coetzee indicated left and pulled off the road onto a red-earth track. They sped along it, raising a tawny cloud that swirled in the SUV's wake, before rolling to a stop on an expanse of graded earth that extended for half a mile in front of them.

'Not exactly Heathrow, old boy, but it serves us fine, eh what?' Coetzee said, in a terrible parody of an upper-class British accent.

Gabriel smiled and got out, wishing, for the thousandth time that he could put a couple of rounds into Coetzee's skull, just to shut him up. He grabbed the attaché case and his daysack.

To their left, a small white plane waited beneath a tree with wide, spreading branches. In its shade, occupying a flimsy-looking camp chair, sat a big man in jeans, chambray shirt and a bush hat. His eyes were obscured by mirror-lensed aviator sunglasses.

Seeing Coetzee and Gabriel, he folded the paper he was reading and dropped it to the ground. He came towards them, smiling.

'This the passenger?' he asked Coetzee.

'I didn't bring him all the way out here to wash the Cessna, if that's what you mean!'

This apparently passed for great wit, and the pilot guffawed, shaking his hand and then coming forward to grasp Gabriel's right hand in an iron grip.

'Name's Brik Todd. Don't get many Pommies out here,' he said, pumping Gabriel's hand and squeezing harder. 'Too soft, I reckon,' he added, winking at Coetzee, whose whinnying laughter set Gabriel's teeth on edge.

Feeling that here at least he could work off some of his building frustration with Coetzee, Gabriel returned the pressure. Smiling broadly, he altered his grip minutely, placing pressure on a nerve bundle he knew lay between the thumb and index finger. Wincing at the unexpected pain, the pilot hurriedly ended the shake.

'Alec Jensen. Something the matter with your hand, Brik?' Gabriel asked.

The pilot scowled and stumped away towards the Cessna, kicking out a couple of grapefruit-sized stones he'd used to chock the wheels.

'I'm heading back to Jo'burg,' Coetzee said. 'Brik'll take good care of you. Have a good trip, yah?'

Five minutes later, after Todd had run through his pre-flight checks, the Cessna was rumbling down the airstrip towards a stand of trees at the far end. With a hundred yards to go, Todd lifted the nose and the plane took to the air. Gabriel turned to his left and watched the ground swing beneath the port wing as Todd banked the plane to the northwest.

The greenish-brown veldt stretched to the horizon, dotted with acacias and other trees Gabriel couldn't begin to name. A sinuous river wound north–south, glittering in the sun like a rope of diamonds on a sage-green velvet cloth.

He watched a huge herd of antelope making their way towards the river, snaking back for a couple of miles.

The Cessna's drone made conversation impossible, which suited him fine.

The flight took four hours. By the time Todd began his descent towards the landing strip, Gabriel felt his body was vibrating in time with the beats of the Cessna's engine.

The landing was rough but secure, and the Cessna rumbled over the ground before Todd swung it in towards a single-storey, cinder-block building. Above its white walls orange-painted steel letters were riveted to a frame:

WELKOM BY NUWE HOOP

'Know any Afrikaans, Alec?' Todd shouted over his shoulder.

Gabriel shook his head.

'It means "Welcome to New Hope". That's the name of our town.'

With his booted feet on Mother Earth again, Gabriel looked around. Beyond the airstrip, he could just make out a cluster of buildings a mile or so distant. Their white shapes floated in the heat haze. He swatted away a fly that landed on his nose and resettled his hat, tugging the brim down to block out the sun.

Todd led him to a white pickup, its sides coated with red dust.

Gabriel climbed in. Todd booted the throttle, spinning all four wheels and raising a cloud of dust before they found traction and the pickup lurched off towards New Hope.

45

NORTHERN CAPE

Todd trundled down the town's main street, a wide, dusty, unmetalled road. No markings, traffic lights, parking meters or pedestrian crossings broke up the tyre-flattened thoroughfare as it ran, ruler-straight, from one end of the settlement to the other.

Something about the dust and the relative absence of vehicles put Gabriel in mind of the one-horse towns in the Westerns he'd been so mad about as a boy. Something itched at the back of his brain. He couldn't reach to scratch it.

'Hotel,' Todd said, pointing at a single-storey building in a ranch house style. He continued pointing, first to the left, then the right. 'Pub, general store, bodyshop, sporting goods. Yah, we have everything we need out here, man. And nothing we don't.'

Gabriel scanned the people thronging the pavements on each side of the street. He realised what had sent his soldier's 'spider sense' pinging. Everyone was white. There must have been a hundred or more people, and not a black or brown face among them.

'Like kaffirs,' he said.

Todd laughed, an ugly sound in the cab's cramped confines.

'In one. This is it, Alec. The capital city.'

'Of?'

'Ha! I'll let Julius tell you,' he said, as he swung the pickup off the main street and down a narrower track towards a fenced compound dominated by a two-storey wooden house fronted by a patch of lawn and a couple of shade trees.

Arriving at the gate, he killed the engine and got out. He looked back in at Gabriel.

'Come on, then. This is why you're here, isn't it?'

Gabriel nodded and climbed out, knuckling his lower back. He reached back in for his bags and followed Todd through the gate and up to the front door.

A furious barking erupted from the side of the house and a large, tawny-coated dog bounded around the corner, coming straight for him. He knelt and let the animal skid to a stop in front of him, its blocky head pushing towards his, slack jaws slobbering as it sniffed his hairline. He offered the back of his hand, fingers curled under, and let the dog sniff, then lick his skin. Apparently satisfied he wasn't a threat, the dog wagged its tail and trotted off, the stiff fur along its spine gradually settling into a softer peak.

'I see you've met Pikko,' a man said from above his head.

Gabriel got to his feet and turned to take in the master of the house whose guard dog he had just charmed into retreat. The master of the house, leader of the BVR and, as was looking increasingly likely, murderer of the fallen Paras and their Botswanan comrades.

Julius Witaarde's bow-shaped mouth was smiling as he held out his right hand. Gabriel noticed a gold signet ring inset with a red seal as he took it. The Afrikaaner's face was composed of angular planes: high cheekbones shadowing a square, clean-shaven jaw, a tall forehead grooved with lines that met in a sharp V between heavy eyebrows. Gabriel estimated his age at somewhere between thirty and thirty-five.

'You must be Alec,' he said, in lightly accented English. 'Julius

Witaarde at your service. Welcome to New Hope, and to my home. Please, come in.'

Glad to be out of the burning sun, Gabriel placed the daysack beneath a coat-rack in the hall. He removed his hat and hung it by the cord over one of the pegs.

Witaarde was wearing khaki shorts and a matching shirt, open at the neck and loose over his hips. Gabriel detected a tell-tale rumple to the fabric over the right side. He followed Witaarde into a kitchen dominated by a plain wooden table, its worn surface scarred by what looked like decades if not hundreds of years of use.

'Drink?' Witaarde asked, standing by a tall refrigerator.

'A lager would be good, if you have one.'

Witaarde smiled, running a hand over his straight dark hair, held in place by some sort of gel into a breaking wave.

'I'm a Boer, of course I have lager!'

He took two bottles from the fridge, flipped the caps off on an opener screwed to the underside of a worktop and motioned for Gabriel to sit at the table.

'*Gesondheid*,' Gabriel said, raising the neck of the bottle and tilting it towards Witaarde.

Witaarde smiled as he clinked his own bottle against Gabriel's.

'*Gesondheid*. I appreciate a man who troubles himself with the culture of a new country.'

Gabriel took a pull on the cold lager, which was excellent: yeasty and lemony.

'My father told me it was good manners.'

'Your father was right. What was his line of work?'

'He was a diplomat. Hong Kong.'

'Ah. Another British colony *vinnig afdraaide gaan*. It's what we say. You know, going downhill fast?'

Gabriel grimaced. It was hard to disagree. In recent years he'd watched as the Chinese had begun dismantling the rule of law and the former colony's independence, despite playing lip service to the 'one country-two systems' mantra.

'You think that's bad,' he said. 'Have you seen what's happening in the UK? They elected a fucking communist, for God's sake.'

'Yah, I saw that. You said, "they"?'

'Yes, you know. The idiots who swallowed Tammerlane's bullshit about free this, free that, free everything for 'the people'. Who do they think's paying for it all?'

Witaarde shrugged.

'Not my fight, Brother, but I feel your pain. It's why New Hope exists.'

Sensing that this was Witaarde's invitation for him to start talking business, Gabriel leaned forwards across the table, pushing the half-empty bottle of lager to one side. Witaarde mirrored the gesture so their faces were only a foot or so apart.

'My friends and I want to help you,' Gabriel said, lowering his voice to a conspiratorial whisper, even though they were alone.

'Help me with what?'

Gabriel smiled.

'Come on, Julius, let's not pussyfoot around. Why do you think I came halfway around the world to meet you? Because I'm telling you, it wasn't for the luxury travel. My kidneys feel like your dog's been chewing on them for the last six hours.'

Witaarde smiled.

'Why don't you tell me what you think you know and we'll take it from there?'

'You are the founder of *Boerevryheid an Regte,* and—'

'Wrong,' Witaarde interrupted. 'That was *my* father.'

'My apologies. You are the *leader* of *Boerevryheid an Regte.*'

Witaarde nodded.

'I am.'

'You believe in the right of white South Africans to establish their own homeland, free of the corrupt control of the black-dominated ANC government in Pretoria. How am I doing so far?'

'Very well. Tell me something, Alec. We have kept a low profile so far. How did you find out so much about us?'

Gabriel smiled and swallowed some more lager.

'My friends and I have what you might call an intelligence department. We make it our business to know about and, if possible, befriend, those organisations around the world that share our worldview. The BVR is one of those organisations. We wish to offer you moral support and something more. May I?' He pointed to the attaché case.

'Please.'

Witaarde shifted his weight in his chair and his hand strayed to his hip.

Gabriel lifted the case onto the table, popped the catches, lifted the lid and swivelled the case round so Witaarde could see its contents.

He had a flashback. A former Delta Force operator named Shaun Cunningham, looking with wonder at a similar sight, moments before Sir Toby Maitland blew his head off by shooting him through the lid. He shook his head to clear the horrific image.

Witaarde closed the lid and regarded Gabriel over the top.

'There's twenty-five thousand US in there,' Gabriel said. 'A token of our goodwill. I'm sure you can put it to good use.'

Witaarde lifted the case down and placed it beside his right leg. The hand hovering by his right hip had relaxed and joined its fellow on the table top.

'Thank you. *Dankie*.'

Gabriel waved his hand.

'Call it a gesture of solidarity.'

'Tell me, Alec, you talk about you and your friends. Who, exactly, are these "friends" and where do they get their money from?'

'Smart question. We have been active for the last fifteen years. Our agenda is one of facilitating separatist movements who reject the global trend towards the mongrelisation of the races. Though this might surprise you, we are also happy to fund non-whites, provided they pursue a strict racist agenda.'

'Why?'

'Why?'

'Yes. Why?'

Gabriel had worked up his script with Eli before she'd left for England. They'd gone for fanatical-meets-just-this-side-of-crazy. Now he tried it out.

'Isn't it obvious? Look around you, Julius. Not here, in New Hope, but in the wider world. Lift your head above the horizon, beautiful though the veldt is. The world is on the brink of a catastrophe. Not climate, either. I am talking about the breakdown of human society itself. Intermingling blood is a recipe for disaster. We are sleepwalking into a racial apocalypse!'

He'd raised his voice and deliberately not wiped away the spittle that had collected at the corners of his mouth. Stopping suddenly, he looked at Witaarde, whose stark blue eyes were shining. Now he'd learn whether they'd pitched it right.

'My friends and I believe we have a God-given duty to halt that,' he finished.

'Amen,' Witaarde said, finally. 'Amen to that, Brother. Thank you for this money. But what do you want in return?'

Gabriel shook his head sadly, letting his mouth curl downwards and his eyes grow heavy.

'Julius, Julius, don't talk like a trader. There is no quid pro quo. We have money, more than we know what to do with. Do you think we're investors, looking for a return? No! I just told you what sort of a world we're trying to create. *That's* the dividend!'

Witaarde held eye contact for five seconds. Gabriel searched deep in those hard, blue irises for a sign of trust. He noticed a faint wrinkle at the corner of the left eye smooth out. *Got you!*

'Come for dinner tonight, Alec. I want you to meet Klara.'

'Your wife?'

'Yes. And the best cook in New Hope. Come at six-thirty.'

Gabriel checked in at New Hope's only hotel: *Die Wit Huis*. It shared little with the official residence of the US president beyond the name. But the manager had been welcoming and had assured Gabriel he'd allocated him the best room in the house. Gabriel thanked him. News of his generosity had clearly spread beyond Witaarde's house.

46

Pikko sniffing his left hand, which was curled around the necks of two bottles of wine, Gabriel knocked on the door of the Witaardes' house.

'It's open, come in!'

A woman's voice. Mrs Witaarde – Klara – Gabriel assumed.

He went in, leaving the inquisitive Pikko keening softly on the stoop. Klara Witaarde greeted him just inside with kisses on each cheek. Her eyes, a softer blue than her husband's, were unadorned by makeup, as was the rest of her pleasant, apple-cheeked face. The constant sun had turned her skin the colour of cinnamon, though she must use some sort of moisturising product, because it was unlined and smooth beneath the weathering.

She wore a loose-necked white cotton peasant blouse above a suede skirt, covered by a flour-dappled apron. The apron was embroidered with the same design as the pennant he'd seen at Yusuf's factory.

She stood back, holding Gabriel's right hand with both of hers. Her smile revealed small, white teeth, and he noticed a tiny triangular chip in one incisor.

'Alec, it's a pleasure to meet you,' she said, 'come inside and let me get you a drink.'

Gabriel followed her into the kitchen. When they reached it, he held out the bottles.

'South African Chenin Blanc and a Pinot Noir. I wasn't sure what we'd be eating.'

Her smile widened as she took them from him, placing the red on the counter and the white in the fridge.

'That's so kind of you. Thank you. And before Julius gets back, let me just say what an incredibly generous gesture you made this afternoon.'

'Call it an earnest of my good intent. I knew Julius would be suspicious of an Englishman arriving unannounced. He had every right to be.'

'Yah, we do have to be careful. Those kaffirs in Pretoria keep trying to penetrate our defences. Lucky for us, we can sniff them out like Pikko hunting *vlei* rats.'

'*Vlei*?'

'It means marsh.'

'You have marshes out here? It looks so dry.'

'No, there are plenty of lakes around here. It's how we get our water. I like to take Pikko with me and he has some fun hunting the rats. Now, what about that drink?'

'If you have any wine already chilled, I'd settle for that,' he said with a smile.

With a glass each, she untied her apron, draped it over the back of one of the hard wooden chairs and motioned for him to sit. As she took a chair for herself, she leaned forward and the front of her shirt gaped for a second, revealing the inner slopes of her breasts.

'So, Alec, tell me about yourself,' she said, taking a delicate sip of her wine.

'Private school in England, then I went to work in the City of London. Finance?' Klara nodded. 'I made my money in investment banking. Cross-border mergers and acquisitions. That's how I met my mentor.'

'Mentor?'

'A very wise man named Paddy Stirling. He showed me how the races were never meant to intermix. He had all this amazing evidence he'd spent decades putting together. He invited me to join his organisation. Basically I never looked back.'

She dropped her eyelids for a second, then looked back up at him. Her expression was hard to read. Lips parted slightly, finger on the point of her chin.

'Does it have a name, this organisation you joined?'

'The Committee for Policy Progress.'

'That doesn't sound very exciting!'

'Paddy always said, "If you're running a group dedicated to racial cleansing, Alec, you don't call it The White Power Commando. Make it sound boring, so people don't notice you until it's too late". I always thought that was rather clever. Not exciting, but definitely clever.'

She took another sip of her wine, regarding him coolly over the rim.

'Does that description fit you, too?' she asked, one eyelid fluttering.

Had she just winked at him? Gabriel shrugged, buying time with a sip from his own glass.

'I'm not sure I'm either, to be honest. I got by in banking because I was good at forming relationships. Clients like that. Paddy says one good relationship with the right person is worth a thousand soldiers.'

'And you think Julius is the right person?'

Gabriel heard footsteps.

'The right person for what?' Witaarde said as he entered the kitchen.

Gabriel stood and turned to greet Witaarde, holding out his hand.

Witaarde ignored it, enveloping Gabriel in a hug noticeable for the wiry strength behind it as much as the affection. He smelled of sweat and something else. Propellant. Witaarde had been shooting. He stepped back, holding Gabriel by both shoulders.

'Here he is! The man with the money!' Witaarde glanced down at the table. 'You've got a drink. Good.'

He rounded the table and kissed Klara on the lips. Then he turned her round and slapped her backside.

'How about a drink for the boss?'

She smiled at him, but Gabriel detected a tremor in the expression. A tightness around those un-madeup eyes. Interesting.

'Of course, Julius. What would you like? Alec brought wine.'

'Red?'

'And white.'

'Red, then. A big one. I feel like celebrating.'

After toasting his new benefactor, Witaarde placed his glass on the table.

'The right person for what, Alec?'

Gabriel focused on Witaarde's dilated pupils. Holding his gaze. What he said next had to be convincing.

'The right person to join a global crusade for white rights and white freedom. For too long, the white race has been cowed into submission by supranational groups like the UN and the EU, communists at home and abroad, and the craven, Marxist-dominated mainstream media.'

Witaarde frowned, grooving deep creases into that high, square forehead. The exact same profile as Mount Fuji, Gabriel found himself thinking.

'The BVR is a tiny outfit, Alec. Yes, we have big plans, but outside New Hope, what are we, really? A few hundred Boers with a dream of a *Volksrepubliek van Suid-Afrika*. Nothing more.'

Gabriel shook his head. He reached across the table and took Witaarde's left hand in his right. Then, improvising, he repeated the gesture with Klara's right hand in his left.

He looked at each of them in turn, holding Klara's eyes for a fraction longer than her husband's.

'Dreams build nations, Julius,' he said in a husky voice. 'Your dream is our dream. We are the connective tissue between dozens – hundreds – of groups like the BVR. Some bigger, some smaller, but all with the same shining dream. Surely you see that?'

'You know what I see? I see empty glasses. Klara!'

She released Gabriel's hand and jumped to her feet.

'I'm sorry, Julius.'

She poured more wine and opened a second bottle.

'What's for dinner?' he asked her.

'I made a pie. That bushbuck you shot yesterday.'

Witaarde turned away, apparently satisfied.

'Come on, Alec, let's leave the woman to her kitchen work. There's something I want to show you.'

Witaarde rose to his feet and Gabriel followed him from the kitchen.

They left the house by a back door. While Gabriel had been inside, the moon had risen and cast a silvery glow over the land stretching away from New Hope.

Witaarde led him to a shed in one corner of his fenced-in yard. Retrieving a bunch of keys from his shorts pocket, he unlocked a sturdy steel padlock and swung the door wide. The smell that emanated from the pitch-black interior was unmistakeable. Gabriel Wolfe was in the presence of death once more.

47

Behind him, he heard a match scraping on a striker. The flare as Witaarde lit a hurricane lamp illuminated a ghastly scene.

The body of a black man sprawled on the earth floor. The legs and arms lay at unnatural angles, as if a sadistic child had twisted the limbs of an action figure.

What remained of the head was the lower jaw. Everything above the teeth, which gleamed in the lamp's flickering light, was gone. The back wall was spattered with blood and brain tissue.

Realising that in his role as a bagman for the Committee for Policy Progress he had no need for a strong stomach, Gabriel allowed himself to wrinkle his nose and gag at the smell, which had solidified around him like a rotting blanket.

'Ha! You money men are all the same,' Witaarde crowed. 'No stomach for anything except your expense account dinners. This,' he jabbed a finger at the corpse, 'is where real men get their hands dirty.'

'Who is – was he?' Gabriel asked, letting his voice falter.

'The latest kaffir to think he could discover our plans and get away with it. ANC probably. Stupid bastards never give up.' He laughed. 'They keep sending their spies and we keep killing them. I tell you, Alec, they're easier to catch than *vlei* rats!'

Still chuckling, Witaarde kicked the corpse, then turned away.

'Come on, let's go. I thought you might like to see that. Call it my own little gesture of solidarity.'

Over dinner, and more wine, Witaarde opened up about the BVR's plans. His eyes were hooded, the lids drooping further with each fresh glass.

'See, Alec, when we started out we knew straight away we'd need money. Your twenty-five K is a pretty gesture, but compared to what we're making, it's chicken feed.'

Klara rose from the table and began clearing away the plates.

'From your winery?' Gabriel asked.

Witaarde guffawed.

'You hear that, Klara? This Englishman thinks we finance the BVR selling wine!'

She laughed. Gabriel observed the way her face twitched as she followed her husband's lead. She looked nervous. What the hell was it?

'Not wine, then.'

'Nah, man. Not wine,' he slurred. 'How about ivory?'

'Ivory?'

'What, are you deaf? Ivory! You know, tusks! Elephants. Here, I'll show you.'

Witaarde levered himself to his feet and stumbled from the kitchen. Two minutes later he was back, carrying a bolt-action rifle, which he placed on the table, the muzzle pointing at Gabriel's midsection. Beside it, he thumped down a long-barrelled revolver, though he retained his hold on the grip.

He tapped the revolver's muzzle against the wooden stock of the rifle.

'Dakota Arms Model 76. Takes a .450 round.' He pointed the revolver at Gabriel. 'Know what this is?'

Gabriel knew the model, barrel length and calibre. He'd had one pointed at him before, by a Mozambican militia commander named Mama Chissano. He hadn't enjoyed the experience then, either.

'A revolver?'

'Yah. A Smith & Wesson Model 629. Twenty-three centimetre barrel, takes six .44 Magnum rounds. You miss with the Dakota, this baby's your last chance.'

'For hunting elephants?'

'For hunting elephants. Take out the tusks, move them on down the line, take a cut of the proceeds. Smooth as a baby's bum.'

'Here in South Africa?'

Witaarde shrugged.

'Plenty of game parks.'

'Further north?'

Witaarde's eyes narrowed. He gulped some more wine.

'Why're you so interested? You want to do some hunting?' It came out *hunnin*.

'Maybe. You know, if you *are* involved in ivory, we could talk more about that. We're always interested in new sources of finance.'

Witaarde laughed.

'Expensive business, fighting for your rights, eh?'

'You could say that.'

Suddenly, Witaarde snapped upright in his chair. His gaze cleared and those hooded blue eyes returned to full alertness. The change in his demeanour was unnerving.

He lifted the Model 629 and touched the foresight to the tip of his nose, frowning. Then he lowered it until Gabriel was forced to look straight down the barrel. Below it, he could see the flat-topped lead noses of the Magnum rounds in their chambers.

'Why are you here, Alec? Really?'

'I told you. To make contact. To invite you to join us in our—'

'Struggle, yes, I heard that part. But look at it from my perspective. You turn up in Vientiane, sniffing around the market, and you ask to meet me. You splash dollars around like sweeties and then give me this bullshit about your cause. Why do I get the feeling you're really just interested in making money? Does this Committee for Policy Progress of yours even exist?'

'Yes! OK, look, I wasn't completely straight with you, Julius. And for that, I apologise.'

'Go on,' Witaarde said, lowering the revolver a fraction.

'That money I gave you? We're really struggling financially. It was a big chunk of our reserves, but we hoped, if we could show you we were serious, you'd cut us in on the ivory. We're also looking at blood diamonds, drugs, people trafficking, whatever.' He spread his hands wide. 'That's it. Now you know everything.'

Witaarde relaxed. He let the Smitty's barrel thump onto the table. A grin stole over his features.

'I don't fucking believe this. The old colonial masters reduced to begging from me!'

'Believe it or not, it's true.'

'The Committee's real.'

'Yes. If we can reach an agreement, I can introduce you to some very powerful people.'

'Powerful poor people.'

'It's a cash-flow issue. They still have connections you could use. In the US, Russia, Israel.'

Witaarde stood.

'I need to think about it. I'll give you an answer in the morning. Stay here tonight. I had Klara prepare a guest room. We'll talk over breakfast.'

The grass towered over Gabriel. He stretched out a hand to move one of the stems aside and winced as its saw-edge cut through his skin. Beside him Smudge, Stevo and the others were also bleeding from their hands and forearms.

Smudge grimaced.

'This stuff's sharper than my bayonet, boss,' he said. 'Look.'

He chopped the last foot from a stem with his bayonet and grabbed it as it fell to the ground. Blood leaked out from between his fingers as he clenched his fist around the green sword.

He stroked it across Gabriel's wrist. The edge bit deep into muscle, sinew and bone, separating the hand as cleanly as a butcher jointing meat. There was no pain. Gabriel watched, fascinated, as his hand flopped to the ground and scuttled away into the undergrowth, leaving a slimy trail of blood.

A crash from the other side of the stand of grass shattered the silence.

Smudge looked up. Gabriel followed his gaze. Smudge screamed. A monstrous-tusked elephant blotted out the sun, rearing on its hind legs before plunging forwards and down. It smashed Smudge's skull into pieces with a trunk like a great, grey club, before trampling his headless body into a red pulp on the forest floor.

Then it turned to Gabriel.

'You're next, kaffir,' it said, in Witaarde's voice.

Its blue eyes flashed, then it swung its massive head left and right, sending razor-edged tusks in a slashing arc through Gabriel's belly. He screamed as he watched his intestines spill into the dirt and shot bolt-upright in bed, the borrowed pyjamas drenched in sweat.

Klara Witaarde was sitting on the edge of his bed. Her face was glistening in the moonlight: *face cream*. He could smell it, and remembered his mother in Hong Kong, coming into his room when he'd had a nightmare. The same perfume. What was it? Pond's?

'Alec, you were screaming. Are you all right?' she asked, holding his hand in hers.

'I'm fine. Sorry. Just a bad dream. Must be the heat.'

She moved towards him and laid the back of one cool hand on his forehead. Her nightgown was pale, edged with lace. The front was a deep V and, once again, he couldn't help glancing at her cleavage.

'You're hot. And you're soaked. Take that off,' she said, pointing at his pyjama jacket.

'But...'

She leaned closer.

'Don't worry,' she whispered. 'Julius is a heavy sleeper. A rhino could come through the house and he wouldn't wake up.'

Gabriel unbuttoned the pyjama jacket and pulled it off. She took it from him and balled it, before tossing it towards the door.

'How about the rest?'

Beneath the sheets he removed the soaking pyjama trousers and handed them to her.

'I should change the sheets for you,' she said.

'Really, it's fine.'

She bit her lip.

'No. It's not.'

'What do you mean?'

'Oh, God!'

She sniffed, and Gabriel watched as a tear emerged from the corner of her eye and crawled across her cheekbone, catching the moonlight like a diamond on her skin.

'What, Klara, tell me.'

'I don't know if I can trust you. If I tell you and he finds out, he'll kill me. He'll kill us both.'

Gabriel sat straighter in bed, his role in bringing Witaarde to justice forgotten for the moment. Now there was another reason to hate the man.

'I won't let that happen.'

She sniffed again and wiped away the tear with a finger.

'Julius, is,' she hesitated, 'a good man. Deep down, I mean. But his ideas, they're so,' her eyes searched the ceiling as if the words she were seeking might appear there, 'unrealistic. I admit I don't like the blacks, but you can't turn back the clock. I just wanted to live in peace up here away from everything. But Julius, he wants a full-blown revolution.'

Her whispering took on a harsher note.

'The fact is, Alec, I'm a prisoner here. We all are. The women, I mean.'

'Prisoner, how?'

'They treat us like slaves. We were told that we would have equal rights in *Volksrepubliek van Suid-Afrika,* but they want to send us back to the kitchen like the eighteenth century never ended. I went to university in Capetown before I married Julius. I was a finance analyst. Now I'm to be a cook and baby machine. Look,' she said.

She pulled down the straps of her nightdress. She leaned forward and twisted so her left shoulder was facing him. It bore a tattoo – three heavy, gothic letters: BAW.

'What does it mean?' Gabriel asked.

'Oh, Alec, that's his mark,' she choked out. 'It stands for *Behoort Aan Witaarde*. Belongs to Witaarde.'

She let her hands fall to the counterpane and, as she did, the top of her nightdress slid down, revealing the tops of her breasts. She made no attempt to cover herself.

Gabriel saw an opportunity. To get to Witaarde, but also to right a smaller wrong. He decided there and then to take a chance. He'd get her away from Witaarde. Who knew, she might even be a source of intelligence they could use later to shut down the BVR.

'Listen,' he murmured. 'What if I told you I wasn't with some white pride group. What if I told you I was here on other business, but I could get you out? Would you come?'

She nodded frantically.

'I would do anything. Just get me away from him.' She looked down at her breasts as if seeing them for the first time. Then back at him. 'He hits me. They all do. Hit their wives, I mean. Look.'

She pulled the front of her nightdress all the way down. Her right breast was marked by a livid purple bruise from just beside the nipple to her ribcage.

Gently, Gabriel lifted the nightdress and resettled it over her shoulders. She frowned.

'Tell me about the ivory poaching,' he said.

She shook her head.

'I can't. I don't know anything about it. He just goes off on trips and comes back a couple of weeks later.'

She glanced at the bedroom door, then rose from the bed,

crossed the room on silent feet and closed it before sitting back down beside him.

'Alec, I want to leave with you. But I'm scared. Anyway, how will you get away? Brik drove you here, didn't he?'

'Yes, but I can steal a truck or something. I'm very resourceful.'

'When?'

'I need to talk to him about the ivory. But after that. The day after tomorrow?'

She nodded, glancing at the door as if Witaarde might burst through at any moment, brandishing the big revolver.

'I can't believe this is happening. You're really going to take me with you?'

'I said so, didn't I? Maybe we can find a way to rescue the others, too.'

'Oh, God, I hope so, Alec. I hope so.' Then she bent towards him and kissed him, lightly, on the lips. 'Thank you.'

Instead of pulling away, she leaned against him, stroking the bullet scar on his shoulder. Her other hand snaked beneath the covers.

'Klara, please, you don't have to.'

'I know I don't *have* to,' she whispered. 'Supposing I *want* to?'

He felt himself hardening in her grasp. Took hold of her shoulders and pushed her, firmly but gently, away. He shook his head.

'I have someone.'

Klara Witaarde stared into his eyes.

'Then she's a very lucky girl.'

She got up a second time and left, kicking the sweat-soaked pyjamas into the corner on her way past. At the door, she turned.

Gabriel released a breath he'd been holding. Was all that real? He couldn't work her out. One minute a frightened enslaved woman, the next a minx, coming on to him while her husband slept down the hall.

* * *

Gabriel woke from a dreamless sleep. No murderous elephants the size of houses. No razor-blade grass stems dismembering him. He had a vague memory of a noise waking him. A nocturnal animal tapping on the window? He turned to find his watch.

And his head exploded in a blinding white flash of pain.

48

Instinctively, he raised his arms to protect himself. The next blow smashed down into his solar plexus, driving his wind from him and leaving him gasping, curled into a foetal position.

Above him, he saw two bulky shapes.

'Here's one to put your lights out, kaffir-lover,' a voice in the darkness said.

The blow connected with his left temple. A high-pitched whine screamed inside his skull. He tasted metal and smelled burnt toast. The world turned orange, then turquoise, then white, yellow, a sickly green, grey…black.

He tried to lift his head. It wouldn't move. He tried again and felt a tearing pain on the left side. A grenade exploded inside his head, filling him with a violent desire to vomit. He lay still, moaning softly to himself until the agony subsided.

He realised he was conscious again. He raised a finger to the side of his face. It felt crusty. He picked at the substance and felt a piece dislodge. He opened his eyes and brought his finger up where he could see it.

The substance on the end of his finger was congealed blood, the colour of molasses. He returned the finger to his skull and felt around, gingerly probing his scalp. He winced as his questing fingertip found a lump. It felt soft in the centre and a fresh wave of nausea engulfed him. He swallowed, hard, and took a few deep, steadying breaths.

* * *

The third time he awoke, he felt something approaching normal. His watch was gone. He looked down. He was naked.

His torso was an atlas of pain, the countries and continents coloured purple, blue, red, yellow and green.

He could smell the rank stink of urine.

The room was ten feet square. No windows. A single door. A bare electric light bulb on a short length of flex.

He heard a key scrape in the lock. Pushed himself back against the wall. Tried to stand. Managed to get into a half-crouch when the door swung inwards.

Filling the frame, Julius Witaarde stood, smiling down at him.

'How did you sleep, Alec? Is that your real name, by the way? We checked your ID, but who knows what those kaffirs down in Pretoria can do.'

'I'm not a spy.'

'No? Then explain all the bullshit you told Klara.'

'I don't know what you mean. I didn't say anything to Klara after she left us alone after dinner.'

Witaarde said nothing in reply. His smile widening, he entered the room and stood to one side. Behind stood Klara. In place of the peasant blouse, suede skirt and bare feet, she now wore a starched, military-style shirt and khaki combat trousers tucked into riding boots.

And Gabriel realised. He'd been played. The oldest trick in the book: the honey trap.

Klara folded her arms across her chest, as if to deny the reality of what he had seen in the early hours of the morning. She sneered down at him.

'I'm a *slave*, Alec,' she said in a whiny, sing-song voice. 'Julius *beats* me. He put his *mark* on me.'

She crossed the room in a couple of long strides and kicked him mid-thigh. He gasped and clenched his jaws to avoid giving her the satisfaction of signalling his pain.

'You pathetic piece of shit,' she said. 'I don't know what sort of women you have in England, but I'm a loyal Boer wife and a proud freedom fighter. There was something off about your act from the moment you turned up in my kitchen. I warned Julius, but he fell for your crap.'

She kicked him again, on the same spot, and this time Gabriel bit his tongue in an effort to stay quiet.

'My tattoo? BAW doesn't stand for *Behoort aan Witaarde*,' she said. 'It's *Beter Almal Wit*. You get that, *spioen*?' Another kick. 'Better All White. And I got the bruise when my horse threw me.'

Gabriel stared up at them both. Witaarde had a pistol on his hip in a brown leather holster. Not the 629. This looked like a basic nine. Klara wasn't carrying.

He calculated distances, angles, lines of attack. If he could get to his feet, he'd stand a chance. Allow them to march him somewhere, slow down, stumble, back into Witaarde, roll under the muzzle and to the side in a *Krav Maga* move, disable Witaarde with an elbow to the side, disarm him, shoot them both, get out, steal a car, get gone.

He pushed his back into the wall and levered himself to a standing position, grunting with the effort and feeling his guts roil again.

Witaarde took a step back, hand on the butt of the pistol.

'Don't even think about it. You make a move faster than a snail, I'll put a round into your belly and we'll leave you out on the veldt for the hyenas. Now, what's your name? Your real name.'

Gabriel inhaled.

'Gabriel Wolfe.'

Witaarde smiled.

'There. That wasn't so hard, was it? Be good and you might get out of this in one piece.'

A phone rang. Gabriel recognised the ring tone. Witaarde frowned and reached into a pocket. The hand that emerged clutched Gabriel's Department-issued phone.

Witaarde glanced at the screen.

'Someone called Eli wants you. Here. Talk to her. If I don't like what I hear I'll slice your balls off and feed them to my pigs.'

He handed the phone to Gabriel.

'Eli, hi, what's up?' he said.

'Not much. I'm stuck at home watching the news. I tried to call Don but his phone rang out. Then I went to Rothford. The gate guard turned me away. A new guy. I'm worried, Gabe.'

'I'm sure it's nothing.'

'Are you? Because I'm not. How about you. Where are you? Did you find the BVR yet?'

'It looks like a dead end. I'm in Jo'burg but the guy never showed. I think that Irishman conned me out of ten grand.'

'Shit! OK, so what next?'

'Return to base, I guess. Hey, I tell you what?'

'What?'

Gabriel looked at Klara Witaarde as he spoke. She was regarding him with cold, dead eyes.

'I'll cook Sunday dinner for you. Your favourite. Roast pork with all the trimmings.'

'What? You know I'm Jewish, right? I mean, that little fact about me hadn't escaped your attention?'

'Yeah, OK, El. Love you, too. Bye.'

Gabriel handed the phone back to Witaarde.

'Who is she?' Witaarde asked.

'My girlfriend.'

'Yeah? Well, you better pray I like the rest of your answers or she's going to be looking for a new man in her life.'

'Ask me anything.'

Witaarde shook his head.

'Not here. You sound too fucking cool and collected despite the beating Duckie and Ruud handed you. No, I think we need to get your defences *all* the way down.' He turned to his wife. 'What do you think, darling?'

She grinned.

'I'll go and run a bath.'

* * *

The horse trough stood in the centre of a barn, its slatted sides admitting the first rays of the sun. The wide, flat shafts captured dust motes that swirled in and out of the yellow light.

The two giant Boers, Duckie and Ruud, had him gripped by the elbows, his arms twisted up behind his back. He trod on a nail buried in the straw and yelped as half an inch of steel penetrated the arch of his foot.

Ignoring him, they frogmarched him over to the trough and pushed him forward at the waist, forcing his head down. He saw himself staring back out of the trough. The water slopped over the rim.

'Put him in,' Klara said.

The giants lifted Gabriel as if he were a child and dumped him into the water. He gasped, expecting cold, but it was oddly warm.

He opened his mouth to speak, then snapped his teeth together as one of the men pushed him by the throat backwards and down. He had time to gasp in a breath before the water closed over his face.

The faces wobbled and broke apart, then came together in hideous grins. He willed himself to stay calm, beginning a mantra Master Zhao had taught him. He knew he could hold his breath for up to two and half minutes with sufficient preparation, both physical and mental. But this wasn't one of those times.

At the forty-five second mark, he could already feel his system screaming for fresh oxygen and had to fight down the urge to struggle against the man's massive fist.

Sparks jumped in his eyes, then he was being hauled up. Choking and spitting, he drew in a huge breath, then started coughing as water droplets entered his lungs.

'Why are you here, Gabriel Wolfe?' Klara said.

The giant thrust him beneath the water again. He'd been expecting time to answer Klara's question and could only snatch a brief breath before the water rolled over his face again.

Thirty seconds and he was on the point of blacking out. He imagined the water flooding into his nose, his mouth, his throat, his lungs, ending it all, never seeing Eli again. Dying in a foreign country and being thrown out like meat for the veldt's scavengers.

He was wrenched up again. He struggled to drag air down, retching and coughing. He didn't think he could take another trip beneath the surface.

'Wait,' he gasped. 'Please, wait. I'll tell you everything. Just don't—'

He saw Klara nod. Heaved air into his tortured lungs. Felt the grip on his throat tighten. Plunged under the water again.

Panicking, finally, he grabbed the giant's wrists, as thick as tree branches, and desperately pulled at them. For his pains, he was thrust right to the bottom of the horse trough. He felt the hard steel bang into the nobbles of his spine.

Goodbye, El. I love you so much. We could have been good together. We could have—

49

ALDEBURGH, ENGLAND

Eli rang Don at home. While she waited for him to answer, she tried to squelch the anxiety knotting her stomach. Something was wrong. Badly wrong. The signal had been as clear as an air raid siren.

'Hello, Eli.'

'Oh thank god, boss.'

'What is it?'

'It's Gabe. Gabriel. He's in trouble.'

'Trouble how? Trouble where?'

'South Africa. Johannesburg. I just called him. He sounded strange and then he said he'd cook me roast pork and just hung up on me.'

'Pork.'

'Yes! You know what that means, don't you?'

'It means somebody was listening in. Someone who doesn't know you're Jewish.'

'I figure he's been captured. Probably by the BVR. They're holding him in a safe house. They'll be interrogating him, trying to find out who sent him. His cover's blown. I don't know how, but it is.'

'Right. One, slow down. Two, take a breath. Three, I need to think. I'll call you back.'

Five minutes later – Eli had spent the entire interval watching the long red second hand of the kitchen clock circling the dial – her phone rang. She stabbed at the green icon.

'Boss.'

'Get yourself to Jo'burg. Do not, repeat *do not*, go sniffing around for intel. If they took Gabriel there, they have people on the ground. Don't turn yourself into a target.'

50

HEAVEN

The sheets were so soft. Who knew Heaven would have such a high thread count? He could smell fresh-baked bread. Coffee brewing. An angel speaking. In Afrikaans.

'*Is daardie kak kop nog wakker?*'

She sounded just like Klara Witaarde. He heard footsteps. Must be Saint Peter. The gatekeeper came into the bedroom. Gabriel listened, wonderingly. Peter spoke.

'Hey, shithead. My wife wants to know if you're awake yet.'

Gabriel opened his eyes. His arms were resting on top of the coverlet. Sun streamed in through a window curtained with off-white muslin that bellied inwards with the breeze.

Witaarde stood over him. He called over his shoulder.

'Yah, he's back in the land of the living.'

'I thought I died,' Gabriel said.

'Me too. How about that! It was Klara's idea to get you out before Ruud pulled your plug for good. That woman has a soft heart.'

Reflecting that any soft-hearted woman who could kick as hard and with as much deadly accuracy as Klara Witaarde was in breach of the Trades Description Act, Gabriel contented himself with a one-word answer.

'Ivory.'

Witaarde sat on the edge of the bed.

'What about it?'

'I want in.'

'I? What happened to "we"?'

'There is no "we".'

'I knew it!' Witaarde said, smacking the palms of his hands together. 'You fucker. You almost had me believing that global white rights story. So, what's going on? Why are you here?'

'You no longer think I'm a government spy?'

Witaarde shook his head.

'Those pussies down south break easier than a Boer virgin. Nobody's stood up to Ruud's bath-time that long. What are you, CIA?'

Gabriel shook his head, seeing half a chance.

'You know what a triad is?'

'Of course! I'm not some *dom yokel*. Chinese gangs.'

'My sister runs one.'

Witaarde's eyebrows shot towards the ceiling.

'Get the fuck out of here!'

'It's true. Her name's Wei Mei. That means Beautiful Plum in Mandarin. The triad is called The White Koi.'

Witaarde ran a hand over his face.

'Prove it.'

'Bring me my phone.'

Witaarde returned five minutes later. He handed the phone to Gabriel. Gabriel called a speed dial number, then switched the phone to speaker. Mei picked up on the third ring.

'BB!'

'Hi, Mei. Listen, no time to explain. I need you to talk to somebody for me. Just answer his questions.'

'OK.'

He handed the phone back to Witaarde. Then watched Witaarde closely.

'Who is Gabriel Wolfe?'

'He is my brother.'

'What line of business are you in?'

'Triad.'

Witaarde smiled.

'What's the name?'

'White Koi.'

'Thank you.'

'Hey!' Mei snapped. 'Wait. Gabriel is with you?'

'He's my guest, yes.'

'Do not hurt him. If you hurt him I will find you and kill you.'

She ended the call.

'Feisty,' Witaarde said.

'She means it.'

'I don't doubt it. All right. We've established your family business is, what, organised crime?'

'That about covers it.'

'Then tell me, Gabriel, why are you interested in ivory?'

'Can't you guess?'

'I know the Chinese buy most of it.'

'That's right. Mei wants to move upstream. Take an interest all the way from the source to the customer. She sent me to negotiate.'

'Why all the bullshit about white rights?'

'I thought you'd let your guard down if I showed sympathy for your political goals. Not everybody welcomes the attentions of the triads.'

'Too fucking right!'

Gabriel sat up, waiting for a burst of pain that didn't arrive. That was good.

'Cards on the table, Julius. I'm ex-army. I have some mates and we're looking for a way to make some serious money for ourselves. We're tooled up and ready to act as Mei's enforcers over here. You could do with some extra protection.'

Witaarde stood.

'Get dressed. Go for a walk. Don't think of running; I'll have someone shoot you in the leg and bring you back trussed like a hog. And then we'll go back to the barn.'

51

With the Englishman gone, the ever-reliable Duckie dogging his tracks, Witaarde sipped the fresh mug of coffee Klara had just placed before him.

'He's telling the truth.'

'How do you know? That whole call thing? He could have set it up. He could have support in Hong Kong.'

Witaarde felt a flash of anger. Klara was a loyal wife and a damn good fighter. But she had a mouth on her, too.

'We nearly fucking drowned him, woman! Nobody goes through that and sticks to their story unless it's the truth. Nobody!'

She sat down opposite him.

'What if it *is* the truth? We don't want a bunch of English bastards muscling in on a very profitable business. Especially not if they're triad muscle. They'll take over, then they'll either kill us or turn us into hired help. Is that your vision? Because it isn't mine. I say call Duckie right now and have him put a bullet in the Englishman's head.'

Witaarde, who'd just lifted the mug to his lips, put it down again. He felt the calmness descending on him. The stillness at his centre where he found the motivation to torture, maim and kill his enemies.

His vision clouded.

He was staring down at a kaffir sprawled before him on the barn's dirt floor. He felt no pity despite the man's horrific facial injuries.

A jagged cut above his right eye was bleeding freely, giving him a red contact lens. His nose had been mashed sideways by a fist or boot forcing him to breathe heavily through his mouth.

Every time he gasped for breath his bloody gums moved against each other.

'One last time, kaffir, who are you working for? The cops? State Security Agency?'

'I told you,' the man mumbled through broken teeth, 'I'm a wildlife photographer.'

Witaarde drew his right foot back and kicked the man in the solar plexus. He groaned and curled into a foetal position as he struggled for breath.

'Listen to me, kaffir!' Witaarde shouted, spraying spittle onto the prostrate figure. 'The only wildlife round here are our guard dogs. You were caught spying. Now, tell me who for and maybe I'll let you go.'

Wheezing, the man looked up at Witaarde. And in that moment, as he registered the hatred in his eyes, Witaarde realised he would never get him to talk.

'You think you're going to set up a white homeland, Witaarde? Not. Going. To. Happen.' He heaved in a breath. 'Fuck you!'

Witaarde shook his head.

'No, kaffir.' He pulled his pistol from the polished leather holster on his belt. 'Fuck you!'

He fired twice, directly at the man's face, blowing the back of his skull away in a spray of blood, brain and bone.

'Julius?'

The vision dissipated. He looked across the table at Klara.

'What?' he snapped.

'We were talking about what to do with the Englishman.'

'We don't kill him. Not yet. If his story checks out, then we could have some very useful support. Think about it, Klara. You know the Botswanans are putting more behind the anti-poaching drive. It's just as bad in Congo-Brazzaville. These boys are ex-army. British Army. They're tough. Combat-hardened. The triad connection could work in our favour. They must have better distribution. We cut out Yusuf and the guys in Vientiane and deal direct with the Chinese.'

She shook her head.

'No. I still say the risks are too high. We should kill him.'

He curled his fingers around the coffee mug. It was still half-full. Hot to the touch. He hurled it in her face. She screamed, leaped from her chair and ran to the sink, reaching blindly for the taps and splashing cold water on her cheeks.

'Don't say no to me again,' he said in a quiet voice, before turning and leaving the room. 'He lives.'

He left the house and climbed into his truck. The engine caught on the first twist of the key and he roared away, spattering the side of the house with grit from the spinning tyres.

He called Duckie, keeping one hand on the wheel and scanning the town for signs of the Englishman.

'Yes, Julius.'

'Where is he?'

'West of town. Big Lake. He's doing some kind of weird exercises.'

'OK. Leave him. I'm driving out.'

'Yes, Julius.'

Witaarde reached the lake in ten minutes. He pulled up behind a thick stand of trees and stepped down onto the earth. The red earth it was his intention, his dream, to turn white.

When he reached the lake, the Englishman was standing at the water's edge, facing across the narrow expanse towards the national park on the far side. His arms were raised above his head, palms pressed together, and, as Witaarde watched, he lifted one foot from the ground and placed the sole against his other thigh.

Witaarde folded his arms and watched, amazed, as the

Englishman held the pose for four minutes. As slowly as a chameleon stalking a moth, he crept closer. The Englishman was chanting. Nonsense words.

He came to within twenty feet of him. The Englishman's eyes were closed, face upturned. How easy it would be to put a 9mm round in the back of his skull and leave him here, just like Klara wanted.

'Hello, Julius.'

Witaarde started.

'How the fuck did you do that? I was silent. I've been hunting out here since I was nine years old. My *pappa* taught me.'

'You might want to leave off the aftershave next time, then. You're upwind of me. I smelled you coming.'

The Englishman opened his eyes, lowered his right leg and turned round to face Witaarde.

'How many men?' Witaarde asked.

'Thirty, including me.'

'You think they're up to it?'

'British Army, best in the world.'

'What unit?'

'Mainly Royal Marines, a few SAS and the rest are Parachute Regiment.'

Witaarde felt a surge of triumph, finally back on top as far as this smooth-talking Englishman was concerned.

'You might want to check how tough your boys really are, Gabriel,' he said with a smirk. 'We had a few Paras up here not so long ago training those fucking kaffirs in Bots. Guess what?'

'What?'

'They're not here any more.'

'No? Did they go back to the UK?'

The Englishman's face was impassive. Witaarde had never been good at reading people. Now he wished he had Klara by his side.

'Nah, man. They went to the big fucking game park in the sky, courtesy of me and my boys. We ambushed them. It was like shooting fish in a barrel. One of them was a kaffir himself, so he's gone to the black heaven. Or better yet, they're all down in Hell.'

He saw the Englishman's lips tighten a fraction. *Not so fucking cocky now, are you?*

'It was their time,' the Englishman said, finally. 'But remember, my boys would be fighting on *your* side. As long as the pay is good, and the action. They wouldn't mind getting into it with some local law enforcement or kaffir soldiers.'

Witaarde nodded. Saw himself at the head of a private army. His own Boer fighters, buttressed by thirty battle-hardened Brits. And who knew, once they'd seen the paradise of the Northern Cape, he'd persuade them to stay on. Join him and Klara. Take wives, build homesteads, raise kids. Witaarde wasn't averse to mingling blood, as long as it was all white. As white as the ivory that was paying for it all.

Standing under the boiling sun, facing the man who had just admitted killing the Paras, Gabriel had to suppress the urge to do him immediately. Witaarde was on guard. His body language showed that, and although Gabriel could try hypnosis, that would require Witaarde to be closer, off his guard and not already highly suspicious. And although he could take Witaarde's truck, which had alerted him way before the drifting aftershave, there was every chance Witaarde would have set up a call-back with one of his men, or the redoubtable Klara. If he didn't call in, they'd be out looking for Gabriel.

Something else was needed.

'Any chance of a lift back to town?' he asked. 'If we're going to talk terms, I'd like to get changed and get a drink.'

Witaarde spread his hands wide.

'Sure! I don't know what the fuck you were doing out here but it's liable to give you sunstroke. Come on, my *bakkie*'s behind those trees.'

. . .

Back in New Hope, Witaarde drove straight to his house and ushered Gabriel inside.

'Klara, we're back,' he yelled. 'Coffee!'

Klara's face was blotched red beneath her tan. She glared at Gabriel as she caught him looking. He looked away.

Once she had served them coffee and left again, Witaarde spoke.

'I'm sorry about the rough welcome we gave you, Gabriel. But look at it from my perspective. I was well within my rights to have you shot and fed to the hogs, or the wild animals.'

Gabriel sipped the coffee. He shrugged.

'I get it. You're under siege here, politically if not physically. I would have done the same in your shoes.'

'Yah, well, thanks. But now I have a different plan. How about a business partnership? You bring in your mates and don't even worry about the guns. I know how hard it is to get them in England, let alone fly them out. Anyway, we have plenty of them over here.'

'Hunting rifles? Shotguns?'

'Sure,' Witaarde said, then grinned. 'Plus M16s, Glocks, even a couple of Vektor SS-77s. You know what they are?'

'General purpose machine guns.'

'That's right. Ivory money buys all kinds of stuff if you know who to talk to.'

'Let's talk about money. My boys get four hundred a day a man, cash, plus rations and a place to sleep.'

'What's *your* day-rate?' Witaarde asked, sipping his coffee.

'No day-rate. I want a partnership.'

'What kind of a partnership?'

'I run your new military wing and handle relations with the White Koi in return for ten per cent of the profits.'

'That's a lot of money. What if I tell you to go fuck yourself and we'll carry on the way we were?'

Gabriel smiled, enjoying his newfound role.

'Simple. I call Mei and tell her you're not interested. Then, one day when you've forgotten all about me, a Chinese-made fighter-bomber arrives in that beautiful African sky above this town and then New Hope gets a new name.' A beat. 'No Hope. Anyone who survives the bombing will be shot. Then we take over the whole trade. I know it sounds brutal, Julius, but it's how they operate.'

He watched as Witaarde's jaw worked, the muscles bunching and relaxing as if he were chewing a particularly tough piece of bushmeat.

'Five per cent.'

'Eight.'

'Seven and a half.'

Gabriel smiled and held out his hand. Witaarde took it and shook it perfunctorily.

'We could take over Yusuf's factory, too,' Gabriel said. 'In time. Mei's very keen on vertical integration.'

Witaarde smiled. An odd expression that got nowhere near his eyes, just that bow-shaped top lip curling.

'I bet she is. I tell you what, Gabriel. How about this? Come on a hunting trip with me. We'll go up to Bots and shoot a couple of elephants, take a chainsaw to them. I want to see whether you can handle the messy side of the business. I need to know I can trust you.'

Gabriel knew he couldn't afford to hesitate. But shooting dead an elephant then butchering it with a chainsaw to get the tusks? Not good. Even if it meant having a chance to deal with Witaarde away from New Hope.

'Fine. I'll get a chance to show you what I can do with the Dakota.'

Witaarde grinned. Gabriel realised the man facing him entirely lacked a sense of humour. Witaarde explained he was going to fly into Botswana in the Cessna and meet Gabriel there. Ruud would be his escort and driver. *And my guard.*

It was fine. Witaarde was approaching his destiny. Just not the one he had planned for himself.

52

KGALAGADI TRANSFRONTIER PARK, BOTSWANA

Four hours in Ruud's company was enough to confirm Gabriel's opinion of the man. Leave his politics out of it, and what remained was a cold-hearted killer. He'd boasted on the four-hour drive of torturing and killing journalists, activists and government security agents. With so little regard for human life, Gabriel could see why slaughtering elephants wouldn't raise a quiver of moral doubt from the man.

And he'd confirmed, willingly, that he'd been a member of the group of poachers, under Witaarde's personal command, who'd murdered the Paras and the Botswana soldiers. Good enough for what was coming to him.

As they entered the park, the black guard on duty shot Ruud a look that Gabriel read as easily as a book. Complicity. He waited until the pearlescent Range Rover was a few miles inside the park.

'That guard know you?'

'On the payroll.'

'So you don't mind using the kaffirs when it suits you?'

'Ha! Why should we? Throw them a few dollars and they'd shoot their own mothers. They're useful, nothing more.'

Gabriel next asked the question he'd been turning over in his mind, as much a brain-teaser as a practical matter.

'The park's a big place. How do you know where to find the elephants?'

Ruud turned and winked.

'Why do you think the guard knows me? They have pretty sophisticated tracking up here. A gift from one of those bleeding heart charities. You know, "Save the Elephants" or some liberal bullshit.'

'And he tells you where to find a herd.'

'In one, my friend. I tell you something else. The locals aren't nearly as fond of elephants as the greenies seem to think. You know how long it takes a single bull to destroy a farmer's yearly crop of sorghum or tomatoes?'

'How long?'

'One night! One, man! Then that poor kaffir is fucked three ways from Sunday.'

As they drove north, Ruud checking a discreet GPS tracker on his side of the steering wheel, Gabriel sorted through the options he'd been considering for despatching Witaarde and getting himself out of New Hope and back to the relative safety of Johannesburg.

The best option would be to shoot him and Ruud and blame their deaths on a rival poaching gang or, better yet, a patrol of Botswanan APU guys. After killing them, he intended to leave the bodies out for the scavengers, just as Witaarde had bragged he did with the dead 'enemies' of the *Volksrepubliek van Suid-Afrika*.

He'd have transport. But would the park guard want to know where Ruud was? Scrap that, he'd be behind the wheel of one of the best 4x4s in the world. Cross-country back into South Africa and avoid New Hope altogether. Now he knew he wouldn't be acting as, what had Britta called him *riddare i skinande rustning* – a knight in shining armour – to Klara Witaarde, he'd be better off avoiding the place altogether.

'You know the best place to shoot an elephant, Gabriel?' Ruud asked, breaking into his thoughts.

'Tell me.'

'For a one-shot kill, you want to hit him in the brain. A heart shot is more of an insurance job. Sure, you can take one down that way, but it's a small target in a big body.'

'What's the shot placement?'

'Side-on; you want to hit him just in front of the ear-crease, where it joins the head. From the front, visualise a point halfway between the eyes. The height depends on if he's got his head up. You ever hunt before?'

'Only people.'

Ruud laughed, a harsh bark.

'Ha! "Only people." I like that. Yah, well, big game is different. You hit a man with a decent calibre round, he goes down, one way or another. Big game is different. Miss the brain or the heart, it'll just take off. A big kudu or a hippo, you put a round in its body it just swallows it up, man.'

As Ruud talked, Gabriel tuned him out. He was thinking through the upcoming confrontation with Witaarde. He'd imagined he'd be travelling alone with Witaarde and had planned simply to shoot him dead once they got to the elephant herd. Rudd complicated the picture, but not by much.

A phone rang. Gabriel paid attention to Ruud's side of the conversation.

'Yah, right beside me.'

—

'The best way to shoot an elephant.'

—

'Hold on. Thirty minutes.'

—

'OK, boss.'

Ruud turned to Gabriel.

'That was Julius. He's found the herd. It's small. Just a bull and two cows plus three babies. But plenty enough for us. It'll be a good haul, too.'

Gabriel nodded. He realised he wanted to take two lives and save six. Was he getting sentimental? He didn't know. Only that he wasn't going to let these men kill and butcher any more elephants.

After half an hour's driving through lighter scrub, Ruud pointed off to the right.

'There's the plane.'

Gabriel followed his extended finger. The Cessna stood out against the brown and green like one of the egrets they'd seen striding along the mud flats skirting a small lake at the entrance to the park.

Beside the Cessna, Gabriel could make out a white pickup – a *bakkie*. But what troubled him was the truck's contents.

53

Next to the *bakkie*, Gabriel could see four brown-skinned men standing alongside a white man that had to be Witaarde.

Ruud roared off the track and rumbled the Range Rover across the dusty earth, slewing to a stop some fifty feet from the *bakkie* and throwing up a dust cloud that drifted across the open ground. It enveloped the loose group of men, forcing them to hide their noses and mouths in elbow crooks or behind hats.

He climbed out and Gabriel followed. As the dust cloud cleared, Witaarde strode forward and stuck his face close to Ruud's. His blue eyes were dark with rage against the dust sticking to his sweaty skin.

'You fucking idiot! Don't you ever pull a trick like that again. If those kaffirs weren't here I'd knock you down.'

The big man's eyes glistened with unshed tears and Gabriel knew where he had seen that level of fear before. A cult compound deep in the Brazilian rainforest. A demented Frenchman named Christophe Jardin – the self-styled Père Christophe – who'd ruled like an absolute monarch until Gabriel had deposed him.

'I, I'm sorry, Julius,' Ruud stuttered. 'I just thought it would be funny to see those kaffirs choking.'

'Yeah, well it wasn't funny from where I was standing. Come on, let's get them organised.'

Witaarde turned to Gabriel.

'Gabriel! How do you like this fine game park?'

'Who are they?' Gabriel asked, pointing at the black men unloading long guns from the *bakkie*.

'They've come down from Congo-Brazzaville to help out. What? You thought it would be just us two? Listen, man, this isn't some fucking ego trip for one of those "white hunter" wannabes. This is my *business*. This is my country's *future* we're building.'

'Sorry, Julius, I meant no disrespect. I was just curious, that's all.'

The apology, which Gabriel had figured, correctly, would appeal to the man's inflated sense of his own importance, worked. Witaarde clapped him on the shoulder.

'Yah, well, that's who they are. You have a problem with any of them, you bring it to me.'

'Understood. When do I get the Dakota?'

Witaarde grinned.

'In a hurry, are you?'

'No. But I like to familiarise myself with any weapon I shoot. SOP: standard operating procedure.'

'Yah? Well, *my* SOP is you get a gun when I say so and not before.'

'Supposing we're attacked.'

Witaarde narrowed his eyes.

'Attacked by who?'

'I don't know, the Botswana Defence Force? Other poachers? Lions?'

'You let *me* worry about security. These boys have seen plenty of action. If I was a lion I'd keep well clear of them. Unless I wanted to end up with my pelt on some millionaire's den floor. As for the army, forget it. They're cowards. After what we did to the last lot, they'll be keeping their heads down for a good while yet.'

'What about other poachers?'

Witaarde snorted.

'Huh! This park is under our control. It's all thrashed out higher up than you need to worry about.'

Gabriel shrugged.

'Fair enough. And they're disciplined, are they? The Congolese?'

'Disciplined? This isn't the British army, my friend. We don't do fucking drill. They're tough, ruthless and efficient. And they can shoot straight. That's all the discipline I need from them.'

Witaarde checked his watch.

'It's going to get dark in a couple of hours. We need to move and Brik needs to get the bird in the air again. He's picking us up when we've got what we came for.'

Witaarde went over to talk to the pilot. He tapped his watch. He must be setting up a routine for bringing him back when the hunt was over. Gabriel watched him gesturing to Ruud, who nodded, climbed into the Range Rover and roared off back towards the park entrance. Gabriel strolled over to the four Congolese poachers.

To a man, they were lean and muscular. All wore a basic uniform of camouflage shirt, trousers and boots. The headgear ranged from wide-brimmed bush hats to baseball caps and a dun-coloured bandanna. One man wore a pair of mirror-lensed Aviators. He grinned at Gabriel.

Each carried a knife in a leather sheath on his belt, plus a machete dangling from a leather or woven sling. The approach was that of his former brothers in the SAS. You chose the clothes and personal equipment you felt best met your personal needs.

Two carried Kalashnikovs, one an antiquated but serviceable-looking bolt-action rifle, one a more modern, wooden-stocked rifle Gabriel couldn't identify at first. He pointed at it.

'*C'est jolie. Qu'est ce que c'est?* It's pretty. What is it?'

The poacher smiled.

'*C'est un* Mauser M98 Magnum.' The last word came out, *Magnoom*.

Gabriel nodded his appreciation.

'Calibre?'

'*Quatre seize*.'

Gabriel nodded again. A .416 round would stop a charging elephant or Cape buffalo dead in its tracks if you were accurate. If.

'Right. Move out!' Witaarde called out. 'The herd's three miles west of here.'

Gabriel watched the Congolese shouldering their gear, including a new-looking STIHL chainsaw on a faded-orange webbing sling.

* * *

After an hour's tabbing through the park, they arrived at a long, narrow waterhole, fringed with trees and waist-high long grass.

They set up camp, although once the food and water had been consumed, Witaarde made a point of him and Gabriel moving to a spot away from the Congolese. They built a separate fire and then spread out sleeping bags.

Witaarde retrieved a bottle of whisky from his knapsack. He unscrewed the cap and took a pull before offering it to Gabriel. Gabriel accepted it, but blocked the neck with his tongue as he brought it to his mouth.

He kept Witaarde company as the man descended into slurring drunkenness, slowing his own speech down to mimic Witaarde's. Around them, the noise of nocturnal animals built steadily, so that an hour later it was a continuous background wail, mixing every type of sound from buzzes and whines to squeals, shrieks, leopard coughs, and an unearthly hum that sounded as though someone had powered up a distant electrical generator.

Witaard tilted the whisky bottle neck at Gabriel.

'No thanks, Julius, I'm good. I want to stay fresh for tomorrow.'

'Yah? Gonna lose your virginity, aren' ya? Bag a big elephan' for me and get 'is tusks out.'

'Do we take the *bakkie*?'

Witaarde rolled his eyes, and Gabriel couldn't tell if it was in exasperation, drunkenness or both.

'Those ears aren't jus' for keeping cool. They can hear real good. Engine noise spooks them.'

'Then how come tourists manage it?'

'Well, for one thing, they don't get as close as we need to. An' another thing is, this is more honest. You know? Like my granpappa used to do it.'

Reflecting that honesty was the last thing he'd have expected as a reason for poaching on foot, Gabriel shuffled a little closer to Witaarde. Witaarde's eyes were drooping. Gabriel knew he had to be quick.

'I know how important *Volksrepubliek van Suid-Afrika* is to you, Julius,' he said softly. 'You really care about it, don't you?'

'Course I care. This is my life. My fight,' he said, punching his chest. 'You know, Mandela had it right. You have to fight for what you believe in. I'm fighting for what *I* believe in.'

'Mandela?'

'Yeah, you know. Mandela!'

'Mandala?'

'What. You deaf, Englishman? I said Mandela. You know, *Nelson* Mandela.'

'Ohh, Man*del*a. Yeah, *Man*dela. Mandel*a*.'

It was easiest with drunks. As long as they were awake, the alcohol did half the work. Gabriel kept repeating the great South African's surname, varying the stressed syllable and raising and lowering his voice in a precise sequence of tones taught to him many years ago by master Zhao.

Behind him, Gabriel could hear the Congolese singing old French songs in exquisite harmonies. Their melodic voices, so surprising given their day jobs, floated across the space between the two groups of men, adding their own sonic colours to the disruption Gabriel was causing to Witaarde's brainwave patterns.

As he drew Witaarde's gaze into his and moved his eyes in synchrony with his voice, Gabriel waited for the tell-tale signs that Witaarde had lost control of his own mind. They came after twenty more seconds.

Witaarde's pupils blew. His breathing settled into a deep, glacial pace, one breath every thirty seconds. His muscle tone slackened.

And, in the flickering firelight beneath a billion stars, Gabriel Wolfe began talking. As the insects chittered, and the eternal battle between the eaters and the eaten gathered pace, he issued instructions and made suggestions for the following day's sport.

By seven, they were on the move again. One of the Congolese had been away before dawn, scouting ahead, tracking the herd. He'd reported back as the rest were eating breakfast.

In a ramshackle patois incorporating French, English, Swahili and Afrikaans, he communicated that the elephants were no more than a mile to the north, foraging in a patch of grassland by a waterhole.

Witaarde turned to Gabriel.

'This is it, my friend. Time to show what you're made of. Because I tell you, man, all that army BS counts for nothing out here. You shoot straight, you kill a tusker and you take the ivory. *Then* I know I can trust you.'

Gabriel nodded grimly. The hunt was nearing its climax.

54

Witaarde settled his bush hat lower over his brow. The sun was blinding, and even with the yellow-lensed hunting sunglasses, its glare was terrific. Like staring into a furnace.

He signalled with a finger to his lips to the lead Congolese, a guy called Amadou, to go 'all quiet'. The kaffir nodded and started signing orders to the other three. They grinned and nodded. You had to give it to those Congolese kaffirs, they enjoyed the sport.

Ahead, the grass speared skywards, increasing from waist-height to over eight feet tall. Somewhere among those breeze-disturbed stems the elephants were grazing.

He saw the topmost branches of an acacia swish violently from side to side, then still. Soft snuffling and parping little calls denoted the presence of babies. No good for ivory but the meat was supposed to be good. *Maybe we'll get our new friend to put a .416 Rigby into their little skulls. See if he's man enough.*

They were downwind of the beasts and he drew their musky stink deep into his lungs before exhaling quietly. Dung, mostly, and something else, something weirdly like human sweat.

Imagine God creating such a huge animal and then loading its face with hundreds of thousands of dollars' worth of ivory. *He gave us dominion and with that much money available, it's our duty to put it to better use.*

He looked left and right. The Congolese had vanished. Just him and the Englishman. *You playing me for a fool, Gabriel? Or are you serious about helping us? Soon we'll know. And if I don't like what I see? Well, one more corpse out here won't make a difference either way.*

It had caused him a moment's pain handing over his father's rifle. But the Englishman needed the Dakota to make a clean, one-shot kill. Witaarde had taken one of the kaffirs' AKs to replace it. Now he held it across his body like a damn guerrilla in one of the northern wars. He patted the 629 in its holster on his right hip. Always good to have backup.

The Englishman slid between two clumps of the monstrous grass, turning to Witaarde and signalling with his eyes. Witaarde had no trouble reading it. *They're in there. I'm going in.*

He nodded and pointed his right index finger. Then he followed close behind, the AK's muzzle pointing at the midpoint of the Englishman's spine. *Don't let me down now, Gabriel.*

He felt a buzzing in his head, and a high-pitched whine. Bloody mosquitos. He slapped at his right cheek.

The Englishman turned and put a finger to his lips. He beckoned Witaarde forward with a crooked finger.

'There they are,' he whispered, close to Witaarde's still-buzzing right ear. 'A bull, a cow and two calves. We kill them all at once, OK?'

'Yah, good plan.'

'I'll take the bull. You kill the other three. Make certain of it, Mandela.'

The buzzing intensified for a second. Witaarde shook his head at the mention of the dead president's name. He scowled. He didn't need an Englishman telling him how to kill elephants.

The Dakota had more than enough power to punch through the skull, but the puny little 7.62 mm rounds he'd be shooting didn't. Not singly. He flicked the fire selector switch to full auto. It wouldn't be clean, but it would be lethal.

He watched the Englishman silently raise the Dakota to his

shoulder. He settled his cheek against the worn-smooth stock and sighted on the bull. Witaarde saw his trigger finger as if through a magnifying glass.

Extreme close-up. Tightening around the trigger. The innocent-looking curve of steel beginning its short journey.

He realised he was holding his breath, let it out in a controlled exhalation as silent as any he'd ever breathed.

He raised the AK and aimed at the cow, ready to rake her and her babies with a blistering hail of bullets.

They fired together. A massive bang from the Dakota and from his AK an insane, juddering series of blasts that merged into a deafening roar. The bull toppled, blood spurting from a head wound, dead centre between its eyes.

He held his finger down on the trigger until the mag was empty. Dropped it out and slammed a new one home and emptied that, too, the red-hot barrel spewing lead into the fallen mother and babies. The corpses jerked and jumped as the rounds smashed through flesh and bone.

The AK's bolt smacked home on an empty chamber.

Ears ringing, Witaarde let the smoking AK drop to the ground. His nose itched with the smell of burnt propellant and hot brass. The coppery smell of blood was thick in the air.

The Englishman picked up the chainsaw. Grinning at Witaarde over his shoulder, he walked over to the dead bull. He kicked the massive head. With a flowing movement, he pulled the chainsaw's starter cord.

The machine kicked into life with a cough. A harsh rasping filled the air. The Englishman blipped the throttle a couple of times, then bent and hit the first tusk with the blade. It bit deep and the engine note deepened then started singing and screaming as he sliced into the skull to take off the tusk.

The second tusk came off even easier than the first.

The Englishman killed the engine and dropped the chainsaw. He picked up one of the tusks and held it aloft in triumph.

Witaarde was pleased. More than pleased. Delighted. He had what he wanted. More ivory to trade. And a ready-made private army of battle-hardened soldiers he could use to smash the opposition. He'd like to see the Botswanans try and shut him down now.

'Come and take a look,' the Englishman called out.

No need for silence now they'd killed the elephants.

Witaarde walked forward, trying to ignore the ringing in his ears. It felt like it was located exactly halfway between them, right at the centre of his brain. Like a damn mosquito had crawled into one of his ears and burrowed in, right *there*. He shook his head and took a few more steps, then came to a stop in front of the Englishman.

He looked at the tusk. Odd. Up close, he couldn't see any blood. Normally the root end was a mess of severed tissue, soaked in the stuff for a foot up towards the point. And why was it forked like that?

He looked at the Englishman.

There was something wrong with his eyes. They were, what was the word, flickering. No. Flicking. Left, right, left, right. The ringing in his ears grew louder. He tried to follow the Englishman's eyes with his own, but the damn noise was too loud.

It stopped. Just like that. He blinked. He could hear birdsong. The swish of the tall grass. His own laboured breathing. The Englishman's voice.

'…three, two, one.'

Witaarde blinked. He looked around him and frowned. It made no sense.

Amadou lay a few feet away, a hole you could put a fist through blown clear through his chest. A red mess already swarming with flies. The other three Congolese poachers lay sprawled in tortured postures.

One was missing half his face and his right hand, red craters blowing out from his khaki shirt. One lay face-up with his belly ripped open and slimy purple-grey intestines coiled beside him. One was on his front, gaping exit wounds in his back revealing splintered ribs and the mushy interior where his internal organs had once been.

He looked back at the Englishman. The tusk he'd been holding was gone. He held a bone-white tree branch in his hand.

'What?' was all Witaarde could manage.

His heart was racing and sparks were shooting off at the edge of his vision. He tried again.

'Where are they?'

The Englishman shook his head.

'They were never here, Witaarde.'

Witaarde grabbed for the revolver on his belt.

55

Even if Gabriel hadn't just brought Witaarde out of a post-hypnotic trance, the clumsy grab for the revolver would have been child's play to defeat. He brought the branch round in a short swing that connected with Witaarde's left temple and sent him to the ground. Gabriel stooped and retrieved the 629.

Witaarde came round a couple of minutes later. Gabriel was leaning back against the dead tree he'd so recently attacked with the chainsaw, removing two of its lower limbs.

'Get up,' Gabriel said, holding the 629 steady, aimed at Witaarde's midsection.

'What the fuck did you just do?'

'I planted a post-hypnotic suggestion in your whisky-soaked brain last night.'

'No! I saw them. The elephants. We shot them.'

Gabriel pushed himself upright and took a couple of strides towards Witaarde, who fell back.

'Look around you, Witaarde. Do you see any dead elephants? Oh, wait. They got up and walked away after shooting your Congolese friends dead.'

'It was us,' Witaarde said in a defeated whisper.

'Yes, it was. I killed Amadou with your Dakota. You killed the others.'

'But, why?' Witaarde asked, his eyes wide.

'You murdered the Paras. I'm an ex-Para. I'm here to kill you in their memory.'

'But the men you promised me.'

Gabriel sprang at Witaarde and delivered a hard-palmed slap to his left cheek.

'Don't you get it? There aren't any men. There never were. I traced you from Botswana to Hong Kong, Dubai and Vientiane, Witaarde.'

Witaarde's face closed in on itself.

'It's him, isn't it? He sent you. He's double-crossed me,' he murmured in a dangerous, low voice.

'Who?'

'You know perfectly well, you kaffir-loving cunt. I'm not playing games with you.'

Gabriel shook his head.

'I don't know who you're talking about, but it doesn't matter.'

'Tammerlane! It's Tammerlane. Your own precious prime minister,' Witaarde yelled.

'Joe Tammerlane?'

Witaarde's eyes bulged out of their sockets.

'Yes! Of course! How many other Tammerlanes are there?'

Gabriel heard the unmistakable sound of pieces clicking into place.

'Tell me.'

'And you'll let me live?'

'Tell me. And I'll think about it.'

'We met at Oxford. Balliol College. We were all undergraduates together.'

'Wait. You said, "all". Not "both"?'

'Me. Joe Tammerlane. And Horatio Bokara. He's the—'

'President of South Africa.'

* * *

As the Englishman identified Bokara, Witaarde closed his eyes. He was remembering a meeting, not so very long ago. Just a few years.

They had chosen their meeting spot carefully. At the heart of the Kruger National Park, five hundred kilometres from Pretoria. The three Oxford graduates, each, in his own way, an idealist, stood beside each other on the south bank of the Letaba River. Here, they felt, they could meet safely.

And safety was key. All three men had to please constituencies who would be shocked if they knew with whom their leaders were consorting. Left, right, black, white: all held fast to their own world views. All were sceptical at best, and downright hostile at worst, to any countervailing belief-system.

They had spent many evenings and nights as undergraduates debating, disputing and, on one memorable night, fighting, about politics.

No two shared the same point of view. Yet each recognised in the others the same ferocious fire. The same obsessional single-mindedness. The same visionary clarity of mind that said, 'I am right. And one day I will prove it'.

Over the intervening years they had followed each other's fortunes as they waxed and waned. And now they had found the perfect confluence of money, power and ideas that would help them achieve their goals.

Three vehicles, a Range Rover, a Mercedes G-Wagen and a Toyota Hilux pickup sat beneath the broiling sun, one hundred metres away. Red dust shrouded the lower halves of their bodywork. Beneath their raised-up chassis, condensed water dripped from the aircon units' bleeder pipes, darkening the earth.

'The next shipment goes to the UAE on Friday,' Witaarde said.

'How much did we get for it?' Bokara asked.

'Three point two million. Your share's in the *bakkie*.' He turned to Tammerlane, the third member of their ill-assorted trio. 'Yours too, Joe.'

'Thanks. So, how's it going?' Tammerlane asked, as Bokara ambled over to the pickup to count his share.

'Slow, to be honest. Believe me, setting up a country takes a lot more than cash.'

'I feel your pain. I might not be setting up a country from scratch, but I'm still trying to recreate one.'

'You do know that Marxism won't work? I mean, look around this continent. The place is littered with basket-case economies because their leaders sided with the Commies.'

'Ah, but that's where I'm different. I'm going to do it properly.'

'And does "properly" include stashing your millions in offshore bank accounts?'

'To be drawn on as and when we need extra cash. For the transition.'

'Or if the electorate kick you out after four years when they've been reduced to eating grass, eh?'

Witaarde laughed loudly at his own joke. With no hard surfaces bar the 4x4s for hundreds of kilometres in any direction, the sound died quickly in the warm air.

Tammerlane shrugged.

'There could be a different electoral system by then,' was all he said.

* * *

'Hey!' Gabriel slapped Witaarde, who'd lapsed back into a trance state. 'What's going on between you, Tammerlane and Bokara?'

Witaarde focused on Gabriel. He glanced down at the Colt then back up into Gabriel's eyes.

'We never saw eye to eye on ideology. But one thing we all knew – still know – is that ideology is nothing if you don't have power. Dreams are fine. But you rule, or you fail. Me, Horatio and Joe, we understand that.'

'But how could you ever make this work?'

Witaarde smiled, though it lacked any human warmth.

'It's not so hard to see, if you look at it right. I want a Boer homeland. Nothing different from what other marginalised groups want or have taken for themselves: Catalonia, Scotland, Wallonia,

Palestine, Israel. They've all either got their own homelands or are pressing for them. Horatio wants a black South Africa. Simple as. No Indians. No whites. He's prepared to try and copy what Mugabe tried in Zim. Blame his country's troubles on the Brits or the UN, or NATO, hell, the EU for all he cares. It doesn't matter as long as it plays well at home.'

'And Tammerlane?'

'Joe wants to create a socialist utopia in the UK. He's mad, obviously, but who cares. That's not my fight. My fight is here. In Africa. In fact, guess what? It all dovetails neatly together. Joe gets a new enemy to rail against. What could be better for a hard-left firebrand like Joe than white South Africans fighting for independence? Meanwhile Horatio gets to burnish his credentials in Africa while he lets me split off and create a homeland where he can banish the whites.'

Gabriel shook his head. It was monstrous. A triple-legged tower of fantasy fuelled by slaughtering elephants. They didn't mind who got in the way of their twisted dreams.

'You're a murderer,' he said.

Witaarde raised his hands.

'I told you what you wanted to hear. You have to keep your side of the bargain. Put that gun down and let me go.'

Gabriel looked down at the revolver's gleaming barrel. Witaarde had put him onto an international conspiracy that would bring down Tammerlane, if not Bokara.

He looked back at Witaarde.

'No.'

He raised the revolver and aimed at Witaarde's head. This close, the round would take his head clean off.

Witaarde flung himself to the ground, crawling on all fours towards Gabriel, who had to take a step back.

He raised his face.

'Please don't kill me, Gabriel. Please, have mercy. I am begging you, man. I have a wife. Klara needs me.'

'Fuck her! She's worse than you, Witaarde. Get to your feet.'

Instead, Witaarde knelt before Gabriel like a penitent before a priest.

Then he reared up and flung two handfuls of gritty red dust directly into Gabriel's eyes.

Gabriel staggered back, keeping a tight grip on the revolver with one hand and frantically trying to clear his eyes of the stinging earth with the other.

'Fuck you!' Witaarde screamed as he ran off into the tall grass.

Eyes burning, Gabriel raced after him. His vision was smeary but he caught a glimpse of Witaarde and fired. He saw a spurt of blood from his right thigh. Witaarde screamed but kept running. Gabriel swore: he'd missed the femur and the artery, both of which would have brought his man down.

Witaarde scrabbled frantically at the thick screen of grass before him and plunged on.

He screamed again.

No! Gabriel had time to think. No human had emitted that unearthly wail.

Gabriel burst out from the grass to find Witaarde turning towards him, wide-eyed, running away from an adult elephant and a calf. The adult – the mother? – had raised her trunk and was trumpeting her displeasure at Witaarde.

Gabriel straightened his right arm and shot Witaarde point-blank, straight between the eyes. His face disintegrated in a red mist as his head exploded. The headless body stumbled forward on dead legs and fell at Gabriel's feet.

Gabriel kept his eyes locked onto the adult female. She stood less than twenty feet from him, legs planted foursquare, ears wide and erect, trunk lashing from side to side. The baby had taken sanctuary beneath her heaving belly, secure inside the four massive pillars of her legs.

Gabriel lowered his right hand, let the revolver fall to the ground and took a slow, deliberate step backwards.

The elephant glared at him, her brown, long-lashed eyes following him as he slid his feet backwards, flat-footed, until he felt the grass at his back. He fought to maintain a wide view of her and her calf, avoiding the tunnel vision inexperienced fighters could let overwhelm them, until all they could see was the enemy fighter.

In the distance, he saw a small herd of elephants. *Go and join them*, he mentally urged her. *Take little Dumbo there and get back to your friends. I didn't come here to hurt you.*

The baby bleated from beneath its mother's downcurved belly. The meaning was as clear as the endless blue sky. Mum, I wanna go!

The mother raised her trunk and blared defiantly at Gabriel, then turned, reaching under her chest with her trunk to caress the top of her baby's head. Then mother and baby lumbered off, back to the herd. And safety.

Gabriel breathed out, shaking his head. He bent to retrieve the 629 and stuck it in his waistband.

He began the walk back to the pickup truck: his ride out of the park.

Inside the *bakkie*'s cab, Gabriel pulled out his phone and made a call.

'This is Major Modimo.'

'Major, it's Gabriel Wolfe.'

'Gabriel! How are you?'

'I'm good. If you get some men to the GPS coordinates I'm going to send you, you'll find four dead Congolese poachers and a South African named Julius Witaarde. He was the leader of a Boer separatist movement called *Boerevryheid an Regte* and the poaching gang that murdered your men and the Paras.'

'You are sure of this?'

'One hundred per cent. He confessed to me.'

'This is most welcome news. Thank you. Do you need help with extraction?'

'No thanks, Major. I have transport here.'

As Gabriel approached the gatehouse entrance to the park, he rolled his shoulders and relaxed, pasting a smile on his face, ready to charm the guard into letting him through. He needn't have bothered. The place was deserted. He cruised past the wooden hut at a nice, easy ten miles an hour and was back on the highway heading towards Gaborone five minutes later.

Ahead was a long drive. But the *bakkie* had water, he could buy food from a roadside vendor and, if necessary, sleep in the cab. Compared to some journeys he'd undertaken, in and out of uniform, that counted as luxury living.

He called Eli and discovered to his delight that she was back in Botswana and waiting for him to make contact.

'I'm waiting for you at the Avani, Gabe,' she said. 'Drive carefully.'

* * *

A day later, as Gabriel was rolling into Gaborone and looking for somewhere to leave the *bakkie*, Major Modimo was speaking to TV cameras outside his office. Before him were laid out the corpses of the poachers beneath tarpaulins, the single white man among them at the front of the tableau.

'These men sought to enrich themselves by slaughtering Botswana's elephants and trading their ivory illegally.'

He paused and pointed dramatically with his pistol at the bodies before him. Cameras whirred. Journalists waited patiently to ask their questions.

'Thanks to the efforts of my men, who found themselves under fire when trying to arrest them, these desperadoes have been brought to justice. Their leader was one Julius Witaarde, the leader of the *Boerevryheid an Regte*, a South African white rights movement. We suspect he was using the cash he gained to finance his operations.

'We are in contact with the South African authorities to discuss further steps to ensure his organisation does not attempt to re-enter Botswana to murder our elephants. I will now take questions.'

Klara Witaarde stared at the screen of her laptop in disbelief. As the journalists squabbled over questioning rights like flamingos at a nesting site, a photo of her husband replaced the live feed. Beneath it, a crawl read:

JULIUS WITAARDE, LEADER OF BOEREVRYHEID AN REGTE , SHOT DEAD BY ANTI-POACHING TROOPS. CONFIRMED AS LEADER OF IVORY POACHING GANG

'Julius!' she screamed, slamming the laptop's lid down. 'What have they done to you?'

She didn't cry. That would have to wait. Klara Witaarde regarded herself as a model of Boer womanhood. Grief was a luxury she couldn't afford right now.

She and Julius had discussed what to do if he should ever be killed. They'd always imagined it would be the ANC or their contracted-out stooges who'd make the attempt. But now it turned out that bloody Englishman had tricked them both into letting him get too close to her beloved Julius. Who was he working for? It was obvious, to Klara at least.

Julius had been too wrapped up in the logistics of the ivory operation to revise who he was doing business with. And now that Commie bastard had sent a hitman to kill the one man she had ever loved. The one man who could rescue their people from Pretoria's grip.

She went out back to the office with the safe key and a look of determination on her face.

They would pay for their crimes. All of them. But especially him.

56

ALDEBURGH

Gabriel and Eli flew back to England together. Don met them with a chauffeur-driven limo at Heathrow, courtesy of the mission's banker. The following day, all three, plus Stella and her boss, were seated at the kitchen table. Cups of freshly-brewed coffee steamed between them. Wind rattled the ill-fitting windows in their wooden frames.

Patiently, and stopping to answer all their questions, Gabriel laid out his actions in Botswana and what Witaarde had told him. When he finished, the room was silent for several seconds.

Eli was looking at Don. He'd steepled his fingers under his nose. His deep frown had turned his eyes into slits beneath his greying eyebrows. Stella and Callie McDonald were open-mouthed. Gabriel distinctly heard two separate snaps as they caught each other's eye and closed them.

'Did anyone just hear me?' Gabriel asked the group. 'I said Joe Tammerlane, poster boy of the hard left and our newly elected prime minister, is complicit in the murders of four Paras and three Botswana soldiers, not to mention the illegal fucking ivory trade!'

'We heard you, Old Sport,' Don said. 'It's rather a question of what we do with what we know.'

Gabriel turned to Stella.

'You could arrest Tammerlane, for a start.'

Callie spoke before Stella could respond.

'It's not that simple, I'm afraid. Tammerlane has surrounded himself with a private security force. We've effectively been sidelined. Assigned to purely criminal offences.'

'But this is about as criminal as it gets,' Gabriel said.

'I know, I know,' she said, with a patient air that merely infuriated him. 'But I can't go charging into Number Ten with Stella here waving our shiny handcuffs. There are armed guards on the gate and they no longer belong to us.'

'Shit! How long was I away?' Gabriel asked. 'Have I come back to the same country I left?'

Don sighed.

'I'm afraid not. Those of us who love this country – as it was and should be – have been fighting a rearguard action. This intel is brilliant, and if we can find a way to exploit it, we have a slim chance of getting rid of Tammerlane and cleaning out the Augean stable.'

The discussion wore on for three more, fruitless, hours. Halfway through they turned on the TV to catch a lunchtime bulletin. The newsreader announced that Joe Tammerlane and his inner circle were at Chequers, the country house residence enjoyed by British prime ministers since 1921. Gabriel grabbed the remote and snapped off the programme.

Stella asked a question that brought Gabriel up short.

'Did you find anything else out about who hired the Syrian to murder Princess Alexandra?'

Gabriel shook his head.

'Nothing.'

'Let's look at motive,' Stella said. 'Who could have reason to want her dead? *Qui bono*?'

'Who benefits?' Gabriel asked.

'Exactly.'

The table fell silent. Gabriel felt himself subsiding into a personal quiet space removed from the others as he turned the problem over in his mind. Yes, who *would* benefit from the death of a princess? He'd never placed much credence in the idea of its being Israeli retaliation for her ill-judged attendance at the charity event, even before they'd proved it couldn't have been Lieberman.

Alexandra wasn't a member of 'the inner circle'. A granddaughter of the old queen, yes, but not what was known as a 'working royal'. No official duties. No state visits. No public profile beyond the occasional appearance in a celebrity magazine. Just a very wealthy young lady who lived in a grand house in England's Home Counties and happened to have a jewellery box full of tiaras.

Why her, then? If you wanted to strike a blow against the monarchy, you'd go for the head, surely? Or if not him, one of his children. Or one of the vanishingly small number two or three steps away from the throne.

Fear of public revulsion? Sure. But you'd get that whoever you killed, such was the love most ordinary people in Britain had for the royal family. As had been proved in the days following the princess's murder and funeral.

He recalled his final conversation with Witaarde. He'd asked him if Tammerlane was involved and, instead of denying it, Witaarde had dodged the question. You'd have to ask him, he'd said.

Narratives flashed through his mind, colliding, sparking off each other. And he knew. Right there. He knew.

The princess was a distraction! It *was* a blow at the monarchy. But it was more subtle than attempting to strike at its heart. This wasn't revolutionary France or Russia in 1917. You couldn't overthrow the monarchy by killing them. This was cunning on a monumental scale. And suddenly, he knew with dread certainty who was behind the assassination. And the knowledge made him feel sick.

Gabriel looked up. Eli was staring at him. Her eyes were searching his. Her forehead was crinkled with concern.

'Are you all right, Gabe? You look pale.'

He swallowed.

'I know who ordered Princess Alexandra's murder.'

Eli and Stella wore identical expressions. Shocked eyes, wide and staring, mouths dropped open a little. Frowns. Callie and Don were regarding him with appraising looks.

'Who?' Stella said.

'Joe Tammerlane.'

'What?' Eli burst out.

'You're not serious?'

'You asked who benefited from her death, Stella. Try this on for size. After her death – which, by the way, he arrived seconds too late to prevent, but still managed to kill the alleged assassin – he gets showered with praise by an already pretty favourable media. The public love him. Then he gives them his "I may be a republican but I just did what anyone would do" speech.'

'His position on the monarchy was hardly a secret, though,' Stella protested.

'No, it wasn't. And that's my point. Boss,' he said, turning to Don, 'you told me he's pretty much placed the king under house arrest. On the grounds of national security, but still.'

'That seems pretty sensible, until they find out who really paid al-Javari,' Eli said. 'There could be another assassination.'

'There's not going to be another one,' Gabriel said. 'Why can't you see it?'

'Because you're not making any sense,' Eli said. 'I can accept him being corrupt. Even being tangled up with the Paras' murders. But this? No. It's too much.'

Gabriel sighed with frustration.

'First you find a pretext to get the ing away from the public eye. You keep him there. Then you find ways to *protect* the other members of the royal family. Then you hobble the armed forces and the police, which, by the way, it sounds like he's doing. And then, bam!' he clapped his hands together, 'you announce that it's time to usher in a brave new world of republicanism. Sling a few more freebies at the populace – give everyone free Sky Movies – and you're home and dry. Welcome to the People's Democratic Republic of Britain.'

'Wow,' Stella said. 'That was quite a speech. And I agree,' she added quickly, as Gabriel opened his mouth to object, 'it's a compelling narrative, but I ask you again. Where's the evidence?'

'I—'

He closed his mouth again. She was right, damn her. Bloody detectives. He ran a hand over his face. His palm came away wet. He felt a ball of tension in his stomach.

Eli rose from her chair and knelt at his feet. She placed a hand on his knee.

'Gabe. You've been under so much pressure. I think this was your brain weaving a conspiracy out of unconnected events.'

'I'm not so sure he is,' Don said. 'Callie, what's your view?'

'Look, I've heard some pretty outlandish tales in my time as a police officer.' She shot Stella a searching glance. 'And, believe me, this is right up there with the best of them. It has the virtue of consistency. Just not evidence.'

Gabriel got up from his chair at the table and went outside. Eli arrived a few minutes later. She put her arm round his waist and looked up into his eyes.

'What is it?'

'This is so much bullshit, El,' he said. 'I'm tired of all this "where's the evidence" crap. It's obvious who's behind it.'

His heart was thumping and he pulled away from Eli as she tried to turn him to face her. On the other side of the car park the sea was roaring in over the stony beach, the sound a harsh '*shush*' as if even the sea wanted him to pipe down.

'There's nothing you can do, Gabe,' she said. 'Callie's right.'

He placed his hands gently on her shoulders and looked into those amazing grey-green eyes.

'You're wrong. There's always something I can do.'

He pulled his car keys from his jeans pocket and dangled them in the foot or so of air between them.

'I'm going for a drive.'

'Want some company?'

He shook his head. Smiled at her.

'No thanks. I need to clear my head. Tell them, would you?'

He kissed her softly on the lips, then climbed into the Camaro and started the big V8 with an unnecessary but satisfying jab downwards on the throttle. He backed out of his drive, across the road and then, slewing round in a tight circle that inscribed black circles on the tarmac, headed back into Aldeburgh. And onwards.

57

CHILTERN HILLS, BUCKINGHAMSHIRE

Gabriel cruised along the Missenden Road, heading for the little village of Ellesborough, deep in the Buckinghamshire countryside. This landscape couldn't have been more different from those he'd seen in Africa. Thick green vegetation, tall hedges, round-shouldered oak trees, blush-red roses clambering over ancient brick walls.

The entrance to the lane was so discreet he almost missed it. But the change in light where the lane interrupted the tall hedge caught his eye and he slowed to a crawl.

Two small steel signs, navy-blue with the legend PRIVATE NO ADMITTANCE in white paint were set into the neatly clipped sides of the hedge. Beyond the gap, a brick wall in an intricate pattern like fretwork, stretched away towards a brick-built lodge house.

He checked the map on his phone. Yes. This was it. Half a mile to the west lay the imposing country house he'd come to visit.

A mile further on he found a lay-by, and pulled in, the Camaro's fat tyres scrunching over the gravelly mud. He popped the boot lid and changed his boat shoes for the hiking boots he always kept there. He grabbed a go-bag containing a pair of compact Zeiss binoculars and a Böker combat knife and shrugged it on.

He checked his phone battery: 89%. Good. He'd checked and double-checked the voice-recorder app and it worked just fine.

Like all the best plans, his was simple. And flexible. No specific tactics, just get inside, find Tammerlane, isolate him, force him to confess, take the recording to Callie and Stella. Job done.

Gabriel climbed over a stile and into a field. The big house was visible on the horizon. Over terrain this friendly, he reckoned on fifteen minutes maximum to reach the target.

A herd of inquisitive bullocks wandered towards him. He kept on in a straight line towards Chequers, clapping his hands and shooing the docile beasts as he came within shouting distance. They scattered before him, bumping into one another and lowing in panic as they collided with each other.

In spite of himself, he saw the humour in their attempts to first befriend and then escape from this marauding human, and laughed. The sound only served to scatter them again and he ended up running through the centre of the animals along a wide processional path they had inadvertently created for him.

Ahead, a small copse of birch and hazel trees offered a convenient observation point. In the cover they provided, he fetched out his binos and surveyed the front of the house and then the sides.

Initially he saw nothing beyond the stately home's imposing architecture of the red-brick Tudor house. Then, from the left-hand corner, he saw what he had been expecting, if not hoping, to see. One of Tammerlane's new internal security goons wandered round to the front door, checked it, then continued on a circuit around the outer wing of the house.

A second man appeared as his partner disappeared, like the the old couple in a weather house. He repeated the sequence of moves in the opposite direction.

Twenty seconds from side to side. Then a gap of four minutes fifteen seconds, then the first guy turned up. Both men were no doubt armed with pistols, but their gait suggested they were less than fully alert. Out here, in the depths of the countryside, maybe they felt safe. There'd be more men inside, Gabriel assumed.

With the second man gone, Gabriel sprinted across the open ground towards the front of the house. He arrived at the front door twenty seconds later. Three minutes fifty-five seconds left.

He raised the heavy iron ring and slapped it against the raised iron boss bolted to the door. Three sharp knocks. Nothing obviously coded, but confident nonetheless.

His heart was pounding and he felt the familiar kick from the adrenaline surging through his bloodstream. He checked his watch.

Three minutes, twenty.

Come on, come on!

Three minutes, five.

He heard footsteps on the far side of the iron-banded oak.

Two minutes fifty-eight.

The door swung inwards at speed.

Gabriel sprang through the gap, arm coming up, fist clenched. The man on the other side didn't stand a chance. His mouth was open to ask a question, but he never got as far as the first letter of the first syllable. Gabriel's closed fist hammered into the soft tissue of his throat, smashing into his larynx.

The man staggered backwards, dropping his pistol as he clutched both hands around his throat. Eyes popping, he could only look in shock as Gabriel pulled the door closed behind him and delivered a sharp blow to the side of his head that felled him like a tree.

Gabriel stuck the pistol in the back of his waistband, and dragged the unconscious man by his heels into a recess behind the stairs in the vast hallway.

Breathing heavily, he straightened and scanned the exit points from the hallway. *Where are you, Tammerlane? Where's your conference room?*

The hallway, dominated by a glossy black grand piano with the lid resting on its stay, offered several exits. Gabriel pulled the pistol from his waistband and checked it. A Glock 19, full mag, ready to go. On the balls of his feet to minimise the sound, he ran down a corridor hung with dusty old oil paintings of generals and nobleman from a bygone age.

He saw a door to his right and stopped, pressing his ear against the polished wood. Nothing beyond but silence, broken, just, by the ticking of a grandfather clock.

He ran on. The corridor doglegged and he came to a second door, guarded by two enormous floor-mounted vases as tall as he was, in some sort of liver-coloured stone. *Porphyry*! The word flew unbidden into his mind.

He listened at the door. Nothing but the rushing of blood in his ears like the North Sea surf back in Aldeburgh.

He heard voices. A man and a woman. They were coming his way.

'When're they breaking?' the male said.

'Don't know. Twelve? Half-past?'

'Don't they ever get tired of gassing?'

The female laughed.

'Not this lot. It's what the comrades love best, isn't it?'

Their footsteps grew louder.

Gabriel estimated he only had seconds.

He looked back the way he'd come. Nowhere to hide in the arrow-straight passageway. He flattened himself into the six-inch-deep recess housing the door he'd just checked.

The guards turned into his portion of the corridor. Still bitching about their masters, like guards the world over.

Gabriel counted their footsteps.

One, two, three, four…

He stepped out.

Smiling broadly, he asked the female guard, 'Where's the loo, please?'

She frowned. Struggling to process the appearance of a clearly unauthorised guest, she paused before answering.

Pausing was the wrong choice.

Gabriel caught her across the left temple with the Glock, felling her like a stunned calf. He drove his left elbow into the male guard's solar plexus, emptying his lungs so thoroughly that he collapsed to the ground clutching his stomach, utterly failing to drag so much as an angel's breath of air into his temporarily paralysed lungs.

Gabriel struck down with a chopping hand, sending him into the darkness with a blow that struck a nerve-rich area at the base of his skull. He relieved both guards of their pistols, kept one and dropped the other into an elephant's foot umbrella stand beneath a mullioned window. He took a bunch of cable ties from his go-bag and bound them, ankles to wrists.

He'd been inside the house for over five minutes now and time was against him.

He ran on, assuming, hoping, really, that the conference rooms would all be on the ground floor, the upper storeys being reserved for bedrooms and the old servants' quarters.

A low murmur brought him to a stop. Ahead, the corridor opened out into a square hallway. A door on the far side led to the gardens. But on the left side of the square space, between two imposing suits of armour complete with ten-foot pikestaffs, was another door.

Beyond it, clearly audible without the need to press his ear against its polished surface, Gabriel heard murmurs, laughter and then, crowing in that familiar confident tone, the voice of Joe Tammerlane.

Gabriel grasped the brass door knob and twisted it, then, a pistol in each hand like an old-time gunslinger, he entered the room.

58

Despite, or perhaps because of, the grandeur of the house in which the room was located, Tammerlane had fitted it out like any one of millions of anonymous conference rooms in hotels the world over.

Whiteboard easels, flipcharts and a laptop coupled to a projector filled the space not occupied by Tammerlane and the members of his inner circle.

Gabriel recognised a handful from the brief moments he'd spent watching television news.

To Tammerlane's left sat Tracy Barnett-Short, the secretary of state for defence. To her left, Ariane Hooper, the home secretary who had done so much in such a short space of time to demoralise and antagonise the police, the prison service and the security agencies.

The men he was less sure of, although one face he did recognise. The secretary of state for the Environment, whose sanctimonious interviews in the election had had even the normally supportive papers questioning his sincerity.

Gabriel heeled the door closed behind him.

'Good afternoon,' he said, holding the pistols wide so everyone in the room would feel they were being aimed at. 'My name is Gabriel Wolfe and I have come here to end your little shit-show.'

The seated politicians all bore an identical expression. One part shock, one part bafflement, one part hatred. Teeth bared. Eyes wide. Faces pale. A couple of the men were grasping the arms of their chairs as if to rise. Gabriel swung the gun barrels in their directions and they sat back down.

'Look, friend,' Tammerlane said, his voice smooth, unwavering, calming, 'I don't know who you are or what you think we've done, but there's really no need for the guns.' He half-rose from his chair. 'Why don't you—'

'Sit down!' Gabriel barked, deriving satisfaction from the speed with which Tammerlane's rear end hit the seat cushion.

'Fine, fine,' Tamerlane said, his voice having risen in pitch by a semi-tone. 'Look, I'm sitting. Now, everyone stay calm, OK? What is it you want, Gabriel, was it?'

Gabriel walked to the end of the boardroom table they were sitting at and took up a commanding position where he could see each one of them and the door.

He leaned forwards and spoke directly to Tammerlane.

'I know about your little business deal with Julius Witaarde and Horatio Bokara.'

Tammerlane's lips twitched. A tiny movement. But Gabriel caught it. He'd been *trained* to catch it.

'I know who Horatio Bokara is, obviously, but the other one?'

'Your other friend from Balliol College, Oxford. Julius Witaarde, which means White Earth, by the way, although I'm sure you know that.'

'What is this about, Joe?' Barnett-Short asked. 'You did go to Oxford, right?'

'Shut up, Tracy,' he said.

'No need to be rude to the lady,' Gabriel said. He turned and pointed his left-hand Glock at Barnett-Short. 'Go on,' a beat, '*Tracy*. Ask him your question again.'

'Who is Julius Witaarde, Joe? And what's this about you and Bokara?'

'Witaarde is nobody. I don't know anyone by that name. Look,' he jerked his chin at Gabriel. 'The man's obviously insane. He's a fantasist.'

'Am I?' Gabriel asked. He addressed the room as if giving a presentation. 'Julius Witaarde was, until recently, the leader of two distinct, but interrelated groups. One, *Boerevryheid an Regte*, is a white separatist movement in South Africa. The other, which finances both that group and some of your boss's own efforts, doesn't have a name, but it's an ivory poaching operation stretching from Botswana to Laos and into mainland China.'

'This is just ridiculous!' Tammerlane said, but his eyes gave him away. They were wild and his breathing was coming in short gasps.

'No. It isn't ridiculous at all,' Gabriel said. 'It was this man's friends who murdered the four British paratroopers last month, along with three members of the Botswana Defence Force Anti-Poaching Unit.'

One of the men, Aldon Hayter, that was it, was staring with frank curiosity at Tammerlane.

'Joe, it's not true, is it?'

'Look at him,' Gabriel said. 'Look at his face. Can't you see? Of course it's true.'

Hayter stared at Tammerlane, and Gabriel was gratified to see the other people doing the same.

Tammerlane straightened in his chair. He ran a hand over his hair, smoothing it into place. Then he swept the others with a gaze all the more dangerous for the friendliness in that famous, Instagram-worthy smile.

'Comrades. A bloodless revolution would have been preferable. But sometimes the greater good calls for sacrifices,' he said, still smiling. 'Think of the good we're doing for this country. Of the good we *will* do.'

Then he turned towards the door and yelled:

'Guards!'

He turned back to Gabriel, his eyes flashing, a triumphant grin on his face.

'Yes, you're right. I do know Julius. And Horatio. I know all about the unfortunate business in Botswana. But one can't run a revolution on buttons, Gabriel. Projects like mine need money. Real money. With big business against me, where else was I to find it?'

Gabriel watched with interest as the other occupants of the table drew away from Tammerlane. Chairs had scraped back, torsos were leaned away from him.

'Witaarde is dead,' Gabriel said. 'So are his men. The Botswanans have shut your evil little operation down.'

Tammerlane's gaze flicked to the door and back.

'They're not coming,' Gabriel said. He held up the pistols. 'Where do you think I got these from?'

'How can you criticise me for what we did out there? I'm transforming a country of seventy-plus million people. How can you weigh that against the deaths of five men and find me wanting?'

'Five men and one woman.'

Tammerlane shook his head.

'No. Julius called me. It was only men out there.'

'I'm not talking about out there,' Gabriel said, levelling his right arm towards Tammerlane.

'What are you talking about then?' Hooper asked.

'Princess Alexandra.'

'What?'

He turned to her, but kept one pistol pointed straight at the bridge of Tammerlane's nose.

'He hired a Syrian contractor killer called Nazir Aboud al-Javari to assassinate Princess Alexandra. That's how he was able to time his intervention so precisely.'

'You're crazy,' Tammerlane said.

Gabriel shook his head. Time for his bluff. The only weak card in his hand.

'No I'm not. I killed al-Javari. But before he died, he confessed. I recorded him. It's what the police call a dying declaration. It's acceptable in a court of law.'

Tammerlane shook his head. Smiled. He actually smiled. Gabriel felt an urge to empty both Glocks into his grinning face.

* * *

Five and a half thousand miles due south, Klara Witaarde was on the phone, talking to a Russian hacker she knew, simply, as WhiteKnight.

'Check your account. The money should be there,' she said.

She waited. Outside, she could hear Ruud butchering hogs. Their squeals, cut off and transformed into a gurgle, soothed her.

As Klara counted the number of death-screams Ruud drew from the pigs, WhiteKnight came back on the line.

'It's there. Thank you. You want me to hit the green button?'

'With all your might.'

Klara watched as the little animated globe on her laptop screen spun, before coming to a stop.

'OK, it's up,' WhiteKnight said. 'Copies to Wikileaks, Buzzfeed, Huffington Post, the BBC, Reuters, links on Twitter, Facebook, basically everywhere.'

Klara Witaarde checked the major global news sites, and her social media feeds, as her late husband's covert audio and video recordings went live, then viral, then global.

One video in particular would do the job, she felt. She played it again. Julius had shot it from a hidden camera in a bag. His voice was rendered with perfect clarity. As was the man he was speaking to, whose face was framed by the fuzzy eclipse of the slit in the leather through which the tiny lens protruded.

* * *

Tammerlane smiled at Gabriel.

'You're mistaken. I had absolutely nothing to do with her death. You saw me. I was on the TV. I explained what happened. I killed the assassin. The Jew,' he said. 'Now, look, I admitted to the business with Julius. But I'm afraid you have no chance at all of getting that to stick. Not least because you won't be leaving here except in the back of a police car. And I—'

'Er, Joe. You need to check Twitter,' Hayter said, in a quiet voice.

The man was staring at his own phone, not looking away from its glowing screen even as he talked. Apart from Gabriel, everyone seated before him took out their phones. He heard a few gasps.

Somebody said, 'We're fucked.'

He stood behind Barnett-Short and watched a video playing on her phone.

Framed in a fuzzy brown ellipse, was the face of the man sitting at the far end of the table.

'Did you make contact with the Syrian yet? The hitman?' the voice of Julius Witaarde asked.

'Uh huh. And he's good, this al-Javari guy?'

'Nazir Aboud al-Javari is one of twenty men worldwide you could trust to do a job like this. Trust me, he's good. '

'He bloody should be, the fee he's asking.'

'Joe, you want him to kill Princess Alexandra. That kind of work, it doesn't come cheap.'

'Yeah, well just as long as he follows the script, I'm fine with it.'

'Did you tell him what you wanted? It sounded pretty complicated.'

'Yes! And it's really not that difficult to understand, Julius. Even for a Boer.'

* * *

Off-screen, Klara heard Julius laugh. She felt her tears begin to flow. She wiped her eyes with her sleeve.

'Oh, Julius. I always said you were paranoid, but thank God you were.'

* * *

On Barnett-Short's phone screen, Tammerlane was still talking. The smug tone survived the phone's tiny speaker.

'I take Lieberman up to the tower. Get him to line up the shot so his prints are all over the rifle, then stand him down. Al-Javari comes up. I kill Lieberman and then al-Javari shoots the princess before taking off. The evidence points to the Jew and I'm left as the saviour of the hour.'

The video began to replay from the beginning. Barnett-Short jabbed the pause button.

Gabriel looked at Tammerlane. His face was drained of colour.

'What are you going to do?' Tammerlane asked.

'I'm going to kill you,' Gabriel said, raising the Glock in his right hand.

59

The door swung wide, banging back against the wall. Three men in black tactical gear burst through, assault rifles at their shoulders, screaming.

'Armed police! Armed police! Get down. Drop the weapons! Drop the weapons!'

Gabriel placed the pistols on the table. He got to his knees, then lay, facedown, on the floor.

Strong hands drew his hands behind his back and he felt cuffs snapping home.

'Stay down,' a voice growled in his left ear. 'If you know what's good for you.'

After being released from custody five hours later, Gabriel found Don waiting for him outside the station in his Jensen. He wound down the window.

'Climb in, Old Sport,' he said with a grin.

'Those armed cops were on the scene pretty quickly,' Gabriel said.

'Hmm, mm-hmm. You took your Department-issue phone with you when you left in such a hurry. I just asked our technical team to switch on the tracker. Bingo! Once I realised where you were going I scrambled a team and waited to see what sort of a stunt you'd pull.'

Then he started the Jensen's engine and pulled smoothly away.

60

PADDINGTON GREEN POLICE STATION, LONDON

In his windowless cell inside the police station designed to hold Britain's most dangerous terrorists, Joe Tammerlane closed his eyes. He lay down on the thin mattress pad on the moulded plastic bench that passed for a bed.

With his arms folded behind his head, he flew back to the day when everything still looked good. Windsor. The wedding day.

After standing Lieberman down, he'd observed the Syrian closely.

Al-Javari worked the bolt on the rifle and the extractor popped the empty shell casing from the breech like a dentist pulling a tooth. He'd been careful to angle the rifle just so, and the brass pinged into the centre of the concrete platform.

The screams of the crowd were audible at this distance, though robbed of some of the higher frequencies.

'Will your prints be on it?' Tammerlane asked, gesturing at the spent cartridge.

Al-Javari shook his head.

'Too hot. The detonation burns off any organic material. It's clean as a whistle.'

Tammerlane turned to Lieberman. Smiled.

The pistol was heavy in his hand. Which was odd, given he'd been told it was mostly plastic. He frowned. He'd always imagined guns to be made of metal.

He'd procured it from the same man who'd supplied the rifle. A Dutch arms dealer allied to his African friend's political party.

'Your part in this is over,' he said to Lieberman.

Lieberman held his arms wide, his deep-brown eyes pleading.

'I did what you asked. Now, make the call,' he said. 'Please.'

'Call?' Tammerlane answered, cocking his head on one side. 'What call?'

'To the people holding my family. You said you'd let them go afterwards.'

Tammerlane slapped his forehead. A silly comedy move. Who did that, really? he asked himself as he pulled out the phone he'd acquired the previous day.

He waited for the ringing to stop. The voice that answered was deep, raspy. Born of a forty-a-day habit and too much cheap whisky.

'It's done?'

'Yes. You can kill them now.'

'All? Kids, too?'

'Yes please, Bashir. As agreed.'

'Can I fuck the woman first?'

'Do what you like, I don't care.'

He ended the call. Lieberman stood like a statue.

'What did you just do? You said you'd return them to me.'

'Sorry. I don't like loose ends.'

The gun bucked in his hand. He hadn't been prepared for the recoil and winced as it twisted his wrist. Lieberman staggered backwards, blood fountaining from a massive wound in his forehead. As he fell, an arc of blood spanned the short distance between them. Tammerlane made sure to be under it, closing his eyes as the hot liquid spattered his face and the front of his suit.

He inhaled once, gripped the still-smoking pistol tighter, squeezed his eyes shut and smacked the barrel against his right cheekbone. He swore at the pain, despite knowing it was coming.

Bending to Lieberman's corpse, he pushed the butt into the right fist and squeezed the fingers closed around it, ensuring the pads made decent contact with the surface. He let it fall a couple of feet away. He repeated the process with the knife he'd used on the cop, leaving Lieberman's stiffening fingers wrapped around the hilt.

And smiled.

Behind him, al-Javari left, his boots scuffing the gritty concrete.

Tammerlane opened his eyes. Sighing with disappointment, he turned over a question in his mind. How much should he tell the court? His part in the revolution was over. But his sentence would end, eventually, and then he'd be free again to take up the cause. He smiled. Because he realised the answer had been staring him in the face all along. Blame the Syrians. Yes! It would work. He began rehearsing his plea to the judge.

61

HIGH-SECURITY PRISON, UNDISCLOSED LOCATION, UK

Joseph Tammerlane's trial took four weeks. During those twenty-eight days, his government was overturned by a combination of actions, civil, criminal and military. A fresh election was held. The incoming government instituted certain reforms to ensure the near-death experience of British democracy could never be repeated.

In his summing up and sentencing, which he permitted to be televised, a first in British jurisprudence, the judge outlined once again Tammerlane's crimes.

He ended with the words, 'You have heard the verdict of the jury. You are guilty on all counts. I hope it will ring in your ears for the rest of your life. You, Tammerlane, are nothing more than a common criminal, a murderer of the vilest kind. You became drunk on power and, in your inebriation, were willing to commit the most heinous crimes in your quest for a utopia that was never going to exist outside the dogma of your own outdated thinking. I sentence you to a whole-life tariff. You will die in prison. Take him down.'

* * *

Tammerlane was not permitted to receive any visitors, bar an official of any religion he might care to entertain. Declaring himself an atheist as well as a Marxist, he declined even this, thin company.

Nevertheless, one windy February day, three months into his sentence, a plain, grey Ford Mondeo saloon rolled up to the gate at the facility housing him.

The guard on duty that morning approached and twirled a finger for the driver to lower the window.

He leaned in, scrutinised the document the driver held out to him and nodded.

The driver rolled up the window, noticing, as he did so, the small black diamond sewn onto the right shoulder of the guard's uniform. The red-and-white barrier jerked upwards and clanged into a vertical position.

The driver drove into the yard, parked, switched off the engine and exited the car. Rounding the back, he opened the boot and took out a supermarket carrier bag.

He walked up to the front door and rang the intercom buzzer.

'Yes?'

'Wolfe.'

The latch rattled and he pushed the door open and stepped into the warmth of the reception area.

The man on reception nodded, handed him a magnetic keycard and went back to his sudoku.

Gabriel walked down the white-painted corridor. At the far end, a single door waited for him. His footsteps rang out on the painted concrete floor.

Reaching it, he pressed the keycard against a black plastic pad standing half an inch proud of the wall.

The lock clicked. He pushed through into the cell. Carefully designed without a single protrusion to which a ligature could be tied.

Tammerlane looked up from a book. Gabriel saw pictures of garden plants. He was wearing a pair of grey jogging bottoms and a sweatshirt in matching fabric. White athletic socks on his feet, which were tucked into the sort of slippers hotels often provide.

'You!' Tammerlane said.

'Me.'

'Come to gloat?'

Gabriel shook his head. He reached into the carrier bag and withdrew a sweatshirt identical to the one Tammerlane was wearing.

'I've come to make good on my promise.'

* * *

The following day, Aisling Connor, the BBC's senior evening newsreader, patted her hair one last time, checked her teeth for lipstick traces in the small mirror she kept in her handbag, then readied herself. She stared into Camera Two's lens, keeping half an eye on its red 'ON' lamp.

Her earpiece clicked.

'Coming to you in five, Ash,' her producer said.

The floor manager signalled for quiet.

'In five, four…'

He switched to hand gestures for the final count, fingers folding down *three…two…*

Finally, he simply aimed his pointing index finger at her.

Aisling assumed her 'serious' face. The one she used to report terror incident, royal deaths and natural disasters.

'The body of disgraced former Prime Minister Joseph Tammerlane was found in his cell this afternoon by prison staff. He had hung himself with his own sweatshirt and was pronounced dead by the prison doctor. The police say they are not treating his death as suspicious.'

After a brief and largely repetitive interview with a BBC reporter outside the gate of the unidentified prison, Aisling continued to the next item.

'In Botswana, a major ivory poaching ring has been rolled up. With connections stretching as far as Dubai and Vientiane, the capital of Laos, the operation was said to have been extremely well-organised, well-funded and utterly ruthless. We go now to Robin Summersby in Gaborone, who is talking to Major Edward Modimo of the Botswana Defence Force Anti-Poaching Unit.'

Gabriel aimed the remote at the TV and turned it off. He gathered Eli closer. She snuggled against his right side and lay a hand across his midriff.

'Are you happy?' she asked.

'Very. Are you happy?'

'Yes. Remember we're having dinner with Stella and Jamie tomorrow.'

'I know. I'm looking forward to it.'

'Gabe?'

'Yes?'

'You know you just said you're happy?'

'Er, you mean ten seconds ago?'

She pinched him.

'Yes! That!'

'Vaguely.'

She popped her eyes wide at the sarcasm and slapped his chest.

'Are you happy with me?'

'What's that supposed to mean? You know I am.'

'Then, can I ask you something?'

'Go on.'

She moistened her lips and in that split second he realised she was nervous.

'I want us to get married. Will you marry me?' she asked.

He looked into her eyes. Saw his future there. Opened his mouth to give her his answer.

His phone rang. He glanced at the screen. No Caller ID.

'Gabriel Wolfe.'

'Gabriel. It's Frank Onagweyo. From Kagosi Group?'

'I remember. What's up, Frank?'

'You know you said I could talk to you about it? The PTSD?'

'Yes.'

'You got a minute?'

'All you need.'

Gabriel looked at Eli, at her expectant face. The crinkle just above the bridge of her nose. Her lips, half-open as she waited.

He nodded, smiled and mouthed, 'Yes.'

Feeling a lightness in his heart that had been absent for a long time, he took the phone out into the garden.

The End

COPYRIGHT

Published by Tyton Press, an imprint of Sunfish Ltd, PO Box 2107, Salisbury SP2 2BW: 0844 502 2061

ACKNOWLEDGMENTS

As with every book I write, the finished story has been shaped by a team of talented and dedicated people whom I now have the opportunity to thank.

My first readers, Simon Alphonso and Sarah Hunt.

My editor, Nicola Lovick.

My proofreader, Liz Ward.

My "sniper spotters": OJ "Yard Boy" Audet, Ann Finn, Yvonne Henderson, Vanessa Knowles, Nina Rip and Bill Wilson.

My cover designer, Stuart Bache.

The members of my Facebook group, The Wolfe Pack.

The serving and former soldiers whose advice helped me to keep the military details accurate: Giles Bassett, Mark Budden, Mike Dempsey and Dickie Gittins.

And, as always, my family.

Any and all mistakes are mine alone.

Andy Maslen

Salisbury, 2020

ALSO BY ANDY MASLEN

The Gabriel Wolfe series

Trigger Point

Reversal of Fortune (short story)

Blind Impact

Condor

First Casualty

Fury

Rattlesnake

Minefield (novella)

No Further

Torpedo

Three Kingdoms

The DI Stella Cole series

Hit and Run

Hit Back Harder

Hit and Done

Let the Bones be Charred

Other fiction

Blood Loss - a Vampire Story

ABOUT THE AUTHOR

Andy Maslen was born in Nottingham, in the UK, home of legendary bowman Robin Hood. Andy once won a medal for archery, although he has never been locked up by the sheriff.

He has worked in a record shop, as a barman, as a door-to-door DIY products salesman and a cook in an Italian restaurant.

He lives in Wiltshire with his wife, two sons and a whippet named Merlin.